DETROIT PUBLIC LIBRARY
3 5674 00736263 6

D1131113

THE SIDE OF THE ANGELS

BY THE SAME AUTHOR

The Forests of the Night
Lucifer's Dream

Jean-Louis Curtis

The Side of the Angels

Translated from the French by
HUMPHREY HARE

G. P. Putnam's Sons
New York

 Published on the same day in the Dominion of Canada by Thomas Allen, Ltd., Toronto.

Originally published in France in 1954 under the title *Les Justes Causes.*

Library of Congress Catalog
Card Number: 56-10225

MANUFACTURED IN THE UNITED STATES OF AMERICA

CONTENTS

PART ONE

PART TWO

PART ONE

France during the post-war period is presented through "case histories" of Partisans, Gaullists, and collaborationists.

CHAPTER I

ARGOS DELIVERED

*

THAT Thursday night, François Donadieu heard two important pieces of news. He would have been more interested in the first, if he had not been so upset by the second: the vanguard of Leclerc's army was reported to have reached the suburbs, and his wife had been waiting for an hour outside the door of his room.

In the vestibule of the hotel François hesitated. Should he turn back, or go up to the third floor? Under the inquisitive eye of the manageress, he yielded to convention rather than to his instinct for flight, and strode eagerly towards the stairs with every sign of happy anticipation. The manageress knew that he had not seen his wife for two years. Some display of emotion was therefore necessary.

No sooner was François on the stairs, out of sight of his pitiless judge, than his face immediately changed expression. The young man looked extremely put out. Indeed, he was so. He dreaded this interview with Catherine. 'She's even spoilt the liberation of Paris for me,' he said to himself.

Catherine was sitting on a step, and the cloud of smoke about her head resembled one of the photographs of ectoplasm taken by those who dabble in spiritualism. The floor round her feet was strewn with cigarette butts. At the sight of her husband, she took the half-smoked cigarette from her lips, stood up and leaned against the wall in an effortlessly contrived, theatrical pose. François stopped short, with a feeling of constriction in his throat. An explosion shook the hotel, followed by a burst of machine-gun fire. François supported his wife with his left arm, while he searched with his right hand for a key in the pocket of his battle-dress blouse.

"I'm sorry that you've had to wait so long," he murmured. "Had I known, I'd have left the key."

No sooner were the words out of his mouth than he recognised their involuntary irony; they were the first he had spoken to Catherine after an absence of two years.

He opened the door and laid Catherine on the bed. She seemed more or less to have lost consciousness, and he wondered what he should do to bring her to. It was no good thinking of cold towels, since the water had been cut off for several days. Should he slap her face? François had never in his life slapped anyone; besides, he felt averse from inflicting such treatment upon a wife whom he was meeting again after so long a separation. At a loss, he sat on the edge of the bed, took one of Catherine's hands in his own, and spoke her name several times without result. He told himself there was nothing to do but wait for her to recover consciousness. With Catherine's hand still held in one of his, he managed to extract a cigarette from the pocket of his blouse and put it between his lips. He then had considerable difficulty in striking a match with one hand, since the other was tenderly engaged with the patient. For a minute or so his attention was wholly devoted to this absorbing little manœuvre. He gave himself up to it exclusively, and after several failures succeeded at last in striking a match only by wedging the box between his knees. He took a long puff at his cigarette and, only then, noticed that Catherine's eyes were open and that she had been watching him all the time.

"How clever you are!" she said.

Automatically he threw away the cigarette, as if the very thought of smoking beside a fainting wife were a solecism, and he felt himself blushing. Catherine's frown was annihilating.

In certain circumstances, Catherine's frown always had been annihilating.

* * *

Above the high, marble chimney-piece a translucent spider's web radiated from a number of luminous centres: bullets had starred the looking-glass. For an instant Lieutenant Bernard stared in admiration at his face, tanned attractively by two months with the *maquis*. In the middle of the web, in the foreground, was his own face, rather Oriental-looking, with tawny marks beneath the eyes. All round it, among the criss-cross markings, at varying distances could be seen the reflections of uniformed men. To the right, the windows were open wide upon a red-tinged sky; sandbags and sub-machine-guns lay against the wall. Here and there were ill-shaven young men in battledress wearing tricolor brassards. Right in the background, a man in plain clothes, looking very official, two colonels, a captain and one or two other soldiers of indeterminate rank, were all bending over a map of Paris. 'The masters of the insurrection,' thought Bernard with rapture. And he, Bernard, had a front seat. He had managed nearly always to have a front seat wherever history was in the making: Cours la Reine, the sixth of February, at Munich, at Toledo during the siege of the Alcazar. . . . There was a noise of voices in the room, of coming and going, of shouts in the corridors, of a woman's laugh in the courtyard below, and further off, over towards the Boulevard Saint-Michel, of isolated shots. Lieutenant Bernard was fascinated by the reflections in the starred looking-glass. He must, he felt, he *must* fix the whole scene in his memory: these febrile groups of men, these 'Paris lads' armed with sub-machine-guns (Bernard actually thought 'Paris lads'), this twilit sky which . . . No, Bernard thought, he really could not speak of the twilit sky resembling a new dawn, it was too much of a cliché and . . . "the woman Narsès, who is the dawn", he could still hear Jouvet speaking this phrase which ended Giraudoux' *Electra*, he was wearing a funny little round hat, and it had been in '36 or '37, a great first night, as exciting as were all Jouvet's first nights. . . . He must remember the red sky, the disciplined disorder, the ringing of the telephone, the machine-gun fire outside, the coming and going of messengers, all Paris bristling with barricades, and himself, at the centre of this symphony of the liberation, an eyewitness, at once witness and actor, not yet thirty, the future in his hands, his kingdom the new world which was coming to birth that night.

Lieutenant Bernard was fascinated by his own image in the centre of the spider's web. He had always had a sense of history, and now he was living in the very womb of history, at the moment of parturition, the most vividly arresting moment both to mind and heart. The looking-glass, starred by bullets, mirrored the men who held all the reins of command, who were the sole masters of the situation. 'I must take a few notes,' Bernard thought, and felt for his notebook in his tunic pocket. At that moment a shattering burst of fire threw everyone to the ground, the spider's web doubled the number of its threads, and Lieutenant Bernard found himself lying flat between a couple of F.F.Is. and a broken bust of Marianne. Like a huge, phosphorescent insect, a tracer bullet passed diagonally across the rectangle of the window.

* * *

Catherine passed a hand across her forehead.

"Forgive me," she said. "I fainted, didn't I? I haven't eaten for two whole days."

The room was dark, and the lights could not be switched on because the current had been cut off. François struck a match. The dim light etched her jutting cheek-bones, her pale and hollow cheeks, a dilated pupil against the darkness. She had certainly become terribly thin.

"Why didn't you write?" she asked in a low voice, just at the very moment that he asked, "Shall we go and try to find something to eat?"

"Why didn't you write?" she repeated. "Or telephone?"

He got to his feet. "Come on; we'd better go and find something for dinner."

He took her by the hand, helped her to get up, and led her towards the door.

"Wait!" she said.

She leaned against the door-frame. He noticed that she too was wearing a very short dress, reaching only to the knees, and wooden shoes. He struck another match, and was shaken by the intensity of Catherine's gaze. It was impossible to tell whether it expressed love, hate, or merely an exceptional curiosity.

"Be that as it may," she said, "we might at least kiss each other, I should have thought."

* * *

Lieutenant Bernard leapt to his feet and ran to kneel by the sandbags at the window. He seized a sub-machine-gun. The courtyard of the Hotel de Ville had emptied in a flash. A crowd of boys was crouching in a gateway; above them an Alsatian headdress beat like the wings of a huge black taffeta butterfly.

'The Alsatian woman's on the job,' Lieutenant Bernard thought, smiling to himself; but almost at once he was ashamed of such sacrilegious mockery. He knew that his cynical intellectualism could often spoil the pure joy of fighting for a cause.

* * *

"We can't cross now," she said.

"Yes, we can. Come on. Don't be afraid."

They went out into the deserted street, walking briskly, till François suddenly slackened the pace.

"Don't be afraid," he whispered. "They won't fire."

Out of the corner of his eye he was watching the barrel of a machine-gun, trained on them from a German strong-point only ten yards away. They moved slowly forward; François felt his wife's nails biting into the palm of his hand. The barrel of the machine-gun, like a telescope, veered round slowly as it followed them. They had to reach the door of the little restaurant on the other side of the street. If only the door was not barricaded! If only that brute didn't fire! It would be too stupid to be shot by that fool, now that it was all over, or nearly all over. They must look inoffensive; above all, not run. If they ran, they'd had it.

"Slowly; we're nearly there," he whispered through his teeth. "Here we are."

The shutters were closed across the restaurant door, but they gave way. They walked slowly in. But as soon as the door was shut behind them, Catherine fell trembling into a chair. At once the manageress came towards them. A group of men and women were lining the closed shutters, gazing out into the street through the cracks. The room was heavy with silence and shadow.

"You've got a nerve, I must say," the manageress said in a whisper.

As if suddenly released, everyone started talking at once.

"They've been going it hot and strong!"

"That couple were crazy to cross the street like that!"

"Only ten minutes ago a chap caught it!"

"Yes; but he ran."

"What difference does that make?"

"The little bastard! All the others have cleared out, and there he stays like a bloody fool with his gun."

"A fanatic. He wants to die at his post. There are a few like that. Tough nuts."

"He's for the high jump, I can tell you."

"Look, the Panther's on the prowl again!"

"It can't have had much luck over towards the Rue Médicis, so it's come back."

"Of course, there are barricades wherever it goes."

"Caught like a rat in a trap."

"Look how pale the little lady is!"

"I suppose you can't give us anything to eat?" François asked the manageress. "Not for me. For her. She's had nothing to eat for two days."

"There's nothing left on the menu, I'm afraid. But there may still be some noodles in the kitchen, with a bit of bread. Marcelle, go and see what's left in the kitchen. Lay places for the lady and gentleman."

"Thank you. That's very kind."

"Not between Frenchmen. It's a matter of course. Particularly on a day like this."

Her face was placid, rather greasy; her little eyes enquiring and kind. She radiated goodwill. Catherine put her chin in her hand and began to weep silently.

"Don't cry, my dear," said the manageress. "The Americans aren't far away now," she added with a little display of patriotism.

"I beg your pardon. You mustn't confuse the issue," said one of the men standing behind the shutters. "It's Leclerc's advance guard, not the G.Is."

"Well, anyway, the Allies," said the manageress conciliatingly.

"Besides," said the man, "it's the Partisans who have liberated Paris."

"Exactly," said the manageress. "The Free French Forces."

"The Partisans, not the Free French Forces," said the man in a nasal, irritated voice, with all the impatience of a purist who discovers wilful error in his opponent's speech.

"I thought it was the same thing," mumbled the manageress. (She took a generously impressionistic view of history.)

"Madame Julienne," sighed the purist with patient reproach, "I have explained to you the difference between Partisans and F.F.I. a hundred times. The Partisans are nearly all Communists,

They are the real resistance. Whereas the F.F.I. are merely little Gaullist waverers."

"Just the same, they're all French, aren't they?" said the defeated manageress.

"Agreed," the purist conceded. "Nevertheless, there are distinctions which must be taken into consideration."

"I'm a Partisan," the man said. "Those chaps over there are F.F.Is."

* * *

Young Thibault Fontanes was greatly interested in the insurrection. With his hands in his pockets, a lock of fair hair across his forehead, he strolled calmly from one barricade to another. He had just accosted a big, simple, rather fierce-looking chap, and now set himself to ask him a few little questions of general interest with all the curiosity of a tourist.

"Oh, so they're F.F.Is., are they?" he said demurely. "And you're a Partisan. . . . Bravo! Besides, your barricade's much prettier than theirs. Indeed, it's a most beautiful barricade."

The Partisan looked Thibault up and down.

"I say, you little runt, you're not trying to take the mickey out of me, are you?"

"Me? Of course not. I'd love to be a Partisan, but it would break my Daddy's heart. He wants me to go into the Diplomatic."

" 'Daddy'!" sneered the Partisan with crushing sarcasm. " 'It's a most beautiful barricade!' Where the hell do you spring from, tick?"

With his hand to his chin, he sketched a gesture of supreme contempt. "Go on, clear off, you little tart!"

Thibault was not the man to be so easily disconcerted.

"Now, don't get angry, Partisan. We don't want to quarrel, do we? Between Frenchmen on such a day as this, it would be most regrettable."

The Partisan opened his mouth to reply; but no sound came. He blushed scarlet, frowning. But he was tamed.

"And really, without wanting to flatter you, I do find your barricade most attractive," Thibault continued. "Though perhaps not quite so agreeable as the one in my part of the town."

"Your part?" the Partisan muttered.

"The Plaine Monceau."

"The Plaine Monceau?"

"Yes. It's true, of course, that the barricades there are not of much use. Necessarily so, since the war is being fought further to the left."

"That's so, the war's being fought further to the left?" the Partisan repeated feebly.

"Of course, don't you see? On the main road that runs south-west-north-east, on the axis Porte d'Orléans-Porte de Clignancourt," Thibault explained with impatient authority. "You may be a good Partisan, but it's clear that you've had no staff experience. . . . Anyway, don't worry about your barricade. The one in my part of the town is smarter, but it has no other merit; they bought it on the black market. Yours is much more authentic."

Having proffered these impertinent remarks, young Thibault put his hands in his pockets, turned on his heel, and began whistling a tune.

"Come back!" shouted the Partisan.

Thibault turned about.

"Are you off your rocker, or do you pimp about on purpose?" the Partisan asked, beside himself with fury.

Thibault modestly lowered his eyes.

"Oh, I'm a very serious character. Besides, I've no sense of humour."

"How old are you?"

"Eighteen and a half."

"You weren't in the *maquis*? No; I'm talking balls; in the *maquis*, with a mug like that!"

"Oh, my face wouldn't have mattered. I'm told that socially it was very mixed."

"You weren't in the Resistance then?"

"You know, at the time I was only a child. . . . Fourteen in 1940. But our maid was in it, if you're interested. Only yesterday she denounced us to the neighbours as Vichyites."

"Well, what the hell were you doing during those four years?"

"Reading the humanities."

"Aren't you ashamed, a big, strong fellow like you?" continued the Partisan.

"To have read the humanities? Yes, a little; it's so commonplace these days."

"You can leave humanity out of this! I'm telling you that at your age, well set-up as you are, you could have gone to the *maquis*. So, I ask, aren't you ashamed to have done bloody nothing while France was fighting for her liberty?"

"France! That's a bit too inclusive. You've got an odd way of writing history, you Partisans."

"Listen," said the Partisan, pale with anger. "If you were my age, I'd have half murdered you already. I'm stronger than you. But I don't hit kids. Now run away; it's time you were tucked up in bed. I don't know why the hell you want to come arsing around here. We don't need idlers in this sector."

"God, what a bore the man is! You'd do better to teach me how to use a sub-machine-gun. It must be a charming weapon. And your sector, as you call it, is perfectly quiet at the moment. Come on, Partisan, make a friendly gesture. Besides, you know, if it's any help, I'm a Marxist."

* * *

"Aren't you eating?"

"I'm no longer hungry, and these noodles are disgusting; they taste of sacking."

"Eat a little bread."

"No; I found a worm in it. Give me a cigarette."

"I've got one Craven A left; here you are. It's my last. I was keeping it as a souvenir."

"Then I won't take it."

"Yes; go on. I shall still have the packet. . . . You're smoking too much, Catherine."

"There's been nothing else to do these last few days. I exchanged my bread tickets for two packets of Gauloise. When did you get back?"

"Will you take coffee, madame?" asked the manageress. "I'm afraid it's national coffee, but still . . ."

"Yes, please. I'd like some."

"Tomorrow we shall have coffee; they say the American rations are full of it."

"Madame Julienne, if you think that the G.Is. are going to distribute food and cigarettes to the French, let me tell you that you're making a big mistake. It's not to revictual a starving Europe that they're making war."

"What a kill-joy you are, Monsieur Émile!" replied the manageress. "When one has starved for four years, one may at least be allowed to hope."

"Between ourselves, Madame Julienne, you certainly haven't starved."

"Go on; and while you're about it, you may as well say that I was in the black market!"

"I don't say that. But what I don't understand is people's mentality. For them the end of the war means cigarettes, coffee and as much meat as they want, silk stockings and all the rest of it."

"Well, that would be a nice change, anyway."

"Madame Julienne is quite right," said another man. "Anyway, what does the end of the war mean to you?"

"It means the end of injustice and the ruin of Nazism."

"Oh, you're austere!"

"What do you mean, austere?"

"Well, ascetic, if you prefer. You're too earnest by half."

"Earnest! . . . I'm merely saying that abundance is not for tomorrow and that the G.Is. are not to be counted on to pamper us. The time for sacrifice is not yet over."

"Really, Monsieur Émile, you talk like a true son of Pétain!"

Madame Julienne burst out laughing at her own joke and everyone else joined in.

"When did you get back?" Catherine asked again in a low voice.

They were sitting opposite each other at the table, at some distance from the group by the shutters.

"In May. By way of Spain."

"Why didn't you let me know?"

He shrugged his shoulders and turned his eyes away.

"You've seen your cousins? And Juliette?" she asked.

"Yes; I've seen them, for one night only. I had to hide, you know. The child didn't recognise me. . . ."

"How is she?"

"Very well. She goes to the village school."

"Poor darling. I haven't seen her since Easter."

"How did you hear I was in Paris?"

"From Roger. I met him this morning. He gave me your address. Why didn't you ring me up?"

"I intended to when everything was over. I preferred to wait, as a precaution."

She raised her eyebrows.

"As a precaution? . . . Oh, of course, you're one of our liberators. You belong to—what do they call themselves?—the Free French Forces?"

The irony was barely discernible.

"You've grown no thinner," she said. "Your stay in London has done you good."

François was silent for a moment, then he said, "I knew that you had gone to Germany, on tour."

"Talk lower. Who told you that? Your cousins?"

"Yes. . . . Why did you go, Catherine?"

She looked suddenly blank. Her features hardened and her eyelids fluttered.

"I had to live. Lambert gave me a good contract."

"You got back all right?"

"Yes, through Switzerland. We were in Bavaria, and near Lake Constance."

Someone near the window shouted, "There's that Panther again! There's no way of escape left for it."

"The fool from the strong-point's got into it!"

"Then we can go out."

"Of course, people are already out in the street."

They opened the door and rushed outside.

"Let's go back to the hotel," said François. "We've got to talk."

"You really think it's necessary?"

"Perhaps not. But you've asked me some questions and I ought to answer them."

* * *

There was a group of F.F.I. at the post in the Préfecture, with an unfurled flag and the Alsatian woman at their head. The German prisoners rose from their palliasses and stood to attention. Lieutenant Bernard had already heard the *Marseillaise* three times that day. Nevertheless, it made him feel emotional. He felt his throat contract. 'What a Boy Scout I am,' he thought. At eighteen, as a member of a student anarchist association, he had written anti-authoritarian articles in left-wing papers, attacking the Army, the generals, the totemism of the tricolor. Those days were over. Now, Lieutenant Bernard was affected by the sound of the *Marseillaise*. Not sufficiently, however, to forget to take note of his immediate reactions. He observed the German prisoners, shabby, standing to attention, and was once more aware that he felt no hate for them. Not even a shade of resentment. Indeed, he felt a vague sympathy for these defeated men, with features drawn and uniforms in rags. He even felt almost embarrassed by the sight of this manifestation which, though inoffensive enough, seemed nevertheless to bear the stigma of vengeance. It was certainly not that he was unaware how horribly the Germans had treated their F.F.I. prisoners. Perhaps these very Germans standing there. . . . And the only sanction imposed upon them was to sing them the *Marseillaise* and show them an Alsatian woman in her country's dress. There was an anodyne quality about it. None the less, Lieutenant Bernard felt slightly embarrassed. Embarrassed for the Germans. Embarrassed for himself. Embarrassed for the Alsatian. . . . Mentally he took a note of his unease, turning it into a phrase for the great novel he had every intention of writing as soon as he was demobilised. It seemed to him that there was something rather noble about *not* hating the Germans when you had been chivvied and humiliated by them for four years, and when you belonged to an organisation against whom the Germans had committed the most appalling atrocities. Indeed the word 'noble' actually crossed Lieutenant Bernard's mind. He discarded it, denied it, but it obstinately returned. All right, then, it *was* noble. He might as well accept it once for all, and question it no longer. Lieutenant Bernard looked at the Germans. He determined to come back to the post later on and give them some cigarettes.

* * *

The Partisan looked at Thibault with suspicion.

"You're a Marxist?"

"Of course I am, my dear chap. All the French upper classes have been Marxist for the last eight days. We haven't got our Party cards yet, but you must give us time to turn round."

The Partisan thought things over; they appeared confused.

"All right, since you're determined to be a bloody nuisance, even a left-wing one," he said at last.

He slipped the sling of his sub-machine-gun down his arm.

"Look. You take hold of the weapon in the left hand, like this. With the forefinger you pull back the breech-block till it's held by the safety-catch. Like this."

"I see. It's quite simple. Up to now I understand perfectly."

"With the right hand you fix on the magazine and push it home till you feel it catch; what's more, you hear a click as well."

"Have you only got one magazine?"

"No, idiot. I keep a spare one in my haversack. After that you've nothing to do but fire."

"At whom?" Thibault asked with interest.

* * *

The street had taken on all the animation of a holiday, its crowds and its excitement. Everyone was hurrying towards the Hôtel de Ville, where, so it was said, the first tank of Leclerc's army had just arrived. To the west a red glow set the sky aflame from some house conflagration over towards the Rue de Rivoli. The crowd was made up of every kind of person: young men with arm-bands and sub-machine-guns, housewives, students in spectacles, clerks carrying brief-cases, a priest with his cassock tucked up to his calves, fashionable women, schoolboys, all mingling with a sort of febrile excitement in which the ideas of victory and liberation appeared to be only secondary to the concrete image of a huge collective game. For, in spite of the machine-gunning and shelling that had punctuated the days and nights of the past week, in spite of the men and women who had been seen to fall beneath a hail of bullets in the very streets, in spite of the wounded borne on Red Cross stretchers, the dark stains on the pavements, and the familiar, provocative presence of danger, it was nevertheless in holiday mood that the city witnessed its liberation. It had something of the quality of a South American revolution, a pogrom, a huge student's rag, a panic at night on a fair-ground: it was a rising of the people of Paris. Men were being killed at the barricades; but the barricades were, at the same time, the subject of numberless jokes, of infinite laughter. No doubt one rejoiced because the Germans were beaten, because four years of privation and fear, of humiliation and discomfort were coming to an end; but, above all, because history was abroad tonight in the streets and because each one felt as though he were playing a part in a newsreel. And whenever history comes within everyone's reach, there is a truce, in which tensions are relaxed, boredom is dissipated, and loneliness dissolved.

Jostled by the crowd, François and Catherine were walking side by side in silence. For them, tonight, no truce existed. François wanted to go with the crowd, to mix with it, immerse himself in the confusion which was at once both so terrible and so good-natured, permit the mass emotion, which so wonderfully enhances the sense of the significance of living, to take charge of him. He would have liked to wander about Paris all night, talk to anyone he met, to everyone, to laugh and sing, drink red wine at a bar, be fired at and come to terms with fear: in brief, be a patriot. He remembered the evening of the 11th November, 1943, in Piccadilly, the sort of joyous madness which had suddenly come upon every single customer in the huge hall of Lyons Corner House, how he had been carried away upon an eddy of rejoicing, in a dance, a chaste and patriotic bacchanal, where chorus girls, elderly spinsters and respectable civil servants were intermingled with soldiers from every part of the world, Americans, huge, bronzed Australians, Indians, French, Canadians, and everyone sang *Tipperary* and the *Madelon* at the tops of their voices, and kissed the waitresses, while a woman dressed in puce, with a black ribbon round her neck, pecked at François' cheek and called him "Ducky". She was crying and shouting "*Vive la France!*" though she had had nothing but a cup of tea and a few wartime biscuits. . . . Though supposed to be so cold and reserved, no one could let themselves go like the English in certain circumstances, or be noisier or more enthusiastic. Bernard had also gone to a Lyons Corner House that night, he remembered. Always elegant and distinguished, an Oriental prince in a khaki uniform, he had brought his mistress, a red-haired dancer called Beryl. Later, as midnight struck, they had all met under the arcades at the Piccadilly end of Regent Street, and someone had said: "I know a new night-club, most amusing, near Tottenham Court Road. Let's go." But they had never gone, because a warning had sent everyone into the shelters. How wonderful London had been then, how good it had been to be alive in those days, in spite of restrictions and bombs, because the atmosphere had been so . . . welcoming, so friendly, beyond anything that François had ever known before. But now London was over and soon life would have to be lived again as it had been in the past.

But tonight Paris was wonderful too, but in a different way, a French way, and François Donadieu bit his lips in annoyance and regret. He had always been haunted by the fear of missing the great occasions, of being denied the best moments of life. He owed Catherine a grudge for having spoilt this day for him.

They climbed up to the third floor. Somewhere a radio was booming—"The electric current will be on all night"—and Catherine sat down in a chair and put her hands on her knees. "Please shut the windows," she said.

He shut the windows upon a rejoicing Paris and turned heavily back into the stifling room, towards the conversation he knew must follow.

"Won't you sit down?" Catherine said.

He took a chair and sat down some distance away. Each avoided looking at the other.

"Would you rather I turned the light out?" he asked her.

"Does the light worry you?"

"No . . . It's for your sake. You're tired."

"I prefer the light on," she said drily. "When you're going to be given the sack, it's better to look the giver in the face."

François looked at her from under lowered lids.

"Why do you talk like that, in your stage voice?"

But he was relieved that she had begun the conversation on a practical level, and that she seemed to look upon their separation as inevitable.

"Leave my stage voice out of it. What do you intend doing?"

"I have no precise intentions."

"Don't be a coward, François. It's odd how cowardly men are in situations like this."

"What do you want me to say that you don't already know? When I went away two years ago, the question was already settled. The question of our joint life. We already knew, then, that it had come to a full stop, that we had to separate."

"Was that why you went away?"

"I went away simply because I was in danger of being sent to Germany."

"It's at least something that you don't pretend it was due to patriotism. . . . But it's disheartening enough that you still maintain this fiction about the Todt Agency! At that time you were twenty-six, and Todt only conscripted boys of eighteen to twenty. Besides, you had a labour permit. You were in no danger. At least, in no more danger than anyone else. No, you went because it was the easiest solution to problems you hadn't the courage to solve on your own initiative. You went because flight, a pretended heroic adventure, is a great deal easier than living with a woman you've ceased to love, easier than earning your living and those of your wife and child."

He rose abruptly to his feet.

"You've become very discursive," he said, his voice trembling.

"I've had two years in which to prepare my discourse."

"In any case, please leave Juliette out of this. I arranged things so that Juliette should be happy, properly cared for and looked after. She's been a good deal happier there, with my cousins, than she would have been in Paris with us."

"It depended upon you and no one else to make her as happy with us."

"No, Catherine, don't be dishonest. You know very well that's not true."

"I know only that your reasons for going were those of self-interest and cowardice."

"You can't believe even for a second that my going was a wrench?"

"No; I don't believe you felt any wrench at all," she said calmly. "You wanted to feel it, you persuaded yourself you did feel it, because it lent your going a heroic, a somewhat theatrical significance, and so concealed your real motives, which were not heroic at all. Oh, I'm not saying you didn't feel any sadness at all, particularly at leaving Juliette without knowing how long you were to be away. Sadness, yes, but no anxiety, no scruples, since you had left her with people who loved her as if she were their own child. You were sad, and you exploited your sorrow, because it gave you importance in your own eyes, made of your departure a sort of sacrifice. . . . It was an evasion, a flight."

"God knows why you should set on me like this!"

"To resolve a subject we've never discussed before."

"What subject?"

"The subject of your hypocrisy. You've got a great talent for it, François, for attributing to yourself the best possible motives, for disguising your shortcomings as admirable actions. It's a pretty widespread talent, but you're a past master at it. The only thing is, I've come to see you as you are."

"My poor Catherine, you're misled by the dramatics of the situation. You're turning me into a theatrical figure. I'm both simpler than that, and not so simple. Everything you've said is out of focus."

"I know I shan't convince you. Hypocrisy and obstinacy go together, a devilish combination. Under that mild exterior of yours no one is harder than you are. Oh, you've remained a Huguenot at heart!"

"I must admit the relevance escapes me. . . ."

"It doesn't escape me. Listen. I was reading Gide's *Journal* earlier in the year. Gide is said to have such clarity, such candour. . . . And he has, about other people! In *L'École des Femmes*, which I read at the same time, there is a wonderful candour; at other people's expense, and at no cost to himself! In his *Journal*, whenever he starts talking about himself, he concentrates, patiently, slily, with a sort of insect tenacity, upon his own self-justification. It's horrible. I wanted to hit him, to bang his head against a wall!" she shouted violently. "It's the congenital disfigurement of the Huguenot, this terrible hypocrisy you've secreted down the centuries. When I read the *Journal*, I recognised you. You spilt out of its pages, only without the talent . . . all that is worst in the Huguenot. We Catholics at least have confession, where we are supposed to reveal our most hideous, most shameful sins. In any case, we make an act of humility, of humiliation even. We know that we are sinners."

"And you come away pardoned, absolved and blest, which is very handy. Listen," he went on good-humouredly. "There's an insurrection going on outside. There may be a civil war tomorrow. Don't let loose a religious one in here."

She smiled weakly. After a long silence, she said, "Are you quite sure that we couldn't try to live together again?"

François closed his eyes. At all costs not that, he thought. He had earned the right to be alone, to be free and irresponsible. He was not yet thirty, and life had barely begun. At all costs, he thought, not that.

"Yes; quite sure," he said in a strangled voice, and his eyes were panic-stricken as he turned them away.

"I know that I haven't been what would be called a good wife," she said softly. "Indeed, I haven't been exactly the sort of wife you wanted. I recognise my faults, you see," she said, raising her head, "I know them and I admit them. I'm neglectful, I was a bad manager, I . . . well, there's a lot that could be said. But now I should like to try to be what you want me to be."

"One can never begin again, Catherine."

There was another silence. She sat still and straight on her chair.

"Very well," she said acrimoniously. "Our separation will be your fault. It's you who want it. And you'll bear the responsibility for it towards the child."

"You've no more desire than I have to start our life together again. I don't understand what you're up to."

"No; you don't understand," she said, her eyes bright with hate.

She relapsed into a prolonged silence. Her breath came forcefully as if something was weighing on her. Suddenly she lifted her hands to her eyes. Repressed fury made her tremble and stammer.

" 'Why did you go to Germany?' The tone in which you asked me that question just now in the restaurant! A tone of noble reproach, of virtuous sorrow! As if I had done something vicious . . . worse, something vulgar, something . . . regrettable! I'm surprised you didn't use the word 'regrettable'. It figures prominently in that measured, discreet vocabulary of yours, doesn't it? 'Why did you go to Germany? It's so regrettable. . . .' You said it as if you were judging me from the exalted elevation of your own moral worth, judging me with a controlled, courteous disapproval, avoiding all anger, all excess of language. You're prepared to forgive me; only, of course, I must understand that I have committed a base and vulgar action and that you find it very regrettable to have a wife capable of thus erring. Because you're one of the righteous, aren't you? You're on the right side of the barricades, in the camp of the Righteous and the pure in heart. Any other man, any true man, would perhaps have insulted me, perhaps even beaten me, and then, his passion spent, he would have taken me in his arms to console me and wipe away my tears. He would have said: 'Of course, you ought not to have gone to Germany, but I know how things were. You were hungry, my poor sweet. You had to work. Oh, well, it's over now. Let's forget it. We won't mention it again.' But not you. The Righteous don't shout, insult, or beat. They merely ask a discreet question in a tone of sorrowful reproach: 'Why did you go there?' That's all. But it's the worst of all! It makes you feel a worm, an insignificant piece of trash. Hypocrite! Well, then, I did go to Germany. Yes, and I acted for the Boches, several times, even in Paris. And I did it because there was nothing else I could do. Do you understand, François? There was nothing else I could do," she repeated, emphasising each syllable. "You were in England, free, well-fed, your conscience at rest. You ate at the table of the Righteous, you lived under the roof of the Righteous, you loved France from afar, it was comfortable and aseptic, and you were able to feel a noble pity for our sufferings—our sufferings, that was the word you used to adorn our privations and our paralysing boredom. You could indulge yourself with dreams of the liberation, see yourself in the army of the liberators. . . . I know, you ran the risk of being killed by the bombs. It's an easy risk to face; bombing doesn't weigh very heavily on the mind or heart. I've also spent nights in cellars and shelters, when we were on tour in the north. It's one of our pleasantest memories. I was frightened, of course, but we all pressed close up to each other, we were brothers and sisters, and after the raid was over we used to laugh and joke, and the barmaid used to stand us a glass of calvados to set us up. . . . Communal perils are not demoralising, even when they result in deaths. What is demoralising is to have to defend yourself all alone, to have to fight all alone, and to be afraid of everyone. Yes, I went to Germany and I played in Paris before the Boches and for them. So what? I don't like the Boches, I find them as boring as a wet day with their martial songs and guttural words of command. Besides, a time came when I never went with them, I found them so boring. And the people from Vichy were sickening. It was the whole system I hated—do you understand? —their propaganda, their obstinacy, their heroism, the whole business of war, soldiering and politics. For me the Germans were a temporary inconvenience, I knew that they wouldn't be here for ever, but that they had to be put up with for a time.

That's why playing for them was of no consequence: as far as I was concerned they were only ghosts, they merely existed provisionally. It was of no consequence and it allowed us to live, to struggle against cold and hunger. Do you understand? I suppose you're going to prosecute us and condemn us, we actors who have compromised ourselves. I've been threatened already. Compromised! It makes me laugh! All right, throw us into prison, if it gives you any pleasure—with half the population of France besides. But I will not tolerate, no, I *will* not tolerate a damned righteous hypocrite saying to me: 'Why did you go to Germany? It's most regrettable'."

Listening to this diatribe, François' mind was beset by a number of disquieting thoughts. He remembered the competition at the Conservatoire when Catherine competed for the prize for tragedy with a rendering from the *Imprécations de Camille*.

"You're being unjust," he said awkwardly. "To listen to you anyone would think that we had a wonderful time in England. A good many of us, you know, made clandestine journeys to France at night by air. Many were sent on missions of that kind. Some of us got killed."

"You needn't throw your dead in my face!" she cried, her eyes wild with fury. "The dead are not an argument. You had your martyrs too, I suppose! I don't care a damn! I don't care a damn for your martyrs or your dead! I'm only concerned with you, and you're alive."

"Do you realise what appalling things you're saying?"

"Perfectly well. But don't expect me to respect your ideas on heroism and self-sacrifice. I can sometimes respect men; never ideas."

"I could have spoken of such a thing as honour, but I can see very well that you're in no mood to listen."

"No; I'm in no mood to listen. It's regrettable. Re-grett-a-ble, isn't it? And you needn't tell me of the wonderful work you did, of the great help you were to the Americans and the English, nor of the years we should have had to wait to be liberated if you hadn't taken part in the fight. No; you needn't tell me about it, because I understand nothing of politics. Besides, just think, I didn't even know that there was a Resistance movement in France. I only heard of it at the beginning of the year. When nearly all France was resisting. I must have been in a daze, mustn't I? Unconscious. I must be one of the few women in France who, with the prostitutes, didn't resist. They'd better put me in a circus and tour France; I could take my place between the calf with five legs and the Siamese twins."

"You're giving a very painful performance, Catherine. Please calm down. If you really are in danger," he added, "you know very well that I shall do all I can to see that you don't have any trouble."

He went close to her and made as if to stroke her cheek.

"Leave me alone!" she cried, dashing his hand angrily aside. "Thank you for your generous offer, which does you honour; truly does you honour. But I don't want to be spared anything. I shall go to prison, if I must, with my teeth clenched and my head held high."

She got to her feet.

"And now it's goodbye. Or perhaps not, since I suppose we shall have to see each other over the formalities for a divorce? As to that, I may as well tell you that I haven't a penny in the world. My tours in Germany, you see, haven't made me rich. But, generous as you are, I'm sure you would never listen to any suggestion of our sharing the costs. I'll send you my lawyer's bill. But you must be in a hurry to join your little rioting friends. Go on, go on. The insurrection's awaiting you."

She walked towards the door.

"Catherine!" he said with a sort of suppressed violence. "Don't go away like this, don't. . . ." He lowered his head, defeated. "I don't know what to say. I don't know. Your scorn appals me. All the same, I think . . . I know that you are wrong, that you are making a mistake."

Now she looked at him without hatred.

"Poor François," she murmured, and there was a sort of indulgence in the tone of her voice. "You know that I am wrong and yet you're not quite sure. When you meet your friends from London, they'll give you back your self-confidence. Your pal, Bernard, the one who egged you on to go to London two years ago, he must be here, fighting on some barricade, I suppose? But what am I saying? Bernard's more likely to be on the staff of the underground movement. Well, go and find him. Go on. Once you're with him, you'll be quite certain again that you're right."

"How you've changed, Catherine. I have never known you so violent, so—I don't know—contemptuous. Do you hate me?" he asked abruptly, and his face wore an expression like a guilty child's.

She shrugged her shoulders.

"It's much worse than that, François," she said softly. "I no longer love you."

* * *

"My dear chap," cried Thibault, "this insurrection is becoming boringly long. What do you say to coming home for a cup of tea? We still have a few rusks and some orange marmalade."

"Are you crackers? I'm on guard. Besides, I don't like tea."

"But you know that it's all over, or practically! You've surely heard what's happened! An officer of the French Army has reached the Hôtel de Ville with a whole bevy of authentic Negresses, straight from Lake Tchad. Come on then, hurry up," he said in his most charming manner. "I'll introduce you to Daddy. I shan't tell him that you're a Partisan—he might have qualms about the silver—I shall tell him that you were Cultural Attaché to the Free French Government. It'll fit in with Daddy's ideas of what that Government is like."

"You natter and natter, it's a wonder where the devil you find all the words. Half the time I don't know what the hell you're talking about."

"No matter. Come along. I must say, taking you home and introducing you to the family—Grandmamma, Daddy, Mummy, Aunt Léonie and my little sister—will be absolutely perfect. Wildly amusing. I've got a girl friend too, Lorraine. She'll just adore your type. . . ."

"Drop it, kid," said the Partisan, nervously moving his feet as if trying to gain confidence. "It's jolly decent of you to want to introduce me to your family, but . . . I can't."

"Now you're playing the shame-faced warrior! What, are you going to stay here all evening? But, my poor chap, all the Germans are dead. Your barricade no longer serves any purpose at all. Besides, look, the F.F.Is. over there have all gone to the Hôtel de Ville."

"I tell you, I've got my orders."

"If I were you, I'd put a major's badge of rank on my sleeve and give all the F.F.Is. I saw wasting their time ten days' detention. You mean to say you're only a second-class private? I've seen a lot of chaps younger than you who were at least colonels."

"They won't last," he said soberly enough.

"I'll stay a few minutes longer to bear you company. You'll tell me about your adventures with the *maquis*, how many Germans you killed and how many French. . . . By the way, which do you prefer killing? Not that it matters. I should like to sit down. Hand me down that Voltaire easy-chair from up there by the iron bedstead. I wonder who the lady bountiful was who contributed a Voltaire easy-chair to the victory? Not a bad idea, mark you. A Voltaire easy-chair is not proof against bullets, but it may be against stupidity. And, you know, stupidity does nearly as much damage as a sub-machine-gun."

Half an hour later, M. Fontanes, happening to pass by, saw his son, Thibault, reclining in a Voltaire easy-chair, a cigarette between his fingers, listening with great apparent interest to the conversation of a fellow with unshaven cheeks, who was dressed in a leather jacket and carried a sub-machine-gun in his hand, behind a deserted barricade, in an operatic *décor* of red sky, smoke and revolution.

* * *

With blows, kicks and insults, the three F.F.Is. threw the bewildered militiaman they had just discovered, hidden at the back of a cellar, on to the straw of the post beside the German prisoners. He was a boy of eighteen, slightly built for his age, with sharp, angular features and dark eyes which looked as though they would be intelligent when life was normal, but present fear had given them an animal-like expression. His shirt hung in tatters from the emaciated body of a prodigal son. From his nostrils and mouth flowed a rivulet of blood. The German prisoners gazed with indifference at this somewhat maltreated vestige of the New Europe. The young militiaman hid his face in his hands and soon his shoulders were shaking with sobs. The German prisoners looked away; one does not watch a man crying. What a story! What an adventure! What a disaster! The young militiaman saw himself at school again, in the second form, sent to Coventry by the other boys because of his blue shirt. At that time he was not yet a militiaman, but was affiliated to his local group of the P.P.F. As soon as he had finished his examinations, he had joined the Militia, and how unhappy he had been! He had had no defence against the great brutes of the Militia, caparisoned as they were in muscle and ideals, but his own poor little hate and his bare nine stone. His hate. When he was very young, they had said of him: "He's a good child, very gentle and well-behaved." And all that gentleness had been corrupted, at first slowly, then quicker and quicker. Why? Why? Had his political choice determined all the rest? Or had the die been cast long before, in the limbo of his earliest years, and his politics been but one manifestation among others of a fatality that transcended his personal consciousness? What part did chance play? And what part instinct? On the threshold of adolescence Garrigou had been seduced, yes, seduced, by Marshal Pétain, by the nobility of his eyes, of his speeches and of his doctrine. He had begun to read such newspapers as the *Révolution Nationale* and *Je suis Partout*, and had found a peculiar pleasure in them, in the vengeful articles branding the Jews, the Freemasons, the Radicals, the Anglo-Saxon capitalists, and the decadent and corrupt bourgeoisie. These articles made his heart beat faster, stirred his mind and his blood, like a stimulating drug. His father was a Pétainist too, at least in the home circle, a Pétainist and an old soldier, and both father and son had the profound feeling of taking part in a crusade. But soon they became aware of their isolation. In some sort they were taboo. It began slowly enough, first with the neighbours, the house-porter, Uncle Jules and the cousins from Pontoise. Then it spread to the shopkeepers. A web of covert looks and wounding innuendo. Being sent to Coventry at school. The mockery, veiled at first, of the English Master, who was clearly immoral and Gaullist. Little by little, the young militiaman began to feel obscurely that his political ideas exuded hatred, and at the same time fed upon it, transforming it into their own proper substance, till a cycle was set up analogous to the cycle of nitrogen. It was a closed circle. He felt he was suffocating. One day, when he could bear it no longer, he had written an anonymous letter to the police superintendent of his district denouncing the master for making overt Gaullist propaganda in school. The master had been sent for to the police station. And what had happened? The next day the master had been back in his place in school, his eye particularly bright, and he had made a little speech to the class: "Gentlemen, one of you amuses himself by writing anonymous letters to the representatives of the law. I must tell him that this form of amusement is very unhealthy. The hysterical old maids, to whom this particular way of passing the time seemed until now to be limited, end up in the madhouse. Moreover, a madhouse is no fun at all, because the only form of shirt you're usually permitted to wear in it is a strait-jacket." It was on that day that, after school, Garrigou was chased by a howling mob of boys during the break, under the negligent eye of a master who had no intention of interfering. They were all Gaullists in that school. And the mockery of the English Master became more blatantly insolent. "Our friend Garrigou," the master always referred to him thus, "our friend Garrigou is the only one among you gentlemen who has an ideal," the boys sniggered, "a spiritual ideal founded upon a just conception of force." The boys laughed. "Our friend Garrigou will do himself the pleasure of reading us that beautiful poem of Kipling's to the glory of England." The boys guffawed. Garrigou found himself obliged to send another anonymous letter, not to the superintendent this time, but to the Kommandantur. The only trouble was that they received so many anonymous letters at the Kommandantur that Garrigou's must have passed unnoticed. The master stayed. Garrigou had not a single friend left, and day by day he sank further into isolation. He no longer spoke to anyone. Besides his school books, he read nothing but newspapers—all the newspapers, from *La Gerbe* to *Je suis Partout*—and a few classics, such as the *Discours* by the Marshal, *Bagatelles pour un Massacre*, by Céline, *Les Décombres* by Rebatet, or *Les Murs sont bons*, by Henry Bordeaux. When he read these papers and these books, he felt that he was justified. "It's I who am right. A day will come. . . ." A day would come when Garrigou would sit upon a National Revolutionary Tribunal. The English Master, the house-porter, the grocer, and some of the schoolboys would appear in turn before him. Garrigou would be at once contemptuous and magnanimous. No, he wouldn't condemn them to death. Merely to hard labour. Not even that; it would be to give them too much importance. He would say to his colleagues on the Tribunal; "Gentlemen, these unhappy people are not worthy of our severity. They are cruelly lacking in intelligence, appear sadly under-developed. Believe me, let us show indulgence." But the day had never come. Herold Paquis might proclaim over the radio that England, like Carthage, would be destroyed, but England had held out, while it was Germany that was falling apart. The Militia became more and more brutal and unrestrained. Garrigou suffered much. On the day Philippe Henriot was assassinated, he had fled and taken refuge with a distant relative at the other end of Paris. The relative had thrown him out; but the Militia had found him again and he had had to stay with them, trying to find a truck that would take them to Baden-Baden; but that month it was difficult to get a lift. So there it was. Some F.F.Is. had found him in a cellar. They might have killed this chick, treason's scraggy fledgling, on the spot. They contented themselves with beating him up a little.

Garrigou was weeping hot tears when someone touched him on the shoulder. He raised his eyes. An officer was standing before him, a lieutenant of the enemy army, a Frenchman. He signed to him to stand up and follow him. 'I'm going to be tried,' Garrigou thought, and began to tremble. He felt a great void inside him. Like a shadow, he followed the officer through a labyrinth of corridors and stairs. At last they came to an empty attic room whose dormer-window looked out upon a prospect of roofs. The enemy officer closed the door and took up his position in front of Garrigou. He had a fine head and looked bronzed and a little exotic. There was a short silence.

"So," said the officer, "you hate us with all your heart?"

What was he to answer? Besides, Garrigou was much too frightened to speak. 'He's going to torture me,' he said to himself.

"Why did you join the Militia? Had you any real reason?"

Silence.

"Look me in the face. I order you to look at me!"

Garrigou made a prodigious effort to lift his eyes, to bear the vivid gaze of his enemy.

"I want to know what goes on in a militiaman's mind, if anything *does* go on there. I'm curious by nature. So why did you join the Militia? Answer me. You had an ideal?"

Garrigou opened his mouth. It seemed to him that the joints of his jaw were of lead. He wanted to speak, but he had neither breath nor words. His throat was constricted. He had opened his mouth in a reflex of fear to prove to his executioner that he was willing.

"Do you hate us?" the officer asked.

Garrigou tried to shake his head, to make the sign for 'No', but the muscles of his neck hurt him, they felt like stretched cords. His head hardly moved. He could not understand the point of this interrogation, which seemed to waver between a game, an interview, and a sadistic prelude to something hideous. . . . Did he hate the officer? No, he was frightened, that was all.

"I could kill you," went on the enemy, carrying a hand to his belt. "I have the right to do so. Perhaps I shall even have the duty to do so."

Garrigous leaned against the wainscoting. He could now no longer take his eyes off the officer's. His heart had ceased beating, his legs felt weak under him, his whole poor little life seemed to hang upon this gaze, upon this invisible, agonising thread which bound him to an unknown face. If the thread broke, it was finished. . . . Suddenly the officer raised his right arm and took a step backwards as if to make a spring. His face gave a little convulsive twitch and suddenly, with the whole weight of his shoulder behind it, he hit Garrigou as hard as he could in the face. The boy fell to the floor. He did not cry out. Slowly he got up, first on to his hands and knees, and then to his feet, sliding up the wall. He was unsteady on his feet and his mouth was bleeding. The officer's bronzed, good-looking face seemed a little shrivelled.

"You hate us," he said breathlessly, "and you had better find out why. We're the victors."

With the back of his hand Garrigou wiped away the blood that was flowing from his chin. He was pale and trembling, and was no longer quite sure what it was all about.

The officer ran his fingers through his dishevelled hair. He seemed to have recovered his calm.

"That window opens on to the roof," he said. "To the left there's an iron ladder. It'll take you down into the backyard. You may break your neck or you may be shot by the F.F.Is. On the other hand, you may manage to escape. I'm giving you the chance. It's perhaps not quite regular, but then today things are not altogether regular. . . . Besides, there's no risk of your doing anyone much harm. You cut a pretty sorry sort of figure and you've got no arms. If you manage to escape, you'll think, later on, that you owe it to a bastard of the Resistance. As re-education perhaps it'll be worth more than two years of gaol. Who knows?"

The officer left the room, shut the door behind him, and listened. He heard a light step, then the squeak of the window opening. He turned and walked away down the corridor.

* * *

The man with silver-pale hair closed the door and locked it. He was rolling his eyes and gasping for breath like someone who has just escaped a mortal danger. He stood with his back to the door, and his huge, pale, bony hands flattened themselves against it like marine creatures stranded on the sand. His teeth chattered. The noises of the street came from the open window. He came away from the door, went to the middle of the room, and leaned with both hands on a table. Little by little his breathing became calmer, but his eyes were still dilated with panic or some sort of horror. He took a key from his waistcoat pocket and opened a drawer. He drew out some papers which he threw pell-mell on the floor; his movements were febrile and arhythmic. Some photographs fell out. They were of young women, one of whom was in German uniform; of a group of soldiers; of a German in uniform whipping, with a long carter's whip, a youngish and completely naked woman, whose back was already a criss-cross of long, bloody weals; and, lastly, of a boy of about eighteen, who had inscribed the photograph: "To my friend, Nicholas Gaudie, a free man, in memory of our discussions in the school yard, 1935." It was signed "Bernard". At last the man took out a cardboard box, fastened with an elastic band. He opened it. The room was very dark. The window outlined a square of red evening sky. The man's movements suddenly gained surprisingly in precision and dexterity. He undid his belt and let his trousers fall. He seized an ampoule from the box, knocked the end off against the table and inserted the needle of a syringe. The man's tall, thin figure was reflected dimly in the looking-glass of the cupboard. He lowered his head and bent his body a little forward. With a quick jab he inserted the needle into the anterior muscle of his thigh. A few seconds later, he placed the hypodermic on the table, pulled up his trousers and tightened his belt.

His features were relaxed, his expression at once serene and melancholy. He went over to the cupboard, turned on a switch and looked at himself in the glass. He passed a hand that trembled a little through his hair, and then, with both hands began smoothing his lean face with a sort of fearful tenderness. At the same time he smiled at his own reflection, while tears shone at the corners of his eyes without in the least altering the calm, almost the happiness, of his expression. He took off his coat and threw it into the middle of the room. Then he placed a chair near the washbasin and sat down. He turned on the tap and let the basin fill, then opened the waste and turned the tap off a little so that the basin remained half full of running water. He drew the chair nearer the basin and, having turned up his left shirt sleeve, plunged his forearm into the water. He tried several positions before finding the one that suited him best. A second later, a razor blade flashed in his right hand. The man closed his eyes and threw his head back. He made a little grimace of distaste; but at once his features regained their calm, which little by little became almost voluptuous. The water went on running in the basin and its little glug-glug made an ironic counterpoint to the sounds that came up from the street. The man's head nodded. He heard loud and joyous carillons sounding through him and out across the city, he seemed to be floating upon a cloud of silver sound, to be cradled upon waves of ringing bells; and he smiled, so happy was his death.

* * *

He looked at her, trying to decipher her real feelings from her thin, drawn, pale face. She bore his look without flinching, and it was he who first lowered his eyes.

"You no longer love me?" he asked. "In that case why did you ask me if I wanted to start our life together again?"

"Because I was afraid," she answered evenly. "But I don't expect you to understand that either. But for the last few days I've been alone; I was afraid, and I thought myself in danger. So I came to find you, a little out of cowardice. However, I can't say that I was certain of what I felt before seeing you and speaking to you. Now I am certain and I'm no longer afraid. Someone told me of what a Jew said when the Germans came to arrest him and send him to a concentration camp. 'Before, I was afraid,' he said; 'now I shall begin to hope.' Let your friends do to me what they will. They won't always be the masters. One day I shall be free."

She opened the door and he followed her automatically, too oppressed to speak. He was a prey to disquiet, humiliation, sorrow and a sort of bitterness. There was nothing more to say. The ruin of what they had once been able to call their 'love' was total, irremediable and final. Going down the stairs behind this stranger with whom for a time he had shared his life, he thought to himself that the break had taken place both more easily and more quickly than he had dared to hope in his most optimistic moments. 'Now I am free,' he told himself, but he could find no relief or pleasure in it. He felt nothing but disquiet, self-discontent and a certain bitterness. 'I failed to take the lead. It was she who did the talking, who overwhelmed me. . . .' The noise of the street came up to them, suddenly grown loud and wild. Below, in the hall, the manageress was screaming with savage exaltation, "Leclerc is at the Hôtel de Ville." A bell began to rind nearby, then another further off, then one by one the bells of Paris joined in a great resounding fugue above the rescued city.

CHAPTER II

A SCAPEGOAT

*

"MONSIEUR Oyarzun's flat?"

The concierge gave him a sharp look. "Fifth floor on the left," she snapped, and went back to her knitting, her expression sour. 'She knows,' thought François Donadieu. Three months after the liberation the face of popular patriotism was still besotted with suspicion and bigotry; and every Frenchman was a patriot, except those who had been thrown into prison. In the well of the staircase the wallpaper hung in great strips from the dirty walls, the banisters were loose, the whole place stank of poverty, with the smell of ill-kept houses overcrowded with anonymous humanity, of stale cooking fat, dust and ammonia. On the second floor Madame Hortense, dressmaker, had earned a swastika, painted in red upon her door. On the fourth floor another swastika stigmatised Monsieur Pfeiffer, violin teacher. Undoubtedly the whole house had been foredoomed. What a martyrdom the concierge must have suffered with such tenants, crucified during four long years for her patriotism by Madame Hortense, dressmaker, and Monsieur Pfeiffer, violin teacher!

The fifth floor. . . . François, out of breath, paused before the door on the left. It was about to open upon the figure, the almost forgotten features of a man whom he had not seen for three years, whom he did not care for and who cared little more for him. They had been at school together. They had maintained, as a result of casual meetings become less and less frequent, the fiction of friendship. In its name Roland Oyarzun had invited François to visit him in this distant suburb: "My wife and I would be very happy if you would dine with us." François Donadieu would undoubtedly have declined the invitation as an appalling bore (half an hour in the Underground, drab suburbs, a wasted evening) if, at the end of the clumsy, rather pathetic letter, there had not been a postscript: "You may or may not know that I have just been released from Fresnes, where my country's justice has confined me for three months. I am, what's more, branded with the stigma of National Indignity. It may be that you will not want to compromise yourself with the company of a pariah such as myself. I shall perfectly understand your discretion and shall not hold it against you. If you do come all the same, I'll tell you of my adventures and we'll have a good laugh together." The postscript explained the invitation: Roland Oyarzun probably wanted to ask his help. Or, at least, he felt the need to justify himself to someone. In these four or five lines, François recognised the tone and manner of his old companion, they were the tone and manner of mediocrity in general —not of mediocrity triumphant, or aggressive, or picturesque, or amusing; no, quite simply of an average mediocrity. First, the affectation of ease: the serious news was conveyed in a few casual words, as an afterthought, as if it were of no importance; then the mixture of anger, defiance and false meekness, common to the persecuted, to the proscribed suffering from their proscription: ". . . It may be that you will not want to *compromise* yourself with the company of a pariah such as myself. I shall perfectly *understand* your discretion. . . ." Then the pretence of lightheartedness—"we'll have a good laugh together"—with which he tried to minimise the calamity under which he suffered, tried to transmute his shame into a subject for joking, and invite François to join him, Roland, in that band of mockers, the condemned of the liberation, who scoffed at the liberators. The pathetic postscript was a masterpiece of clumsiness, but doubtless Roland had congratulated himself on his brilliant diplomacy: "Listen to this. Isn't it subtle?" he must have said to his wife. François seemed to hear him speaking. "You see, Donadieu won't dare not come after this for fear that I shall take him for a coward." In fact, François had accepted the invitation out of pity, not from any fear of what Roland might think of him. From pity! What an encumbrance pity could be! One damned the importunate, raged at the thought of a wasted evening, at the prospect of three or four hours of boredom, of a melancholy return journey in a suburban train at one o'clock in the morning. But, with death in one's heart, one accepted the duty in the name of old acquaintanceship and one's memories. So François had bought a good bottle of wine, and some *pâté*—the shortages of the time authorised the gesture—and he was determined to be friendly to the very limits of exhaustion and, if there were some service he could render, then to do his best to perform it.

He knocked twice on the door. His heart was beating fast, from breathlessness and, a little, from anxiety. Of what could they talk without embarrassment? It was true that Roland Oyarzun was very far from being shy; besides, the sort of familiar contempt, or perhaps condescension, with which he had always treated François, should do something to ease their meeting.

"Who's there?" a voice asked from behind the door.

François gave his name. There was a scraping of the key in the lock, a rattling of chains, an impressive sequence of metallic sounds as if a drawbridge were being lowered. The door was partly opened and a shadowy head appeared in the aperture. It seemed to be making an inspection of the landing, the walls, the well of the staircase. "Come in!" Behind his visitor, Roland without a word embarked upon the complicated operation of closing the door, adjusting the chains and pushing home the bolts. Cordial phrases of greeting flowering on his lips, François had launched out upon friendly, stammering speech: "My dear chap, how glad I am to see you again, how is . . . ?" He fell silent, frozen by something sinister, something awesome in this ceremony of the keys. He stood mute and abashed, the box of *pâté* under his arm, the bottle of Burgundy in his right hand. At last Roland Oyarzun had finished. He announced in a tone of pompous sarcasm: "Since I have been involved with my country's justice, I take certain precautions, which I do not believe to be altogether supererogatory."

He turned towards François, whom he could barely see in the darkness of the little hall.

"You weren't followed outside?"

"No. What an extraordinary idea!"

"It's not an extraordinary idea at all. I'm being watched. Come along in," he said, pushing François by the shoulders.

An unshaded lamp lit the tiny dining-room. After the darkness of the street, the brilliant light made François blink. A crackling noise of frying came from the next room. Roland skirted the table and the full light fell upon him. François was shocked. He remembered a young man of twenty-five, athletic-looking, his features rather imperious, his physique a little heavy, a little massive perhaps, but young and dominating. But now in the face and body before him, though François could distinguish the lines he had known, they were changed and blurred, as if some angry hand had taken pleasure in remodelling a beautiful waxen image, had transformed it into a caricature of itself, imprinting upon it the stigmata of age, almost of dissolution. The body was still tall and straight, though the shoulders sagged; the shrunken chest no longer filled the too-ample clothes. But, above all, the sunken face showed the signs of disaster. The mouth was framed in lines, the skin had turned yellow and dry, the eyes no longer shone with that permanent light which had once lent so much life, albeit a wild, disquieting life, to the adolescent face; they were now dull and sad. Nevertheless, Roland Oyarzun gazed at his friend in silence, his expression indecipherable. When he had finished inspecting him, he heaved a sigh.

"It's terrifying," he muttered, as if speaking to himself.

"What?"

"It's terrifying how you've changed. You've aged appallingly I wonder if I should have recognised you in the street."

"Really! You haven't grown any younger yourself, you know.'

"I imagine not. But in your case it's quite shocking. Besides, you're going bald in front and over the temples."

"We're getting on for thirty, my boy."

"You show it too. In the old days you were always rather young in appearance. Indeed, you remained young-looking for a long time. Oh well, that's finished now. Really, I should never have believed that three years could age anyone so much. It was in '41 that we last met, wasn't it? Yes, I remember, in the Underground! My brother-in-law was with us."

"You, at any rate, haven't changed in character. You never hesitated to say disagreeable things to your friends."

François forced himself to laugh aloud. But it raised no echo. Oyarzun remained immobile. His glance now rested on the bottle of Burgundy and the box of *pâté*.

"What have you brought along?" he asked heavily.

"Oh, nothing much; a little wine and some *pâté*."

"You'll pay me the compliment of taking it home again," Oyarzun said curtly. "You were afraid of the food, were you?

Or was it the delicate thought of showing charity to poor suburban pariahs? You shouldn't have done it, my boy. We may be in the soup, we may live in two fifth-floor rooms in a working-class, suburban block, but when we ask a friend to dinner, there's enough to eat. Thanks for the generous thought, all the same."

"Listen, Roland. You needn't be angry. With the present shortages, it's quite natural that . . ."

"You'll pay me the compliment of taking your food home again!"

'This is a good beginning!' François thought bitterly. Poor Oyarzun was running true to form. His innate asperity was aggravated now by the smart of an open wound. The evening did not promise well.

"Are you aware," he said with a sort of forced good nature, "how you've greeted me? Why, you haven't even shaken my hand! You've done nothing but abuse me."

Oyarzun's lips parted in a pale smile.

"You know my character. I'm a hard and brutal man. And with you I make no pretence. Besides, I've been involved with the law. So, you see, I'm a little crazy. I've lost my good manners. At Fresnes one tends to lose one's manners, especially when one's forced to live with common criminals. Put down that bottle and the box of food, stop looking so embarrassed, and come to my arms."

He embraced François with an unexpected, almost savage strength. His voice suddenly broke and he launched into a sort of hurried, whispered rhapsody.

"You're my only friend. You're the only man in the world to whom I can talk. I've no one left. Not a soul. Only my dear old Donadieu, my old school friend. I'm surrounded by enemies, brutes, filthy beasts who are out for my blood. Since they shot Jacques, I've no one left. I'm all alone. I thought of you. We never see each other, we don't agree about things, we've nothing in common, but we understand one another all the same, don't we, old chap, eh?"

He pushed François from him with both hands, holding him by the shoulders, and gazed into his face. There was uncertainty in his expression and his chin trembled as if he were about to burst into tears.

"You won't let me down, will you?" he appealed.

François had reddened. This was too much! 'What the devil of a predicament!' he thought.

"You won't let me down?"

"Of course not, old chap. What do you think?"

"I'm very unhappy," he went on, clutching François' shoulders. "Without friends I can't live."

"Is your wife here?" François asked to change the subject. "You know, you've not got a bad place here," he continued easily. "It's small, but snug. . . ."

"You'll see my wife in a minute; and don't try to be polite about this horrible hole."

He was leaning with all his weight on François' shoulders like a man about to faint, while fixing him with an implacable, glassy stare.

"I'm done for, if you let me down. They're out for my blood. I don't know why they released me, but I do know that one of these days they'll machine-gun me at some street corner. At Fresnes, imagine it, even pimps and murderers were calling me a filthy traitor. Me! Me, who always placed France first! Me, who would have died a hundred deaths for France! And if I wasn't killed in '40, during the war, it was no fault of mine. Me, a traitor! Because I was with Bucard for six months. Because I was an instructor with the League of Youth. Because my brother-in-law was a member of the Militia. As if they hadn't already shot Jacques! As it if wasn't enough to have murdered him! They condemned me to National Indignity," he went on with a mournful little laugh. "National Indignity! Doesn't it make you sick? Me, the son of Commandant Oyarzun."

He suddenly released his hold and, straightening up, passed a hand across his brow. The gesture had a curious stress of its own. Until then he had been natural and spontaneous. The gesture bore a suspicion of theatricality.

"Some days I think I'm going mad."

François was angry. It was worse than he could possibly have imagined. How intolerable people were with their personal revelations! They invaded your life with their sordid dramas, their dirty linen and their eyes imploring help. . . . 'As if,' he thought, 'I hadn't any worries or problems of my own. But I don't throw them in other people's faces; I try to solve them on my own.' Under the pitiless light of the naked bulb, he gazed at Roland

Oyarzun s huge, shattered body, at the ruin of what had been, but a few years before, an athlete, an adolescent crowned with radiant youth. 'The man means nothing to me,' he thought. 'He's a bore. Why the devil did I come? If he's been unjustly treated, what can I do about it? I'm not to blame. It has nothing to do with me.' But pity stirred in him, sickly sweet.

"Calm down", he said gently. "I understand very well how you feel. But, anyway, Fresnes is over now and you won't be bothered any more. You'll see, the whole thing will settle itself."

"It's easy enough for you to talk. The whole thing will settle itself! No matter: it happened. I got three months in prison. I'm an outlaw in my own country. They've destroyed . . ."—he was seeking words, his fingers spread out before his face—". . . all that was most fundamental in me, most essential to me, my own conception of myself, do you understand? Listen, it reminds me of a phrase of Montherlant's that I once learnt by heart. I still remember it. 'I have nothing but my own conception of myself to sustain me upon the seas of extinction'," he quoted with a certain nobility, and then threw his companion a glance that was at once timid and crafty.

François remembered this phrase of Montherlant's all the better from the fact that it was he who had made Roland read the page upon which it occurred. Suddenly François felt a sharp and poignant pang, for the little phrase, coming out of the mists of the years, tore at his heart and burst suddenly into a whole sheaf of remembered sensations: patches of sunlight on the flagstones of a courtyard, the denticulated foliage of the limes, the dusty warmth of a July afternoon, sounds and light shimmering, a snatch of dialogue from two young, boyish voices. "What do you think of it?—Marvellous!" and the joy of admiring and sharing one's admiration like a treasure which, instead of decreasing, must increase tenfold by being shared with another. The little phrase seemed no more now than a rather vain piece of rhetoric, and today François could no longer discover in it the quality that had enraptured him at sixteen. Yet the mere rhythm of its syllables seemed to pulse with a life other than its own.

"I see you remember it, too," Roland Oyarzun said. "It struck you at the time, when I read you the text."

So he was appropriating the discovery. A strange error, since

Roland had always professed the greatest contempt for literature and all writers, with the exception of political writers. He used to read nothing at school but Maurras, Bainville, and the *Action Française*. His admiration for that page of Montherlant's had been no more than a friendly gesture towards François, a lazy concession to a comrade's predilections, in short an act of courtesy, as one pretends for a moment to be interested in the art of the Ming period or in the track performances of Ladoumégue if, by chance, one happens to find oneself in conversation with a sinologue or a champion runner. (It is also true that Montherlant might be considered a right-wing writer, which, in any case, would have assured him Roland's adherence in the name of spiritual solidarity understood in its widest sense as, for instance, a member of the Ku-Klux-Klan, who, being strictly puritanical, was a stranger, even hostile, to every manifestation of aestheticism, would nevertheless shake a decadent artist by the hand, since all white men must unite against the black peril.)

"By the way, he's in trouble from what I see," he went on. "He's being attacked in the Press. He's been purged too," he said with the bitter pride of an aristocrat who, on climbing into the fatal tumbril, chanced to recognise André Chénier among the condemned.

François smiled.

"Yes, he also," he said, but his tone was so discreetly ironical that it failed to reach the level upon which Roland Oyarzun could distinguish irony. This required a fair degree of emphasis.

"Do you smell burning?" asked Oyarzun, sniffing immoderately and rolling his eyes in alarm. "I bet it's the potatoes. Simone asked me to watch them. Whatever we do, we mustn't give you a burned dinner. Come on. Let's go and look after the food."

He preceded François into a tiny room, lit by a sort of garret window which opened upon an interior courtyard. There was a gas stove in one corner, a tin bath in another, and a sink which doubtless served both for personal ablutions and for washing-up, for there were toilet articles, tooth brushes, a comb and a looking-glass, alongside the kitchen utensils. The effect was squalid and depressing.

"Beastly, isn't it? And yet it wasn't easy to find, I can tell you. But Simone was so fed up living with her family. As you see, we can't keep the children here. My in-laws are looking after them for the moment. By the way, I haven't asked you for news of your wife and child. Are they well?"

"Very well, thanks," François replied briefly.

"You've got your child here with you?"

"No; she's in the South, but I shall be going to fetch her soon."

"How old is she now?"

"Seven."

"Seven! Good Lord, already? But of course you married out of the cradle. . . . My children are three and two. Your wife's well?" he insisted.

"Yes; very well."

"You ought to have brought her along with you, then!"

He was looking at him sideways, expectantly. François knew his Oyarzun well enough to be sure that he would not stop at merely giving him significant openings.

"Catherine and I have separated," he said. "We no longer see one another since I came back."

"I knew it," said Oyarzun. "But I wanted to find out whether you would talk to me about it. So you've separated. Ah, well, I always thought your marriage was unstable, that it wouldn't last. Besides, when you leave your wife for two years to go and play about in London, what can you expect? And so you've separated? Well, well. But it must complicate things for you, doesn't it?" he asked with visible satisfaction.

"It complicates nothing at all."

"But what about your daughter Juliette?"

"What about her? Juliette's still my daughter. I pay for her keep and allow my wife to go and see her as often as she wants."

"And you're going to leave things like that? Supposing your wife should claim sole custody of the child?"

"It's very unlikely. Catherine has her career."

"By the way, talking of her career, she must have had a bit of trouble, too, hasn't she? Because during the occupation she played for the Germans, even went to Germany. She must have had trouble?" he insisted hopefully.

"You seem to be very well informed. No, Catherine has had no trouble. She was in danger of being prosecuted, her name appeared in the lists of the proscribed, but it stopped short there.

No proceedings have been taken against her. I took care of that."

He regretted having let slip that last phrase. Already Roland was responding in his sardonic way.

"Of course, you're one of the big bosses nowadays. Well, don't let's exaggerate; one of the smaller bosses. . . . Anyway, part of the outfit. In with the boys who count. A member of the Resistance! . . . You pull the strings. Christ, when I think of you at school! Little Donadieu, for God's sake! Well, that's how it is. You write in the Resistance Press, while I've just come out of prison. I've read your film reviews, you know. Not bad, not bad at all. And how's your friend, Bernard?" he added, looking mysterious.

"Very well. But you seem to be peculiarly well informed about me. May I ask . . . ?"

"Oh, we have our little sources of information, you know, we victims of the Liberation. We have our secret service and keep our little lists. Do you mind? After all, we have to look after ourselves. But it's all right, my boy; don't you worry. I'm only joking. Just a sly dig in the ribs for you, that's all. Who informed me about you? You forget that your goings-on are known in Sault-en-Labourd, and that I get letters from Sault-en-Labourd. Besides, I saw your wife once or twice during the Occupation. I knew that you had gone to London, swept off by that fascinating Monsieur Bernard. I used to know Bernard, you see. Well, 'know' is saying a lot. He was in the Remove at Louis-le-Grand when I was in the First Form. I think I may have spoken to him casually once or twice. I remember him because he was friends with one Gaudie, Nick Gaudie. They were never seen apart; and these inseparables became famous because of the extraordinary contrast between them. Bernard was always as smart as you like, impeccable, you know, out of a bandbox; while Nick was disgustingly filthy, a real gutter-snipe. This Nick, by the way, I don't know if I was seeing things, but I thought I recognised him one day in a German uniform. Perhaps it wasn't him, but if it wasn't it was someone damned like him: a big chap with hair so fair it was almost white, and as thin as a lath. I met this Boche at the entrance to the Underground. Naturally, I stopped, riveted, my mouth hanging open. 'Gaudie!' I said mechanically. The Boche looked at me for a bare second. If it was Gaudie, I must say he had his wits about him; he didn't give himself away, not a sign.

He went on down into the Underground and left me standing there like a bloody pillar of salt. Funny, wasn't it? But to come back to Bernard. So you know him. In fact, they tell me you're like a couple of love-birds. I don't know how you can stick a chap like that, a tailor's dummy with the gift of the gab. Even at Louis-le-Grand I couldn't stand the sight of him. Besides, he was an anarchist in those days. He used to write poems of revolt against the flag and what have you. A holy terror. And today he's editor-in-chief of that brilliant rag, *Horizons*, into which you excrete your articles. Aren't I right?"

'My God,' François thought, 'how cheap he is! Even in detail: "a sly dig in the ribs," "you *excrete* your articles," he can't miss. How sad to be so cheap.'

"Well!" cried Roland, banging him on the shoulder with his fist. "I've been pulling you to pieces, eh, old man? I've not changed, you see; as assertive, as malicious as ever. But you forgive me, don't you?"

The subject of François' troubles and sorrows had clearly cheered him, but he was soon wallowing once more among his morose, unhappy thoughts.

"In short, one way or another, they've done us all down." ('They' for Roland Oyarzun meant collectively everyone he believed to be obstinately set upon his destruction: before the war it had meant the Jews and the Freemasons; today it meant the Resistance. In general, 'They' stood for the other side in direct proportion to its responsibility for the sorrows of the world and those of Roland in particular. 'They' represented the sinister conspiracy of hostile forces. The mental universe of Roland Oyarzun was not unlike that of a Papuan savage.)

He was turning the potatoes over in the pan, his body bent backwards to avoid the spitting fat.

"By God, we live in a hell of a period! You know I've been sacked from my job?"

"No. I didn't."

"But of course. National Indignity necessarily carries the sack with it, didn't you know? For five years, in my case. They might as well condemn us to starve to death, my wife, my children and myself. National Indignity!" he suddenly shouted aloud, and began rummaging among the potatoes with such a violence of righteous anger that he might have been chastising the injustice of men or of the gods themselves. "It's that, that, that which gets me down, which is killing me! But you, Donadieu, know what I am, what my origins are, and my ideas. For all that you've become a swell member of the Resistance, for all that you know nothing whatever about politics, and you have never known anything about them, admit it, for all that you went and joined de Gaulle like the nitwit you are"—he was becoming violent, but knew from experience that François would accept this sort of outburst with calm—"you won't pretend that I'm not now, or ever have been, anything but a patriot?"

"No, no; of course not. Calm down. Besides, how am I to judge? I don't even know why they shoved you into gaol. You merely told me in your letter that you had been released from Fresnes; that's all."

"Just wait. You shall hear the whole story. I asked you to come here to tell it to you. In order to justify myself. No," he corrected himself awkwardly, "I didn't ask you only for that. I wanted to see you too, see my old friend again, naturally!" he added with such patent insincerity that François was taken aback. "I'll tell you all about it after dinner. I hope Simone comes in soon. She went to take the children back. Christ!" he sighed. "To be compelled to get rid of the children at night because there's nowhere to put them to sleep! But you see how things are with us? No money, no work, no resources, no redress for five years, with two children and a hovel to live in. And I who long for a son. A son of my own whom I would have formed with loving care like a masterpiece. But how can I have a son as long as we're compelled to live in a hole like this? You see how the bastards have succeeded in depriving me of everything, even of the joy of paternity."

"You've got two daughters. . . ."

"That's not the same at all!" he interrupted impatiently. "Girls don't count. Of course, I'm exaggerating. But one's not truly a father till one's the father of a boy. Besides, you know, my daughters, poor little mites, I hope they'll alter as they grow up, for at the moment they're as ugly as sin. I don't know where they get it from. My father was a good-looking man, my mother was only too beautiful, poor thing. My wife is charming; besides, she's exactly like her brother, Jacques, who was beauty incarnate. As for me, I've always been considered a fine figure of a man. I'm not vain, but the truth is the truth. Well then? Christ!" he shouted, pulling his hand away as a drop of hot fat fell on it. He blew on his fingers. "Hell, it's hot!" He blew again. "Well, there it is, old man: I've no right to have a son. Because, apparently, I'm a traitor. National . . ."—he blew on his fingers—". . . Indignity!" He shook his head. "National Indignity," he repeated softly, dreamily, as if modulating in a minor key after the original exclamation had exposed the theme in the full dramatic plenitude of a major chord. "No; you see from whatever angle I look at it, the expression seems to have nothing to do with me. Me, the scion of the Oyarzuns. The son of Commandant Oyarzun."

"By the way, how is your father?"

"Very well. He's a monk."

"What?"

"Father went into a monastery in '43. He'd been obsessed with the idea of a vocation for some time. There's drama there too. We seem to be a family for drama. Fated to it. Anyway, he went into a monastery. I haven't seen him for two years. He wrote to me the other day. An admirable letter, old man. I carry it here, over my heart."

His voice had grown gentle, a sort of glow of adoration irradiated his features.

"And your mother?"

"Don't speak of her. Do you mind?" he said without anger. "Besides, why do you ask? You know very well what happened; all Sault-en-Labourd was full of the scandal just before the war. My mother chasing my father round the house in his nightdress with a service revolver, then threatening to kill herself. Scenes which wavered between comedy and tragedy—in fact, hell. When he wanted to enter the Order, all hell broke loose. My mother refused her authorisation out of sheer spite. The Bishop of Bayonne intervened. At that time I was in the Army, and I couldn't follow closely what was going on. Something happened that I didn't understand or, rather, which was kept from me. Something that, on application to Rome, made the annulment of the marriage possible, or so I gathered from the vague hints I received." He frowned with the effort of thinking and remembering. "Although I have always wondered whether a marriage can be annulled when consummation has taken place. . . ." He fell to thinking again and was silent for a moment or two, fork in hand, standing by the stove upon which the potatoes were browning. François had sat down on a stool. "And whatever my father's principles may have been as regards conjugal morality, there is no doubt that the marriage was consummated at least once, since here I am. In short, my mother finished by giving way. And there you are. My father went into a monastery, my mother lives in concubinage in Paris with another man, I've come out of prison, having lost my job, my reputation, my rights as a French citizen, and my greatest friend, my brother-in-law, murdered by the cads of the Resistance. The fate of the Oyarzun family! A real tragedy."

"Yes. The subject has even been treated in classical times."

"To hell with the classics! You always confound life and literature. You were always mouthing quotations and pedantic allusions. Hitler sent the Jews to concentration camps. He ought to have sent the writers there too."

"He in fact did so."

"Oh no! And the proof is that they're still about today, muscling in with their frenzied pens, and their hearts full of hate. They persecute the chaps who wished to remain loyal to France in her hour of trial."

"You forget the writers whom the Germans shot."

"They'll be avenged. Your friends from London understand shooting very well too."

"I don't want to start an argument. It's quite clear that on some points we shall never agree."

"No; we shall never agree. Anyhow, talk to me no more of literature and writers. As a breed they make me sick. Do you still want to write?"

"No; I gave up the idea long ago," François muttered as if he were excusing himself; and he blushed again, saying to himself: 'Why am I so shy in the presence of fools?'

"You're quite right not to pursue the idea," said Roland with satisfaction. "I remember that at seventeen or eighteen, at school, you were always talking of writing. I suppose you discovered you had no talent. If all the pretentious clots who write showed the same sense as you do, the country would be much better off; if no one wrote at all it would be perfection. I scorn all men of letters and, generally speaking, every other sort of artist too.

I spit on them. They're parasites upon society, foul little lice."

"Even Montherlant, whom you were quoting a moment ago?"

"Certainly not. He won the *Croix de Guerre*. He was wounded seven times in the stomach by exploding shells. He's proved that he's got sand in the belly. A virile type. Besides, he belongs to the opposition."

"The opposition?"

"Against the corruption of democracy. Haven't you read the *Solstice de Juin*?"

"Yes; I have. What's more, it's the book he can't be forgiven for today."

"But mark well, all he says about the zodiac and the swastika is ridiculously absurd, insane nonsense. Besides, he sucks up to the Boche, and that I don't care for. I've never been able to stand the Boche; on that point I agree with Maurras, and I'm against the Fascists of *Je suis Partout*. But I'll explain to you in detail my moral and political position. To come back to the *Solstice en Juin*, all that's pro-German in the book is bad. But everything he says against democracy is meticulously right, absolutely first-class. It's inspired. He's hit it off exactly. Forgive me. It's not surprising that it's made your little Israelite friends foam at the mouth."

"What do you mean by my little Israelite friends?"

"Don't play the innocent; it's well known that you went and joined the Jewish-Marxist coalition."

The phrase belonged to that particular kind of rather puerile teasing which is current among old friends, it was one of those jokes which make sense to the initiated, because they belong to a whole system of allusions, of intimate references which at once evoke a whole realm of common experience; thus, even when the passing of the years has utterly changed both the physical and moral characteristics of those involved, even to the point of rendering them unrecognisable, the little joke, spoken by one of them at a chance meeting, establishes at once a fugitive and, more often than not, quite artificial intimacy. Thus, every 'old boy' possesses a certain number of personal keys, by whose means, having opened one by one the stubborn doors of memory, he can hope to regain the classroom and the playground of his youth, until the day when, having renounced a mental gymnastic which forgetfulness, indifference and arthritis have ultimately made too laborious, and for that matter vain, he no longer, as a frail septuagenarian, bothers to con over his little stock but uses it purely as a signal of recognition. At this stage, in fact, the schoolboy jokes, now utterly meaningless, but none the less conducive to an automatic and knowing smile upon lined and bloated faces, have become the passwords of a freemasonry, the rallying cries of a cast. They delimit a privileged section in the vague social amalgam, define a political or religious allegiance, and provide the individual, lost in the void, with the resource of belonging to an Order. Thus Roland Oyarzun's teasing, flung out like the battle-cry, "Mountjoy Saint Denis!" was obscurely pursuing a double end. On the one hand it was intended to underline his standing as an old pupil of the Fathers and, by extension, his adherence to a still stable bourgeoisie, which remained capable, for all the convulsions of the period, of watching over the safety of its members: a precious conviction in this hour of loneliness and confusion. On the other hand, it was intended to lead François Donadieu gently back from the enemy camp to the common Fatherland, which was not France as a whole, but a France shorn of the Communists, the Freemasons, the Jews, of all foreigners, whether naturalised or not, of the Resistance, of the Gaullists and of sundry other undesirable elements of the French community. And the speaking smile with which he accompanied his joke seemed to imply: 'In spite of your political aberrations, it remains perfectly clear to me that you are still really on the same tack as I am, that you belong to the same race, and that you bear indissolubly graven on your heart the convictions that make us brothers.'

"I'm convinced that fundamentally you have remained sound," he went on, "in spite of the peculiarities of your behaviour. Have you kept your faith?"

"That's a difficult question to answer."

"Difficult? One either has faith or one hasn't. I know that faith with you Huguenots . . ." He made a vague gesture with his hand, as if faith among Protestants were as uncertain and incomprehensible as the religious thought of Hottentots. "Anyway, you still practise your religion, I suppose?"

"I seldom go to church these days. But, tell me, where do you stand?"

"As far as I'm concerned, there's no question about it at all.

I'm a Catholic to the last gasp. Which doesn't mean to say that I communicate every Sunday. But I'd die, if it were necessary, in the defence of Catholicism. After all, the Church is part of my inheritance. Like Maurras, I'm a Roman."

"Catholic and French for ever," drawled François.

It was another school joke, the counterpart of the first.

"Precisely, old boy. I wish Simone would come back. I don't know what to do with these potatoes," he muttered, leaving for the moment the defence of the Holy See to turn to more trivial things. "Perhaps I ought to salt them? Where is the salt? Help me look for it, Donadieu. Come on. Lend a hand. You weren't invited just for the fun of it! For God's sake, where's the salt!" he shouted in pretended fury.

This heavy joviality, produced in the manner of hearty student high spirits—the laughter and good humour of bohemian poverty —created a silence which François, try as he would, could find no way of breaking. For here, indeed, the poverty was too glaring, and Roland was no longer twenty; it was not an occasion for laughter, even courageous laughter, and François felt embarrassed as if he were hearing salacious anecdotes told by an old man. No doubt Roland Oyarzun dimly perceived that his gaiety rang false, or failed in its object, or in any case was out of place, for he went on more normally: "Well, of course, I don't spend all my time shut up in church. That's quite true. It's the feeling that counts. I'll make an admission which will surprise you. You know what a terrific womaniser I was and all that— mad about women, always after a bit of skirt and so on? Well, you can believe it or not, but I've never been unfaithful to my wife. Not once. And we've been married five years."

"Bravo. But I don't see the connection."

"What connection?"

"Between being faithful to your wife and your Catholic faith."

"You must be half-witted if you don't see the connection. Why do you think I've abstained from betraying my wife?"

"It might be because you're in love with her."

"Nothing to do with it! Hundreds of men love their wives and are unfaithful to them. It's the known dichotomy between the heart and the flesh. Elementary! You seem to me a pretty poor psychologist. It's just as well you're not a novelist, your readers have had a lucky escape."

"It might also be because you've had no inclination to be unfaithful, the game not being worth the candle."

Roland started as if under the lash of an outrage.

"What, no inclination to be unfaithful? What do you take me for? What right have you to suggest that I've had no inclination to be unfaithful?"

"None, none. Calm down. . . ."

"I have restrained myself from being unfaithful to her," Roland announced forcibly, "because my religious convictions forbade it."

"Right. I believe you. You must have suffered much."

"Suffered?" he asked, genuinely surprised.

"A womaniser like you. You said it yourself."

"Oh, yes, of course. Yes, certainly. Naturally, it hasn't always been easy, particularly when one has had the success I've had. Nevertheless, 'suffered' is saying a lot. It's all a question of moral discipline. Tell me, have I changed much physically?"

"A good deal, yes."

"You don't have to tell me!" he said peevishly. "Naturally, I lost a good deal of weight in prison. My physical coefficient is not what it was. But I shall recuperate! I intend to find a job in one of those physical culture centres. The Desbonnet method, you know. After all, I've got my diplomas as an instructor, and I held a job for four years in the State schools. By the way, you'll have to help me over that."

There was a ring at the door. Roland went to open it. Between the metallic sounds of the opening and the shutting of the door, from the kitchen François heard a brief whispered interrogation. "Did you see anyone? Did the concierge say anything? Is everything all right?" Simone came in. François remembered a rather soft little woman with delicate features, completely subject to the overwhelming authority of a young husband who, at that time, reunited in himself a diversity of attractions; good looks, preminence in all sports and physical exercises, and a good education. At that time people said of Roland Oyarzun: "He's a young man who'll go far." Simone, the daughter of a school porter, thought that she had married the offshoot of an old military family from the provinces, a sort of Pyrenean junker. Roland talked emotionally of his father, Commandant Oyarzun, and of the battle honours of the 49th Regiment of Infantry. Such a show of military swagger and social lustre dazzled the young girl. Besides, Roland was her brother Jacques' greatest friend. Romance flowed into her grey life. From the first day, Simone gazed upon her fiancé with all the ecstasy of a happy slave. François remembered having met them both in the company of the young brother-in-law in the Underground in '41. Jacques and Simone resembled each other like a reflection in water resembles a sunlit face. The boy's nervous grace was transmuted into languor and softness in the girl; the refulgence of the one was dimmed, as if veiled, in the other. The three years that had elapsed had marked Simone less hardly than her husband, or, rather, they had not marked her body, her cheeks and her eyes, but, more dramatically perhaps, her general appearance. François retained the memory of a young girl neatly, perhaps a little over-elegantly turned out. The woman who came towards him, her hand outstretched, was a slattern. The neglected clothes, the thin hair upon her neck and shoulders, the worn shoes, the dirty finger-nails—François took in the extent of the disaster in a single glance—were symptomatic, over and above her poverty, of an irremediable negligence and surrender. This woman had lost her self-respect, her humble everyday courage. 'What on earth have I come here for?' François asked himself once again. He felt his throat constrict with compassion, yet a cruel phrase took shape in his mind: 'the dregs of society'. 'What have I come here among these dregs for?' He felt resentful, against Roland Oyarzun, against 'these people who mean nothing to me', whom he knew only by chance, who were now drawing him into their lives and flaunting their wretchedness before his eyes. Now, and what a bore it was, he would have to return their invitation, play the part of family friend, exhaust his good nature. He remembered a phrase that Catherine had used: "You think of nothing but escape." Well, yes, it was true; he longed to escape from pathetic, malodorous humanity, break loose from respectability, pity and guilt, repudiate every obligation and all sad things, and reach a sunlit land where, at last, he would have the right to live in the implacable innocence of a child. But François knew that there was no such sunlit land upon earth; he knew that he would have to stay and be caught in the mire of compassion.

"Do you recognise our old friend?" thundered Roland. "He's changed and grown suddenly old, but he's recognisable all the same. You see, he's come, answered our call at once. A good sort, Donadieu! And mark well," he said, addressing himself to François, "we were sure you would come at once, but the times we live in are so base, cowardice so widespread these days, that we wouldn't really have been surprised if you'd turned a deaf ear to us. We, who have been prosecuted by the law, who have become compromising pariahs, we should have thought it perfectly natural if you'd let us down."

"Roland hasn't altered," Simone put in. "You can't change him. He's always joking."

At last they sat down to dinner. Roland, large and important, played the part of a man of the world entertaining a friend at his table. Simone was the distracted hostess, much too absorbed in her duties of supply to be able to take part in the conversation, except for a few meaningless interjections, "yes", "no", "really!", "impossible", "what a pity!", "today as ever is", thrown out at random. The preparation, but above all the ordering and managing of the modest meal for three people caused her as much worry and bustle as if it had consisted of twelve people on an official occasion. She was always getting to her feet to visit the kitchen to see if all were going well. She made mistakes, bringing the sugar instead of the salt, oil instead of wine, apologised with a nervous laugh, upset some sauce on the table. She rolled the first mouthful of each dish round her tongue with the expression of an official taster or perhaps the dread of a chief cook in the service of an Oriental despot; and she watched the faces of the two men for the reaction which would either bring peace to her soul or plunge her into despair. Meanwhile, her husband talked.

"Well, as I was saying, I was with Bucard. Yes, I joined the ranks of the Francisme, with Jacques, who was not yet at that time my brother-in-law. I stayed a little more than six months with Bucard. Was that, in your opinion, a crime? Particularly as I left the Francisme with a good deal of fuss and loss to myself when once I got the hang of what it was all about. Because, in the end, I did come to understand. Too bloody simple-minded by far! Idiot that I was, Francisme for me stood for the youth of the country, for decency, was a phalanx of honest, manly chaps. Bucard I saw as a man who was trying to save what still could be saved, a character like Ernst von Salomon's *Réprouvés*, with patriotism aglow in his heart; all right, I know what you're going to say, that that phrase served as a motto to *Je suis Partout*, but that makes no difference; besides, if you'll allow me to say so, the policy of *Je suis Partout* implied something of the sort, it was a fighting paper; the crowd who wrote for it, Lesca, Laubreaux, Rebattet, were tough. In short, Bucard, in my eyes, was the real leader, don't you see, the only leader who could set up a true French Fascism—not a nitwitted fop like La Roque, who had the chance of a lifetime on the 6th February, 1934, and didn't know how to take it, the fool! So Bucard, for me, represented manliness in every sense of the term."

He paused. With his eyes half closed, a secret smile upon his lips, he gazed at François like someone preparing an effect. With a little crow of laughter, he arched his eyebrows with a falsely ingenuous look.

"Well—can you believe it?—it wasn't like that at all! . . . Not at all, not at all!" he repeated. "When at last I understood what was going on, as the result of a chance incident, I was furiously angry. Jacques, my future brother-in-law, wanted to stay all the same. Of course, he was only a boy at the time: eighteen. 'Oh, so you want to stay all the same,' I hissed at him. 'Yes, Roland,' he said. 'Why the hell should I care? I should merely find it rather fun.' 'Oh, so you'd find it fun, would you?' I said. I went up to him and . . . poor boy, I'm sorry about it today, because he was a good boy, he didn't see the harm, and now that they've murdered him. But, at the time, I thought it my duty. I gave him a terrible blow. I was mad with rage at the thought that he wanted to stay in that kind of . . . that he wanted to stay there, in spite of everything, and that one day or another he'd be lost. And so, in the end, he came with me all the same, in tears, his face bleeding. I was distressed to have had to hit him, but what else could I do? I looked upon Jacques as a brother, I felt responsible for him, for his behaviour, for his purity. So we left the Francistes. A month later I married Simone."

He placed his hand upon his wife's with a gesture at once affectionate and protective.

"How did it happen that your brother-in-law was . . . ?"

"I'm coming to that. It was last May."

He narrated the circumstances of his death. It appeared that Jacques, who was a bit crack-brained, had decided, after the unfortunate experience with the Francisme, to enlist in the Militia.

Roland had done his best to dissuade him, not that he was prejudiced against the Miltia or against Darnand, but simply because he was reluctant to see Jacques embark upon an unknown adventure. But instead of succeeding in dissuading him, it was Roland himself, so infectious was the young man's enthusiasm, who had very nearly followed him to the recruiting office. "You'll see," Jacques said, "the Militia is quite different from what it was like with Bucard. They're wonderful chaps, real fighters. Besides, I want to live, I want action. The maxim of the National Revolution, Work-Family-Fatherland, bores me stiff, you know. Pétain's a grand old man, but he's not up to date, behind the times. The future is with youth and with violence. There's no one about Pétain except priests, elderly maiden ladies, colonels and Boy Scouts. You can't remake Europe by sitting on the fence. We must march hand in hand with the Germans. We must be strong, strike at the terrorist bastards, fight, use our muscles. You're behind the times, old chap." That was how Jacques talked. And Roland was at once shocked in his convictions, for he hated the Germans and venerated the Marshal, and assailed with the tenderness of a father who watches the first kicks of his baby son. He had replied, "Very well, Jacques. Since you believe it to be your destiny . . ." So Jacques had donned the khaki shirt, the cross-belt and the black boots. Roland, having renounced adventure in order to assume the duties of a family man, had rather sadly continued to exercise his profession of physical instructor in the school where Simone's parents were the caretakers. A year earlier he had performed the same functions at the League of Youth near Vichy. At the school he made moderate Vichyist propaganda among his colleagues and pupils. For, after a period of live pro-Fascist sympathy, which had culminated precisely, at the very beginning of the Occupation, with his adherence to Francisme, Roland had retreated a little from this position, particularly when the Germans invaded the Free Zone, and he had confined himself to obedience to Vichy and loyalty to the Marshal, a discreet position to which, nevertheless, the reading of *Je suis Partout*, an intransigent anti-Semitism, enlivened by Anglophobia, lent the indispensable note of vigour and mordancy. From time to time Jacques visited the young family, notably for the christening of the second daughter, to whom he acted as godfather, holding her at the baptismal font like an "avenging angel" in his uniform. (Roland actually used the words "avenging angel", which did not fail to surprise his guest, since the poetic designation contrasted ill with Roland's normal vocabulary. Where had he come across it, François wondered. He felt, too, that an avenging angel, whether symbolic or not, was an embarrassing adjunct or, at least, somewhat out of place, at the tender rite of baptism.) In the previous May, the group to which Jacques belonged had been stationed in the neighbourhood of Guéret. They came to grips with the regional *maquis* in a number of skirmishes. A short while before the Liberation Jacques was made prisoner with two of his comrades in an ambush. He refused to give any information about the local Militia, its plans, or the names of its members. During a German attack, Jacques' two comrades managed to escape and join the Germans. The members of the *Maquis* had to pack up and get out. It was then that Jacques was killed.

"How did you learn the details of the story?"

"One of Jacques' companions, who managed to get out, came and saw us last July. It was he who, with the help of a German soldier, buried Jacques on the site of his execution."

Simone was snivelling quietly into her plate. She got up and went into the kitchen. Roland assumed a judicial air.

"The leader of the *maquisards* who assassinated Jacques," he continued weightily, "was named Bernard. In the underground movement he was known as Coriolanus."

"Bernard?"

François raised his head to meet the inflexible glance which was turned upon him at point blank range.

"Yes; Bernard."

"You've no proof."

"Bernard either killed or ordered my brother-in-law to be killed with a shot in the back of the neck. I can produce a witness whenever you like."

"It's nothing to do with me. I'm sorry your brother-in-law should have died in that way, but it's not for me to judge Bernard. He was fighting. There was a war on."

"One doesn't shoot prisoners."

"The Germans tortured and shot most of the *maquisards* who fell into their hands."

"An army of occupation protects itself against terrorists by martial law. But for once I'm prepared to share your point of view and call the German reprisals against the *maquisards* 'crimes'. Very well, then: tell me why what is labelled a crime when committed by the Germans or the Militia should no longer be so when committed by the *maquisards*."

"It's the intention that makes the crime."

"Really. The intention makes the crime. The end justifies the means. When the intention is pure, murder ceases to be murder. I appreciate the delicacy of the distinction. Your casuistry is admirable, you chaps from London. But I'm a casuist too. The intentions of the Germans were equally pure, in their eyes; they wanted to edify Europe, to defeat Bolshevism. As far as that goes, my friend, there are only honest men on both sides of the barricades; the Militia and the Resistance were of equal worth."

"Once again, it's not for me to judge Bernard."

"Very well. You follow the gospel teaching of 'judge not'. But Bernard judged. Your friends on the Committee of Purification, they judge. And I, who have no blood on my hands, who am guiltless both before my own conscience and before my country, I have been judged by the patriots of the Liberation. In whose name?"

François made no answer.

"I'll tell you. In the name of hate."

François put his head in his hands.

"Listen, old man, I didn't come here to have a philosophical debate on the subject of justice. I came here to see you and to help you, later on, if I can. Frankly, you're wearing me out."

There was a mocking gleam of triumph in Roland's eyes.

"Simone," he called, "please bring the cheese and the white wine. Our friend's worn out."

He laughed loudly and disdainfully and smote François on the shoulder.

"You old idiot! Shall I tell you something? You make me laugh. You make me laugh because you're just an old fool of a Huguenot: full of goodwill, but a bit simple when it comes to politics. You never have understood anything about politics. That's why I forgive you for being a friend of Bernard's and for writing in his filthy rag. But don't worry about what I've told you of the death of my brother-in-law. I don't hold you responsible, of course. The murder of my brother-in-law is a matter between myself and the gallant Monsieur Bernard. And it's between us two that it'll one day be settled. It will be settled, old man, I'm telling you. But you've got nothing to do with this, I look upon you as completely inoffensive. Do you even know why you went to join the Gaullists in London? My good, honest Donadieu! Don't look so angry, old man. I'm only teasing you, just being malicious, as always, but I'm fond of you, you know. Do you remember how we used to argue at school in February '34? Even then you always found argument immediately exhausting. You were a timid little democrat, conscientious, and worn out."

"When face to face with a hidebound, loud-mouthed Fascist."

Roland roared with laughter.

"Loud-mouthed—you've said it, old man! And if they think they've shut my mouth with all their nonsense, three months in prison and an iniquitous verdict, they've got another thought coming to them, the bastards! Because, I can tell you, my boy, the wind will change. Today we've still got to keep mum; we live under a reign of terror. But history shows that Thermidor invariably succeeds the Terror. Tomorrow we shall speak."

"I hope so. I'm simply a conscientious democrat: I hope that everyone will be allowed to speak, that every party may have the means of making its voice heard."

"Our voice will be terrible."

"*Dies irae, dies illa!* Our poor country's poisoned for ten years."

"For ten years? You forget our sons. You forget the sons of those who were imprisoned and shot by the Liberation. You've created a dynasty of outlaws within the country."

"Our sons will take no interest in our quarrels. They'll be interested in football and the cinema. The politics of today will seem as far off, as boring, as vague and complicated as the Dreyfus Case seems to us."

"You're wrong. There'll be dynasties of Pétainists and collaborators, as, since 1793, there have been dynasties of Royalists, inveterate enemies of the régime. Poor democracy!"

As soon as the meal was over, François left. Oyarzun insisted upon accompanying him to the Underground.

"Listen," he said. "There was something else I wanted to ask you, but I didn't like to do it upstairs in front of Simone. Will you go and see my mother? Here's her address. I cannot—indeed, I will not go and see her; it's a question of self-respect, we've not been on speaking terms for three years. I'm not concealing from you that it's a somewhat delicate mission. My mother hates me. Or, to be more precise, she has never forgiven me taking my father's part against her. At the moment she's living with a rich man. A shady type, I think, black market and so on, but rich. During the Occupation he helped a number of Jews, laden with gold and foreign currency, across the demarcation line, and I wouldn't be at all surprised if he didn't give more than one of them away to the Gestapo, having already confiscated their luggage for himself. Well, you know the kind of low blackguard I mean. I've no love for Yids, but all the same. Anyway, my mother lives with the bastard. Well, there it is, old man. But, if I don't find some work pretty quick, my wife, my children, and I are all bound to die of starvation. I'm telling you, quite frankly, how things are. If I went and asked my mother for help, she'd crow over me, as you can well imagine. It'd be a bit too humiliating. After all, I've got my pride. I don't want to give her the opportunity of crowing. So you'll go and see her, as if on your own initiative. You'll tell her how desperate our situation is, my wife's and mine. You'll do the necessary, I know, as diplomatically as you can, for though you may be a fool in politics, when it's a question of sensibility, the emotions and so on, old man, I'm certain you know your stuff. I've no fears about that. My mother's mad; but perhaps she's not completely inhuman. You'll go, old man. If she refuses, well, I'll go and see her myself. But, I'm telling you, there'll be a row, and I don't answer for the consequences."

This crowning imposition on top of everything else! François was staggered. He could barely see his companion's face in the darkness of the street, but his voice, sharp and rasping, retained its arrogance even in petitioning a favour. The December night was cold and damp. A group of young men, well muffled up, passed close by them in a cloud of American tobacco. They were singing an American dance tune at the top of their voices. With their forefingers moving rhythmically about their ears, they strutted by like a band of lascivious Negroes. Roland Oyarzun grunted like a pig, as if unable to contain his contempt and indignation.

"Gaullist youth!" he exclaimed with a sort of irritated rattle in his throat.

François could not help laughing.

"You laugh, do you?" said Roland. "There's nothing to laugh about. By God, they're a fine lot, the youth of the Liberation! Between a couple of summary executions, they dance a war dance like the cannibals that they, in fact, are."

They reached the Underground.

"Goodbye, old man," said Roland. "Thanks for coming. I've had a wonderful evening."

He held the hands of his old friend in his. He suddenly became hazy with emotion.

"Friendship, there's nothing to beat it! You know, when I think of our schooldays I feel like weeping. When I see myself in the looking-glass and see the sort of fellow I've become and then remember the chap I was only ten years ago, I could cry like a calf. Ten years! Really, life's very odd. When I think how life changes us, destroys us little by little, disfigures us, breaks us up—sometimes I think that we begin to die at eighteen. Time—by God, what a mystery it is!"

François was about to hurry down the steps to the Underground. He was held back by a hand on his sleeve.

"Listen," said Oyarzun in a hollow voice. "I hate to ask you such a thing, but . . . Frankly, I don't know how my wife and I are going to eat tomorrow. If it's not a frightful bore, could you lend me two hundred francs?"

CHAPTER III

FRAGMENTS FROM A DEAD WORLD

1

ROLAND OYARZUN had not always been victimised. At four years old, for instance, he had won First Prize in a baby show organised by the town of Bayonne. This distinction, acquired at so early an age, augured well for the future.

He was a pretty, plump child with curly hair. His mother spoilt him and was fond of walking under the "*Arceaux*"—the ancient main thoroughfare of the town which had something Spanish about it—accompanied by the child, held on a leash by a nurse, and a greyhound, held on a leash by an orderly. Clothilde Oyarzun was causing a revolution in the Basque town with her fashionable clothes: dresses made by Poirier, audaciously short, with the waistline round her hips, embroidered with gipsy motifs, four rows of huge pearls decorating the bust of an empress, and a cloche hat pulled down to her eyebrows. An accomplished woman of the world, she knew how to display the most elegant culture: accompanying herself on the piano, she could sing the great arias from *Hérodiade* or *Samson and Delilah* in drawing-rooms where her contralto voice made the chandeliers jingle. She read much: Victor Margueritte, Raymonde Machard, Pierre Frondaie, Claude Farrère, and vehemently discussed the emancipation of women, a burning topic, at Bayonne, during the 'twenties.

Lieutenant Oyarzun admired his wife. But, desiring a manly education for his son, he did his best to see that the boy should escape as much as possible from the coddling of the gynaeceum. He told the orderly to take him for walks alongside the barracks: the spectacle of martial force on parade, so he thought, would suggest the proper tone to his infant sensibility. Lieutenant

Oyarzun's son became the mascot of the garrison. The men made a pet of the little fellow with his brown curls. And so, as in the case of the Emperor Philip the Arab, whom Barrès evokes so admirably in a celebrated passage, "the army rather than the temple influenced his childhood", Roland was torn between the maternal boudoir, a sort of submarine grotto hung with green velvet, bright with glass objects and mirrors, in which Clothilde, wrapped in a dressing-gown the madder red of soldiers' trousers, floated like some formidable sea-nymph, and the purlieus of the barracks, the domain of the young recruits, jaunty and licentious, swaggering in their peaked caps; between Venus Anadyomene and Mars the Conqueror. And Lieutenant Oyarzun arranged matters so that the balance inclined in favour of Mars. Whenever the feminine pole appeared to be exciting too lively an attraction, he did not hesitate to react with severity. It was thus when one day he surprised little Roland before a looking-glass, a cloche hat on his head, roguishly posing in a style clearly inspired by Clothilde. The boy was apparently copying his mother. Lieutenant Oyarzun restrained a desire to laugh. 'He's becoming affected,' he thought, 'we must stifle these mincing ways once and for all.' His expression severe, he went towards the boy. Roland stood still, petrified. Lieutenant Oyarzun snatched off the hat with the same quick gesture with which an officer, convicted of unbecoming conduct, is degraded. He smacked his son lightly and said: "Don't ever start this foolishness again." Roland burst into tears and was inconsolable till nightfall.

When Roland was about thirteen he became aware that a growing and dramatic tension existed between his parents. He had already witnessed painful scenes. He had seen Clothilde, her hair in disorder, wrapped in her madder dressing-gown, come out of the conjugal bedroom followed by her husband, his expression furious, his cheeks waxen. Another time he had heard scraps of a dispute, obscure phrases flung out like whistling knives. One of these phrases had enlightened him. He loved his father devotedly. It hurt him to see him humiliated. For him, Edmond Oyarzun had always represented strength, heroism and manly virtue: doubtless a formidable, but nevertheless a tutelary, divinity. Clothilde represented a sort of equivocal opulence, a beribboned disloyalty, coquettishness, capriciousness, the pernicious deeps of feminine inconstancy.

Lieutenant Oyarzun had inherited the family house at Sault-en-Labourd, a neighbouring town. He there installed his wife, sent his son to board at the local school, of which he himself was an old boy, and, as he was extremely devout, consecrated himself from then on to the promotion of his own spiritual welfare. He visited Roland at school each week and spent every other week-end with his wife, as much to give the lie to gossip as from a sense of duty and a taste for self-mortification.

Roland revealed himself to be but an average pupil except in French history at which he excelled. Having 'got' religion, he had founded a semi-sporting, semi-pious society called the "Congregation", and had set himself up as a friendly guide to the youngest boys. He found a certain exaltation in this part which, with its attendant functions, was approved by the school authorities. At sixteen, the crisis of that ungrateful age was made manifest in him by an access of acne and, almost equally striking, of lyricism. He composed a "Congregationalist" hymn and a didactic poem inspired by the *Roman de la Rose* (it was about a violet, France, threatened by a horrible thistle, called Democracy, and happily rescued by the Chevalier Fleur de Lys).

A good football player, he enjoyed at school a popularity which was only tempered by discreet mockery. The preternatural gravity with which he preached to the younger boys even earned him certain malicious nicknames, such as "the Reverend" or "Baden-Powell". On the whole the masters recognised his good qualities. But only the boys knew another side of his character, the hidden reverse to his religious fervour: a delight in scabrous talk, an obsession, loudly proclaimed, with women and woman's mystery. He had a fund of dirty stories and of wanton songs. Thus, according to the day and his mood, there issued successively from the young man's lips the most edifying discourse and the licentious chronicle of *Marius the Bigamist*, a nobly inspired marching song and the shocking refrains with which soldiers divert themselves: *Trois Orfévres* or *Les Filles de Camaret*. He who had written verses in honour of the Chevalier Fleur de Lys showed himself, in theory at least, not merely commonplace in his attitude towards women, but positively vulgar. His vocabulary had a dismaying precision. The most clear-sighted of his contemporaries realised obscurely that all this was merely showing off, youthful bragging, a young cock playing to the gallery, his feathers erect. They perceived that the true Roland was rather the young leader who, in shorts, his face serene, his gaze direct, subdued a group of little boys with his exhortation.

He had no friends, his strong emotions found their outlet by preference in the relationship of a master and disciples, a horse-breaker with young colts, with his little band. To tell the truth, he allied himself successively with companions of his own age, but these experiments failed one after the other. On each occasion Roland set out under full sail towards an ideal of brotherhood so exalted, so dramatic and so intense that the selected guinea-pig, exhausted by the first onset, beat a hasty retreat. So highly charged a relationship frightened off even the nicest natures. Roland began at once to speak of a communion of souls, of spiritual emulation, of a political crusade; he happily envisaged the death of the two friends, cut off in the plenitude of youth, by the same shell, upon the battlefield. The sensible lad called upon to share this high destiny modestly excused himself: he preferred, he said, motor-bicycles. Moreover, Roland was extremely unreasonable; he was jealous, meddlesome, easily disappointed and quick to blame, as well as being exhaustingly romantic: in fine, he was an appalling bore. Hence he had no friends. As a result he took an extremely pessimistic view of the human heart. Between pursed lips he would let fall remarks of a disillusionment that had nothing to learn in acerbity from La Rochefoucauld, though their expression might be less classical: "Friendship?" he would say. "It's all balls. Don't make me laugh. In this world men have but one consolation, and that's a bit of skirt." And if he saw no masters about, he would begin to sing:

Les filles de Camaret
Se disent toutes vierges

or perhaps:

Le cordonnier Pamphile
A élu domicile
Près d'un couvent de filles.

Among his contemporaries one of the nicest was François Donadieu, a good, rather quiet boy. Roland bullied him a good deal, being one of the disquieting type who attacks the slightest sign of weakness, making game of it, trampling it underfoot, perhaps because they have within themselves a fount of secret weakness like a unstaunched wound. But upon young Donadieu he used his claws in vain. The boy possessed vital and unsuspected resources, a hard shell that was proof against anything. He drew back, readjusted his shell and then, the danger over, became as nice again as ever. The secret was a simple one: Donadieu regarded Roland as being something akin to a character in a play. He thought him comic and rather pathetic. He found him amusing. Roland's rudeness and insults did not touch him. In the end Roland began to suspect that this pale, thin Donadieu was made of some strange infrangible material. From that moment his attitude changed. He still teased him, but good humouredly, and allowed a certain rough affection to show through. "Donadieu," he would say, "you're not such a fool as you look. At bottom, you're not a bad chap", or: "I curse you because you're so wet, but I like you all the same", or again: "I can't make out how it is: with your beastly white face, your skinny, round-shouldered body and your nut full of Huguenot ideas, I ought to spit on you. Well, I don't. I can take you. I can take you better than I can anyone else here. One can say anything to you and you listen as if one was God. I can confide in you; you're my dustbin." And as the parodies of Reboux and Muller were then going the rounds of the school, he added in imitation of them: "I shall open my heart to you. Follow me, sweet Receptacle."

The school was not so out of the world that the rumour of political events did not reach it. A swindler had recently shot himself at Chamonix. The shot tore aside a veil. The "crimes of a corrupt system of government" were brought to the light of day. Parliament reeled. The scandal, which filled the daily papers, brought into the realm of reality the extravagant plots, the stir of crime, of Balzac and Eugène Sue. The school, both masters and boys, was immediately, as was the whole of France, divided into two camps. One side voted the Republic to the gallows, crying aloud for its demise. They recalled Panama, Madame Hanau, Oustric, a whole sequence of shameful crimes. The other, clinging to their democratic beliefs, protested that the republican idea must survive even the failure of its institutions. If, they said, a single scandal sufficed to condemn a system, what system could endure? They spoke of the Queen's necklace and the assignats.

"You're a fine lot, you democrats!" crowed Roland Oyarzun,

the unchallenged leader of the reactionary opposition. "It's done pretty well, your bloody democracy, eh? Pretty good, isn't it? You're just a lot of bewildered wets, putrid sentimentalists, bleating sheep. Do your noses have to be shoved into your own midden before you can understand what it's all about? Let's have a king straight away who'll clean up the mess!"

This was the sort of invective he used against the left wing in the school, which was represented by François Donadieu and a few unimportant boys. The right, on the other hand, which was largely monarchist, consisted of the strong, boastful boys with social pretensions; they talked loud and had a gift for abuse. The left, humanitarian and at a disadvantage, allowed themselves to be scoffed at while wrapping themselves shiveringly in the Declaration of the Rights of Man. Argument was impossible because the two sides spoke different languages: the right expressed itself by concrete examples and abuse, the left had recourse to flat abstractions.

"Look at the little weaklings!" Roland cried. "They don't make up one proper chap between them. I don't suppose the lot weigh ten stone. They're last in gym and want to have political ideas. The fools would kill France to save radicalism and Freemasonry. Dirty Girondins, you've given the country over to a Jew adventurer, a cheap crook."

"It's no worse than giving it over to an Italian schemer and a Scotch banker," the Left answered woefully.

"Shut up, Donadieu. You've no right to speak. In the first place because you know nothing about it, in the second place because you stammer, and in the third because you're so biased that your opinion's discredited in advance: you've never forgiven Henry IV his conversion or Louis XIV the Revocation of the Edict of Nantes. Your ancestors should have cleared out to Prussia."

"They would have been joined there by the emigrants of '89."

"Or to Geneva to join Calvin the Torturer and Jean-Jacques the Visionary."

"Anyway, it's better than to be foreigners in your own country, like the Royalists."

François Donadieu was one of the few Protestant pupils admitted to the school. This was due to a tradition of gratitude which went back to Combes and the Disestablishment. At that time many of the expelled priests had found refuge in certain Protestant families, a hospitable gesture which put a term to the old religious antagonisms. These pupils were naturally exempt from attendance at the religious services. They had the right to leave the schoolroom before the long evening prayer was said. Roland Oyarzun was the only boy who, in the heat of political argument, thought to underline the heretical persuasion of his opponents. The rest of the boys were unconcerned. For a long time past in Sault-en-Labourd there had been a tendency for the consciousness of contrasting faiths to diminish, though the Huguenot community, a minority, lived somewhat apart and without real contact with the Catholics.

A few days later the excitement among the boys reached a climax. François Donadieu, a day boy, had been commissioned by the boarders to buy the daily and weekly papers secretly, since reading the secular Press was forbidden. Each day therefore the boy brought in a huge stock of newspapers hidden under his thick black woollen cape. He had then to distribute the papers surreptitiously to those interested. Every shade of opinion, except Communism was represented. *L'Action Française* and *Candide* went to Roland Oyarzun, who immediately made a dash for the lavatories in the yard with a haste that implied gastric disorder rather than mere intellectual impatience. *Le Jour*, *L'Echo de Paris*, *L'Ordre* and the rest were read in the attic or in a hidden corner of the courtyard by little groups or, by individuals, under desks in school. They learned that thousands of demonstrators had tried to take the Chamber by assault to cries of: "Down with the thieves! Into the Seine with the members!"; that there had been fighting on the Place de la Concorde; that in the end the police had received the order to fire on the crowd and that French blood had been shed.

In those cold, sunny days of February an unprecedented excitement pervaded the old school. The older boys from the classes of philosophy and rhetoric played no football, the game of the winter term. Gathered together in a corner of the yard, beneath the leafless planes, they discussed the successive phases of the confused crisis which was shaking the country. Or sometimes, to avoid the rebuke of the supervising master, since stationary groups were not allowed during the recreation period, they walked up and down the yard like seminarists: parallel rows of three or four boys, face to face, each row taking it in turn to walk backwards. Their black or grey smocks caught in at the waist with string, their clogs clapping on the hard ground—for at this time the schoolboys of Sault-en-Labourd, whether they were rich or poor, still wore in winter felt slippers and wooden clogs—they talked in great bursts of southern, sing-song speech, while the cloud of their breath formed and dissolved, like a Pythian exhalation, about their young faces glowing in the cold. The younger boys, who did not read the papers, went on playing marbles, their winter game, and looked respectfully at their talkative elders; while the master in charge, as the procession passed him, caught the clash of passionate argument. "It was Chautemps who gave the order to open fire.—No, it was Frot.—It was Daladier. —It's been impossible to find out. . . .—The Leagues were responsible.—It was a plot of the Croix de Feu.—La Roque's a traitor.—The Fascists have failed in their *coup d'etat*.—They dispersed voluntarily on the evening of the seventh. . . .—. . . to shoot down Old Contemptibles!—. . . and what about the dead Communists, then?—Tardieu said to Thorez: 'I've put you in prison before and, when I can, I shall do so again.'—. . . an attempt by the Fascist reaction!—Blum's a traitor!—. . . the police were crazy, without orders, without the Préfet.—. . . the shooting in the evening was ordered by the Home Office.—If only Doumergue had refused. . . .—The Trades Unions are fighting among themselves.—Incompetent agitators!—Radical-Socialist bastards!—Chautemps' maffia. . . .—They're all in the Stavisky business together.—Lyautey ought to form a government with Chiappe.—. . . reactionary groups, enemies of the people!—The Fascists have a corporative programme.—. . . a Mussolini-like dictator.—. . . swindlers and murderers!—Only Maurras has a policy.—. . . against the whole tendency of history.—The French will never accept a king.—. . . an outdated ideology.—Jews, Freemasons and foreigners under the orders of an international adventurer.—. . . shame when the eyes of the world are upon us."

All these boys, as is usual at their age, were without exception proud and ardent in their patriotism, but they expressed it from different points of view, from irreconcilable and antagonistic systems of thought. They loved their country equally, but they could only approach its reality through opposed and dissimilar means. It was not even sure that the reality itself was the same for each of them. And this indeed is one of the most normal and yet concerning enigmas of social life: the teeming variety of political choice. What are these "opinions" for which so many men are prepared to sacrifice their quiet, their happiness, their life itself—for politics, like religion whose place they so often usurp in men's hearts, have their heroes and their martyrs. How deep do the roots of these "opinions" go! Certainly, they attain to the fervour and violence of the passions, and it is then that, of all human passions, they become the most ambiguous, the least defined. Many believe that they are fighting and dying for an idea, when in reality they are fighting and dying to avenge a father's humiliation, compensate for an unhappy childhood, escape from the torments of remorse, affirm their own courage or genius, or satisfy by a devious road the pangs of a hunger they have perhaps never learnt to call by its right name. They believe themselves to be fighting for the City divided against itself when in reality they have never ceased to fight against themselves, inhabitants as they are of an interior Argos, haunted by mysterious Furies, beneath the lowering of strange storms. More subtle and curious yet is the self-deception by which the adherent of a cause can persuade himself that he is possessed by a burning faith in the "destiny of Man" when, from a thousand little traits, a thousand indications, it can be seen, however obscurely, that he is creating his own illusion, playing a part, dancing before a looking-glass. Nevertheless, should it happen that he come to be shot, the proud defiance that he hurls at his executioners before he dies will find a place in the stories little children are given to read, to teach them what true grandeur may be.

The boys, divided more or less into a right and left wing, though they came from the same backgrounds and were undergoing the same spiritual training, held therefore different and almost irreconcilable ideas upon their country. Roland Oyarzun, leader of the right, had elaborated a conception that was both physical and dramatic. France, ancient and noble land of fields, forests and sweet villages, who should have dominated the world, was wasting away, devoured by foreign parasites, given over to accursed races, corrupted by Satan-inspired doctrines. ("I hope," Roland said seriously, "that Aristide Briand is in hell.") This land must be saved by the sword, regenerated by fire. One must die for it in the apotheosis of a civil war. Roland Oyarzun did not reason about his love. He lived it, he felt it beating gloriously in his veins, he sang it in his anger and in the insults he hurled at his adversaries. François Donadieu, on the other hand, the timid spokesman of a still more timid left, flattered himself that he was a rationalist. He believed in the indefinite Progress of the Species, in the Perfectibility of Man, in the possible founding of the Utopian City. For him France was the nation who, intelligent and enlightened, had massacred her tyrants and discovered the great principles of liberty long before the rest of the world. He loved her in Voltaire, in Victor Hugo, in Jaurés. Roland loved her in Joan of Arc, in Louis XIV, in Maurras. They were both of good faith, but their good faith was mutually exclusive.

From behind the window of his room the old Superior of the school looked down sadly upon these children already caught up in the foul eddies of the century. He had himself spent his early years within the walls of the school at the period of Latin speeches and flowery rhetoric. He, too, had walked up and down the yard with his companions, but they had never talked of politics. The echo of national events only reached them from afar: Boulanger's campaign, the deaths of Gambetta and Victor Hugo. The masters talked much of the Encyclical *Rerum Novarum*; they were concerned about anti-clericalism, whispered to each other the name of Jules Ferry, and quoted the speeches of M. Albert de Mun. There was no disagreement. There was no poison in the air. But the Republic of his youth was still decorous, the Socialist tribunes, the right-wing orators, were at one in their patriotism and in their common regard for honour. Had they not proved this in 1914-18? Since the Armistice, the face of the world had each day become more lowering, more formidable, hitherto unknown forces were ranged against each other in irreconcilable antagonism, and the Republic, overwhelmed by problems too vast for it, incapable of adjusting itself to the modern necessities of a changing world, had begun to look inwards, fascinated by the petty strife of party politics, the sterile alternations of the parliamentary game, and had become the ineluctable prey of two equally flagitious types of men: the hidebound ideoogist and the arrant scoundrel. The processes of corruption had been swift. It was difficult to be a republican under a government that had made an international sharper the secret master of the country and had protected itself from the fury of the people with a burst of rifle-fire. The whole business was nauseating. Must one admit that democratic institutions bore within themselves the seed of their own disintegration?

'Poor children,' thought the Superior as he looked out through the window at the philosophy and rhetoric classes perambulating the yard. He pitied them in their need to quarrel over their opinions. In the old days it was enough for a man to devote to public life only what was strictly demanded of him by his duties as a citizen. Today, political doom had seized men by the throat, and the sons of men, and would never more let them go. More than that, it had set division between them. But the fight itself was a dubious one, for all values had foundered in the confusion and even words no longer bore their true meaning. A word such as "nationalism", for example, once as limpid as the word "liberty", assumed variegated moral hues according to the viewpoints of the political parties, became in turn, as with these boys who were bandying it about between them at this moment, the standard of a sacred crusade or the black emblem of a class, its greed, folly, and pride. 'They read the propagandist Press with its lies and hatreds.' The Superior was aware that the newspapers were illicitly imported into the school, a discreet inspection had revealed it to him, and he even knew the name of the smuggler. He thought it useless to take rigorous action against an evil which, in any case, he would have found it impossible to prevent and which, moreover, did not rank at the head of the official list of prohibitions. (Had it been a question of pornography, he would have acted at once.) Young Donadieu had preferred to disregard the regulations rather than ignore the pressure of his companions: in the circumstances a minor fault, particularly since the boy was irreproachable in other ways. The Abbé Decazes was more concerned about young Oyarzun. There was nothing against him, at least from the point of view of morality. All the evidence was in Oyarzun's favour: his good behaviour, his patriotism, his evangelism among the younger boys, his popularity, his energy, his success at games. He had the stuff of leadership, of a commander of men. Certain reports had reached the Superior of Oyarzun being overheard shouting soldiers' songs and telling his companions dirty stories. The Superior was not unduly concerned. These, he thought, were unimportant peccadilloes at an age when the sap is rising and the soul is so often obscured by the vapours of the instincts. No; what disquieted the Superior had little to do with these minor distresses, but had he been asked, "Why are you anxious about Oyarzun?" he would have found it impossible to give any precise reply. It was a vague intuition, an indefinable disquiet. The sort of disquiet we suffer in the presence of an actor who takes infinite pains to move us, yet does not quite succeed in doing so: the ultimate note of sincerity, which compels our total adherence, is lacking. And yet the analogy was at fault, for Oyarzun was certainly not playing a part, poor child. .,. . It was rather the disquiet we feel before a man whose joviality is excessive, who is manifestly forcing his gaiety, who laughs too loud, while his eyes belie him, a haggard look dulling their brilliance from instant to instant and giving the lie to all his fine assumption of euphoria. Was Oyarzun unhappy? Was he hiding some sorrow, some secret anguish? The Superior had heard of Madame Oyarzun: she was the talk of the town. Everyone knew that her marriage had gone to pieces, and that Major Oyarzun had to all intents and purposes separated from his unworthy wife. Yes, it must be that: the boy was suffering in silence, hurt in his love for his parents, ashamed at heart. Yes, *perhaps* that was it. If someone had asked the Superior, "Why are you anxious about Oyarzun? There's no better boy in the school," he would have replied: "I don't know. But when I pray for our children, and I pray for them every day, it is Oyarzun above all whom I commend to the Divine care."

2

The events of February had resounded through every school in France. In some schools in Paris they even became the basis for children's games. The son of a politician, who at that time was playing a leading part in the affair, was compelled by his companions to represent in his own person the Government and the mobile guards: he was made to fire upon the demonstrators, a turbulent crowd of children, who hemmed him in all sides, crying, "Into the Seine with the members!" Very much against his will, the boy had to pretend to point a rifle and fire it to unconvincing cries of "Bang, bang, bang!"; but the wounded demonstrators, having rolled upon the ground to the accompaniment of the most appalling groans, immediately got up again, miraculously recovered, so that in that particular school the popular uprising would undoubtedly have succeeded. One of the most implacable demonstrators was a small boy of nine years old, Thibault Fontanes, a brilliant pupil in the seventh form. When he grew tired of fighting, he announced that the mobile guards had been slaughtered a long time ago, that the Chamber was on fire, that the bodies of the members were floating in the Seine, and that all that remained to be done was to form a new government. "I am dictator," he announced. "You, Bergeaud, can be my Minister of Justice; Legouvé can be Ambassador to Germany; Clodowitz, my Chief of Police. Why don't you shout: 'Long live the Leader!'?"

At this level, every utterance took on a frankly epic quality: blood-baths and feats of prowess predominated. "My father killed three Communists.—He leapt on to the horse of a mobile guard, wrenched his weapon from him and kept up the struggle for over an hour.—You didn't see him, you liar. You were in bed at the time!—My father took a photograph.—How could he? It was at night!—A cad called my father a dirty Fascist. My father gave him a black eye and socked him one on the jaw. You ought to have seen the cad measuring his length on the ground, his mouth agape and not a tooth left in his head. . . .—Now they're advancing and take cover behind the colonnades of the Chamber. Bang, bang! Two mobile guards have copped it. . . .—Bang, boom, bang, bang, they retreat, advance again, take the Concorde bridge with a rush, bang, three chaps have gone down in front of me." They talked of the rising as if they had been there, using many onomatopoeic sounds, slogans, gestures and marvellously expressive mimicry. Thus the squalling of a choir of brats became the accompaniment to the drama which ended an epoch.

Young O. Bernard and his friend Nicholas Gaudie had done better than mime the popular uprising in a school yard: they had taken part in it. It was true that they were already grown men. It was difficult to imagine two more dissimilar beings. Bernard concealed a Cartesian severity behind the slightly fleshy mask of an Assyrian god. Over Nicholas' features, his head resembling an anaemic Viking's, played the light and shade of alternating moods. Bernard was precise and methodical; he would have appeared aloof had it not been for his eyes which, set in a handsome, golden face aglow with friendliness, could establish an immediate personal contact with anyone who spoke to him. Nicholas was shy, nervous, and retiring. Bernard, so perfect were the proportions of his body, appeared tall though he was only of average height. Nicholas, but an inch or two the taller, but bonily thin, his neck emaciated, his shoulders already rounded, gave the impression of being immensely tall and gawky. His bony face seemed all the harder for the flat thatch of silver-pale hair above it. At school he had been nicknamed "the Condor", and it was true that there was about him something cruel, something proud and at the same time sad, as one likes to imagine there is about those great birds of prey which hang suspended in the upper airs above the glaciers. "Your name doesn't suit you at all well," Bernard told him. "Gaudie means joy. You're sinister." Nick mumbled some horrid insult and added, more intelligibly, "As for you, I should like to know what your Christian name is. You've never told anyone yet. O. Bernard! What does it stand for: Octave? Onésime? Orion? Origen? Oleaginous?" "I wouldn't mind Orion; it's the name of a star. Origen I won't have, since I've no desire to be called after a man who committed such a horrible outrage upon himself. But Octave fits me like a glove: it's a romantic Christian name and everyone knows that I look like Lord Byron." The two friends differed also in their manner and behaviour in society: Bernard, supple, courteous, adapting himself to his surroundings with the ease of a chameleon; Nicholas, stiff, aloof, disapproving, even surly. With so many reasons for misunderstanding and disliking each other, they were nevertheless inseparable, not in obedience to the supposed law, indeed far from being proven in real life, that insists upon the "attraction of opposites", but rather because these two very different characters had a single passion in common: a love for Lautréamont. At first sight it might appear that this was a somewhat tenuous link between two beings who differed in everything else, but their love for Lautréamont was but the symptom of more profound and more general affinities. They had discovered that they were the only two boys in their class at Louis-le-Grand who had read the *Chants de Maldoror* and were capable of quoting from it by heart. At that date this was a sufficiently rare taste, Lautréamont being known only to a very few initiates, and it sufficed to bring the two schoolboys together. They often walked up and down the courtyard declaiming turn and turn about.

Each night, plunging my spread wings into my tortured memory, I evoked the image of Falmer,

or that other terrifying Nocturne:

Each night, at the hour when sleep has attained the highest degree of its intensity, an ancient spider of the larger sort slowly protrudes its head from a hole in the ground at one of the intersections of the corners of my room.

Nick spoke in a toneless almost shaking voice as if he felt these superb rhapsodies of destruction in his very bones; Bernard, on the other hand, spoke the lines with a more certain artistry, doubtless more concerned with the rhythmic beauty of the text than with its intellectual implications. For them Lautréamont was one of the stars, more distant and more strange than the rest, of the constellation in which shone Baudelaire, Rimbaud, Mallarmé and Apollinaire. Those of their companions who were interested in poetry were still at the stage of Verlaine. Besides, Bernard and Nick passed as being "advanced", and they knew that they in fact were so. But whereas Nick insisted fiercely upon the distinction, was delighted to voice his contempt for the "Philistines", the "bourgeois", the "idiots" (epithets which frequently recurred in his conversation), and lived with dramatic intensity the spiritual revolution upon which he prided himself, Bernard seemed to reconcile within himself revolutionary convictions and the ability to have a good time, the desire to "change the world" and the delightful enjoyment of the world not yet regenerated. Nick hated authority, the police, the Army, the Church, family tradition, Racine, Barrés and the Archbishop of Paris. He *really* hated them. He insulted "coppers" in the street which led on several occasions to his being taken to the police station by these painfully outraged officials and to his being temporarily expelled from school for some days. Bernard professed to hate the same things as did Nick, but he found it extremely agreeable and stimulating to be taken by his father to dine with the President of the Council or with some minister in office, he tenderly loved every member of his numerous family, wept when listening to the choir at Solesmes, was capable of admiring a sensual and melancholy page in *Du sang, de la volupté et de la mort*, and, had the Archbishop of Paris spoken to him, would doubtless have replied with the most charming good manners. Nick on the other hand would have addressed the prelate with cold overfamiliarity and would have asked him some scurrilous question upon the subject of his housekeeper. To sum up, Nick represented the inspired revolutionary, prepared to give his life for the cause and to sacrifice more promptly still the lives of others to it. Bernard's was a richer humanity, more complex, more supple, he was the exquisite flower of a civilisation which had built the cathedrals, of a race which had attained to the highest consciousness of human destiny when the Pharaohs had created the Pyramids among the sands. On the first page of a notebook which he always carried upon him, Nick had written a dozen "fundamental" formulae, key quotations which served him as a philosophy of life. For example,

Beauty is convulsive or is not,

or, again, this *Proverb* of Blake's:

Prisons are built with stones of Law, brothels with bricks of Religion.

Bernard thought the same, but this did not prevent his owning to a weakness for the unconvulsive beauty of Puvis de Chavannes' frescoes, or whenever he had enough money, going off to one or other of the two most luxurious "establishments" (one on the Left Bank, the other on the Right) where the politicians of the Third Republic found relaxation from the fatigues of power in the fatigues of love. Bernard had not yet reached the legal age, but at seventeen he looked over twenty, and if by chance the doorkeeper had refused him entry, a telephone call to one of the ministers, friends of his father, and clients of the house, would have smoothed out the difficulty. He returned from these discreet expeditions in a state of languor, his heart overflowing with gratitude, his mind disposed towards universal indulgence, secretly reconciled to a social order which placed at his disposition, in circumstances of elegant and aseptic luxury, a host of such concubines as Solomon himself never enjoyed, he who, the master of a thousand wives, had sadly concluded that "Woman is more bitter than death". Bernard told Nick about these visits to the palaces built "with bricks of Religion". He could evoke their pleasures with a gentle persuasiveness, with the tremors of a tender oriental sensuality, till one might have thought that his lips were distilling the "essential oils" of the Song of Solomon and that for him happiness was inconceivable except in immediate proximity to these wonderful gatherings of Shulamites, fair and dark and auburn, where there was even a Venus from Senegal: "*I am black, but comely, O ye daughters of Jerusalem*"—and where about the man-king they displayed the whole florid range of their singular charms and intoxicating perfumes. And since he was naturally kind, a trait which did not fail to add lustre to his visits to the grand seraglios of the great democracy, he suggested to Nick that next time he should take him and pay for him, since Nick was very short of money. From time to time Nick accepted with a certain haughtiness and he never said thank you, judging doubtless that a disciple of Lautréamont was above such polite conventions, or perhaps that a son of the decadent bourgeoisie, such as Bernard, had no right to expect gratitude from those who deigned to accept his charity for he still remained in their debt. (Nicholas Gaudie, the son of a stockbroker, seemed to forget that he himself came from the hated bourgeoisie. It was true that his father, who was excessively mean, allowed him practically no pocket-money.) Thanks therefore to the generosity of his friend, Nick was able to make use of the republican concubines, but this privilege, which his contemporaries at Louis-le-Grand might well have envied him, in no way modified his views about the world and French society in particular. In angry little poems he exploded a whole diversity of institutions, poured derision upon a number of generous emotions, patriotism, veneration for the dead, belief in religion. These explosive little works were circulated secretly in the school, several were even printed in one of those innumerable private reviews which young boys publish with their friends' money and which are read by no one, one supposes, but their contributors. Nick's poems found their inspiration in the most aggressive sort of violence; they were much concerned with obscenity, scatology and incitement to murder:

Dans le ciel abject pour constellations ovipares
Le dauphin-gladiateur aux prunelles de basilic
Les girls de Mayol aux cuisses hilares
Martèlent à coups de talon
Le vagissement des coïts cantharidés
Les pupilles de la Nation violent les Carmélites hélicoïdales
Et des larmes gonococciques
Ruissellent le long de la Sainte Epine,

etc., etc. The piece was called "*Elévation*". There was another called *Ballade des petits Tréponèmes* (it was clear that the theme of veneral corruption haunted Nick's imagination) in regular octosyllables, of classical workmanship and laboured horror. Another, somewhat esoteric to tell the truth, illustrated, so Nick said, an obsession with death:

Or je n'ai plus présentement mémoire
Orge sanglant des champs opératoires
Hors jeu sur la table de laque noire
Orgelet dévorant l'œil du Cyclope
Or gelè des aurores boréales
Heure jolie de ma chute dans l'infini
Argile ingénue distraitement effritée.

Bernard also wrote somewhat "advanced" poems, though they were more traditional in inspiration. One of them, called *Van Gogh*, evoked a Provençal countryside glittering in the sun, striped with lines of green and yellow, and ended with a crashing alliteration:

Cicadas chisel the silicates of the sun

which, being admired by Nick, filled Bernard with pride, for his friend was difficult to please and not at all generous with his compliments. Bernard's most ambitious work, *The Great Manœuvres*, of three hundred and fifty-seven lines, written in June 1936, was a violent indictment of war, the Army, militarism, the Fatherland and the cult of the flag. It contained every cliché of anarchism: the plotting of international capitalists, the collusion between the Sword and the Church, the cynical trickery of cenotaphs and Armistice Days, the criminal folly of General Staffs, of the French Academy, of patriotic emotions, of the famous and immoral artiste singing the Marseillaise, her bosom draped in a fold of the flag, before an audience of generals, bishops, bankers and aristocrats, all the good old imagery of popular revolution was made use of in this diatribe in verse, but renewed, galvanised by a deliberately eccentric syntax, a verbal excess and the presence of a variety of linguistic forms which, until Malherbe, had held an honourable place in poetry: the pun, the Spoonerism and the play on words. These were the first lines:

L'arme à la bretelle
Les pauvres conscrits trainent la jambe lamentablement
En chantant faux un refrain martial
"*Ils ont la mine bien piteuse,*
Ils l'ont vraiment bien miteuse,
Et la voix pâteuse,
Pense le capitaine asthmatique et ulcéré.
La chair à canon est un peu avariée cette année.
Qui m'a foutu
Ces dégénérés
Du Front popu?
Pas cadencé urche!"

One would not offhand have supposed that the author of this truculent and nevertheless somewhat facile poem was young O. Bernard, who appeared more of a dandy and an aesthete than a firebrand. Nick, on the other hand, could be seen from afar to be quite the dirtiest of all the boys at Louis-le-Grand. He refused to wash as part of his system of flouting the conventions as well as from a desire to scandalise and displease. Bernard wore immaculate linen, attended to the crease in his trousers, and selected with perfect taste his expensive ties bought at Charvet or Barclay or, better still, when he had been to London in the holidays, at a little shop in the Burlington Arcade which supplied the Duke of Kent and Noël Coward. One day Nick roughly reproached him with his vanity and the excessive pains he took with his personal appearance.

"You've got a taste for luxury in the blood. You're still a slave to the manners of your class. A decadent little bourgeois, that's all. Really, I don't understand you. Why on earth do you want to spend all that time on dolling yourself up?"

Bernard surveyed his filthy companion from head to foot. "Out of respect for the human countenance."

The reply was given with a certain arrogance. Nick blushed to the eyebrows and bit his lip. It was their first quarrel. (There were to be others later, notably on the occasion of the 6th of February.) Bernard was suddenly intuitively aware that what Nick hated most was not so much social injustice, but the natural injustice to which he owed his skeleton limbs, rounded shoulders, and the gangling awkwardness of his graceless body. He wanted to destroy the world because he could neither dominate it nor clasp it to him. The thought only touched Bernard in the most fugitive way. In any case he would have discarded it as mean and tendentious; indeed, he took the view that one must guard against explaining human conduct by the unstable variations in the individual, as a point of view it was an over-simplification and somewhat unworthy. (Certainly it is an incomplete view, for if it is true that men rationalise theoretically, construct abstract principles and doctrines out of their most secret hurts, their hates, their fears and their shame, they have at the same time the strange power of transcending both their doctrines and their wretched secrets in outbursts of generosity, in self-forgetfulness and in sacrifice; thus the first term in the mysterious human equation is a little mud, a little absurdity and a little deceit, while the second is an almost divine truth: the Fall and the Redemption coexist and are fused through all eternity.) So Bernard would have discarded the horrid thought (that Nick was not so much a revolutionary as a pathetic figure, unhappy and embittered), because he attributed genius to his friend, and genius, like Caesar's wife, must be above suspicion, a pure incorruptible flame that nothing merely mediocre can dull. Bernard really thought that Nick had genius, and he was not mistaken to the extent that one can call genius that raging, tragic demon which causes certain adolescents to utter such awe-inspiring cries; then, the demon grows quiet, the adolescent becomes a man, dies of tuberculosis, or goes to Ethiopia in search of gold; or, again, becomes a political militant, another expeditious road to extinction. But perhaps the highest genius is not so much to utter at sixteen the cries of an old man possessed, but at eighty to speak still in the accents of eternal youth. Bernard submitted to Nick's ascendancy, which called everything in question, scoffed at everything we hold most dear and most sacred, but under whose aəgis the mere fact of living became an unexpected and dramatic adventure. It was thus that one day, though trembling with apprehension, he took his friend home with him: how would Nick react to the rich and bourgeois Bernards' flat, to his friend's room, hung with reproductions of pictures, to his parents, his sisters, his brother, his grandmother? . . . Nick's manner towards the family was icy, though they laid themselves out to be hospitable—but then the first page of his notebook bore Gide's apophthegm: "Families, I hate you all!" In his friend's room he looked at the portraits, the photographs, the well-known reproductions the engravings, with the insolence of a valuer. Catching sight of the "*Ignudi*" from the Sistine Chapel, he shouted, "Why not the Farnese Bull or Niobe!"

"I quite like," Bernard protested feebly, "the Promethean power of these. . . ."

"Boom!"

"What did you say?"

"I said: Boom! Everytime you hurl at my head a phrase such as 'Promethean power', or 'Dionysiac exaltation', or 'the delicate enormities of the Middle Ages', or 'Pantheistic excitement', or "the seminal germination of the universe', I shall say: Boom!"

"But then conversation becomes impossible," said Bernard ingenuously.

"Yes; it becomes impossible. If you can only talk in clichés, commonplaces and half-baked romantic phrases, it's better to shut up."

He continued his inspection, only to stop suddenly before a photograph of the Apollo Belvedere.

"Hullo. I haven't seen this crooner before," he said. "Or is he an Italian tenor? You must have photographed him when he was singing *O Sole Mio*. Tell me, is that his usual get-up for recitals? It must be most stimulating. He's not badly built but, in his place, I wouldn't have a permanent wave. Or is it a wig"

Bernard was shaken.

"As for that Goya," Nick went on, "I could understand your choosing it for your grandmother's room: a sylvan ball in the taste of the eighteenth century is sweet and charming, eminently suitable for old ladies' boudoirs. But for yourself you should have chosen the Goya of madness, the Goya of the shadows, Saturn devouring his children, Spanish peasants impaled at Napoleon's orders, or the Witches' Sabbath. The authentic article, in fact."

That very evening Bernard confided an account of this memorable visit to the journal he had scrupulously kept ever since he was fourteen. "He destroyed everything," he wrote. "A tornado has passed through my room and through my conceptions of art. Nothing remains; and here I am with empty mind and hands and before me the intoxication of new beginnings. This afternoon he seared me with humiliation and shame. Tonight I am grateful to him though I shall take care not to let him know it; he'd only laugh in my face. He's a demon. His friendship both appals and exalts me." He added in a final entry: "Another matter for vexation: he now knows that I'm called Odilon. He didn't flinch when he heard my grandmother call me by that ridiculous Christian name, but there's no doubt he'll use the discovery to harass me with his mockery. I really owe Daddy a serious grudge for having called me Odilon merely because he was devoted to the work of an artist who bore the same name. I know that Odilon Redon had a sort of genius, but really! It makes me think of M. Homais, who called his children Athaliah and Nicomedes. Luckily, my surname is also a Christian name, so that everyone calls me Bernard; it does equally well for both acquaintances and friends."

Nicholas Gaudie had the good sense not to be facetious on the subject of "Odilon" and never called his friend by that name; but it did happen from time to time, though rarely, that when an argument about art or literature became heated, he would throw it in his face by saying something like: "You, my dear Odile, who have a cult for Bonnat," or perhaps: "Odile, my dear girl, I must inform you that Madame Cora Laparcerie is to give a lecture in the *Université des Annales* on M. Jean Richepin and will declaim some of the late lamented poet's verses."

In fact, on that particular day, Nick wished at all costs to be present at the lecture of Jean Richepin. He applauded frantically at every opportunity, cried and sobbed at the extracts from *Chemineau*, and when it was all over rushed up to the lady lecturer waving a copy of one of the poet's books, insisted that she should inscribe a dedication in it, and, as he kissed Madame Laparcerie's hand, he bedewed it with his tears. Five minutes later he had collected about him an audience of four or five old ladies in the ante-room of the *Salle Gaveau*, and was reciting Jean Richepin with a ridiculous grandiloquence which was a superb parody. The old ladies were carried away with emotion, while in another corner of the ante-room Bernard was wiping the tears of laughter from his eyes.

This was all part of what Nick called, as did the other boys of Louis-le-Grand, a "canular"—that is to say, a systematic and sustained joke. But there were more sinister tricks than this. One day Nick, having slipped unseen into the school linen-room, hid in a cupboard and waited patiently for the seamstress to come and open it. When she did, he leapt out at her and ran away, leaving the poor woman in a dead faint at the cupboard's foot. This experience left her for ever afterwards with serious heart trouble. Naturally, she had not had time to recognise him, and, later on, Nick went out of his way, whenever he met his victim, to ask after her health with the most touching interest. He made her tell him the story of the "boy who had jumped out of the cupboard like a devil" and always condemned severely such appalling behaviour. The seamstress, much affected, always spoke of Nick in the highest terms: "He's a good boy, Monsieur Gaudie is, whenever he meets me he always asks after my poor heart. He's very civil and polite." And on these days Nicholas Gaudie's eyes blazed with a truly demoniac light. 'He's a Sadist,' thought Bernard, who knew the whole story. He thought it sad and disgusting and it displeased him that Nick, in his ethic or aesthetic of outrage, sacrilege and destruction, should have attacked a seamstress. He told him so.

"That's the whole point," Nick replied, "the cream of the joke lies in the fact that my victim is *really* a victim: a defenceless proletarian, an honest 'woman of the people'. If I had shortened the life of a commanding general, a banker, an armaments manufacturer, I should be a lover of justice, a Don Quixote. But I've shortened the life of a 'poor working woman'. That really is evil in its pure state, that really *is* destruction. I'm a murderer. And not only unpunished, but liked and esteemed by my victim. You must admit it's magnificent. Besides, I've so much enjoyed the experience that I've sworn to do it again at the first opportunity."

All this talk was not mere boasting. A few months later the seamstress did in fact die of a heart attack. Nick came to school wearing an enormous black arm-band.

"I've gone into mock-mourning," he said.

Bernard was the prey to contradictory emotions. On one side, all that was spontaneously good and compassionate in his nature was revolted, overwhelmed with horror: it was that part of him which derived from social and religious atavisms, though Bernard had no religion and had to make an effort to remember that in some people's eyes he belonged to a well-defined social group. It was also the side of him which he owed to education: he had been taught as a child that one must not harm one's neighbour, that it was wrong; that, on the other hand, one must succour one's neighbour, particularly if poor and defenceless. There was also the humanist in Bernard, a sage of the old school, an enlightened pagan who believed that even a slave was a man and who placed above all other virtues those of justice, moderation and magnanimity: this side of Bernard deplored Nicholas Gaudie's act as being in bad taste, a vulgar and ill-considered gesture. Thus the descendant of the biblical patriarchs and Seneca's spiritual heir consorted to condemn in accordance with somewhat different criteria, or reflexes, Nicholas Gaudie's attack upon a humble servant. But there was still another Bernard, there were two or three others, for whom Nick's 'crime' was intensely exciting. There was the exuberant dilettante, invincibly attracted by everything that was outside the platitudinous daily round of things already seen and known, the devotee of William Blake, Thomas de Quincey, Lautréamont, Nietzsche—for whom the substance of the world was energy eternally renewed, cruel often in its manifestations, and a stranger to our poor morality. Beyond good and evil, the forces of instinct eternally create and destroy thousands upon thousands of images which, terrifying, militant and incomprehensible, are yet indescribably beautiful. Murder can be a fine art, cruelty excite the nerves better than can music, madness cast a brilliant ray of light into the abyss of the unconscious or the unseen, and Rome was well worth burning to acquire a new sensation. Considered in the light of these aesthetic conceptions, Nick's act and the young man's eminently Maldororian attitude took on a quite different significance. Indeed, Nick was at one with Maldoror and those other sinister heroes who kill coldly, without faltering, for the mere pleasure of killing, and add to the beauty of the crime itself the infernal refinements of sacrilege and derision. Bernard, at eighteen, was subject to these outdated fascinations: the disquieting thing was that he was to be still subject to them ten years later. Clearly, Lafcadio had passed that way. (The importance that Lafcadio's 'gratuitous act' had for the boys of the 'twenties and even of the 'thirties is a very curious phenomenon indeed.) It was wonderful to tell oneself that one knew, that one actually had for intimate friend a flesh-and-blood Lafcadio, less charming of course than Gide's, but quite as resolute, and who had *really* killed. It was delightful to be able to boast about it. One could say quite casually, "I've got a friend who has killed a seamstress."

"What's that? What are you saying?"

"Well, he simply killed a seamstress, that's all."

"But why? Was it a sex crime? Did he do it out of jealousy?"

"Good God, no! She was sixty at least."

"Then why in the world did he do it?"

"How should I know? Perhaps he killed her because she had a squint. Or because her breath stank. Or for no reason at all, simply because she happened to be there. What does it matter?"

"But, look here, it's simply monstrous. You can't go about doing things like that. He's in prison, I hope?"

"Not at all. You see, he accomplished it with diabolical cunning. It was the perfect crime. He couldn't conceivably be arrested; there's no proof, no evidence at all. I must tell you he's a pretty clever sort of chap."

"Didn't you tell the police?"

"Tell the police? What next! Why on earth should I? He's the most charming fellow and I'm very fond of him. Most amusing, too!"

For there was also in Bernard—and at moments he was aware of it—something of futile worldliness, of silly intellectual snobbery, and this side of him would have sacrificed anyone and anything for the sake of a witticism, while literature and the arts were almost as much an occasion for shining in society as they were objects of pleasure.

Nevertheless, he had a feeling that his intimacy with Nick, already shaken by the 'murder' of the seamstress, was shortly to be disrupted. The fact was that the two boys seemed to be taking divergent paths: Nick, the path of gratuitous and indiscriminate violence; Bernard, that of "progressive" humanism. They were united in their admiration and love for Lautréamont, the young iconoclast to whom they attributed all that was finest in adolescent rebellion. But, as soon as it became necessary to define the rebellion's object, they fell apart: for Nick it needed no justification, it was the apocalyptic shattering of a contemptible universe; for Bernard it concerned the honour of the human state (he was beginning to read Malraux) and its object was to ameliorate the condition of the world and hasten on a socialist society. Indeed, Bernard thought that honour was to be found only among the left wing, "like any half-wit!" Nick complained in exasperation. He thought, too, that intelligence, the spirit of critical enquiry and sound justice, was the perquisite of the left: an unimportant and very comprehensible bias in a young intellectual of the 'thirties, who belonged to a good, rather "advanced" bourgeois family, and whose father was an intimate friend of Léon Blum's. On the February day of the popular rising, Bernard and Nick had mingled with the demonstrators, Bernard as an eager spectator, Nick merely loitering in the capacity of an amateur of disorder. They were surrounded by men and boys wearing bérets who, armed with cudgels, their aspect fierce and determined, clamoured in unison, "Death to Daladier!"

"How convinced they seem," signed Bernard. "I wish I could feel a little of their conviction."

Nick shrugged his shoulders.

"They're morons," he said. "Look at their brutish faces. They're worth no more than the scum they want to destroy. I'd rather be governed by a lot of Marseillais thugs under the orders of an international swindler than by a band of *Froides Queues*[1] or National Volunteers. Decomposition would set in all the more rapidly."

Bernard did not respond to what, in his eyes, was a melancholy paradox. A little later, he said, "This is not the place for us. We should have joined in with the Communists marching down the boulevards. I'm glad the communists are demonstrating. Without them, the whole thing would be much too like a Fascist or para-Fascist Fronde."

"Do you think the little innocents spawned by drivelling Moscow are any better than the Fascists?"

[1] Literally "Cold Tails", the nickname of the reactionary Croix de Feu movement of the 'thirties.

"Listen, Nick. To quote Aragon like that is a bit too facile, isn't it? You can say what you like, but the Communists are the only party that the reactionaries really fear, the only party that's organised, disciplined and coherent. I know some Communists, they're very good chaps, and I feel sympathetic towards them. That's why I'm glad, and reassured, that they've come out into the streets today. I feel justified in being here myself."

"You flirt with the Communist Party like a whore. Join it and shut up. But I warn you: 'if you do join, I shan't speak to you again. I don't care; you're more profoundly bourgeois even than I thought: you flirt with the Reds out of snobbishness and stupidity. You bore me."

Bernard contracted his jaw. When he spoke, his voice was cold and trembled a little:

"You know, you rather bore me too. Your nihilism doesn't lead anywhere and . . ."

"I don't want to get anywhere."

"Perhaps not, but it's also curiously old-fashioned: nineteen twenty-five and Dadaism. You may think it picturesque to play the adolescent terrorist, but unfortunately, my dear chap, you bear no resemblance whatever to Fantin-Latour's young Rimbaud or Salvador Dali's Lautréamont. You should cast yourself for another part."

"It was the first time that Bernard had attempted malice, for which he had no natural aptitude. Only cold fury could have drawn so unkind a remark from him. Nick trembled all over, as he had on the day Bernard had spoken of the dignity of the human countenance. He was about to reply, when a burst of fire split the air in two and the crowd poured back upon them like a huge wave; there was a brief, shocked silence, followed almost at once by a roar of furious anger, and cries of: "The bastards! The bastards! They've given the order to fire!" Dragged along and jostled by the crowd, the two boys were soon lost in the growling, eddying mass surrounding the Palace which, with its Corinthian pillars, resembled, above that angry sea, a melancholy Temple of Iniquity. There were several more shots fired; men fell and their blood flowed. The gentle and happy post-war period of the Charleston, of prosperity and of hope died then; civil war had burst upon the world.

3

In the corner by the window Clothilde Oyarzun was sewing. Statuesque, her hair piled above her forehead in heavy golden coils, she somewhat resembled "the Angel in the House" so often reproduced in the illustrations of parish magazines. A rather too luxuriant angel, perhaps, to ring quite true. She was sewing. This benign domestic occupation suggested the calm and peace of a family circle. Yet Clothilde's expression gave warning of a storm in the offing. She was listening to her husband and her son airing their views, like two shepherds in an eclogue. Since coffee, they had not addressed a single word to her. For the pair of them she hardly existed at all. Roland was filled with admiration for his father. 'When he looks at him like that with his mouth open,' thought Clothilde, 'one might think he was going to bleat like a sheep. A halfwit distraught with love. That a little boy in short knickers should think his father the most wonderful man in the world is all very well. But at eighteen! Of course Edmond always made a lot of his son. He treated him like a man, spoke to him as an equal. Children are very sensitive to that sort of thing. As far as I was concerned, for five minutes I'd stifle him with kisses and stuff him with chocolates. Then I'd get bored with him and send him away. In fact I used to hand him over to the orderly. All the same, he might show me a little affection. After all, I've been a good mother to him. At any rate, *he* has nothing to reproach me for. I used to bully him a little, but it was for his own good. What are they talking about now? Still this tiresome revolution that didn't come off. How maddening men are with their politics! And they talk and talk, and listen to themselves orating, and get excited about absurdities. Clowns! Women are not so futile. When Edmond talks in that sententious way, it drives me crazy. One might take him for a clergyman. Where have they got to now? The revision of the Constitution. God, how unhappy I am! And, really, to ignore me like this becomes in the end merely insulting.'

The husband and son were sitting a little away from her and rather behind. They had the slightly ceremonious air of a conversation piece.

"For ten years Tardieu has been pressing for a revision of the

Constitution," Commandant Oyarzun was saying, "but no one would listen to him. Every time he gets up to speak, every single time, you see, the radical maffia start shouting him down. The incontestible and uncontested integrity of such an opponent as Tardieu makes them literally wild with rage."

"You've seen what they're saying in the *Populaire*: they're asserting that Colonel de la Roque has been financed by Tardieu out of the secret funds."

"The *Populaire*, like the other Marxist and para-Marxist papers, doesn't stop short of libel. As we know, newspaper editors drew on the secret funds, you remember Tardieu's article: 'This Silence about Secret Funds!'—so why not the leader of a League?"

"It's like that story of the cheque-stub with the name 'Tardie' on it. . . ."

"The whole thing was forged, of course, to discredit their accuser. It's absolutely inconceivable that Tardieu should have had any relations, even the most distant ones, with Stavisky. There can be no doubt, and for my part I'm profoundly convinced of it, that that man's hands are clean."

"You have the gift of second sight, of course," Clothilde said, without raising her eyes from her work.

Her remark was not taken up.

"Colonel de la Roque has failed to be the man of the hour," Roland went on. "If he really has been financed by the agents of the Republic, it's not surprising."

"This appalling business has proved, only too evidently, alas! that the leaders of the Leagues are not revolutionaries or, more precisely, true men of action. They're theoreticians. There are moments in history when hesitation is fatal. If Bonaparte had hesitated on the eighteenth Brumaire, the face of the world would have been changed, to quote a famous phrase. By the way, if you have an essay on Pascal in your examination this year, try to get the quotation in. You'd do well to make a note of it, in any case. A well-placed quotation influences the examiner in your favour. But to return to our muttons, a last minute hesitation sounded the knell of Boulangism. La Roque missed an opportunity which won't present itself again. He should not have dispersed his troops. His proper tactics, of course, were to make a junction with the Patriotic Youth and the National Volunteers and to hold his ground at all costs."

"What a pity you weren't there," sighed Clothilde. "You could have given him your advice. I don't know why you don't found an organisation of your own. Since you are Béarnais, you could call it the White Tuft, in memory of Henry IV. You would be known as the Tuft-hunters. . . ."

"I fear we're boring your mother, Roland," the Commandant said courteously. "Forgive me, Clothilde. Let's talk of something else."

"Of course. Why don't you talk about the tactics of a flanking movement as you did the other night? You never finished winning the Battle of Austerlitz."

"You forget my dear, that Roland has to go up for his examination this year and that he has to pass a history *viva*."

"Oh, of course, and I hope he passes this time. Because, if he fails again and if that means that you'll spend the whole holidays going over the coalitions under the Empire and the victory of the Marne all over again, you can go to the mountains without me. I shall go to the sea."

"Don't put yourself out for us," Roland said.

"Oh, I know very well that you'd be delighted to be alone with your father! You put me in my place, don't you? Thanks very much! You appreciate, of course, Edmond, the respect your son shows his mother."

She got up and went towards the staircase.

"I'll leave you to your strategy," she shouted as she went up stairs. They heard two doors bang.

The Commandant put his head in his hands.

"Roland, you shouldn't have answered back like that, it was insolent."

"Listen, Daddy. I can't stand it," the boy faltered. "I can't stand it when she talks to you in that tone. . . . I . . . It makes me wild! And when she's sarcastic, I could hit her!"

He clenched his hands. There were tears in his eyes.

"Hush, hush. You must be patient, my boy. Your mother is nervous, unstable. And it's true that when we're together we don't pay her much attention. We neglect her a lot."

"I can't help it. I've got nothing to say to her."

"You must make an effort, Roland, even if it's only from charity."

His expression was gentle. He was kind. Roland stifled a sob.

Suddenly, there was a noise like thunder overhead, followed by a metallic roulade. The two men jumped. They recognised the sound of the old out-of-tune piano in Clothilde's room, and the first chords of an operatic aria.

"She'll break the piano," said the Commandant.

"She's banging on it like that on purpose to annoy us."

Clothilde was now singing at the top of her voice:

Mon cœur s'ouvre à ta voix
Comme s'ouvrent les fleurs
Au baiser de l'Aurore . . .

"Delilah's great aria," said the Commandant in astonishment.

"She's not singing. She's roaring. It's too much!"

"What are you doing?"

"I'm going up."

"Roland for God's sake, don't make a scene. Roland!"

But the boy was already running up stairs. He kicked the door open. Without ceasing to sing, Clothilde glanced sideways at him. He was standing in the doorway furiously angry, a lock of hair across his forehead. He took three paces towards her and, with a sudden blow, shut the lid of the piano. Clothilde uttered a piercing scream, and twisted forwards on her seat.

"You've pinched my fingers! Murder! Help!"

She leapt to her feet, upsetting the piano-stool; then ran to the window and tried to open it. "Help!" she cried. Roland seized her roughly by the arm, turned her round and pushed her towards the centre of the room. As she was trying to hurl herself towards the window again, a hand hit her hard across the cheek. Stunned, panting for breath, Clothilde remained glued to the spot. The scene had not lasted ten seconds.

His arm still raised, Roland was appalled by his act. He ran from the room and rushed downstairs. The Commandant came to meet him.

"What's happened? You didn't . . . ? Good God!"

Roland sank into a chair.

"I'll go up," the Commandant said.

"No, no. Please stay here. I lost my head. I wanted to stop her rousing the neighbours."

A month later, it was Speech Day at the school. Clothilde and the Commandant were present, smiling and relaxed, like a tenderly united married couple: typical "parents". A nervous crisis or two, torrents of tears, lacerating forgiveness, and a mutual non-aggression pact had sealed a temporary reconciliation between the three members of the family. The Commandant was above all concerned with keeping up appearances. On her side, Clothilde was delighted to play the part of a model wife in public. Sitting in the front row of the gathering, upright and discreet, she typified in this scholarly and catholic setting with its old-fashioned, lavender and rose charm, a great lady of religious society, a pillar of the Church.

Behind the scenes of the little improvised theatre, Roland Oyarzun was powdering his face with an excessive and ridiculous energy. He was shivering with stage-fright. François Donadieu, his sleeves rolled up, his hands sticky with grease-paint—he was doing duty as make-up man—was encouraging his friend.

"Look at me," Roland groaned, gazing at his face in the looking-glass. "I look like an old witch."

"Don't be an idiot. You look wonderful."

"They'll roar with laughter when I make my entrance."

"I tell you, you look very well. No joking."

"Why on earth did I consent to play Athalie? Oh, damn, damn," he said tremulously in a small voice.

"All the same you could hardly have played Eliacin, with your size and weighing thirteen stone."

"Joad! I should have chosen the part of Joad!"

"You're the only one who could play Athalie. Your features are good and with your brown skin your beard won't show. Wait a minute. Don't move, and I'll put your crown on."

"Fix it on firmly, then. You know what'll happen: it'll start slipping off in the middle of a scene. As long as I don't trip over my train! Christ, look at my face! God, it's awful! You've given me too much eye-black. I look like a singer in a night-club."

"No; like a wax doll. Wait a moment. I'll take some of it off."

"Hurry up. I must go to the lavatory. I want to go every ten minutes. This tangle of robes makes it so damned convenient!"

And Athalie, her skirts raised to her thighs, streaked off like a meteor in the direction of the lavatories.

The three knocks were struck and the curtain rose. The great cadences of Racine filled the sudden silence. In a corner, backstage, Roland studied his lines and bit his nails. He looked pale and drawn.

"It's your cue, Athalie," whispered Abbé Lacroux, the producer.

"Jesus, Mary, Joseph," the apostate Queen murmured piously. She made the sign of the Cross, then, like a sleep-walker, to the accompaniment of the silken rustle of her pompous robes, she emerged slowly from the shadows.

There was a wave of excitement among the audience, the Commandant's eyeglass leapt involuntarily from his eye, Clothilde's mouth fell open, the Superior clutched the arms of his chair. The personage who appeared on the stage was no schoolboy disguised for an innocent school play. Fantastic, sheathed in the rigid folds of her gold and velvet robe, her tiara crowning a brow wreathed in noble, black locks, it was the accursed Tyrian herself, the daughter of Ahab and Jezebel, advancing with slow steps towards the young Eliacin, her hands extended, groping, her eyes unseeing, like a blind ghoul. A torch-bearer illumined the spectre's way. She halted. She sighed profoundly. Her eyes once more became conscious of the world around her, and bent their convergent fires upon the face of the young Levite. Suddenly, she recognised the graceful "traitor" who haunted her dreams and plunged the "homicidal steel" into her breast.

O ciel! plus j'examine et plus je le regarde,
C'est lui,

she announced in a rasping, trembling voice. Abner pushed forward a seat and assisted the Queen to sit down. She questioned the young boy. She seemed to devour him with an octopus- or vampire-like gaze, and then, overwhelmed by a strange emotion:

Quel prodige nouveau me trouble et m'embarrasse?
La douceur de sa voix, son enfance, sa grâce
Font, insensiblement à mon inimitié
Succéder . . .

At last she smiled at him, extended awkwardly towards him her fingers laden with rings, as if she had the desire, but lacked the courage, to caress that downy cheek. Already her voice seemed to coo with a curious tenderness, for one could not have said whether her words betrayed the calculating intriguer or the mere avowal of an old woman charmed:

> *Enfin, Eliacin, vous avez su me plaire. . . .*
> *Vous voyez, je suis reine et n'ai point d'héritier. . . .*
> *Je veux vous faire part de toutes mes richesses. . . .*
> *Je prétends vous traiter comme mon propre fils.*

And while her lips intoned the insidious offer, she moved her head in a slow, Hebraic rhythm, as if the scene of the Temple evoked in the infidel Queen's blood, subject as she now was to the cult of a hostile god, the atavistic recollection of metric recitations, of sacred versicles learnt by her ancestors as children under the ferule of a Scribe. The torch-bearer was standing behind her and Athalie's shadow, falling upon a column, reflected in exquisite outline the whole heredity of Israel.

Clothilde held her breath as she gazed upon the scene.

A little later, backstage, Roland was congratulated by the Abbé Lacroux and by his comrades: "You were marvellous.—Very good, Oyarzun; you played it extremely well.—At the beginning, I thought you were going to fall into the percussion." He was delighted and modest, blushing with pleasure under his make-up. "I was in a terrible funk!"—so ingenuously happy that François was almost touched. 'What a good chap he is!' François said to himself. 'He has no malice. A bit loud-mouthed, a bit of a tyrant, a little mad, but sound at heart.' Roland held up his bedaubed face for François to wipe. Roland talked, chattered incessantly in the exaltation of his dramatic triumph. François did not listen to him, but watched with fascination the features emerging in their original nudity as the thick layer of grease-paint dissolved. Seen thus from above—François was standing and leaning over the sitting Oyarzun—and from close at hand, they appeared somewhat disquieting: an intense animal life seemed to shine through the vivid eyes, the mouth was a little thick, the nostrils quivered incessantly, while round these central features so violently alive, the rough, blue chin, the cheeks, the shining forehead, lay like dead mineral surfaces, marked here and there by disgusting little imperfections: enlarged pores, spots, blackheads. It seemed to François that here was a face defenceless and pitiable, and for an instant or two he was sorry for it. Perhaps the human face should not be looked at from too close? In silence, François continued to wipe it, as if it had been the bloody face of a dead boy upon which he was gazing for the last time, the tragic masque of Athalie.

Some time after this, during the first days of the holidays, he met Roland Oyarzun in the road.

"Where are you going?" the latter cried. "To the Navailles Tower? What are you going to do up there? Dream? All the same, may I come with you, poet? By the way, you haven't congratulated me on getting through the first part of the exam."

"I haven't had the chance. But I was glad of your success."

"Oh, don't exaggerate. When you've been failed twice, you can't talk of success any more. All the same, I'm jolly pleased. I had a cracking good mark in history. The Prof. who examined me was drivelling with admiration. It was the Battle of Austerlitz, did you know? My father made me sweat it up with a map, a fortnight before. But, Christ, the Latin! Guess what I got to translate? An ode of Horace, for God's sake! If it had been Caesar, all right! One can always manage Caesar somehow. Legates having been sent, ablative absolute, the town surrendered, principal clause, in order to avoid being pillaged, subordinate clause. Caesar's in the bag."

"Particularly when you've got a passion for generals."

"Of course. War, conquest, tactics, that's what I like. While, as for that Horace! Besides, I hate syrabites."

"Sybarites."

"What?"

"It's sybarites, not syrabites."

"You can't ever let a mistake pass without correcting it, can you? You're a pedant! Always trying to humiliate me."

"Surely it's better to correct a mistake, isn't it?"

"And when, for once, I use a difficult word, too! Oh well, no matter. I was talking of those swines of Romans. They disgust me. They thought of nothing but eating and doing all sorts of dirty things after their banquets. The only ones I like among them are Cato the Elder, Coriolanus, Scipio Africanus and Julius Caesar. I should like Antony well enough if he hadn't killed himself for the sake of a woman. A great captain does not kill himself for a woman."

"I like the Antonine emperors: Trajan, Hadrian, Marcus Aurelius."

"Marcus Aurelius, that ink-slinger, that . . . that . . . philosopher! No, thanks. He won't do for me. Ah, but I see what it is! You salute a colleague! You've just passed brilliantly in philosophy, though you don't say anything about it! I'm being sarcastic, aren't I, old man? I say, while we're on the subject, it's making me sweat having to spend another year at school, when all my friends have left. Well, all my friends in our class. There'll only be Loustalot, and he's a dolt, and a Socialist, like you, only with you one can argue seriously. And I mean: seriously. When do you leave?"

"At the beginning of September."

"Are you going to live in a hostel?"

"No. I'm going to board with a cousin of my father's. He's a pastor in the suburbs."

"My poor chap! You have my sympathy."

"I don't mind."

"I know. You're a good Huguenot, brought up on the Bible. You know, you ought to become converted to Catholicism. At least, it's a bit gayer: Gregorian chants, pomps and ceremonies, a magnificent liturgy. . . ."

"Thank you, No. And, anyway a Catholic like you hasn't much chance of converting me."

"And why not?"

"Because you're only a Catholic for the sake of appearances. You haven't even got faith."

"You're damned impertinent! You've no right to say that! How can you say I haven't got faith?"

"I divine it. I sense it."

"You sense it, do you? Too bloody clever by half. Let me tell you this: I've got faith to such an extent that I don't even ask myself the question of whether God exists. I don't ask any questions. I practise blindly."

"That's exactly what I'm saying. What about love. What place has it in this formalism?"

"What are you talking about? Love?"

"Exactly, love. In Latin, *caritas*. The love of God and the love of one's neighbour."

"If you mean that I don't love my neighbour enough," said Roland angrily, "I don't know what more you want. What about my Congregation? The hours I've spent with the little boys teaching them civics, games, and energetic, open-air morality, to make tough, decisive men of them. According to you, all my devotion counts for nothing, does it?"

"I don't say it doesn't count. But you must admit that you like that sort of thing: being in command, the prestige of a leader, para-military exercises and your popularity with the boys."

"Bravo. Go on. Humble me. Mock. Insult. Oh, you're a typical Frenchman of today: petty, mean, your mind closed to all grandeur, incapable of being disinterested. A Frenchman of the brothel and the card-table!"

"I make use of neither the one nor the other."

"You'll come to it. I predict it!" Roland roared. "Your arse on a chair in a café, that's how you'll spend your days in Paris. A card-player! You make me sick, the whole lot of you. When one thinks how low France has fallen, beside a Germany who is rearming and preparing to violate the Treaty of Versailles."

"What are you talking about? What has the Treaty of Versailles got to do with our discussion? We were talking about my leaving for Paris. You get excited, mount your high horse, and all about nothing."

"All right. It's much ado about nothing. To hell with it!"

"All right, to hell with it!"

"I don't mind telling you, Donadieu, there are days when I could scrag you."

"Have I annoyed you? I'm sorry. I didn't intend to."

"Oh, yes, of course, your intentions are always good. You'd wring some innocent person's neck with the best intentions in the world. Robespierre! I hate virtuous people of your type," he shouted. "They're soft, they never quite give themselves away, they throw vitriol in your face, and when you tell them that it burns they're astonished: 'What, really? I'm so sorry, I thought it was whey'. And to crown all they're persuaded of their good intentions!"

François was not unduly worried: Oyarzon had accustomed him to this sort of outburst. He knew an infallible method of quieting his companion: first, place a hand on his shoulder; then, "My dear chap, calm down. You're wounding me now. And you know that I'm very fond of you."

The effect was immediate.

"Misunderstood," Roland murmured. "That's what's the matter with me: I'm misunderstood."

"What nonsense! Everyone likes you at school."

"I've no friends," he moaned, growing more and more sorry for himself. "I've acquaintances, that's all. No friends."

"You're too exacting, that's what it is."

"Exacting, yes. When you're as exacting as I am, you're condemned to go through life alone."

In an access of emotion, he developed the piteous theme. The ideal in this world was always jeered at. Woe to the sensitive. Those were in luck who had a stone in place of a heart. One might just as well throw oneself into the river, if it were not for one's religion and a father who understood. The great lout, eighteen years old, with good muscles, an excellent centre-forward, had tears in his eyes. His voice faltered and he was making visible efforts not to burst into sobs. François was more embarrassed than moved. Oyarzun had no shame. Trying to look as if nothing were happening, François cast anxious glances at the rare passers-by.

"My dear chap, you're being much too pessimistic," he said pacifically. "You ought to know that I, at any rate, understand you."

"Nobody understands me! No one knows what goes on in here!" Roland cried, striking his forehead with his fist, as if his brain were in process of secreting, unknown to everyone, the *Maison du Berger* or the *Tristesse d'Olympio*.

"When are you leaving for the holidays?" François asked to cause a diversion.

"Tomorrow."

"In that case, if you're going to stay all summer in the mountains, we may not meet again before I go away."

"Good God! Yes. I hadn't thought of that."

The prospect suddenly released a great sentimental effusion.

"What fools we are to quarrel like this on the eve of our separation. To think that our life together is over! And the old school! I remember when we were still in short trousers, in the Sixth Form. It only seems like yesterday. My dear old Donadieu, you'll forgive my having maddened you so often by calling you Calvin? Yes, yes. Don't protest. I did, often. I made you very angry. I can't help being malicious, you know, it's my nature.

I'm an aggressive type. But you don't bear me a grudge, do you?"

François assured him that he didn't; he bore him not the least grudge in the world. But when Roland accused himself of being malicious, François wondered which he imagined to be most in need of commiseration, the victim or the executioner.

"Well, I must run now, I've a meeting of my group leaders at three o'clock," said Roland, having quite recovered his serenity. "If you only knew how wonderful these boys are: at fourteen, they've already got a sense of duty—and what energy! Well, goodbye, old chap. We'll meet again next year. I'll write to you. Send me your address."

He mounted his bright red bicycle and went off down the hill at full speed, singing the first bars of the *Artilleur de Metz.*

François walked on up to the top of the hill. There, on a knoll, stood the old dismantled castle called the Navailles Tower. The site had a certain romantic beauty, for it lacked neither ivy, mountains on the horizon, nor a certain melancholy. François often came to sit in this high place. A few hovels and kitchen gardens clung to the side of the knoll, recalling a century when the people of Sault-en-Labourd built their houses and spent their lives cowering in the shadow of the castle. Beyond the river, too shut-in to be visible, the countryside of Béarn stretched away unspectacularly peaceful, a country of small fields, jealously divided by hedges of blackberry, a land of small individual proprietors, with a field of wheat here, of maize there, a few vineyards and many spiky conifers. On the horizon, the peaks of the Pyrenees mingled with blue thunder-clouds. Once this land could have contained within its borders the ambition of a boy on the point of leaving school. He would have gone from school to his father's shop, to his workshop, to his forge, or to his farm by a natural transition that had always been foreseen. But now, in the 'thirties, the land could no longer feed them, it was said, the small business-man feared the end of the month, the workshop dismissed its workmen, while the doctor and the solicitor no longer had the means to retire, money was scarce, and work too, there was nothing for it but to emigrate. In old Béarn, the old Basque land, the second son of large families sailed for the Argentine, shod in sandals, a béret on his head, a sack over his shoulder and twenty francs in his pocket. Thirty years later he came back, comfortably off, to be known as "the American", and to build himself a villa on the coast. But not for ages past had the Argentine enriched its immigrants. There was nothing for it but to go up for the universities and the competitive examinations, a more uncertain expedition. It was in the 'thirties that young Frenchmen began to be haunted by a lugubrious obsession with diplomas. The lower middle class of artisans and small shopkeepers impelled their children towards the liberal professions and the civil service, sometimes from a desire to "raise themselves", but much more frequently from anxiety for the future and a longing for security. It was the advent of hard times.

François Donadieu had no precise vocation. Since he had to choose a profession, he had proceeded by a process of elimination. A doctor? No, he had a horror of everything to do with illness, decline and death. A business-man? He had no arithmetic and no cunning, he would be bankrupt in a week. The Army? There was too much discipline, too much mathematics, and he had no taste for authority or uniforms. Manual work? François was no draught-horse, and after all he had studied Virgil and Descartes. A solicitor? Papers, dust and the grind of the law. His mother would have been happy to see him a pastor, but she did not know that he had found (and adopted) atheism at twelve years old, when he had read the work of M. Camille Flammarion on the subject of the plurality of inhabited worlds. A schoolmaster? Too humdrum and too dreary. The magistracy? The obstacle of the law again. So there remained nothing but the competitive examinations for the Civil Service, and for that there was no need of a vocation. François did not conceal from himself the modesty and mediocrity of his ambitions. He counted on Paris, the unknown, and luck. He had a vague appetite for life, and wanted above all to remain available without very well knowing for whom or for what. He was thin, light, rather timid, with a tendency towards dreaming and absentmindedness. His face was weak, unfinished, his hair pale, but there was a certain romantic sensitiveness about him, and an air of integrity and honesty. He looked down at the curving, mossy roofs at his feet, at the wide expanse of the countryside, the misty outline of the mountains, and the sky rose-tinted by the setting sun. He thought: 'In the midst of all that, I don't amount to much,' and again, 'Why am I here?' and: 'There are two thousand million souls in the world. Does one soul really count for much?' He remembered also a phrase he had read in a Russian novel: "If God doesn't exist, everything is permissible." Nevertheless, even in the perspective of Divine non-existence, François knew very well that everything was not permitted to *him*. For example, even if he could do so with absolute and guaranteed impunity, he would not steal ten francs from a millionaire. He was physically incapable of performing an act of theft. Nor did murder hold any attraction for him: what a vulgar, repugnant thing killing was! He knew, too, that if he gave his word he would keep it. He disliked lying. Besides, he was bad at it. With regard to the flesh, there were no problems there. A moderate interest bounded by a zone of disgust for everything that was blatantly and indecently physiological. He had heard that this disgust was due to a moral perversion known as "angélisme", a too idealistic philosophy, but this had not impressed him much. 'On the whole, I'm a very reasonable sort of person.' He thought that as a young man, and as a man, he would doubtless be reasonable too. His ideal was to achieve an equilibrium in life, to be generous without folly, and enthusiastic without being silly. He would read much, take an interest in literature and the arts, and listen to a lot of music. In politics, he would be on the left, because the capitalist structure, etc., but not a Communist, because of the liberty of the individual, etc. He was holding a book in his hand, *Jean Christophe*. He liked the book. He thought that Romain Rolland was the greatest writer of the century, an eminent and distinguished thinker.

He went down towards the town.

"You're late," said Mme Donadieu.

"It's hardly half-past seven."

"We dine at seven. What were you doing?"

"I met Oyarzun. We stayed late, talking."

"I'd rather you didn't have anything to do with that Oyarzun boy," said M. Donadieu. "I've got nothing against him, but his mother's got herself talked about a good deal."

"And for far too long," added Mme Donadieu.

"All the same, I can't drop him because of his mother. . . . He's a good chap."

"If your eye offends you, pluck it out."

"But I'm not offended," he answered thoughtlessly.

"François!"

He longed to answer back. But he clenched his teeth and sat down at the table in silence. He made a wry face as he began to eat his soup. It was made of pumpkin, which he loathed.

"François! Grace!" said Mme Donadieu with an air of rebuke.

"I'm sorry. I forgot."

He put down his spoon, clasped his hands together on the edge of the table, and stammered out the prayer in three seconds:

"Bless us, O Lord, and this food of which we are about to partake to strengthen us in Thy holy service. Amen."

"There was no need to say 'we'," remarked M. Donadieu with logic, "since you were saying grace for yourself alone. We have already done so."

"It was a royal plural," François sighed.

The joke seemed to amuse no one.

'When I get to Paris, I shall only eat what I like. I shall not say grace any more. I shall come home at any hour. I shall go to church from time to time, so as not to break altogether with a faith that may have some sense in it.' He remembered that he was going to live with his clergyman uncle and that doubtless this luxurious programme might prove difficult of realisation. He looked at his parents, his young sister, his brother, and, confronted with their honest faces, felt a pang of remorse. The house might be a little dull, a little severe, but it was also a tabernacle of rectitude. Nothing despicable had ever entered in. 'All the same, my childhood might have been freer and happier. I grew up in a network of prohibitions and was soundly scolded each time I tripped. I was certainly never pampered. On the whole, I was bored, without always being aware of it. Perhaps that's why I'm not naturally gay. Oyarzun has often told me that I've got a face like an undertaker. He exaggerates. My features bear the imprint of a noble melancholy.'

When he had swallowed the last mouthful, he waited till his father had finished reading aloud an article about the murder of Chancellor Dollfuss (M. Donadieu enjoyed reading the newspaper to his family). Then he said good-night to his parents and went up to his room. He untied his tie and took off his coat and shoes with relief: it was another whim of his family's, this desire to see him wearing a tie, confined in a coat, and shod with leather even in the hottest of the dog-days, when most of his friends wore open collars, short sleeves and sandals. The window of his room opened upon a ravine in whose bottom a stream slowly trickled. The three or four tanneries of the town stood on the edge of this stream, which filled their reservoirs. François sniffed the animal smell of the tan and the hides, through which he could detect another odour, fainter, more countrified—that of the fresh bark. Herds and oak woods, all Béarn was summed up in this violent, musk-like odour which mingled with the scents of the night. "*I breathed the healthy smell of tanneries,*" Francis Jammes had written, and François, who liked the poem very much, recited it to himself. On the further bank was a sixteenth-century house which had belonged to the Grammont family; the wonderful wooden balcony had recently fallen down during a storm. Working-class families, with innumerable children, had found more or less satisfactory homes in the rooms of this stately ruin in which Henry IV had often stayed. Further off there were tiled roofs, a steeple, the hillside blue in the dusk, and Venus already shining at its crest. Frogs were croaking in the stream. Some distance off the boys of a club, who practised playing the bugle on summer evenings, were croaking too: their fanfares shivered the silence in intervals unknown to western music, but with an impetuosity which, in default of tune, at least gave evidence of the power of their young lungs. These were the only noises in the town, at this house when Sault-en-Labourd gave itself up to sleep, and soon they would fade into the silence of a night like every other night in Sault-en-Labourd. François got into bed, a book in his hand, but his thoughts wandered beyond the narrow room, beyond the smell of tan and bark which he had known since his earliest infancy, beyond the town and towards the borders of sleep and forgetfulness. He floated now among the nebulae, and saw his whole life, past, present, and to come, as a series of detached scenes which he could judge from afar. He could look upon his life as if he were already dead. Who are you, François Donadieu? A single soul among two thousand million souls, renewed three times a century through thousands of centuries. Who are you? Which of these scenes, already touched by oblivion, will you choose to preserve? Time passes, time passes. . . . Listen to the ticking of the invisible clock on your breast. Two thousand million souls, and a single life for each of them. Two thousand million souls, François Donadieu, and there is no one in the world but you.

CHAPTER IV

FRAGMENTS FROM A DEAD WORLD (CONCLUDED)

1

FRANÇOIS worked five hours a day for an insurance agency, classifying and typing policies and modifications to them. The job gave him enough money to pay his board at the pastor's and left him about a hundred francs a month for other expenses and pocket money. He was supposed to be preparing for the competitive examination for a clerkship in the Ministry of works. In fact, his two first terms were given up to discovering and exploring Paris. Not daring to trust himself to the buses, whose routes seemed to him utterly incomprehensible, François spent hours every day in the Underground, going from the Sainte-Chapelle to the Louvre, from the Butte Montmartre to the Arc de Triomphe, making journeys of infinite complication and appalling length.

He also read an enormous amount. While most boys of his age were reading Breton, Cocteau, Malraux, Aragon, and Céline, he discovered Barrès, France, the Claudel of the *Grandes Odes*, the Maurras of *Antinea*, Péguy, Apollinaire and, with extraordinary, almost sacrilegious audacity, Gide. He was, however, bored by the latter's lesser works. He finished *L'Immoraliste* in the greatest perplexity, wondering why on earth the hero was considered immoral: was it because he bathed at dawn in those icy coves at the risk of catching pneumonia? François could only see in it rash silliness. But the *Nourritures*, ah, the *Nourritures*! Drunk with its poetry, François walked in the Luxembourg Gardens, reciting, "Nathaniel, I will teach you fervour," he stroked the bark of the chestnuts, chewed grass, dreamt he was a faun, and whistled the themes of Debussy's symphonic poem. (The young man was certainly rather young for his age.) Never for François had the world been so concrete, so luminous, or run so smoothly. It was also, no doubt, due to the fact that after the confinement of Sault-en-Labourd, he was making his first tentative but intoxicating experiments in youthful liberty. Was the universe really so vast? Could one walk for whole hours together in public parks, objectless, intent only upon oneself and one's own whims?

From Roland Oyarzun, now in the Philosophy class, he received letters which might have been written by a nincompoop of thirteen. The hand was round and naïve, so was their content. Roland declared that he loathed philosophers as much as he loathed writers. To be obliged to sweat blood over the *Discours de la Méthode* when Hitler was re-establishing conscription in Germany, was proof enough that the youth of France was condemned to impotence and irresponsibility. On the 6th of February, 1935, Roland attended a morning Mass, and prayed for "the repose of our martyrs' souls". (He had annexed to himself those who had been shot the year before.) "To change the subject, the old school is doing well. Last Sunday we defeated the thrusters of the Immaculée[1] by six goals to two. I scored two myself." But life did not consist wholly of triumphs. "I have had a great sorrow. A member of my Congregation, Bridoux—you remember him?—has died of appendicitis. Poor boy! It was he who would have had the Cross of Honour this term; I pinned it to his shroud. No other news to give you. Goodbye, old chap. All the best."

On a Sunday in May, François went to the Colonne concert and found himself sitting next to a fair-haired, thin girl, dressed in blue. Before each piece she read the programme notes with great care. François thought she was rather pretty. She let her programme fall. They both bent down to pick it up, their hands touched, they blushed. François stammered an apology, she whispered, "Thank you," and, since the conductor was raising his baton, they recovered their calm and turned back towards the sea of faces alive with pleasure and aesthetic anticipation. After the first movement, they exchanged a remark or two in an undertone about the quality of the performance: an admirable tempo, yes, but the tone. The brass was too loud, wasn't it? On the other hand, the flute . . . At the *largo ma non troppo*, François was troubled. At the *scherzo*, he thought that the girl

[1] The Immaculate Conception, a school from a neighbouring town.

was very nice, that her little nose had great distinction and that her mouth was adorably shaped. At the final *rondo*, he was in love.

In the interval, they went over the programme together, talked of Johann Sebastian Bach, and came to the conclusion that they had the same tastes in music. God, how pretty she is! I ought to have put on my new suit. What's happening to me? Really, she seems to be as much taken with me as I am with her. Can it be true? "The second movement of Mozart's D minor piano concerto. Do you remember it?" No; she did not. François hummed the theme quietly into her ear as if he were imparting a confidence. Her face, framed in fair hair, lit up at once: yes, yes, of course! La, la, la, la, la, la . . . Wonderful! It had a tender, almost childish delicacy, a heavenly romanticism, like an angel rocking the cradle of a little child. She had heard the concerto on the wireless, played and conducted by Bruno Walter. Of course, one couldn't expect it to be done so well today. She sighed. No, not so well. She sighed again. But after the dramatic *allegro*, almost Beethovian in its violence, the piano announced note by note the angelic little lullaby, then the violins repeated and developed it, without losing any of its airiness. François listened in ecstasy, despite the regrettable absence of Bruno Walter.

They saw each other again. Catherine Monnet was taking a course in secretarial work, but dreamt of nothing but the theatre. Her parents would not hear of it; they thought only of marrying their daughter off. François was shocked at so philistine a point of view, so bourgeois a prejudice against the profession, etc. They talked bitterly of parents' lack of understanding. They quoted Gide's phrase, "Families, I hate you all!" with a certain pleasurable audacity. They were at one in the cult of the Pitoëffs. Catherine had sophistication, taste, and had read a certain amount. She initiated François into the modern drama, led him to discover Pirandello, Lenormand, Passeur. On his side, François became passionately fond of the theatre, and of the magic phantoms of the cinema. It was a wonderful term. So wonderful, that he had to pay for it in failure at the competitive examination. But that was of no importance: he was nineteen, he was in love, life was wonderful and beautiful.

October. Roland Oyarzun, who had just been failed for the

second time in his philosophy examination, accompanied François to Paris. He was going to try another year of study at the Louis-le-Grand school. The Commandant did not hesitate at any sacrifice to assure his son a career. Roland was frantic with happiness. In his first week at the school he managed to get out surreptitiously one late afternoon, joined a band of Camelots du Roy who were patrolling the Boulevard Saint-Michel with sticks in their hands, and fought like a demon in a row with a hostile band of young Communists. With a black eye, a broken tooth, and his clothes in tatters, he spent part of the night in a police cell, in a state of euphoria bordering on ecstasy. Action at last! At last he had fought for his ideals! He had broken the bastards' heads! He had become a man. From now on his life would be militant and wonderful. In using his muscles at the expense of the nasal cartilage of an adversary, Roland Oyarzun had experienced the most voluptuously exciting moment of his life. To tell the truth, he knew no other, for the concern he felt for his physical and moral health had, up till now, caused him to fight shy of the diverse resources available to the needs of a youthful instinct.

François Donadieu was no fighter and, at this period, completely ignored politics. He learnt without emotion that Italian troops had crossed the frontier of Abyssinia, while a delirious crowd, massed in the Piazza Venezia, cheered Mussolini and shouted: "Death to the Negus!" These huge, primitive, operatic scenes took place in an unreal world, boring in its confusion: the world of history on the march. François thought his destiny was not bound up with Ethiopia, but with a pretty profile framed in fair hair. François was not thinking of marrying in the immediate future. "Later on, when I've done my military service and got a job." The idea of marriage attracted him for several reasons: in the first place, as a young provincial of the 'thirties and a Hugeunot who had been pretty strictly brought up, François could not conceive that he could have Catherine outside of marriage; in the second place, the title of 'husband' hallowed that manly independence to which boys, who have been somewhat suppressed at home, so ardently aspire; finally, the idea of a home of his own was very much to his liking. If one had decomposed his love for Catherine into its constituent elements as one decomposes the spectrum, one would have found: animal desire, all the keener for his total ignorance of the flesh; an ingenuous admiration for Catherine's "artistic gifts", with the refrain of "she's a brill-iant-ly clev-er girl, intelligent, cultured"; a desire to love and the exaltation of being in love, both part of that comedy which men play for their own benefit, from puberty to old age, and in which the pure and simple invention of the sentiment of love so closely resembles, and so often replaces, the true sentiment itself; and finally one would have found laziness, a self-abandonment to the easiest course, for it is easier to be in love and to play at being it than it is to prepare for examinations and earn one's living, for love, or its simulacrum, is an excellent alibi for irresponsibility, even when one happens by chance to die of it. Needless to say, François did not discern these motives till much later. For the moment, he was devoutly floundering.

The idyll was approaching its climax. From kisses to caresses, François was growing bolder, persuaded that he must surmount Himalayas of reserve, of virginal modesty in his little friend. Catherine's surrender had for setting the Monnet drawing-room, hung with brown and yellow curtains, furnished in the decorative style of 1925, with low seats in the shape of curule chairs, pearly lampshades, bronzes, a print representing the modern girl of the period, her skirts up to her knees, her waist round her buttocks, stroking a greyhound. Upon the divan, among cushions as idiotic looking as dahlias, were two almost life-size dolls: Pierrot and Columbine. The debilitating ugliness of this fussy *décor* would have been enough to cool the blood of any sensitive boy. But François had not yet learnt to recognise ugliness in furnishings and objects. He even thought the Monnets' drawing-room smarter than that of his parents (when, in fact, what was known at the Donadieus' as the "drawing-room" was a bare, admirable room, its floor tiled in red, its walls plastered, with, as the only piece of furniture, a Navarrese chest in black oak, as simple and magnificent as an old *hidalgo*).

About a month later François asked Simon, the pastor's son, to come up to his room. Simon had noticed at dinner that his young cousin was silent and pale. He expected "sensational" revelations. He lit his pipe, sat down in an armchair and waited.

François, looking extremely embarrassed, walked up and down the room without being able to broach the subject that worried him. He talked of the news: the Italo-Abyssinian campaign, sanctions.

"Come to the point, my boy," Simon interrupted briskly. "Leave the Negus alone. You don't care a damn about him anyway."

"Don't look at me. It embarrasses me. And promise not to jaw me afterwards."

"What silliness have you been up to? Have you stolen Mamma's jam?"

"Don't laugh. It's very serious. It's simply terrible! I . . . Promise you won't blame me or kick up a fuss."

"Christ said, *Judge not.*"

"I've told you about Catherine?"

"The girl you go to concerts with?"

"Yes. You know I regard her as my fiancée?"

"You have every right to. Though I think you ought to have begun by introducing her to your family and perhaps to us too.'

"I'm going to marry her."

"I should hope so, since you look upon her as your fiancée."

"You don't understand. I'm going to marry her at once, in a fortnight or a month at least. I've *got* to marry her."

Silence. Simon drew at his pipe. Then, gently: "Of course you'll marry her, François. As soon as possible. I'll be your best man, if you like."

François' cheeks were scarlet.

"Don't you blame me?" he murmured.

"You have sinned. I'm sorry both for you and for the girl. Poor children, it seems to me you're making a bad start."

"If only you knew how ashamed I am! The very idea that I'm going to be a father . . . At my age! I'm not twenty yet. It's as indecent as a farce at the Palais-Royal. Doesn't it seem like that to you?"

"It isn't paternity that's idecent; it's sin."

"I can't help it. I have no sense of sin."

"Don't say silly things like that, please. What are you ashamed of if it isn't of having sinned?"

"I'm ashamed because . . . to begin with, because you're there and you're thinking . . . it's as if I were naked. Then, the idea of having a child. . . . Like cats or rabbits! I don't see myself as a father. That's what it is! It's a mockery! Good God, I've only been shaving for six months! Everyone will laugh at me. I shall die of shame. I know I shall.

"My poor chap, no one's going to laugh at you."

"How are my parents going to be told? You know it's going to make a frightful scandal."

"It's not that I'm worried about. If I were you, I should be more concerned to find some way of keeping my wife properly."

"I don't know which way to turn! And how's she going to tell her family? It's even more difficult for her."

"I repeat, that's not the important thing. How are you going to live?"

"I don't know. I'm in a frightful mess. But just to think: a child! I could cry. . . . If only Catherine could be wrong! . . . It seems that one can sometimes be wrong about these things."

"How has Catherine taken it?"

"Pretty well. She didn't seem worried. Not at all. Happy, rather, and moved. Yes, I think that she was touched, happy at the idea that we should be getting married very soon. . . ."

"I'm going to say something wounding and you must forgive me, but I wonder . . . Are you quite sure that she's a 'good' girl, if I may so express it?"

"Catherine's the best girl in the world, and the purest! She only yielded to me because she loves me!"

Simon whistled softly.

"She 'yielded' did she? Heavens!" he murmured sympathetically. "Well, since you're such a conquering hero, my dear François, you'll have to think now of becoming a good husband and supporting a family, of being a father."

On being told of this premature marriage, about which they had not been consulted, Donadieu's parents reacted, not unreasonably, by asking peremptorily: "What are you going to live on and how are you going to support your wife?" To this purely economic cry of alarm were added a variety of moral considerations ("you have behaved badly"), sentimental ones ("it's very ungrateful of you to behave like this . . ."), and even theological ones ("what makes it worse is that she's bound to be a Catholic. No Protestant would place herself in the position of having to marry in a hurry"). There were five indignant pages, overflowing with reproaches, nearly all well-founded, and admonitions, nearly all reasonable, which was very depressing. François was angry and distressed at the same time. He bore his parents a grudge because of the suffering he was inflicting upon them. He bore himself a grudge because of the folly of his own actions. At the same time there was a certain satisfaction mingled with his anxiety: he was escaping from the clutch of the adult and parental world and was becoming integrated as himself. He was achieving autonomy.

The wedding, which took place in the middle of winter, was a pathetic and chilly occasion. Only the touching youth of the two victims saved it from total gloom. Catherine was dressed in a cheap coat and her teeth chattered. François, pale, thin, and hollow-cheeked, resembled one of Picasso's little blue Harlequins. One wanted to roll them up in an eiderdown and give them a hot toddy. Except for the witnesses, Roland Oyarzun and the pastor, there were no guests, the ceremony was "strictly private": to be exact, the privacy of blank poverty. Afterwards they went and had luncheon at a fixed-price restaurant on the boulevards and everyone made heroic efforts to be gay. Over dessert, Catherine wept the tears which had been threatening all morning. A girl must have a sort of natural genius to be able to renounce the pomp and ceremony of a proper wedding without a certain anguish. Or, on the other hand, she must be passionately in love with the man. Frankly accepted, in a spirit of kindness and love, the meagreness of the wedding would have been perfectly tolerable, as is everything that achieves transfiguration through the heart or the intelligence. But, undertaken in shame and bitterness, it became a refinement of torture. Catherine had suggested a honeymoon. To make it possible, François had had to resort to borrowing money from Simon. They went to the Basque coast ("I want to know your country," Catherine said), but the Atlantic greeted them with tempestuous weather: squalls, torrential rain, waves sixty feet high breaking over the jetties and promenades. Prisoners in their hotel, the young couple dragged themselves backwards and forwards between their room, where in spite of everything they managed to kill time, to a communal lounge where they read old magazines and smoked endless cigarettes. Though barely perceptible, there was yet a certain constraint between them, like a sort of mutual grudge. After the ecstatic chatter of the weeks before their marriage, they now no longer had much to say to each other and, secretly horrified by the spectre of their own silence, they hoped that the child who was to come would fill with his prattle the abyss of their torpid silence over which the night cast the frail bridge of their interlaced limbs and mingled breath.

At last their weary, lonely stay in the empty hotel, haunted by the furies of the Bay, came to an end. They took the train back to Paris with relief. In spite of her condition, Catherine intended taking lessons in acting, while François would have his daily work with the insurance firm and would give some lessons in a private school to augment his salary. This would mean that they would spend several hours away from each other every day, a prospect which they nevertheless found encouraging. Hope was renewed in their hearts; and with hope a little happiness, and so a little tenderness. Thus, speaking of the immediate future, they deplored the necessity which compelled them to work apart for long hours each day, when it would have been so delightful to be always together. And in expressing their regret they were sincere, for the certainty of being separated for the greater part of each day was so painful to them that they were able to feel a sort of vague gratitude to each other, a lessening of their apathy, to such an extent that they began to be in love once more. After the painful experience of their Basque stay, they needed to be reassured, to persuade themselves that nothing was lost, that they had not jumped blindly into an unhappy adventure; and the words and gestures that they exchanged in a corner of the empty compartment, rocked by the noisy rhythm of the train, were really the first tendernesses of their life together.

2

They went to live in the Rue de Vaugirard, in a flat found by Simon, and were not unhappy, at least in the first weeks which were devoted to furnishing. Their days were arranged in such a way that they really only lived together in the evening. At half past eight, François went out, drank a coffee at the bar on the ground floor, and took the Underground. He had to change twice and stand all the way, and he spent his time looking at his reflection in the window: 'Bad complexion. Eyes tired in the morning. Liver, perhaps? Ought to consult a doctor. I'm getting older.' By nine o'clock he was in the office. Noon: a light vegetarian luncheon in a pseudo-Russian restaurant of the neighbourhood. At five o'clock, homeward bound. At this hour he could have a few moments to himself, except on those days he went to fetch Catherine from her dramatic lesson. He could loiter along the quays if the weather were fine, or pay a long visit to a free library, skimming through books taken at random from the shelves, in the practice of that strange means of evasion, relaxation and liberation whith is open to the twentieth-century man-in-the-street: snuffling at the universe of print.

There was also the cinema, for which François had discovered an avid appetite. He remembered that at Sault-en-Labourd, on the rare occasions when his parents had allowed him to go to the cinema, he had spent enchanted hours in the little public hall where the audience assembled on Sundays. Sitting on a wooden bench, five yards from the screen, among the children of his own age, he forgot everything in screaming with them "Look out! Behind you!" to the hero upon the screen who could not see the traitor brandishing a dagger at his back; while the pianist played the *Hungarian March* on the old out-of-tune piano (in emotional scenes or love scenes she played Schubert's *Ave Maria*). What films were shown at Sault-en-Labourd in those days? *The Hunchback of Notre Dame*, *Blackmail*, *Surcouf*, *Mysteries of New York*, and Jacques Feyder's wonderful *l'Atlantide* (oh, Napierkowska's lascivious dance!), *Broken Blossoms*, *Cobra* (oh, Valentino's eyes!) and, above all, the film whose fantastic oddities were to haunt little François' imagination for a long time to come: *Metropolis*, the German delirium, the robot woman with Brigitte Helm's timeless, frozen beauty, the mechanised crowds of proletarian slaves, dwarfed by the Babylonian architecture. Never, never would François Donadieu forget *Metropolis*, which, in a condition of hypnotic stupefaction, he had seen at the age of six or seven. Today, like many young people of his age, François cultivated a conscious taste for the cinema and interested himself in every aspect of that impure but captivating industry; in short, he prided himself upon being a connoisseur and delighted in using the amusing phraseology of the films: tracking shot, focusing, wipes, close-ups, flash-back, sequence, panning, cutting, etc. But what, rather ingenuously, he sought in that cave of shadowy figures, was the bemused expectation, the being taken out of himself, the magical stupefaction that a silent little boy had once known.

His wife's days were widely different. Catherine got up late, tidied the little conjugal flat lazily and disgustedly, for she disliked all housework. She then dedicated two full hours by the clock to an operation which was at once both ardent and chaste: dressing. Sitting at her dressing-table, she gave herself up to its complicated rites: cleansing the skin, depilation, massage, astringent lotions, hair-brushing, manicure, pedicure, successive trials of rouge, creams, unguents, powders, scents, till at last her face for the day, differing entirely from the one with which she had woken up, had assumed its definitive aspect. Dressed and spruce, she went downstairs in her turn, ordered a coffee and two *croissants* at the bar on the ground floor, made a few household purchases, bought a fashion or film journal, and went upstairs again. She then rested for a while on the couch with the radio turned on, and did a little knitting for the baby's trousseau. Towards the middle of the afternoon she went out; according to what day it was, she visited a friend, her parents, or went to the school of drama, which consisted of two or three hundred boys and girls of her own age. In this nursery of the theatrical art, the boredom of her days dissolved, Catherine began to live again. She liked what she called the "ambience" of the school. ("There's a wonderful ambience at the school, the chums are marvellous, the principal's a darling.") When the principal called out her name, signalled her out from the mass of pupils, when he told her to climb up on to the stage to give a young actor his cues or herself to play some part she had learned on his advice, then she knew a strange glow of happiness. The principal's familiarity of address, his affectionate roughness ("You're Armande, my dear, not Bélise! Don't be so finical. You're playing an hysterical old woman! Don't stick your bottom out, darling, do you mind? Why do you have to walk like a duck? Ar-tic-ul-ate, my child, don't swallow the ends of your lines, and I shall be pleased with you. . . ."), the usual encouragement from her companions ("You're doing it very well, darling," "Really, you've improved no end since last time!" whether said simply or impressively, was the loyal homage of one craftsman to another . . .)—all this, though she was more or less aware that it was the mechanical etiquette of the place, nevertheless enchanted her as the tangible signs of popularity, the expression of a pervasive kindness. The true pleasure she derived from acting, from declaiming some text hallowed by the centuries, was increased tenfold by the artificial warmth, as glowing and exhilarating as a crackling of electricity, created by the genial familiarity of the principal and to which the two or three hundred young bodies under the frosted glass of the school acted as conductors. She went from one to another, calling them by their Christian names, asking for news of someone absent, delighted to hear that Gaston Baty had engaged him for a walking-on part in his forthcoming show. Her delight was due to the *esprit de corps* and sense of comradeship which were an indispensable part of the place, to such an extent that the news of some success achieved by a pupil transfigured every face by a sort of conditioned reflex so close to the true emotion that it was practically indistinguishable from it. In effect, the qualities upon which these young people prided themselves above all were those of the heart, an organ one was too discreet to mention by name, but which was indirectly alluded to by all kinds of appropriate mimicry: "Feuillère certainly has a wonderful technique, darling, but she lacks . . . you understand . . . that!"), and one placed one's hand in the neighbourhood of one's epigastrium while, open-mouthed and wild-eyed, one gasped for breath as if suffocating in the crisis of a heart-attack. This signified that there existed on the one hand such a thing as professional mastery, craftsmanship, and on the other hand one's own quivering talent. Catherine had become expert at these expressive little pantomimes. Yes, decidedly, she loved the "ambience" of the school. Here was the kingdom of art, of the creative urge, the world of school and lessons indefinitely prolonged, the chaste ante-room to a future which might bestow such wonderful gifts. The future. . . . Catherine bit her lip as she thought of the embryo swelling within her and which would soon compel her to give up what had become the salt of life to her. She felt a little surge of regret. Why had she committed this folly? Why had she married François? "I was young. . . ." Indeed, she had been young, she had been a whole year younger on the fatal day of the concert. . . . She tried to reconstruct the "chain of circumstances" that had resulted in the little shared flat in the Rue de Vaugirard; she assembled her memories as if they were a pleading for the defence. Yes, François had attracted her at once. His adolescent charm, his shyness, his boyish devotion. Then, that Sunday afternoon in the empty flat: delusion. 'Besides, I have no propensity for that side of love. I don't love François in that way. Do I love him? Yes, of course, but . . .' But he so often irritated her! He behaved in such a way that one always had the impression of being inferior to him in generosity and considerateness. His patience was maddening. He practised a sort of insidious diplomacy of which the unavowed purpose was to prove that he was always right. Oh, but he was a good man, and a good-natured one! But it had not been long before Catherine had noted in him irresolution, a dislike of exerting himself, something weak and flabby, a tendency to give up the struggle. For instance, in theory, he should have been preparing himself for his Civil Service examination. He had ordered pamphlets and searched the bookstalls for second-hand books. He knew the administrative hierarchy and the rates of pay by heart. But he never opened any of these text-books on law or political science. He spent nearly every day reading Tolstoy or Balzac and, when Catherine on one occasion smilingly remarked upon it, he assumed the condescending air of one who has for a long time past nourished high designs, but fears that he is not altogether understood by the vulgar. "My dear," he replied with the greatest good nature, as if he were explaining a somewhat difficult idea to a backward child, "my dear, don't worry, I know what I'm doing. General culture is also important in the examination, you see. I'm not wasting time," and he returned, quite tranquilly, to *Anna Karenina*, a somewhat unexpected prolegomenon to a clerkship in the Ministry of Works. He was capable of considerable perspicacity about other people, but appeared singularly mistaken about himself. When, in the evening, he came to call for his wife at a little bar near the school, where the pupils met after work, he assumed a certain stiffness and constraint of manner which implied a comparison to his own advantage, between his personal refinement and the disorderliness of the young actors. His ceremonious politeness concealed a subtle reprobation, and Catherine could decipher without difficulty what every line in his fixedly smiling face proclaimed: "Note my courtesy towards these young people. My poor sweet, I don't know how you can stand them, but, well, since it's a necessary part of your profession, I'm prepared to put up with them." At these moments she could willingly have killed him. Nevertheless, she believed that she detected in François' haughtiness a provincial bashfulness, above all an invincible shyness. The ease, the assurance, and the animation of the young actors crushed him. Secretly, he was jealous of them, as he was jealous of their beauty which was often surpassing. Those were feelings which one could understand, with which when it came to the point one could sympathise, provided they were avowed. But François probably did not admit them even to himself. He would not have allowed himself to show envy or resentment for anything in the world. He said with compressed lips: "It's not a proper circle of acquaintance for you, Catherine. Those boys seemed to me a pretty mediocre lot on the whole, don't you agree? I shouldn't like you to become too familiar with them: they're not of a type to suit you, I'm sure. Oh, yes, I know that a certain intimacy of address is the proper form among actors, but all the same. . . . Frankly, I'm not at all sure that contacts of that kind are a good influence for you." And his distant gaze, his pursed lips, and his polite reticence, all proclaimed that, out of regard for his wife, he was seriously understating the facts, and that he really had to overcome considerable reluctance in order to cross the threshold of the little bar. Catherine was by turns demoralised and defeated or burning with resentment. "You annoy them too!" she shouted at him one day. "When you're there, they cease being natural, and become vulgar on purpose. It's not only because you're my husband, but because you're so different from all of them! I feel the same way too. As soon as you come in, I cease being natural, I feel embarrassed, and I want to go away at once. You don't get on with them, you see. You're not one of them. And you can't adapt yourself. In the end this dichotomy makes me feel that I'm two people, that I'm leading a double life, that there's some sort of duplicity in my behaviour. I feel a sense of guilt. You make me feel that there's something wrong in my behaviour." On another occasion, at the end of her patience, she cried: "Why do you come to fetch me when you dislike them all so much, and find their company so unbearable? I can come home alone. You can wait for me there. It would be much better. Oh, I'm so happy at the school with all my friends! Good heavens! Mayn't I be happy for even four hours a week?" As soon as she had said it, she realised how atrocious her admission was. François' face winced as if he had been hit, there was a flow of blood to his cheeks and a moment later they had turned ghastly pale. His lower lip trembled and two large tears, as involuntary as the blood, gushed from the young husband's eyes. Distracted by remorse, as a moment before she had been by anger, Catherine took him in her arms and they both wept, two abandoned children outrun by life and the world who no longer knew to which saint they should dedicate themselves. That night, they felt closer to each other than they had ever been before.

But two days later, punctual, stiff, sadly and silently disapproving, François pushed open the door of the little bar and froze the happy, schoolgirlish laugh on Catherine's lips.

He, too, had his grievances. He thought his wife frivolous, lazy and egotistical. He blamed her for neglecting the housekeeping, which was true, for cooking abominably, which was true, and for wasting too much time on her appearance, which was also true. In François, a long line of Béarn Huguenots, self-indulgent and authoritarian husbands, devotedly cherished by their slave-wives, trembled with scandalised indignation. In his own family, François had seen his father, enthroned like some majestic pasha, the unquestioned master, while the women of the house busied themselves around him. When he happened to raise his voice, it was Jupiter thundering while the world around fell silent, and the dog took refuge beneath the furniture with his tail between its legs. And this respect, this almost religious reference, this devotion so freely rendered seemed the most natural thing in the world, manifestations that it never entered anyone's head to question. The house was organised round the *pater familias* like the solar system round the sun. Still completely impregnated with this patriarchal conception, François Donadieu found himself married to a wife who impudently disregarded the customary married relationship. In place of the deferential slave, he was allied to a self-centred creature who was completely occupied with herself, each of whose gestures underlined her autonomy and independence, and each minute of whose life seemed to declare: "Look, I have made you a royal gift: my young body, my unspoiled youth. Render me the homage which is my due. I am your luxury, the ornament of your days and the reward of your nights. Permit me to care for so precious an object. It is true that you are the man—that is to say, the one who works and deserves to be loved. Nevertheless, I too am a person with her own tastes, aptitudes and activities, her own territory into which you have no right to pry. We are equals, but naturally, from a tradition of courtesy which goes back to Tristan and Iseult and to the troubadours, I am an equal who has the right to a certain supplementary consideration, an equal who is slightly privileged: indeed, the adorable frailty of woman, etc. So, brute male, while I varnish my nails, just adore me and shut up." She didn't imply anything quite so brutal or so summary as this, but she was not far off it. Under cover of the doctrine of the equality of the sexes, the world had fallen into a matriarchy, and new values ruled the young couple's lives. In François Donadieu, a husband out of the pages of Moliére, was daily chagrined and offended.

Nevertheless, he was just, and willingly recognised that there were a number of good qualities to be placed to Catherine's credit: a certain immunity to purely material circumstances, frankness, a gaiety of spirit and temper which often lent their life in common the charm of a picnic, of bohemian casualness. These were not exactly the virtues whose worth François, as a provincial and descended from a long line of Protestants from Sault-en-Labourd, could recognise; but, simply as a young man, he could appreciate them.

Thus they lived in somewhat unstable equilibrium. Their usual relations could be summed up thus: intermittent goodwill, rare quarrels, prolonged silences. They had adopted, once and for all, a certain conventional tone which might be designated as that of "newlyweds", and though they were not entirely taken in by it, there was a tacit agreement between them to maintain it. The cinema, popular entertainers and women's journals had codified this artificial language in which there was an affectation of originality, humour and a certain conscious and wayward fantasy. When one makes the gestures and uses the vocabulary of fondness, it is not absolutely indispensable to be in love, provided always that one can play the game for long enough: some of this absent fondness ends by crystallising around the words which evoke it, so true it is that with many people the appearance of reality takes the place of reality itself.

As regards their finances, they were not very well off, since

François' salary was but modest. The Monnet parents-in-law helped a little. The prospect of grandchildren positively made them quaver with emotion, and each quaver was worth a ham or half a dozen of burgundy to the young couple. Nevertheless, the young people had little appearance of prosperity.

About the sixth month of her pregnancy, Catherine fell ill: a general debility. François worked two hours longer at the office. He now had no time to himself.

At last the child was born. The father gazed upon the horrid, squalling little bundle of pink flesh with a mixture of consternation and sheepish pride. The doctor had had to use instruments to extract the puny creature whose face was purple from asphyxia and the will to live. Catherine, lying exhausted in the bed, looked like a dead girl.

Mme Monnet came and installed herself in the flat. There was a long period of peace. Catherine had no more liking for children than she had for cooking or sweeping carpets, but she played with Juliette as if she were a doll. The grandmother played the part of nurse, and revelled in it. Catherine would have been incapable of boiling a feeding-bottle or washing nappies. Mme Monnet performed these operations as if they were sacred rites, deriving an almost mystical happiness from them. From time to time Catherine fondled and cuddled the infant, kissing it with awkward ardour, till they both grew exasperated and tired of each other; then Juliette began howling and Catherine at once handed her over, complaining that her daughter did not love her. François cherished Juliette with a certain absence of mind.

For three months, Catherine, who was much weakened, was condemned to a sofa, and appeared to have forgotten her fancy for acting. But the vocation returned with returning health. She began to speak of "my lessons" and of having received "a letter from the principal . . .". It was decided to confide Juliette to her grandmother's care, for as long at least as she remained small enough to be a tie. François would pay her keep. So Mme Monnet took Juliette to live with her. The young couple found themselves alone again. Catherine returned to her lessons without being able to conceal either from herself or her husband her relief and gratification. Life blossomed again.

* * *

When Roland Oyarzun thought of François Donadieu's marriage, when he remembered the shy, childish couple they had been, he shrugged his shoulders with commiseration and perhaps a certain disgust. How crazy it was to go and get married at twenty, to allow oneself to be hooked by the first one that came along! Roland wouldn't have let himself be caught like that! He wasn't born yesterday. He didn't go through life with his eyes shut. On the contrary, he saw things clearly, with pitiless realism: that was Roland Oyarzun for you. Besides, he avoided women. He intended keeping himself clean for the woman who would be his legitimate wife and the mother of his sons. Yes, sir, clean; that's what I said. And if anyone wants to laugh, he'll get a clip on the jaw. Of course, that didn't put a stopper on dirty jokes, lewd songs, or a bit of bottom-pinching at the palais, or even going along to the brothel with the chaps. As for a bit of Rabelaisian fun, a bit of frank talk, a bit of wit, Roland knew just where he stood: he was a real Frenchman, always with a quip to make you roar, or a clever piece of backchat—not one of these dubious foreigners who couldn't look you in the face, Yids from the ghettoes of central Europe, who pullulated these days on the Boul'-Mich. No; there was nothing of the cosmopolitan intellectual about Roland, nothing of the dispirited refugee: he was the hearty type, Mme Angot's sort. But mind this: when Roland goes to a brothel, it's just to kick up a shindy, that's all. As for anything else, listen: Roland has no wish to poison his blood, no desire to compromise his health. What's more, fun for fun, Roland prefers running the hundred yards with the chaps on the sports ground; it's healthier and more effective. If François Donadieu had only gone in for athletics, he might have had some chance of becoming a man, a real chap. From the virile discipline of the sports ground he would have derived lucidity and energy. He would not have fallen into the meshes of love. But athletics, him! At school he always had his nose in a book. Certainly, he had passed his examinations brilliantly. But what good did that do him? He was hardly fit to earn his own living and his wife's today. And, in any case, what did this Baccalauréat examination matter? It was nothing but a manifestation of the equalitarianism of this bloody democracy. As if there were no natural hierarchy among men. Now that every little shopkeeper's son wants to take the examination, the competition has become so severe that the whole thing's impossible, perfectly ridiculous. Besides, all the Jews of central Europe apply to enter the French schools now, and all the girls want to take the examination too, instead of devoting themselves to cooking and darning. So, naturally, what with the Jews, the girls and the sons of every shopkeeper in France, there's a pretty good crowd in June to write essays on the comparative merits of Corneille and Racine. How do you expect the true young Frenchman to make out with all this disloyal competition? And disloyal it is. Isn't Roland Oyarzun in a position to know it? He is at Louis-le-Grand and he has friends who are up for the final part of their examinations. Well, among sixty scugs (the new boys are called scugs: always a bit of time-honoured fun, what, jokes and so on)—among sixty scugs, then, there are at least twenty Jews. Yes, sir, twenty of the circumcised in a class that represents the flower of the youth of France. That's where we are after seventy years of democraggers. And what's more, they're intelligent, the Yids are. You can't deny them brains. But what do brains amount to? They're unnecessary. The true Frenchman has no need of brains. He's French, isn't he? And that's enough. He understands things by instinct. He's got a wonderful instinct, an instinct bestowed upon the land of France, upon the genius of French writers, upon the majesty of French cathedrals, etc., but Roland's not going to orate about this for long because, once again, he's not an intellectual, thank God, but he suggests you read the works of Charles Maurras. As for Maurras, well, to be frank, he's beginning to run off the rails, the old beaver, don't you think? Integrated nationalism, the monarchical idea, and watchfulness towards the East are all very fine. But to hell with it! We're living in the twentieth century, aren't we? You can't ignore what happened in 1793, 1830 and 1848. The only form of government that has a chance of succeeding today is National Socialism, because it knows how to combine desirable social reforms with the fight against Communism. Hitler's experiment is interesting. In any case, it's succeeding, and a policy that succeeds is, by definition, a right policy. It would be much better to consider an alliance, rather than to go on barking at the eternal Germania in old-fashioned Germanophobic rage, as Maurras does, shaking his Félibre goatee. Of course, one can't deny that Maurras is the incarnation of the highest expression of French thought, but he is old. A new generation is rising which looks across the frontiers at the ranks of the *Ballila* and the Hitler-Youth and dreams of what a French Fascism might become. So, when Maurras wants to restore the tendentious figure of Henry IV . . . It's not with a king that we shall stop this mounting tide of Jews, Freemasons, foreigners, Communists and other riff-raff. With Fascism, possibly. You know, at school, when one talked of a king, the Radical-Socialist chaps, with Donadieu in the lead, laughed inimically. But when it was a question of Fascism, they foamed at the mouth with rage. Because, you know, Donadieu positively allowed himself to have political opinions, the wretch. The little fool was a socialist. And now he's married, and has no future, he vegetates in a sort of black cess-pit, for all his examination certificates and reading. Roland would go and see them, poor children that they were; he'd take them some boxes of *pâté*; he'd take them out to dine in a restaurant one Sunday. Not too expensively, of course. A discreet charity. Tact was necessary in life. And Roland prided himself upon possessing that very gift. He had the delicacy of the wrath of God.

* * *

However, France was rotting away ever more quickly, by a process of acceleration that might have been represented by a mathematical formula as with falling bodies or explosions. Germany and Italy openly mocked her supineness: the first occupied the right bank of the Rhine; the other, following the example of the great democratic nations, proposed to acquire colonial possessions for herself, and with bombs of mustard gas blithely burned an ancient, half-naked, Christian people, armed with assegais and amulets. The great democracies, masters of vast empires, which they had acquired through kindness, persuasion and good works in the previous century, protested in the name of humanity. They wished to apply sanctions, naturally applied them incompetently, and thus effectively hastened the Italian conquest and, of course, obtained for themselves the conqueror's goodwill. The Republic was much too moral to occupy the left bank of the Rhine. Marianne contented herself with occupying the factories to the tune of an eighteenth-century pastoral entitled *The International*. Red flags flowered at Parisian windows in a fascinating fever of scarlet. A great thinker of the French Right, M. Henri Béraud, wondered whether England should not be reduced to slavery. The project was not proceeded with. It was an interesting one, of course, but perhaps a little Utopian. An anti-Communist plot was discovered and baptised *Cagoule*. Its intentions were, perhaps, not to be taken too seriously; it was symptomatic of a state of mind. But among the conspirators there were some, indeed, who aimed further than merely defeating Communism: they openly desired the triumph of Hitler's Germany, for such was their hate for the republican system that it did not occur to them that its destruction might be paid for too dearly by the defeat of France. Public opinion, utterly disoriented, did not know how to choose between Cagoulards, Communists, who were pacifist at that time, and the impotent radicals. The nation read *Paris-Soir*, the illustrated papers, learnt the meaning of sex-appeal, and enjoyed films about gangsters. Many Frenchmen, revolted by these signs of decadence, looked beyond the frontiers to where the Hitler Youth and the Young Fascists, rivers of force and life, marched beneath unfurled standards. The grand temptation of Fascism rose over Europe like a dawn alternately fanatical and poisonous. Everywhere, in Germany, in Italy, in Roumania, in Belgium, in the Scandinavian mists or under the Castilian sun, Fascism celebrated, sometimes in broad daylight, sometimes in catacombs, its bitter mysteries of love, violence and blood. In face of such enchantments, the old decaying democracies had nothing to offer but their decrepitude, the long list of their scandals, two or three languishing principals and the game of destroying notoriously rotten politicians. Europe's political Left had for too long decried the idea of patriotism, the idea of order, the idea of authority, had for too long mocked at the sources of youth's enthusiasms: in the name of what could it exhort the young to struggle against Fascism? It was necessary to have an old, well-founded faith in democracy, a stubborn attachment to certain Épinal prints—the taking of the Bastille, the soldiers of Year II, Gavroche at the barricades—to go on preferring the utterly shameless thing the Republic had become to the radiant visions of Fascism. But every Frenchman had been conscripted, and every conscript retains, locked in his heart, a sentimental feeling for the uniform, which never dies. The International Exhibition was inaugurated amid the builder's rubbish. Everyone was singing *La Cucaracha*, *Tout va très bien*, *Madame la Marquise*. Would the Trojan war take place? Louis Jouvet, rigged out like a black Samuari, murmured each night in the velvet frame of his theatre: "One minute of peace is always worth the having."

* * *

Juliette lived with her doting grandmother, and her parents went to see her three or four times a week. At first they went together, but later on, because of the marked preference the infant showed for her father, separately. Sunday is a day of family sacrifice: the infant was put to sleep in a pram, which François pushed, and they went gaily for a walk in the town. Catherine leant upon the arm of the head of the family. In passing she glanced into the few shop windows that were open: they were not a bad-looking couple, ridiculously young, and nice enough. She assumed at once and spontaneously the unsophisticated, tender air which suited the part of the charming young mother. The Sunday promenaders were her public. This little private part she played was not, however, exciting enough to counterbalance her disastrous boredom. The great boulevards, the Champs-Elysées, the embankments of the Seine, so delightful on weekdays, became depressing on Sundays.

"It reminds me of my childhood," Catherine said, "when I used to go for a walk with my parents. When I got home, I used to go to my room and think about suicide."

"As far as I can see, you were always a bit off-hand as a child. A little ray of sunshine in the house."

"You sound very bad-tempered."

"Do you think these walks amuse me, either? Besides, a man pushing a pram looks a pretty sort of fool."

"Oh, you know men can look pretty foolish anyway, and without pushing a pram."

"Thanks."

"Oh, for God's sake, don't begin again. Look. Let's go home. We've been out an hour. It's quite long enough."

"Your mother doesn't think it's long enough. She's so particular."

"Oh, leave Mummy out of it. It's a jolly good thing she's taken Juliette on. And it's not for the sake of what you pay her either. Oh, anyway, let's change the conversation. Shall we go out tonight? Let's spend the evening at the Dôme. I'll telephone Nathalie."

The prospect of "going out tonight" at once alleviated the boredom of the day. Their step was more sprightly as they returned to Mme Monnet's house.

Nathalie, a friend of Catherine's at the school, was the daughter of Russian refugees. Although she had been born in the Place de la Bastille, she had an accent so exotic that it was impossible to tell whether it was natural or merely a parody. She magnificently rolled her r's. Partly for fun, and partly from natural instability, Nathalie exaggerated every quality that appertained to that character which, in the 'thirties, was already somewhat old-fashioned: the beautiful, temperamental, bohemian exile. She had enormous eyes, made to look larger still by make-up; some deep-sea dream seemed to stir behind her dilated pupils. Her accoutrements—tartan blouses, Byzantine jewels at neck and ears, her feet naked in monk's sandals—lent her beauty, which was real, a vaguely outlandish and eccentric quality. She always looked as if she had either just come out of an oriental bazaar or was about to go to a fancy-dress ball. Her repertoire of romantic gestures were also, even in 1937, completely dated, except for François and Catherine, who saw in her something very 'authentic'. Nathalie drove a knife into the palms of her hands once a term, drank ink at the least provocation, sipped ether in an abstracted manner, threatened to throw herself out of the window or, alternatively, on the crest of some celestial happiness, she kissed every friend she met upon the lips while addressing them as 'little father'. Or, again, when giving a party to a dozen friends round the samovar in her tiny room, and wishing to offer them something choice in the way of entertainment, she never hesitated to take off her clothes and dance, naked and with perfect gravity, while reciting the *Chansons de Bilitis*. The first time that François Donadieu had the gratification of seeing this performance, he thought, Moliéresque husband and provincial Protestant that he was, that this immodest dance was the prelude to a bacchanalian orgy in which both he and his wife, whether they wished it or not, would be compelled to take part. He would willingly have left the low haunt, in outraged modesty and extreme alarm, taking Catherine with him. But he did not dare, and was much relieved when, the dance over, Nathalie, to the applause of the audience, covered her limbs with a dressing-gown. The intention was art, not debauchery. Later on, François became accustomed to the charming habits of the intelligentsia; he even became brave enough, on these nights at Nathalie's, often to ask in a sort of choral repetition for 'the dance of Bilitis'. Nathalie never had to be asked twice.

Thanks to these minor eccentricities, the young woman had succeeded in creating for herself among her contemporaries at the school a reputation for rather wild romanticism and for disquieting originality. Her acting, monotonous and inexpressive, her hands glued to her sides and her eyes vacant, was considered to have genius. And, as a matter of fact, ten years later, this style became extremely fashionable among young actors (vacuity becoming an 'admirable sobriety', etc.). Naturally Nathalie's 'particular line' was strictly limited to tragedy: Ibsen, Strindberg, and darkest Anouilh. She lacked humour to a dismaying degree.

Catherine and François often met her in the evenings at the Dôme. She spent a great deal of the night there, sitting with Scandinavian or South-American tourists, who were still seeking, in a Montparnasse that had become commercialised and was no more than half alive, the memories of the great period of Foujita-Modigliani-Hemingway. The whole quarter was no more than a half-dead tourist centre, severely hit by the slump; it had become a sort of unprosperous annexe to the great boulevards, with its huge half-empty cafés and bars, and its night clubs in which an occasional provincial might still consent to buy a bottle of champagne for a bored professional hostess. The great wave of success had ebbed long ago, and the embanked neon signs, stretching along this desolate shore, but accentuated the more cruelly its melancholy. Nevertheless, the Dôme still brought together a few artists, bearded and unknown, the simulacra of another age, and visiting strangers. It was in this company that Nathalie gave rein to her gifts. François and Catherine spent one or two nights a week in the Dôme, in the same spirit that certain bourgeois go to Mass: out of class discipline. They were that 'modern and artistic young couple'. This bi-weekly rite at the Dôme permitted them to cherish their own inner dreams of themselves. As soon as she saw them, Nathalie waved her arms like a semaphore. She shouted: "There you are at last, darlings!"

and as soon as they were near enough kissed them in turn upon the mouth with the tender concern of an early Christian receiving the brethren in the catacombs. One evening Roland Oyarzun, whom they had met by chance, accompanied them. When the introduction had been made, Nathalie kissed him on the mouth too, a liberty which caused the young man, entirely given up to games and politics as he was, a mortal fright. Roland was living in the Latin Quarter as an extra-mural student. He had left Louis-le-Grand and was working (still at his philosophy) with a private crammer. Nevertheless, he still played football and frequently took part in fights with political adversaries. This rowdy, perpetually reprieved student life suited him admirably. Physically, he had become a pretty superb animal, and a good deal of ill-will was needed in order to perceive the faults in the superb machine: a perpetual and excessive mobility of feature, a quivering of the nostrils, a spasmodic contraction of the little muscles under the skin of the cheeks and temples, a plethora of almost imperceptible twitchings betrayed unstable nerves and internal disharmony. His face, which very nearly possessed the classical shape of an antique marble, was far from having its noble serenity. And, finally, his voice, which was more rasping than ever, sometimes had intonations which were frankly unpleasant. Nevertheless, all in all, Roland Oyarzun was a fine figure of a man. His height, his gladiatorial shoulders, his thick hair and above all his brilliant eyes, sparkling with wild flashes, all declared his blooming youth. It was the first time that he had been to the Dôme. And seeing at the neighbouring tables nothing but foreigners who were speaking German, Norwegian or Spanish, he secretly threw them suspicious and disapproving glances, as if these perfectly respectable tourists were so many spies in the pay of an enemy power. Indeed, as far as he was concerned, all foreigners, no matter who they might be, were *a priori* suspect. "Damned foreigners," he said. "We French open our frontiers to all these degenerate foreigners who come and lead an easy life here, marry our girls, and carry off all the best jobs. Later on, everyone will complain that there's no outlet for French youth." If it were pointed out to him that these people seemed to succeed very well in their studies and on the whole passed difficult examinations very successfully, he replied: "But I never said they weren't intelligent. I said they were degenerate.

There's a difference." One gathered that, as far as he was concerned, intelligence was a minor quality, a negative quality upon which he had no wish to pride himself, and that he was quite content to leave its possession to these sub-human hordes, who sprang from the Carpathians, to take the Sorbonne, the Quai d'Orsay and the Conseil d'État by assault. On one side were the French, builders of cathedrals, peasants by race, logical and circumscribed, while on the other were these active, poisonous parasites, Jews and other kinds of Dagoes. It was the foreigners who introduced "into our homes" Marxism, psychoanalysis, Cubism and other filthy subversities. Nathalie having gone to the lavatory in the basement, Roland leant across the table towards François. "Who is this Yid?" he asked.

"Nathalie? She's not a Jewess. She's a Russian of the most orthodox kind."

Faced with such deplorable blindness, Roland shrugged his shoulders.

"She's a Yid," he repeated decisively.

"No, my dear chap, I assure you she's not. You can't have looked at her properly. Besides, one of her uncles is a priest in the Orthodox Church."

Roland laughed contemptuously.

"Her uncle a priest? You ingenuous little fool, don't you know that the Jews'll tell any lie? I tell you: it was quite enough for me to hear her pretty theories about marriage: it was just Léon Blum warmed up. She's a Yid! She kissed me on the mouth, the bitch. She must have syphilis, and did it on purpose to infect me."

Panic-stricken at the very idea—he had a horror of venereal disease—he spat a number of times under the table, took a handkerchief from his pocket and frantically rubbed his lips with it. François and Catherine protested: Nathalie was their friend, and they would not allow . . .

"I don't care a damn if she is your friend! It's nothing to congratulate yourselves on. Christ, if she's given me syphilis! It'd be just like the Yids, a trick to poison the French race!"

"You're mad!" François cried, exasperated by such obscene stupidity.

"You think I'm mad, do you? It's quite clear you've never read Drumont!"

Nathalie came back. From some residue of good manners,

Roland calmed down. But from his lowering expression they felt, with the exception of Nathalie, who was quite unaware, that a storm was threatening and liable to break at any moment. It did break. Not all at once, no. There were warning flashes of lightning, a muttering of thunder, by way of a prelude. In the first place, about Gide. Nathalie mentioned the author of *Nourritures terrestres*. Roland started at the mere mention of his name. He fulminated. Gide! That ignoble corrupter. That iconoclast. "He has profaned everything!" That destroyer of Christianity. That filthy degenerate. That accomplice of Yids and Reds. That anti-imperialist. That vile, unclean monster. An incarnation of the Devil. Any government with self-respect would banish him, have him whipped in the market place, and burn all his books. He quoted Henri Béraud: "Nature has a horror of Gide." He quoted Henri Massis and others of the monster's adversaries. If Roland had a son, he'd rather see him dead than reading Gide. Yes, sir, I mean it! At last he consented to calm down a little. He took great gulps of night air to slow down his heartbeats, which had become dangerously accelerated in the exaltation of his anathema. He asked for some lime tea. Nathalie, who had drunk five or six brandies, stroked his temples with the ends of her fingers.

"You mustn't get so excited, darling," she said with a Dostoevskian and slightly drunken effusiveness. "If you don't like modern literature, we won't talk about it any more, that's all."

With an outraged expression, Roland Oyarzun took François across the table to witness.

"There, she's becoming familiar now. I told you she was up to all the tricks."

"What are you whispering about, darling?"

François was twisting on his chair, half amused and half afraid of a flare-up: and, indeed, the people at the next table, Argentines, were beginning to look at them. They went on to talk of the International Exhibition, which had just been opened with great ceremony on the half-finished sites.

"It was a bloody fine show!" cried Roland. "Our Yid ministers, MM. Blum, Abraham, Cohen and Moch, received by the band of the Guard playing *Fiers Gaulois à tête ronde*! To hell with the Russian pavilion, anyway!"

"Yes, and what about the U.S.S.R. pavilion?" Nathalie asked.

"Isn't it magnificent? Not as good as the German one, nashurally not, but all the same . . ."

Catherine admired the new Palais de Chaillot with its statues and Paul Valéry's noble words carved on the façade. The Popular Front régime was wonderfully intellectual. Had they seen Jean-Richard Bloch's play ("Well! Well!" sneered Roland), called *Naissance d'une Cité*? It seemed that it was very intellectual. No; no one had seen it. Nathalie had recently seen *The Battleship Potemkin* again at Studio 28. Won-der-ful! A grr-eat work! That sequence, darlings, that sequence on the steps at Odessa when they machine-gun the crowd. Her eyes rather vacuous, her hair dishevelled, Nathalie pretended to machine-gun the Dôme's customers. "Bang, bang, bang," she said. "Won-der-ful! Bang, bang, bang."

"My God, your friend's as tight as a fart," Roland exploded.

"Nathalie, darling, don't you think we'd better go home?" said Catherine.

The Argentines turned to look at them frowningly.

"Bang, bang, bang," continued Nathalie, shooting the Argentine woman with fatuous ecstasy.

"She ought to be in a madhouse!" Roland muttered.

Nathalie tried to get to her feet, fell back on to the seat, and tried again.

"I'm fed-up with all these bloody fools ogling me," she said. "I'm going to enlist."

"What?"

"Yes, darling. I've wanted to for a long time. I'm going to enlist. The 'Ternational Brigades. Shpain. Franco's bastard. I'm going t'enlist. Darlings, come wish me to t'recruiting offish."

"You're crazy, Nathalie. Sit down."

"Recruiting offish, I shaid."

"But it's shut now. It's one o'clock in the morning."

"Don't care. Can't wait another minute. We'll make 'em open. 'Ternational Brigades. It's Malraux recruits. Nice chap, that. Very good fellow, Malraux. Russian temperament."

"Do be reasonable, Nathalie."

"Don't be bore, darling. Lesh get out this bloody plaish."

She began hiccoughing, and turned towards the Argentines, who had been mildly amused by the scene.

"Finished ogling me, you dirty Fascists? Hic. Look at their

bloody capitalisht mugs! Going t'enlisht. Fed-up. 'Ternational Brigades. Hic."

"So she's a Communist into the bargain. She would be!" Roland said.

Nathalie annihilated him with a slightly glazed look.

"D'you know, little father, you're beginning to be a bore. Hic. Ah, but, but," she cried with the pompous, stammering indignation of the inebriated, "you're a Fascist too, are you? Get out of here, you toad."

In the circumstances, anyone but Roland Oyarzun would have smiled or, at worst, gone away, without taking Nathalie's invective seriously and above all taking care not to answer her. But Roland was not the man to laugh off an insult even when it came from a pretty girl in a state of insobriety. As if moved by a spring, he leapt to his feet. The two adversaries confronted each other, face to face.

"Now she's insulting me, the bitch!"

"Dirty Fascist! Hic."

"Slut! Yid!"

Nathalie jumped on to the seat and, seizing a glass, broke it over Roland's head. Roland smacked her face. The waiter intervened; so did the Argentines. Like a war-horse smelling gunpowder, Roland began neighing with the joy of battle and began hitting out in all directions with his fists. Nathalie, having received a blow on the jaw, fell across the table with blood streaming from her face. François was jostled about, hurled from one table to another; he tripped against the knees of an abundant woman from Auvergne who was eating a raspberry ice and reading Montherlant's *Les Jeunes Filles* (she was an epicurean woman from Auvergne who accumulated her pleasures). Prey to a sacred frenzy, Roland Oyarzun fought like a hero.

The intellectual and Russian evening ended, about two o'clock in the morning, at the local police station.

3

When he saw the tall, bony woman, outrageously made-up, enter his parents' drawing-room, Bernard was stunned. He recognised her at once. She searched the large gathering for him.

Having discovered him, she came towards him, her hand extended, a smile upon her lips. Bernard was paralysed with surprise, and he had reason to be.

"My dear," she cried before he had had time to utter a word, "how are you? You must introduce me at once to your father and to M. Blum."

She spoke with a strong foreign accent, which was probably German, and her voice had extremes of pitch, like a young boy's voice when it's breaking.

"Do you mind telling me . . ." Bernard began in a low voice.

"I'm sure you don't remember my name," the extraordinary apparition interrupted. "Lotte Müller, an Austrian subject, victim of the Anschluss, do you remember? I told you the dramatic story of my escape. You promised to introduce me to M. Blum and to your father and to other important Frenchmen. It's to do with forming an anti-Nazi committee consisting of all the German and Austrian refugees. Come on, come on, hurry up and remember, you giddy young man!" she cried with a roguish laugh, giving Bernard a tap on the shoulder.

Several people turned round, staring at the tall girl with red hair. M. Bernard senior, while continuing to talk to one of his guests, kept on glancing towards Lotte Müller; and it was true that the new arrival with her long, awkward, bony body and her bright red hair, with her dress in the fashion of 1930, stood out among the correct, elegant crowd of the fashionable cocktail party.

Young Bernard was a pitiable object, such was his concern anger and disquiet.

"Listen," he said. "The joke's in very bad taste. Get out!"

"I've had to pay a hundred francs for the hire of my clothes," the lady replied between her teeth. "Do you think I'm going to give up after that? The fact that I borrowed the hundred francs off you the day before yesterday is neither here nor there. Besides, I'm in a terrible funk, and it's heaven. My dear," she went on, resuming her strange, hermaphroditic voice, "introduce me to your father." And then, under her breath: "If you try to throw me out, I shall scream and create a scandal." Aloud: "I'm so terribly, terribly anxious to meet the liberal minds of your happy country."

"I'll pay you out for this, I promise you."

M. Bernard senior came up to them, his eyes short-sighted but alive behind his spectacles. He was smiling with an air of vague perplexity. He looked like Émile Zola.

"Father," said Bernard, "may I introduce Frau Müller, an Austrian refugee. I've spoken to you of her, I think."

"An Austrian refugee." exclaimed M. Bernard. "That's very interesting indeed. Mademoiselle Müller, I'm very glad that you were able to come. I am sure you have a great many interesting things to tell us."

He took her hands in a warmly sympathetic clasp. Bernard wiped his forehead. Already a number of the guests were surrounding his father and the young woman. There was a murmur of interest, a flow of introductions. A week after the Anschluss, a refugee could not fail to arouse the interest of people who were obsessed by the thought of recent events and by the threat which weighed upon Europe. Frau Müller was surrounded, she was inundated with questions from all sides: How had she succeeded in escaping? Had she been in danger? Political squibs before the arrival of the German troops? What exactly had happened in that tragic week? Frau Müller replied with guttural loquacity, in a French which was correct enough if interlarded with a few Germanisms. Bernard moved away, unable to bear the spectacle any longer. He was pale. He went over to the bar.

"Pierre, give me a large brandy," he said to the man in the white coat.

"Are you feeling ill, M. Odilon?" Pierre asked with respectful solicitude. "It's too hot and stuffy in here."

At the Bernards', Pierre combined the functions of chauffeur, valet and butler. At the annual cocktail party given for *Germinal*, the weekly paper of which M. Bernard was Editor-in-chief, he filled the office of barman too.

Bernard swallowed the brandy at a gulp and turned scarlet in the face, his insides on fire. "Beast. Bastard. Shit," he murmured, savagely.

"What?" asked Pierre in surprise.

"I wasn't talking to you," said Bernard drily.

"If only *he* didn't cause a scandal. If only *he* didn't push the joke too far. *He* was capable of doing so, the shit. I'll lay into him tonight. I'll have the hide off him."

He was sick with apprehension and anger. It was appalling to think of what might happen. Good God, the cocktail party for *Germinal* was a serious and important affair! All right-thinking Paris—that was to say, all Socialist Paris, or at least all left-wing Paris—was crowded into the Bernards' big drawing-room; and tonight Léon Blum was there, his tall, aristocratic figure, his spectacles and his greying moustache dominating the gathering. Julien Benda was there too, Cassou, Geneviève Tabouis, and half a dozen members of parliament, a Dominican Father from *Sept Jours*. Good God, it was absolutely impossible to take in people like that! One really could not make game of certain people, certain ideas, certain beliefs. A practical joke was the greatest possible fun, but one really must have a sense of the limits to which one could go. Bernard, boiling with rage, kept his eye on Frau Müller, who looked leonine and rather disquieting beneath her mane, and in the astonishing black silk dress which was garnished with a huge bunch of white flowers at the left breast. The young woman talked incessantly, doubtless detailing the objects of an anti-Nazi Committee of Action. People were listening, nodding their heads sympathetically. When Bernard saw Léon Blum join the group his heart almost stopped beating. He had an affectionate admiration for Léon Blum, who was an old friend of his family.

Someone pulled at his sleeve. He turned round to find his young sister, Jeanette.

"Loulou," she said, "who is that Müller woman? It's a hoax, isn't it? A practical joke?"

"No; of course not," he feebly protested.

Jeanette's eyes were bright with laughter.

"She looks awfully like your friend Nicholas, don't you think?"

"Yes; it's him all right."

"I thought so," she cried. "He's wonderfully made up."

"I don't know what the devil to do. Do you think Daddy has recognised him? You don't? You must try to get him outside on some excuse or other."

"What, do you mean to say you weren't in on this?"

"Are you crazy? He never told me a thing; just arrived out of the blue."

This time Jeanette laughed aloud.

"That makes it funnier still! The boy's a genius."

"A genius!" Bernard muttered. "That's what you think. Don't

you see how low, how base this joke is? He's scoffing at us. Mocking us, mocking me, Daddy and the paper. I knew he was capable of anything, but all the same . . ."

"All the same, it's a scream. Look at him."

"I assure you it's no scream as far as I'm concerned. Go and tell him he's wanted on the telephone. No; he'll guess that it's me. Christ, what are we to do?"

"He's a jolly good actor, anyway. Look at him."

They uttered a cry of surprise at the same moment as did the group round Frau Müller. She had removed her mane, revealing a boyish head with short, very fair hair. There was a horrified silence, and then Frau Müller's guttural voice was heard calmly explaining:

"The Nazis cropped it."

* * *

Bernard succeeded in getting Nicholas Gaudie out of the drawing-room and shutting himself in his room with him. They fought. Bernard was the stronger and anger lent him strength. Half lying on a sofa, his wig at his feet, his dress torn, a little blood at the corner of his lip, Nick resembled a huge marionette that giant children had amused themselves by destroying. Or perhaps, with his shaven head, bony and painted under the feminine fripperies, he resembled Death as seen by a Surrealist painter, a protagonist in a macabre dance for an illustration to the *Fleurs du Mal*. But the piercing glance he gave his opponent was not that of a marionette. It was alight with human hatred. Bernard, leaning against a chest of drawers, was still out of breath from their short fight. His forehead and his hands were wet with sweat and he was wiping them with a silk pocket handkerchief.

"You're nothing but a dirty little Jew," Nick said in a furious voice.

"Do you know, I've been waiting for you to use that phrase." His voice too was trembling with anger and want of breath. "I've felt it coming for months. At last I know what you're really like. You're just a poor devil of a spiteful anti-Semite. A poor fish."

"Anti-Semite? You fool, you don't know the first thing about me. But I assert that your pretended liberal-mindedness has never been more than a bluff, the pretensions of a worldly little tart. As soon as your interests of race or class are threatened, your liberalism disappears with a bang. M. Hitler's only got to tease a few of your racial brothers (oh! 'racial brothers'! that's a good expression, I must remember it) and you become a militant, humanitarian war-monger. Can you imagine Lautréamont excitedly denouncing racialism as you do weekly in your father's paper? You've evolved in the last two years. Your moral development's very fine, isn't it? Nearly as fine as Puvis de Chavannes'."

"We're living in the twentieth century: nihilism's an obsolete system."

"Perhaps; but it's a logical system."

"When I denounce racialism, as you call it, it's not as a Jew, but as a man. Indeed, it needed anti-Semitism for me to realise that I was a Jew. I'm not defending my race, that would be racialism too, I defend the dignity of man . . ."

"Boom!"

". . . the dignity of man which at this moment is being violated in Germany in the persons of the persecuted Jews. If you don't understand this evident fact, we've no more to say to each other."

" 'I defend the dignity of man!' When are the meetings at the Vel' d'Hiv'? You've already marched with your fist clenched from the Bastille to the Nation. You look well in the part."

"Your sarcasms don't impress me."

"If there's anyone more noisome than the conservative, jingoist bourgeois, it's the hypocritical liberal who conceals his jingoism under a parade of modernism. In fact, I can see no difference at all between you and Déroulède. Tomorrow you'll write about the country and the flag between a 'cultural' piece by M. Jean Cassou and a homily from Jacques Maritain. 'Cultural!' It's your friends of the Popular Front who have invented that adjective. All you're good for is to kneel down and be kicked in your large idealistic backsides."

"Systematic abuse is proof of impotence or stupidity."

"Whereas the ineffectives who were surrounding me a little while ago doubtless represented the fine flower of French thought? Poor fools. Hitler will sweep them away like dust."

"Of course, that's what you want to happen."

"Yes, it is, and with all my heart. And what's more, I want to be in the front row to enjoy the sight, and if I'm asked to lend a hand, my happiness will be complete. I've always nursed the dream of firing a revolver into the backs of a French officer and a French 'humanitarian' thinker."

"You hate yourself. You hate humanity as a whole, because you hate yourself. I've known that for a long time."

"I suppose you've been reading a popular pamphlet on psycho-analysis, price seventy-five centimes?"

"There's no point in going on. Get out! Your practical joke didn't amuse anyone, it failed dismally."

"It amused me and I don't ask more. I'll leave you, brave heart. And since your father's paper adopts the policy of the hand extended 'to our Christian friends', I advise you to make a pilgrimage to Notre-Dame de Chartres while reciting Péguy. You'll be complete then."

With these words, Nick picked up his red wig, and adjusted it upon his head, then, getting up, he smoothed down his creased dress and went with dignity to the door. Bernard, going to open it, could not help smiling to himself. After this scene in which they had torn each other to shreds, the spectacle of Nicholas Gaudie disguised as an Austrian woman and compelled to assume this fictitious character in order to get home had an absurd and incongruous humour about it.

This quarrel did not put an end to their relationship, in the first place because Bernard was incapable of bearing anyone a permanent grudge, and secondly because he continued to feel for Nick a secret admiration. The boy was odious, of course; one could, perhaps, even say that to a certain extent, and upon a certain level, he was narrow-minded—perpetual sneering is more the sign of a psychological moron than of a sophisticated man; but it was impossible to deny that he showed, within his shabby universe of derision and negation, a startling comic invention, an extraordinary vitality, shot with brilliant lights. What Nicholas Gaudie lacked least was undoubtedly logic. If one accepted, even for an instant, and as a hypothesis, his basic postulate (the insignificance of all things, the unpardonable hideousness of humanity in general, and the eminently desirable consummation of a total apocalypse), if one accepted this hypothesis, one could only admire the precision with which Nick deduced all the consequences. He was perhaps only a sorry, quarrelsome clown, but one had to admit that his outlook achieved a certain kind of perfection. Bernard even felt disposed to recognise that Nick's insolence and intolerance had a certain liberating quality, a certain power of "cleansing"—added up in fact to a cure, an intellectual irrigation. Two hours spent watching Nick was as efficacious to the soul as reading the great iconoclasts: Voltaire, Swift, Rimbaud, Alfred Jarry. But then, again, Bernard was divided against himself, torn between his profound taste for anarchy and his respect for certain moral values. He had professed to hate war out of sympathy with an old tradition of popular revolt. And now he was adopting a warlike policy out of racial solidarity, family conformism and humanitarian conscientiousness. He was not unaware of the contradiction. Like a good deal of the French left-wing Press at that time (the Communists went into reverse after the Germano-Soviet Pact), M. Bernard's weekly, *Germinal*, was ferociously anti-Nazi and ceaselessly preached resistance to Hitler. At the time of Munich, it showed a certain wavering, since the French public, taken as a whole, had decided in favour of the negotiations, and acclaimed the negotiators; later, it joined in the chorus of protest against Munich, and from that moment never stopped asserting, right up to the 2nd of September, 1939, the necessity for war. This was a perfectly reasonable position and could be supported by all sorts of sound arguments. But war does not become any less of a lottery when one has been denouncing for years the supposed "necessity" for war, attacked militarism, the spirit of revenge and even the idea of patriotism itself. And this had been, up to the moment the Nazis gained power, and even later, *Germinal's* general "line". This had been Bernard's most constant attitude, voiced in his anarchist poem, *Les Grandes Manœuvres*. The menacing expansion of the Third Reich, Hitler's anti-Jewish policy, the influx of Jewish refugees, the first manifestations of French Fascism, the wave of anti-Semitism that had been aroused by the Popular Front and which newspapers such as *Je suis Partout* fanned each week, all these new elements in the situation overset some of his earlier convictions. He discovered at the same time that he was both a Jew and a Frenchman, and this double discovery was richly instructive. To be a Jew was of no great significance in itself. It was of not much more importance than to be called Iturralde and to know that your great-grand father had come from Pamplona, round about 1840, in order to establish himself as a greengrocer in Bordeaux; but Grandfather had been brought up by the Jesuits and Daddy was a Colonel and read the *Revue des Deux Mondes*. Being a Jew only began to signify when people, hearing your name, glanced curiously, and sometimes suspiciously, at you; when your non-Jewish friends turned away to say with some embarrassment: "Oh, yes, I know that chap, he comes from Germany, he's an *Israelite*." M. Bernard senior was accustomed to say: "I first realised that I was a Jew when I was fifteen, at the time of the Dreyfus Case." In the same way, his son could have said: "I first realised that I was a Jew when I saw anti-Jewish cartoons in a section of the French Press." Up till this time he had had but an abstract awareness of this quality of being a Jew, for, like the man named Iturralde, who was aware that his distant origins were Spanish-Basque, it had no effect upon his ideas or upon his life. Many Jewish friends came to the Bernards' house, and also many non-Jewish friends. At school Bernard had had Jewish friends and—he disliked using the horrid offensive term—Goy friends indifferently. The Bernards' ancestors had established themselves in Paris about the middle of the eighteenth century. And from this derived young Bernard's other discovery—the fact that he was French—so infinitely more significant than the first. For the fact of speaking and thinking in French, of having first opened his eyes upon the brightness of a French sky, and of having been educated at a Parisian school, these things, yes, these were of importance. Not that these things were matters of any peculiar privilege, no more, indeed, than if he had been born in London or Munich, but they were things that must be taken into account. It signified something, too, to have had a great-uncle shot under the Commune, and a father who had been a liaison officer between 1914 and 1918. And by a mental process, apparently unlikely, but at bottom perfectly natural and even inevitable, his consciousness of being a Jew accentuated and irradiated the fact of his belonging by language, intellectual training, and a thousand vital and indestructible links to the historical and geographical accident called France, to the land in which a Jewish family, round about the year 1750, had found a welcome and a refuge. It was thus that, under the pressure of events, young Bernard's lofty internationalism, his anarchical convictions, and his aggressive censoriousness came into conflict with the newly discovered necessity to recognise himself to be a Frenchman and to act as such.

It must be added that this conflict, for Bernard, was not of a particularly painful character. He was not the sort to break down ten times a day—indeed, he was not in the least emotional about it, except occasionally in his articles in *Germinal*, "emotion" being an attribute of the rhetoric which is, or at least is thought to be, so important an ingredient of political articles: "the profound emotion which every Frenchman has felt at the announcement of . . ." He was much too interested in himself, and in the act he put on for his own benefit, not to be most agreeably diverted by the clash of his own contradictory tendencies, the complex and sometimes discordant play of his own intelligence and sensibility. (He also kept assiduously a careful journal of his inner life.) It was thus that he was alternately either saddened or amazed, according to the hour and his mood, by the realisation of how little real love lay behind his faithfulness to democracy. He had, in fact, to admit to himself that only a very great effort could shake his olympian indifference to the condition of the oppressed proletarian masses. 'Basically,' he thought in his moments of cynicism, 'the lot of common humanity really doesn't interest me. I don't care a damn about the working classes. I haven't a shadow of true sympathy for them, or any feeling of common humanity with them. In fact, I don't like them and I have to kick myself to feel concern for them.' But if he found it difficult to raise enthusiasm *for* the proletarian classes in their hardship, their sweat, their abortive attempts for freedom, their hopes and their miseries, to be moved simply by the sight of a mechanic in overalls, he found it on the other hand all too easy to be *against* such people and institutions as were traditionally concerned to keep the proletariat in servitude: the rich upper middle class, the Comité des Forges, the Trusts, the City, Wall Street, the Faubourg Saint-Germain, the technocrats trained at the Polytechnique or the Centrale, the Diplomatic Corps, Salazar, Franco, the Vatican, etc. But these aggressive feelings, which he liked to call "revolt", were but an aspect of that destructive energy, that sullen pleasure in repudiating and combating which glows eternally in the heart of man: sometimes it even coincides with their thirst for justice. Oh, yes, it was easy enough to be against these official or hidden powers (the dictators, the magnates in heavy industry, the higher clergy . . .), because destructive criticism costs nothing, one can just go to it. But love, in its true sense, is a more onerous virtue and that is why, when soldiers and revolutionaries abound, saints are so rare (it is true that this particular psychological type has no useful place in modern political life). When he exercised in *Germinal* his youthful, vigorous aggressiveness *against* the oppressors of the proletariat, young Bernard was able to assure himself that he was fighting *for* the oppressed, for suffering humanity, that he was therefore being noble, was "on the right side of the barricades", which did not fail to appease his vague and fugitive scruples, those of a comfortable bourgeois, and gave him a pretty high opinion of his moral quality. Thus he was able to transmute a pure negation into a warm, positive heartfelt emotion. But, too subtle, too intelligent, too finely sensitive and perceptive to be his own dupe for long, or become the political Tartuffe who is the great comic character of the twentieth century—as obese, as self-indulgent, as florid as the original, but how much more knavish in his ingenuity—Bernard intermittently perceived his own subterfuge and analysed its secret machinery. "I'm playing the part of a young and ardent socialist of 1848, of the period when Socialism was a vocation, indeed a religion. Whereas, in fact, my sole preoccupation is with myself, my future, and my standing in the world. Only three things interest me: women, the political game, and myself." And since he had not the bedrock faith of a Louis Blanc, a Prudhon, or a Blanqui, he could at least lay claim to the elegance of a Byron and die, if he had to, for a cause in which he did not overmuch believe, as the playboy Byron had died for the freedom of Greece. This was called "lucidity", one could even add the word "despairing", "despairing lucidity", a desire to "serve" allied to an incurable scepticism, to fight without faith for a cause: and this was the century's new disease, evidenced by such men as Montherlant and Malraux—and when all was said and done one was in good —indeed, choice company. . . . Bernard sometimes envied, or pretended to envy, the admirable conviction of certain young Communists, their chastity, which is indeed touching, their discipline, their disinterestedness, their acceptance of ultimate sacrifice—all those things by which these boys and girls resemble in moral beauty the early Christian neophytes (and to find a similar chastity it had to be sought for at the opposite extreme, in the ranks of the young followers of Maurras and among the young Fascists). He used to say, "If only I had their faith!" as say debauchees on awakening when a vision of cloistral peace and retreat haunts their weariness and their disgust. This pathetic fallacy, common to the ordinary intelligence, can become, when expertly handled, a luxury of the emotions, and Bernard had a natural taste for luxury in all its forms. As he bought his ties at Charvet, so he adopted and made his own the moral attitudes of the best authors. 'Can one,' he asked himself, 'become a member of the Party without believing in the ends that Communism seeks?" He asked himself this question in solitude. He asked it, even more freely, in public—in short essays published in the more precious of the little reviews, or in front of his friends. It became a question of good form, a question of luxury.

His father entrusted him with certain investigations for *Germinal.* The trade of journalism, in so far as it was exciting, lively and picturesque, amused Bernard very much, in the same way that, on a somewhat higher level, he was amused by political activity. He went to Spain and spent several days in Madrid. He was the youngest correspondent on the Spanish front. Dressed in boots and a leather jerkin, he was under fire (though it was fairly dark at the time) in the trenches of the University City. Before the period 1940-5, this was his first real contact with the "militants", with the "people". He was attracted by the natural simplicity, and the sort of combre ardour of some Spanish men and women. He had an affaire with a bronze-skinned woman partisan named Teresa. These experiences which, though brief, were profoundly lived, brought him exaltation. He returned to Paris bursting with excitement, enthusiasm, and zeal. He talked of enlisting in the International Brigades. M. Bernard senior set about quelling this particular eruption, which, in any case, found its outlet in a series of articles published in *Germinal.* The Paris of those years was far from being intolerable to those who earned an easy living and were invited to all the First Nights. Bernard did not enlist.

He continued to see Nick from time to time. The boy had rented a horrible attic in which, never very clean himself, he lived in the midst of an exuberant squalor, as if he wished to bring the nightmares of the *Chants de Maldoror* to life:

I am filthy. Lice gnaw me. Swine when they gaze upon me, vomit. I know neither the waters of rivers, nor dew from the clouds. Seated upon a shapeless piece of furniture, I have not stirred hand or foot for centuries.

To say that the chairs at Nick's were shapeless was an understatement. They hardly existed at all. The ragged pallet which served him for bed should remain nameless in any language. It stank powerfully. Nick had, of course, broken off all relations with his family and society in general. From time to time he took home to his hovel an ageless prostitute, found God knows where. His clothes resembled those of a cut-throat, one of Eugène Sue's criminals, of the footpads so often reproduced in the old popular novels. This was doubtless intentional: a way of making himself contemporary with Lautréamont. Passers-by turned to look at this apparition from another century, this starveling ghost from the pages of *Les Mystéres de Paris*. Nick's general attitude was one of sardonic scoffing, with a sort of underlying bitterness, and Bernard could no longer conceal from himself the fact that Nick, half-mad and half-genius as he was, hated him, "probably because he is jealous of me—of my looks, my elegance, my money. Of my looks above all. But he probably doesn't even know it. What an unfortunate fellow he is." Nick, nevertheless, still fascinated him. So, once or twice a month, he went to see him, climbed the six storeys to the dark cave where this tall, strange, poisonous beast wallowed in his filth. Once there, he pretended to have a cold in the head in order to have an excuse to raise to his nose as frequently as possible a handkerchief steeped in Russia leather. The beast was fascinating, but its lair stank excessively.

* * *

"*De profundis morpionibus*," loudly sang the young male voices. 'A students' party,' François said to himself. He was on the point of going downstairs again: he did not much care for that kind of thing. Unfortunately, the door opened and a boy appeared with an empty bottle under his arm. From inside Roland had seen François and he shouted jovially: "Donadieu! Come in, you old bastard!" and François, looking very awkward, went into the little smoke-filled room where some huge men, as herculean as Roland himself, paid no attention to him, went on talking indeed as if he had been no more than a little cat or a canary. Roland forced a glass of red wine into his hands and, with an imperious gesture, commanded him to join in the general gaiety. It was as if he was inviting a tom-tit to dance the cake-walk. François knew neither the words nor the tune of the ballad with the Latin chorus and it seemed to him both interminable and rather disgusting. He was sorry he had come. "Really, as if I cared a damn any more for Oyarzun! But I was so bored this evening. . . ." He looked round his friend's room, or rather at as much of it as he could see through the smoke. Fastened to the walls with drawing-pins were pictures of naked, or nearly naked, women; clearly they had been cut out of those specialist magazines that appear with alluring titles, printed upon art paper. On the table was the classic skull, crowned with a cap, lying between a tobacco jar and a pipe. There were a few, but not many, books. There was only one thing missing: a cutty. Nothing betrays people so much as their surroundings. Having seen this room, one no longer wished to know the owner. Besides the pictures of naked women, there were several photographs: Commandant Oyarzun, Charles de Foucauld, Chartres Cathedral and a masked man who was at once small and imperious-looking, a 'leader' probably.

When they had exhausted their repertoire (which included *Les Filles de Camaret*, *Trois Orfèvres* and other cradle songs), the louts at last departed, to François' great relief. Roland was delighted with himself. He banged his chest with his clenched fists like a gorilla.

"Well, old man, life's good at twenty when one's fit and strong! What d'you think of my room? Pretty good, eh? A real student's room. You've seen the skull? A friend in the Faculty of Medicine gave it to me. I've got a lot of friends, you know—wonderful chaps always ready for a fight or a song. And they're real Frenchmen, too, with sand in their bellies. You saw them drinking good red wine and singing good old-fashioned songs, but you mustn't think that they're only out for a good time. They're pretty serious chaps too. Like those pin-up girls there on the wall. I've stuck 'em up all round to liven the place up a bit, and because it's the proper thing for a student of our age to have a few erotic pictures about. Eternal woman, you know. After all, the instinct's there, isn't it? But don't make any mistake about it, my friends and I are more often on the sports ground than in the brothel. Besides, brothels, as far as I'm concerned . . . We're more serious-minded than you might think. Supposing I told you that last week we went on a pilgrimage to Chartres, reciting bits of Péguy on the way? Of course, I didn't recite, because I'm not an intellectual—I was an intellectual last year, but this year I haven't the time, politics are too absorbing—but the others, why they know whole pages of Péguy by heart. Have you never made the pilgrimage to Chartres? Oh, of course, I'd forgotten: you heretics don't believe in the Virgin. All the same, you ought to go with Catherine. By the way, how is your wife? And you? Still regretting being married? Ha, ha! That was a good one! All right, old man, don't blush. I'm only joking, putting you on the spot, as usual. You think I'm malicious, don't you? Tell me, do you still see anything of that frightful Yid, Nathalie, whose face I smacked? You still do? Listen, Donadieu. I'm going to give you some friendly advice: drop her. After all, Donadieu, you were brought up in a religious school, you belong to a good family, you've got proper principles. Why do you mix with foreigners, parasites, enemies of your country? We're living in decadent times and one must react. You know that I went to Nuremberg last summer with a party of friends? It was wonderful. We came home overwhelmed by it all. Overwhelmed and, at the same time, profoundly humiliated, because we compared the Third Reich with the Third Republic, and the comparison was enough to make us die of shame. You can't imagine, you simply cannot imagine what Germany's like today, purged of Jews and foreigners, socialised, regenerated by that man of destiny, Hitler. You can't imagine what the nocturnal ceremonies were like at Nuremberg. Oh, they've got a theatrical sense, the Germans have! Those silent files of young men, a human tide, a disciplined torrent, a river of youth, beauty and virile energy. . . . Under the innumerable banners, waving and floating in the breeze, under the banners, the standards and the flags, in the night—men and banners sculpted against the night by the floodlights. It was indescribable. I had tears in my eyes and my knees shook. All the Frenchmen present felt the same thing. And there were some very important chaps there, you know—intellectuals, writers, politicians, diplomatists. . . . We were all quite overwhelmed. Nuremberg! All my life I shall remember the sight. And so, you can see how beside it France of the Third Republic . . .

It makes one despair. But one must act. A few sound, resolute chaps are sometimes enough to save a country from its decadence. Besides, that's how Nazism started in a Judaised Germany in 1930. But we have got leaders in France too. There are still Frenchmen who love order and want to restore it. I am one of them."

He got up. Despite the nervous tic that affected his temples and cheeks, despite the disquieting, over-dramatic expression of his face, he remained good-looking. Speaking forcibly, he continued: "Order. That is the only truth, Donadieu. I believe in order. There's nothing doubtful about me, nothing suspect. I'm clean through and through. Discipline. Healthiness. Integrity. You know, I think I shall become a professional soldier, like my father. I failed for Saint-Cyr, but there are back doors into the Army. I'm joining in October. I've applied for a colonial regiment."

* * *

There was something of a dramatic scene. By chance, Catherine discovered that François and Nathalie were meeting on their own. She so arranged things as to surprise them together. She had no real proof of betrayal, but her jealousy none the less burst furiously upon them. She was profoundly hurt. She gave vent to her passion like a Maenad. There was, of course, a break with Nathalie, beautiful, dreamy Nathalie, so wonderfully romantic, so Russian, so much admired. Catherine insisted that François should tell her the truth. He took her at her word and replied quite simply that he had indeed succumbed several times to Nathalie's pressing advances. Catherine kept on repeating incredulously: "You . . . you. . . ." "Yes, I," he said with the ghost of a smile. "Nathalie has a passionate temperament and it was she who ran after me, you know. But, I thought . . . Frankly, Catherine, I thought you knew and that you didn't mind, that it wasn't contrary to your modern conception of marriage, that in fact . . ." She looked at him in horror. He extended his hands, palm upwards, the fingers spread, like a man assuring you of the purity of his intentions. He looked like a Moroccan Arab protesting his honesty. Catherine fell weeping on the bed. "Go away!" she cried between her sobs.

But, of course, he did not go away.

* * *

When Mme Monnet fell ill of an embolism, they had to take Juliette, who was now nearly three years old, back again. The little girl found it difficult to accustom herself to her new home and her new family, and she did not accustom herself at all to the way her mother looked after her. She did nothing but cry and scream. Every time Catherine brushed her hair, one would have thought from the child's yells and her mother's frowning face that she was being scalped. Until now, Juliette had always been kept so neat and clean that she resembled one of those infants who appear on posters advertising some nourishing food. From now on her appearance was poverty-stricken: dirty fingers, snotty nose, soiled clothes. As she could not afford a nurse, Catherine had had to give up her dramatic lessons. "The sacrifice of my career", as she called it, but more exactly the sacrifice of those delicious, irresponsible three or four afternoons a week spent with young, good-looking delightful and vivacious friends, caused her to become severely depressed. In one month she lost twelve pounds and her complexion turned a leaden grey. She was becoming ugly. François Donadieu sadly contemplated the certain wreck of his home. He was overcome by a feeling of impotence and resignation in face of the inevitable. Naturally, he had failed his examination a second time for want of serious preparation. On the other hand, his salary as a junior clerk had not been raised. Keeping a wife and child necessitated prodigies of management. Since his marriage, François had never had the money to buy a new suit. And now shame prevented his going to bookshops in his filthy old mackintosh, with the bottoms of his trousers frayed and worn shoes, which he no longer took the trouble to clean every morning, since considerable courage is required to perform day after day, when one is poor, those unwearying little actions which dissimulate the truth, preserve appearances, and keep alive the last dregs of human pride. As he walked along the quays, at that hour when the lights of Paris begin to glow, he was overwhelmed by his own penury. 'I wonder sometimes whether I exist. From the very beginning of my life I've failed all along the line. It may be that Catherine hates me. I know that I'm horribly tired of her. As for the child, it's her misfortune to have been brought into the world by parents like us.' He remembered that a few years earlier, during his last holidays at Sault-en-Labourd, he had felt pain and anguish in thinking of his own infinite minuteness lost among the two thousand million human beings who inhabited the globe. In the Christian view, indeed, a single soul, no matter whose, was beyond price, mattered as much as all souls past and to come, *existed* in its own right in the sight of God like some infinite treasure infinitely to be desired. . . . François had doubted this marvellous fact. But at that period the die had not been cast, the future was still a closed book, and in that future François had the right to place his hopes. Today the future was barred, François judged his existence completely futile, a flagging little life that could be rubbed out without changing the order of a world in which it would leave no trace. . . . He went towards the entrance to the Underground, a single grub amid an uninterrupted flow of grubs. 'A down-and-out,' he said to himself, 'is luckier than I am: he's alone for keeps."

The future was barred. There was only one possible solution still remaining. A solution which was both mysterious and perhaps secretly desired: war.

* * *

"This talk of war makes me rather anxious. I don't know if it's safe to keep Juliette with us in Paris. What do you think, darling? Think what might happen if we were bombed. You know, like in that futuristic Wells film, *Things to Come*. It would be too awful. I'd rather know that Juliette was safe far from Paris."

"I'll write to my cousins in Béarn. They're rich farmers. Two sisters and a brother, and they've got no children. I'm sure they'd adore Juliette."

"Of course we'll pay them for her keep."

"Of course. Juliette'll be very happy in the country. The fresh air . . ."

"Really, I think all sensible parents ought to consider . . ."

"And then you can take up your drama lessons again."

"Oh, I'm not thinking of myself."

So, a few days before the meeting at Munich, François took Juliette to his farmer cousins in Béarn. He travelled by night, third class; he slept with Juliette in his arms. There was an indignant fat woman on the opposite seat. At last she could bear it no longer and woke him up with a broadside.

"Young man," she said severely, "you must not go to sleep when in charge of your little sister. For the last ten minutes you've been holding the child upside down."

* * *

"Nick, what are you doing?"

"Get out! It's usual to knock before entering someone else's room."

"I did knock, but you couldn't have heard. What are you doing, Nick?"

"Get out, I tell you."

"No, not that. I'll stop you. . . ."

Bernard hurled himself upon his friend and tried to take the hypodermic needle from him. Nick caught him by the throat. He was beside himself, convulsed with rage and hatred. Bernard broke free and, rushing to the window, threw the needle out. As he turned, Nick, eyes ablaze, rushed at him.

With a blow from his fist, Bernard stretched him out on the floor.

He went down on his knees and frantically smacked the still face.

* * *

"What a wonderful welcome I had at the old School! The Principal was delighted to see me back again, he had tears in his eyes. Everyone was sweet. Such darlings."

* * *

"*My dear old chap, as you can see from the stamp, I am writing to you from Sidi Tigrane in southern Morocco. I am in a splendid regiment, with jolly good chaps, real proper brave Frenchmen. The life suits me perfectly. Of course, one has moments of depression. It's the fault of the country. Then one fights a bit or goes and gets drunk at the bar at the corner of the street. It's kept by a Jew on whom we play all kinds of practical jokes. We laugh a lot here. They're tough chaps, but amusing. We've been on an exercise for the last three days. I'm writing to you on a drum outside my bivouac. Before me stretches away the uninhabited desert. The Goums have lit a fire and are singing their nostalgic songs. The camels swing their heads to and fro in silhouette against the evening sky. It's superbly exotic. You're a bit of a poet, and you'd love this landscape. It's the very essence of Pierre Loti. Goodbye, old man. Think occasionally of the desert-wanderer lost beneath the African sky and don't forget to write to him. Yours as always.*"

* * *

"Now that the child's gone and I've got a bit of time to spare, I'm going to re-read all the classics, systematically. Recultivate my mind, as it were, from the beginning."

"That's right, a good idea you recultivate your mind from the beginning."

* * *

"Buy *Je suis Partout*! A special number about World Jewry. Sensational revelations."

The Bonnet-Ribbentrop Pact. The Russo-German Pact. Danzig. We are going to die, we are not going to die for Danzig. George VI in Paris. *L'Entente Cordiale. La Cucaracha.* "A moment's peace is always worth the having." Danzig. Corridors, pacts, agreements. Special edition of *Je suis Partout*. The war. We've been damned sensible sending Juliette to the south. The defence of human dignity. The Committee of Defence of the Intellectuals of . . . *La Cucaracha. Tout va très bien, Madame la Marquise*. Recultivate my mind from the beginning. Civilisation through war. The war for the defence of civilisation. The die is not cast, the die is not cast, you're only twenty-three. "Total Apocalypse." September the second, nineteen hundred and thirty-nine. In face of fire and sword, France was prepared for every sacrifice.

CHAPTER V

FOR WHOM ARE THESE SERPENTS?

1

THE dread horror was upon him: a shapeless shadow that gradually filled all space, blocked every avenue of escape, was crushing down on him. Roland Oyarzun's forehead was bathed in sweat, and he knew that he was going to die. But the shadow was taking human shape. It was gradually becoming opaque, a retributive figure emerging from the mirror, rising from the depths of the lake of glass, at once concrete reality and its own reflection, growing continually larger though its features remained obscure. Roland started to groan. Simone awoke and shook him by the shoulder as hard as she could. He woke with a start and was quiet.

"Your nightmare again," Simone sighed.

She switched on the light.

Her husband's haggard and streaming features still bore signs of the appalling struggle he so often waged with the unseen. The light of the bedside lamp made him blink his eyes. He was breathing heavily like someone who has just been half asphyxiated. Simone leant on an elbow to look at him.

"What exactly is your dream?" she asked.

He looked at her dully. She had an attractive round face with pretty but irregular features, crowned with curl-papers. The pouches under her eyes made her look as pitiful as a scolded child. If she had taken better care of herself and had been better fed, she would have been charming. But rationing, worry and the sleepiness of five o'clock in the morning did not suit her.

"I've told you already: it's a sort of shadow on top of me, crushing me."

"Is it always the same?"

"Pretty much the same every time."

"How horrible. Why don't you go and see a doctor?"

"And what do you suppose he'll say? He'll only recommend rest and proper food. That's easy enough today, situated as we are!"

"I read in the papers that nightmares are due to . . . I don't remember, but it advised going to see a psychiatrist."

"Don't be absurd. Psychiatrists are all charlatans."

"Perhaps not all of them, you know! I'm beginning to be anxious: your nightmares are becoming more and more frequent."

"It's since Fresnes. I shall never recover from those three months in prison."

"But you'd had them before, hadn't you?"

"Yes; but less often."

"Can you remember when you had one for the first time?"

"During the war, I think. No; before. I seem to remember having them when I was fifteen or sixteen. But, since Fresnes, they've been terrible! Fresnes is the cause of all our misfortunes. National Indignity. . . ."

"Oh, please don't start all that again! We had much better try to go to sleep. It's five o'clock; we can still sleep for a couple of hours."

"I'm not sleepy."

"Read a book. Don't just lie awake or you'll start going all over the old story again; Pétain, the Liberation, prison, National Indignity, Jacques' murder, and this and that. Listening to you always going over the same thing is driving me mad. You must turn over a new page, Roland. You must look to the future."

"The future. That's a good one! I have no future any more. They've stolen my future from me. They would have done better to shoot me."

"For God's sake, don't begin again!" she cried, her curl-papers shaking. "Shall I put the light out? It hurts my eyes. Let's try to sleep."

"I tell you I couldn't sleep a wink. Leave the light."

Simone sighed in perplexity. Then, coaxingly, she rolled over against her husband. Without deigning to look at her, Roland disengaged himself with a movement of his shoulder.

"I don't want that either," he muttered. "Under-fed as I am, it would only need that to put the finishing touch to my physical condition. Wait at least till I've put on a stone."

Simone turned her back and moved away, protecting her eyes from the light with the crook of her arm. She was not offended by her lord and master's disdain. Roland had trained her to humility, to the docility of an odalisque. She had accommodated herself to this servile condition partly out of love for her husband and partly through the natural resignation of her poverty-stricken origins. Would she have protested if he had beaten her? But Roland did not beat his wife. Apart from his foolishness, he was a model husband.

"Simone," he called after a moment's silence.

She was on the point of going to sleep again, and stirred a little.

"What is it now?"

"Donadieu's going to see my mother today."

"Let's hope she understands the position. . . ."

"I'm afraid she'll refuse point-blank. You don't know her; she's a terrible woman."

"You should have gone yourself. I advised you to. You ought to have taken the first step. Your visit would have flattered her. 'He's given in at last!' she would have said to herself."

"That's exactly what I didn't want her to be able to say," he muttered bitterly. "Do you expect me to humble myself before her? No fear."

"It's not very much of a humiliation when it's one's own mother. Besides, a moment of shame's soon over; and when you're situated as we are . . ."

"That's women all over. When it's a choice between honour and their stomachs, it's always their stomachs they choose. So you could have borne my going to Canossa!" he added pompously.

"I thought she lived at Neuilly," said Simone, her voice heavy with sleep.

"God, how on earth did I come to marry a half-wit," he murmured as if to himself.

Beside him on the pillow a light snore rose from a bundle of curling-papers.

* * *

"How are you, darling?" cried Clothilde Oyarzun in a piercing voice.

She buzzed like a huge yellow wasp as she crossed the drawing-room. A heady scent emanated from her imposing figure. She held out at arm's length a strong, dimpled hand upon which gleamed a huge diamond. Her nails, the colour of ox blood, sought François' lips as if of their own volition. Clothilde gave her hand to be kissed like a priest presenting a relic, or a bishop his amethyst ring.

"Cocktail?" she asked with a sort of hoarse, worldly abruptness.

Without waiting for a reply, she opened the two doors of a cabinet of polished wood. Crystal gleamed. François was startled by her theatrical entry and by the fact that she called him familiarly "darling" when he had never before spoken a word to her in his life. She must have learnt the role of a woman of fashion in some book on etiquette, and had decided to play it for all it was worth in order to impress her visitor. Clothilde Oyarzun! The dangerous woman of Sault-en-Labourd, whose scandalous name everyone whispered with a half-amused, half-disapproving smile. The war had promoted this little provincial madam to the rank of a cosmopolitan performer, by turns using the sharp accents of France or the guttural ones of Germany, clothed by the great dressmakers and hung with jewels. She moved against an appropriate background: white fur rugs on the floor, huge screens of frosted glass, covered with heraldic birds, cleverly sinister pictures (one of them blatantly and theatrically sadistic), and a bookcase showing the pink, green and blue backs of the Pléiade edition of the classics: works which were there in a purely symbolic capacity, since it was happily not necessary for Clothilde to go to the trouble of reading them; no doubt she remained faithful to the Frondaies, Dekobras and Paul Marguerittes of her youth.

Clothilde poured out the cocktails, her Olympian figure bending forward, a well-preserved Hebe of fifty. François noted that she had kept her beautiful golden hair. She was attractive and rather sinister.

"Tell me about Sault-en-Labourd," she cried gaily. "You are the son of Donadieu, the tanner, aren't you? That's what I thought when you told me your name over the telephone. Sault-en-Labourd! It must be five or six years since I last went back. Goodness, yes; I left it in '39, the winter of '39. You know, of course, that I'm separated from my husband? Yes; it was then we separated. You knew my husband?"

"No; I hadn't the pleasure. . . ."

"I expect you've heard from Roland that he's become a monk? Oh, my dear man, my life has really been quite a novel. It would take me hours to tell it you."

She sat on the edge of the table and crossed her Amazonian legs, which the short and ample skirt, in the "*zazoue*" fashion of the end of the war, revealed to the knees. She produced a startling cigarette-holder in solid gold and at least eight inches long, fitted a Pall Mall into it and drew a puff, her eyes half-closed. 'Dietrich's pose in *The Blue Angel*,' François thought.

"Do sit down; that chair's quite comfortable. There's a box of cigarettes beside you. Do you like Pall Mall?" (She pronounced it Pole Mole, believing this to be correct.) "I like them best. We've got a friend, a staff officer, who keeps us supplied."

For an octopus with tentacles in every corner of the black market during the occupation, in close relations with the Allied staffs under the Liberation, this was typical.

"He supplies us with an excellent Scotch too; it's very useful."

François had no time to ask himself who the other person included in the "us" might be—no doubt it was the successor to poor Major Oyarzun. Clothilde listened to news of Sault-en-Labourd with amused and condescending curiosity, like a great lady who remembers with simplicity having played as a girl with the peasant children about the farms on the family estate. Everything to do with Sault-en-Labourd took on in her words a quality at once anodyne, tender and slightly ridiculous. To listen to her one would have thought that society existed at Sault-en-Labourd, and that to her infinite boredom it had spent its time running after her. Like most human beings, Mme Oyarzun longed to aggrandise herself. Any audience suited her. She would have boasted to the plumber, unless he was young and attractive, in which case she would have put him to other uses. Rich, lacquered with a certain Parisian varnish of which she was alone in not perceiving that it was of poor quality, she had not yet acquired sufficient assurance to be able to dispense with showing off. She had guessed, at first glance, that her manner and the luxury of her apartment intimidated her visitor; but she was wrong in thinking that he was subjugated. Indeed, one can be intimidated by people whom one despises or laughs at to oneself. Timidity is not always founded on a sense of inferiority, but often upon the consciousness that the social game is weighted against us, that our opponent is using cards that we don't possess (money, power) and knows nothing of ours (sensibility, culture, etc.). That is why the rich who are stupid have such paralysing power, while with those who have some intellectual qualities one feels oneself very soon to be upon an equality. These know that we may be holding undisclosed trumps. Clothilde Oyarzun was not a millionaire, she was merely one of the innumerable people who had grown rich under the occupation, but for François she represented, none the less, the class of big capitalists, or perhaps more exactly, François knew that she thought that she represented for him the big capitalist class, and this was enough: automatically his muscles, his looks, his voice, his attitude approximated to the idea that she held of him, became modelled upon the humble image elaborated by that sly, middle-class and obtuse mind. Sitting on the edge of his chair, his manner constrained, his eyes fluttering, not knowing what to do with his, hands, he talked much lower than usual in a hardly perceptible throaty whisper. To everything that Mme Oyarzun said, he replied with eager, assiduous smiles, hoping to flatter and please, and while outwardly he was all cringing courtesy, he hated himself secretly for so mean a compliance; and this was how a young intellectual of the Resistance behaved when face to face with a trollop who had grown rich by dishonest dealing.

"What's happened to old mother Lardenne? Does she still wear that flat hair-style and the family cross between her breasts? God, how funny it was! I remember evenings when we played bridge with old mother Lardenne. She had a tame stork that walked about the room on its long legs with a little leather bag tied under its tail in case of accidents. God, how funny it was! And the old Vincenot ladies, are they still alive? They must be a hundred. The eldest, Augusta, told me off for swimming. 'It's not seemly, my little Clothilde.' I can hear her still. 'It's not seemly, ladies in our position should not show themselves in public in a bathing-dress.' Of course, I scandalised all those good people. They ended up by thinking me a renegade: I was a traitor to our class, you understand. But, after all, what can you expect?

I was a vital, healthy girl, I never could bow to provincial austerity, I've always been independent and to the devil with the conventions! Those evenings with the Vincenot ladies, what torture they were! I used to take ages over dressing, out of bored anticipation, and say to my husband: 'Edmond, do we really have to go to those old ladies? Send the maid to make our excuses, say that I've got a headache.' My husband had more respect than I for tradition. 'My dear, I know that you'll be bored to death, but you can bear one evening a month, can't you? The old ladies adore you so, they'll be so disappointed. Come on, pluck up your courage, put on your black dress, the one with the highest neck-line.' "

François listened, wondering how anyone could manage to relate with such calm audacity so many lies in such few words. Mme Oyarzun certainly had a nerve.

He was in a hurry to broach the reason for his visit: to get help for Roland. When telephoning the day before, he had been careful to say: "Your son has asked me to seek an interview." Mme Oyarzun must know therefore that he had a mission to perform, that he was acting as an ambassador. But whether from a sense of self-protection or out of sheer malice, she carefully avoided any mention of Roland, and behaved as if François had merely come to see her as a friend, without any particular object, a fiction which did not tend to decrease the young man's embarrassment. On two or three occasions, determined to come to the point, he was on the verge of beginning the sentence he had prepared in agreement with Roland. If he so much as succeeded in getting the first word out, Clothilde immediately interrupted: "Another cocktail, darling?" or "Dear old Sault; I really think I shall have to go and spend a few days there," with a smile, a brilliant glance, which quite clearly underlined her disinclination to embark upon a boring discussion, or at least her desire to put it off.

There was an interruption: a man of about fifty came in, tall, dapper, wearing suède shoes, scented and beringed: astounding elegance. Unfortunately, he was none the better looking for it. He had the sort of puffed-out face which is the result of unhealthy fat and bile which cannot have smelt pleasant in the early morning. At five o'clock in the afternoon, it was already rather high. His mouth was disgustingly loose; his chin, swollen like shirt frills, looked as if it had been sculptured from whipped cream. However, his eyes sparkled with a disquieting intelligence, while his forehead, covered with tufts of thinning hair, nevertheless still had a certain nobility. François noticed his tiny ears, which might have been of a precious white enamel, while his hands resembled little pink claws. Clothilde waved her hand and cigarette-holder in his direction. "The Baron de Pauillac . . . ," she said, as if she were introducing "the King of Diamonds". Then, pointing to François, "Alex, a neighbour of mine in the country, a charming young man from Sault-en-Labourd, Monsieur Donadieu." François got to his feet and shook the beringed hand. Supposing the title to be authentic, what musty ley of the obscure provincial nobility could have produced this poisonous fungus? (But was the title authentic?) The "Baron" was a mixture of the clubman of 1900, the socialite of 1925, and the crook of 1945. That is to say that he was wholly disgusting. He typified that ambiguous type, the suspect man of affairs, the chief of international prostitution, that an actor like Jules Berry had so magisterially created in the cinema, in those realist films which were fashionable under the Popular Front. Many people, nevertheless, saw in him both distinction and charm, women in particular gladly allowing themselves to be seduced by this filth. Few people perceive infamy when infamy has a name, manners, an American car, and so on. François, on the other hand, saw it at once and trembled from head to foot. His uneasiness was immediately increased, his voice fell a semi-tone lower and he appeared paralysed, physical symptoms that Mme Oyarzun and her companion put down to lack of sophistication, but which were due to an allied distress: the horror of honest hearts in the face of ordure.

Clothilde had picked up a newspaper that the "Baron" had brought in with him. She read some of the headlines aloud. Reports from the Pacific: Japan was likely to surrender at any moment. The daily news of the purge: collaborators condemned to death, to life imprisonment, to national indignity, to ten years' hard labour. The High Court went briskly about its business of perverting the ends of justice. Ubu-Roi is dead, long live Ubu-Roi! The shops today would meet the coupons for chicory, margarine and macaroni; on the other hand, there would be a decrease in the ration of meat. Suddenly Clothilde waved the paper in the air and burst out laughing. A caricature showed the Minister of Food in the guise of Marie Antoinette, crook in hand, wig awry, saying with a gesture of disdain: "Have they no meat? Then let them eat offal!"

Clothilde laughed till the tears poured down her cheeks.

"Let them eat offal!" she repeated between two paroxysms of laughter. "Look at her with her crook! She doesn't want to be bothered, she doesn't care a damn about the hunger of the poor, she's above all that! The people have been liberated, haven't they? Very well, now that they've got back their honour, they can damn well starve!"

The "Baron" smiled and so did François. The caricature really was funny, and there was something catching about Clothilde's harsh gaiety. So the woman was capable of humour, and of humour of this particular kind: wounding, corrosive. He would have admired it had he not known that, like the Marie Antoinette of the cartoon, she was contemptuous of the misery of the people. Her laughter was not an expression of revolt. Instead, it betrayed a certain complicity: since the politicians who had come out of the Liberation were showing themselves not only impotent but cynical, careless of the needs of the lower classes while well-fed themselves, morality had become a vain word, honesty a myth, and everyone had to fight for himself by no matter what means in a society where the weakest were condemned to go hungry: thus Clothilde and her like were justified, as are wild beasts among the other wild beasts of the jungle. And Clothilde's laugh carried no condemnation of an injustice; it merely confirmed with a sort of low satisfaction an existing fact.

"I like these caricatures very much. They tell the truth. They show the world as it is," she said with a shake of the head.

She went on looking at the paper and began reading another headline in a nasal, acid, pointed tone:

"The Profiteers will Disgorge. Well, it's none too soon, the scandal has been going on long enough!"

She took the two men to witness; her eyes flashed with wholly admirable malice.

"You see, my dears, the profiteers are going to be made to disgorge. Really, the Government isn't as weak as people say. It's taking action, at last, actually taking action!"

She read the brief paragraph: "The profiteers will disgorge.

An order in the *Official Journal* stipulates that illicit profits obtained between the 1st of September, 1939, and the 31st of December, 1944, will be confiscated by the Treasury."

She put the newspaper down on the table and drew a long puff at her cigarette.

"You see, Alex," she said with an amused and virtuous air, "you have always said that this Government would be unable to make the black marketeers give up their gains. You're wrong. They'll disgorge. The *Official Journal* says so. We can sleep easy."

She glanced at François and laughed her little, rippling laugh.

"Any way, Monsieur Donadieu, this order will not affect you any more than it does us. You didn't make a fortune during the occupation, did you?"

"No, madame," he stammered like a half-wit. Then, continuing miserably, "As a matter of fact, I was in London. . . ."

"Alex!" she cried enthusiastically. "Monsieur Donadieu was in London! In the Free French Forces, of course?"

François bowed his head.

"Alex, Monsieur Donadieu was in the Free French Forces. How fascinatingly interesting! My congratulations, young man, my congratulations. I'm proud to have a hero in my house. You must come and see us again, come to one of my cocktail parties, and I'll introduce you to all our friends; they'll be delighted. I'm at home on Tuesdays."

She raked the London hero with a fierce and exultant glance; she took him all in from head to foot, and his Adam's apple too; the whole of him could not have weighed much more than nine stone and he dressed, apparently, at the Belle Jardinière.

François did not answer. He felt himself shaking frenziedly inside, but he did not answer: he had not accomplished his mission. There must, however, have been a disquieting gleam in his eye, because the "Baron" interrupted; a controlled, ingratiating smiled curled his lip.

"Don't mind her, my dear chap. Clothilde loves teasing her best friends; she's got so much vitality, it has to come out in one way or another. But, believe me, we have every sympathy for those who showed themselves to be on the right side. Were you in the Air Force?"

"No; on the staff. Propaganda and recruiting."

"On the staff. Someone had to be, of course. But you were exposed to the bombing like everyone else. The bombing must have been terrible, wasn't it?" he asked in a tone of polite interest.

"Yes, pretty bad, particularly the first time. One became accustomed to it. When there was a warning nearly every night, and . . ."

"Of course, of course, one can become accustomed to anything," Clothilde interrupted impatiently.

"Is it true," the Baron asked, "that the English coined a satirical phrase for people who talked of nothing but the bombing, that they called them 'bomb bores'?"

"Yes, certainly, I remember. Bomb bores! Well-bred Englishmen never spoke of the bombing."

"Bomb bores! That's good. How would you translate it? *Les raseurs du bombardement?* No, it's too long."

"It's difficult to find an equivalent in French. Perhaps, the *bombarbeurs*, for the alliteration."

"Oh, very good, very good! The *bombarbeurs*! Do you know the story of the chap who was found by the air raid wardens after a frightful bombing sitting on a lavatory seat among the rubble? 'You're not hurt?' they asked him. But he merely looked rather astonished and, showing them the handle of the chain still in his hand, said: 'It's most odd: I merely pulled the plug and the whole house came down.' "

François smiled politely. He had heard the story over and over again. It was as old as the blitz.

"It's a delicious story," Clothilde exclaimed.

"And so characteristic of English humour," said the Baron. "You must admit that they're a very remarkable people."

"Remarkable."

"And, after all, they have suffered as much as we have," said the Baron scrupulously, as if he himself had undergone years of physical and mental torture, "they've suffered as much as we have and yet they're united, they have none of our internal divisions."

"And what a sense of social order!" said François. "To think that the black market practically doesn't exist over there. We, as a nation, with our thousands of spivs, cut a very vulgar figure in comparison."

He lowered his eyes, happily content, delighted to have loosed his arrow. There was a brief silence.

"You're quite right," said the Baron. "I must leave you, my dear sir, but I hope to see you here again. Meeting you has been a pleasure."

The atmosphere was sensibly cooler. Relaxed, perfectly at his ease, François shook the Baron's hand. When the latter had left, he turned to Mme Oyarzun. She looked displeased.

"I must go," he said, "but before I do so, I must carry out my mission. I told you over the telephone that Roland commissioned me to come to you."

"Yes, and what then?"

Mme Oyarzun's voice had become hoarse and brutal.

"He's having a very difficult time just now."

"What has that got to do with me?"

"He seems to think you might be prepared to help him."

"Really?" she said calmly. "He thinks I might be prepared to help him? Why? Why should I? Because I'm his mother? Ask him if he ever behaved towards me as a son should behave towards his mother. It's all very well appealing to people for help when one has need of them. But first it's necessary to have shown them a little . . . I don't know, affection, respect."

With colour mounting to her cheeks, one hand on her hip, she suddenly spoke with greater vehemence.

"Why should I help him, why? He's always behaved towards me like an enemy. His father and he were both in league against me. Do you know that he hit me one day? No doubt he didn't tell you that. Well, you ask him about it. Ask him how he raised his hand to his mother. What about that! A family's all very well, but it's a lottery. If the wrong number turns up, it's best to stop at once. That's what I've done. I've made a family for myself elsewhere, since mine was no good to me. I don't care a damn for the morality side of it. And I don't care a damn for other people's opinions, and that goes for yours too, Monsieur Donadieu," she ended defiantly.

"It's not for me to judge you, madame. Your son has charged me with asking for help on his behalf, and it's not a job for which I have any liking, I can assure you, so I shall content myself with . . ."

"That's just like him, sending someone else! He's a coward.

He wouldn't come himself because it would have humiliated him, so he can think of nothing better than sending a friend as an ambassador. That's him all over!"

* * *

At that instant Roland, sitting opposite his wife in the tiny kitchen, was looking at his watch.

"He must be with her now. Do you think he'll succeed?"

Simone raised her eyes from the sock she was darning.

"How should I know? I hope so."

"She's quite capable of refusing, you know. She's a frightful bitch and she hates me. If she does consent, it'll only be from vanity: she'll want to make a great gesture of generosity in front of witnesses. If she refuses, I don't know what's going to happen to us."

"Why don't you look for work? You ought to. . . ."

"Shut up!" he shouted, beating the table with his fist. "You don't know what you're talking about. A hundred times a day you repeat the same thing: find work, find work! What certificates have I got? What references? It's not much of a reference to be condemned to National Indignity, you know. Every door would be closed to me. We're condemned to die of starvation with our children."

Simone began sniffing and crying gently without ceasing to ply her needle.

"Yes, yes," Roland went on in a low, dramatic voice. "French justice has condemned us to starve, me and my children. If we don't get this help tonight, I'm telling you, dearest, I shall put my head in the gas oven. You can go to your parents with the children. I can't go on any longer, I can't. I'm fed-up."

Simone let her head fall on to the table, and now she sobbed out loud, without restraint, like a little girl.

* * *

"Madame," said François, "who am I to judge your son or to know how badly he may have behaved toward you? I merely know that he is in an impossible position: he has been sacked, he has no work and he has a wife and two children to keep."

"Why did he make such a swaggering idiot of himself during the war? He's always had his head stuffed with politics, and that's his father's fault. The fool was a follower of Pétain. He only had to keep it under his hat like everybody else. What did most of the population of France do? They kept it under their hats. They smiled at the Germans with whom they had to live, they had the Marshal's portrait in the hall, listened to the British radio every evening, and in August 1944 exchanged the Marshal's portrait for General de Gaulle's, and there, with a little sleight of hand, who was to know? They hung flags out of the windows for the *Maquisards*. And that's how one behaves when one's civilised. But he, fool that he is, talked to everyone about his ideas for a National Revolution, about his plan for Europe and God knows what other nonsense. He wanted a 'clean' and 'integrated' France, he said. As if France hadn't lost her maidenhead years ago! He wanted to—how did he put it?—'renew' the youth of France. I ask you! He simply asked to be put inside. Well, he'd have done better to do a little work rather than play the super-patriot. Or, anyhow, if he really wanted to distinguish himself, he might have had the sense to go over to the *maquis* in '43 or '44. He'd have been a colonel today. But, oh no, it has always been a case of lost causes with him. Do you know what's the matter with him? He's a schoolboy. He's never grown up. In fact," and she tapped her temple with her forefinger, "he's a moron. And that's his father's fault, too. He gives the impression of being quite a man, doesn't he, with his imposing presence, his loud voice, and his political arguments? Well, he's a moron."

"You may be perfectly right. But all the same he's your son and he's unhappy. I think you'll help him, won't you?"

Clothilde took a long pull at her cigarette and the glance she gave François was terrifyingly hard. Her answer fell like the knife of the guillotine.

"No."

* * *

"Don't cry," he said softly, caressing his wife's hair with the tips of his fingers. "She won't dare refuse. She won't dare. Don't cry."

* * *

"It would be altogether too easy, wouldn't it?" went on Mme Oyarzun. "Besides, I never give way to special pleading. You understand, don't you, Monsieur Donadieu? Never. The more you plead for him, the more obstinate I become. You could go down on your knees and you'd have no greater success. I have a horror of importunity. People who ask favours of you are swindlers."

François got up.

"In that case there's nothing for me to do but go. Goodbye, Madame."

"Wait a minute. Wait a minute, Monsieur Donadieu. You'll tell my son that he's old enough not to need an intermediary. If he wants help, he must come and ask it himself. I've never seen him humbled before me. Well, I want to see him imploring me, standing there where you are. I want to see him humiliated!" she cried, raising her clenched fists to her eyes in a furious, mad gesture. Out of breath, she was silent for a moment. Her eyes flashed. She wiped the corners of her mouth with a little handkerchief and began murmuring in a low voice as if to herself: "Then, perhaps, I might give him the money he needs. . . . Who does he take me for? I'm not a money-lender or a mutual benefit society. He's thirty, isn't he? Let him look after himself. I manage all right, don't I? Or let him write to his beloved father; he'll get some good advice from that quarter. Two morons, that's what they are, one turned to religion and the other to politics, because they don't know how to manage their lives. Two morons who manage to get away with it in their own worlds."

She looked at François as if she did not recognise him and had no notion how this stranger came to be there. From the fleeting blank look in her eyes, the young man understood that Mme Oyarzun was not unaffected by her age; indeed, for a few seconds, she seemed older in spite of the cunning make-up, the golden hair, the perfectly controlled figure. Suddenly she came to. She gave him a brilliant smile, and her whole personality, voice, glance, face, bearing, as if some internal machinery had begun to function and suddenly created a metamorphosis, changed almost without an instant of transition, and with superb and terrifying precision, from ill-natured ratiocination to worldly affability.

"There it is, Monsieur Donadieu. You've done your duty by your friend, that's splendid. Come and see me on a Tuesday at seven o'clock. I'm always at home on that day. We'll talk of Sault-en-Labourd. I've been delighted, really quite delighted, to meet you."

2

On leaving Mme Oyarzon, François went to the Rue Mazarine, to the editorial office of *Horizons*. He was accustomed to meet Bernard there every Friday in the late afternoon. He would hand him the typescript of a film review for publication the following week. Usually they dined together, or at any rate had an arrangement to do so, though it often happened that Bernard was prevented from doing so at the last moment: he had to meet Malraux, or interview an American general, or more frequently still, entertain one of his mistresses. Indeed, Bernard's love-life was extremely complicated. Unable to stand monotony and taking his pleasure only in variety—"I am condemned to polygamy," he was accustomed to say—he had to expend treasures both of ingenuity and cash to assure himself a satisfactory succession of concubines. This was his major worry, the great concern of his life. He might have contented himself with the resources offered by one or another of the houses whose high tariffs guaranteed the quality of their goods. But, though he was far from holding these venal loves in contempt, he had reached, he declared, the age when a man feels the need of a certain reciprocity and wants this somewhat summary and brutish act to be surrounded with all the tender delights of a personal sentiment. Thus he had one friend who, though not particularly beautiful, was both intelligent and sensitive, for a love-tenderness-esteem relationship; another, a Creole, for a love-passion relationship; a third, a twenty-year-old shorthand-typist, for freshness; a woman of fashion, for love-sophistication; and all this without taking into account the nameless women met by chance in the streets at night, or the lady-like inmates of a respectable brothel: these last two categories interested only the animal man in him. This realisation in post-war Paris of the dream of an Oriental harem became for Bernard a most arduous enterprise, to which he devoted all the resources of a shrewd intelligence and a sure talent for organisation. To begin with, he had had to train himself to discipline his erotic moods by spreading them, in accordance with a fixed time-table, over the days of the week: Monday and Thursday, sentiment; Tuesday and Friday, passion; Saturday, freshness (because shorthand-typists, work girls, seamstresses and so on have only Saturday nights free for the combined joys of the cinema, dancing and love); Wednesday, animality. As for love-sophistication, there was no definite day, for women of fashion, torn between dinners, first nights and fancy-dress balls, are incapable of any sort of constancy in their appointments; he therefore permitted the nights consecrated to this particular form of love to be imposed upon him by the calendar of social events, as Catholics allow the liturgical calendar to determine the dates of the movable feasts of the Church. His greatest difficulty was to ensure the complete separation from one another of these various domains of love; it was essential that the mistress-passion should know nothing of what her lover did on those days when he was not available to her, for such a discovery might well end in assassination; and, conversely, the mistress-freshness had to be kept in ignorance of what went on in Bernard's flat when she was not there—that is to say, every night but Saturdays, for such a discovery might well end in suicide. It was a matter of minute organisation and of a variety of precautions about telephones, confidences and meeting-places; and all this often gave Bernard a headache, conscious as he was that the least mistake, the least slip, might have fatal consequences: a couple of revolver shots for himself or a tube of veronal for an innocent girl.

In spite of all the anxiety and the excessive expenditure that the proper running of this constantly renewed harem cost him, Bernard could not have resigned himself to simplifying his way of life, to sacrificing for the sake of peace and quiet and pecuniary equilibrium the richness and variety of an erotic ambience which he affirmed was the salt of life to him. In these methodically regulated excesses Bernard manifested neither the stupid satisfactions of a vulgar seducer, nor the morbid tastes of a depraved libertine, nor the pride of a classic Don Juan, but simply the warm and endearing fervour of a contemporary of Hafiz, of a young Caliph for whom woman alone is worthy to captivate men. From time to time from some intellectual whim, snobbery, or a desire to be "in line" with the period, in imitation of Malraux' characters, he gave it to be understood that he had inclinations towards fetichism, or that he liked whipping, or that he enjoyed strange practices with women, or that he sought in love "the alienation of another's freedom", or some nonsense of that kind; he even succeeded in persuading himself of it. In fact, the idea of administering the whip to the pretty creatures would never have occurred to him: he used more tender methods towards them and he had, for each one of his three or four contemporary loves, a special place in his admirably compartmented heart.

So, divided between love, politics, journalism and society, Bernard had little leisure to devote to his friends. Nevertheless, since those August days, he had managed to dine a dozen times with François Donadieu. He had commissioned him to review films for *Horizons* which was a most friendly and creditable gesture of confidence, since he had no assurance beforehand that François could write decent criticism. But Bernard made gestures like this: brilliant, lucky, endowed with a host of minor talents, pampered by life, he was also a good friend.

When François entered Bernard's office he found there a contributor to the paper, the Abbé R., and two or three young men and women dressed in black sweaters and corduroy trousers. The presence of these people whom he did not like made him diffident. He took his seat in an armchair at the end of the room and bit his nails while waiting to be alone with Bernard. The feeling of boredom, restlessness and vague depression that he had felt for several days grew worse. He watched Bernard, who was talking to the Abbé with particular cordiality, and for several seconds ceased to have any feeling of friendship for him. 'I must talk to him of Roland Oyarzun,' he thought. 'And this time I must have the courage to talk firmly and, if necessary, disagree with him. He's been dominating me far too long,' he thought a moment later, almost in spite of himself. He turned the thought over in his mind and was somewhat ashamed of it. 'So Roland Oyarzun's misfortunes,' he thought, 'are only a pretext for me to oppose Bernard, because Bernard's dominance is beginning to be a bore.' This somehow seemed rather dishonourable, but François was in no mood for an examination of conscience. His visit to Mme Oyarzun had "put his nerves on edge". He made no attempt to analyse the reasons for his disquiet, for they were not yet very clear. 'But, since I came back to France six months ago, things have not gone well. I'm not happy.' He hated the way the Abbé planted himself with his legs apart, like a lout ready for a fight, and puffed at his pipe like the Curé of Clément

Vautel. François had a Protestant distrust of soldier-priests: "He that liveth by the sword shall perish by the sword." He hated the way the young people in black sweaters behaved in the office, smoked, lolled in the chairs with their legs over the arms as if they had been at home. "The casualness, the stupidity of these young animals!" he thought. How old were they? Eighteen, twenty. Who were they? Certainly not *the* youth of France. There was a youth of France in the schools, the universities, the workshops and the factories. But these boys and girls, dressed like terrorists in an operetta, had nothing in common with that youth, they had nothing in common with youth; they were not young. They belonged to a type which at that time was to be met with all over the place: in newspaper offices, at cocktail parties, on varnishing days, in the cafés of the Left Bank, everywhere where there was a chance of publicity, profit or graft. Like the horned beasts which dispute the centre of the road with humans in certain Indian towns, they behaved with the utmost freedom, clothed as they were in a spiritual taboo which assured them total immunity. This taboo's name was: "the Young". They feared nothing and inspired the public with reverential awe. "The Young," the public murmured indulgently, "the Young. . . ." Sometimes a small detachment of this august herd made its way between the tables on the terrace of the *Flore* or the *Deux Magots* and forced the clients to buy little pamphlets of twenty pages or so. "Poems of the Young," they said and the clients hastily paid up. They were often to be seen in the houses of publishers, where, having grazed at the buffet till the last pastry was gone, they insulted the master of the house, who piously published them six months later. It must be admitted, however that, unlike the sacred cows of India, they were never seen to defecate in the street.

Bernard always had some of these young people about him and did not seem to mind.

As for the Abbé R., he typified a new version of the pre-war priest militant: the anti-clerical, gallican, Marxist priest. He violently attacked the Vichyite bishops and cardinals, roundly told the Roman Church its business and filled Bernard's paper with resounding phrases of spiritual thunder. From his "horizon blue" forebears he inherited his burliness, his forthright speech and, final touch to a highly coloured presence, the pipe stuck in his mouth. There the resemblance ended. The "horizon blue" priest had been simple, vulgar, something of a card and generally uncultivated. The *maquisard* priest was a delicious mixture of St. Thomas Aquinas, Hegel and Brother Jean of Entommeures. He haunted the purlieus of the intellectual world, took luncheon with Gallimard and supped with Camus. He had plans for the reform of organised labour. He spoke at meetings. Before the spectacle of such copious, diverse and noisy activity, one wondered whether the Abbé R., ever found the time to say Mass. But this was a mere detail! The defence of modern spirituality was well worth a Mass. In his articles the Abbé R. examined "contemporary problems" as a specialist: the condition of the Negroes in America, the situation in Indo-China, strikes, the wages of the working classes—everything, in fact, but the daily executions of Frenchmen in Paris and in the provinces. He did not flinch at Brasillach's death. And since François Mauriac from time to time attacked the excesses of the purge, he one day took him sharply to task by saying, if it can be believed, that justice was an aspect of charity, and that therefore there could be no true charity without justice, an argument that F. Mauriac disdained to pursue. But, in general, the Abbé R. did not concern himself with the purge, either in praise or blame. He was concerned with black men, yellow men and with the workers. He was a sufferer from that sublime sort of long-sightedness which is known as "a broad view of history" or "a great sense of synthesis". Indeed, when one's eyes are fixed upon the horizons of the world, one may be forgiven for failing to notice a few bloodstains at one's feet.

The reasons for which this firebrand of the new Christianity had chosen to exercise his talents in *Horizons* were not altogether clear, except, of course, to the extent that they derived from that general tendency which for some time past had moved the intellectual and advanced elements among the clergy to draw nearer to the militant left wing, where atheism and anti-religious combativeness were obligatory. They were received, according to circumstances, either with a sort of smirking sympathy—"our Christian brothers"—or with an ironical tolerance. It was up to these new priests to show that, if the Church had for too long allied itself to the ruling classes, those days were at an end: from now on the Church would fight beside the humble and the oppressed. This attraction towards the left was in part doubtless due to a real passion for justice (particularly in the early days of the movement, at the time of Lamennais and Montalembert, and later, that of Sillon); but there were, too, more disquieting ingredients: a temporal calculation (the concessions to the left were considered to be the only means of "recovering" the masses) and a certain snobbery (the intelligentsia delighting in the game of revolution). There might also be discerned in it a certain taste for excitement combined with a general lowering of piety, for it is more amusing to take part in the quarrels of the world than to live according to Christ, it is more amusing to be an Abbé concerned with meetings and newspaper offices than it is to be Bernanos country priest or a worker-priest. Thus, at the beginning of the second post-war period, the Church hummed with petulant Levites who interpreted the gospel in terms of the class war and had abandoned the Latin of the liturgy for the French of a sergeant-major who had received the Holy Ghost. Under the pretext of making the rites of religion intelligible to the general public, they succeeded in depriving them of all poetry without in the least clarifying their obscurity. Others devoted to football, camping, propaganda, or the elucidation of sexual problems (at educative meetings held for the benefit of the young) the time that once would have been reserved for visiting the sick and relieving the poor. But after all, they were not St. Vincent de Paul, but modern young priests, and they certainly knew more about the methods of legitimate birth control than they did about how to behave at the bedside of a poor woman suffering from generalised gangrene. In brief, the Church was making a serious effort at rejuvenation, at adaptation; only a few elderly, old-fashioned priests still professed the obsolete Christian teachings concerning the separation of the spiritual and the temporal, the meaning of suffering, sin, redemption and grace. Their younger brethren preferred motor-bicycles and illustrated pamphlets upon "what every young Christian girl ought to know".

Bernard had accepted the Abbé R.'s collaboration in the most natural manner in the world, because on the morrow of the Liberation an open-arm "fraternity" was all the fashion: Communists and monarchists, priests and anti-clericals had each and all been equally part of the Resistance. Besides, Bernard himself had a very welcoming disposition, was open-minded, free from prejudice and sectarianism, and was incapable of really hating. When he did take sides, and he did so tenaciously and systematically, his beliefs remained abstract. They did not become incarnate. "I should have made a very bad Fascist," he used to say, "because I don't believe in Evil. To be a good Fascist one must believe that Evil is a German, or a Jew, or a Mongol, or Aristide Briand, or Stalin, and this belief must be tainted with execration, it must have a flavour of blood and murder. Fascism is a religion of human sacrifice; it is directed at the nerves and the intestines. The only trouble is that I have no gift for violent emotion." Intellectually an anti-clerical, an anti-militarist and an anti-bourgeois, Bernard was nevertheless perfectly prepared to entertain the most cordial relations with an officer or a priest; while the bourgeoisie formed the familiar frame in which he lived —a state of affairs which, in words at least, he deplored, but of which he had never had the courage to free himself. In short Bernard did not belong to that species of mankind, in truth as disquieting as albinos or kleptomaniacs, who at the mere sight of a *soutane*, badges of military rank or a hooked nose, grind their teeth, roll their eyes and foam at the mouth.

He was therefore delighted to publish the Abbé R.'s articles under the title of *The Tribune of Freedom*, and even thought it rather smart to have a priest as contributor; it was one more originality to place to the editor's credit. But these same rather doubtful associations were to be found in other papers of the period, these marriages between Red and Black, Marxism and Christianity, under the common banner of Resistance and Fraternity. Men of the most opposite views, but united by war, now met again in Ministries and newspaper offices at an hour when they might hope to reap the fruits of secret action and found a group or a party upon the martyrdom of old comrades shot by the Germans.

Bernard had founded *Horizons* with the financial backing of a banker and the goodwill of the Ministry of Information. At a time when the paper quota was compelling newspapers to reduce their size, *Horizons* bore every material sign of prosperity. It was in need of no more than a hundred and fifty thousand readers for the appearance to be matched by the reality. Bernard wrote the editorial, a brilliant review of the political events of the week. The rest was filled up by a disparate team of activists (or of needy people like François).

At last the Abbé R. left, Bernard sent away the young people and François was able to approach the desk. They shook each other by the hand. Bernard said: "Why are you always so aloof? Is it shyness, pride or what?

"Let's say that it's partly shyness, partly indifference and partly dislike. I don't much care for the Abbé, and since he never seems to notice my presence . . ."

"It's not up to him to make the first advances. He ignores you because you ignore him."

"All right; let's go on ignoring each other."

"It's an attitude that most people find displeasing. You make enemies by it."

"I'm not important enough to have enemies."

"In any case, it's a silly way to behave: nobody knows whether it's shyness or arrogance. If they think it's the first, they won't do anything to help you out of it; if the second, they turn their backs on you and bear you a grudge. You should be more adaptable, quicker on the uptake and nicer."

"Why should I coerce myself?"

"Social life is a coercion."

"When one has ambitions. I have none."

"It's not a question of ambition," said Bernard drily; it's a question of harmony and ease. You know, I'm telling you for your own good. I should like to see you a little more sociable, that's all, but, of course, if you prefer to remain in your own shell, have it your own way."

The interview was beginning badly. François felt unhappier still because he knew that, on this point, Bernard was in fact perfectly right.

"Talking of enemies," he said, "I know an enemy of yours; he really wishes you harm."

"There are a good many who wish me harm."

"This one is determined to murder you."

"Confound him! Let him do his worst."

"He accuses you of having killed his best friend."

"Does he indeed!" said Bernard. But his expression showed a sudden interest. "Come on. Tell me about it!"

"It appears that when you led a detachment of *maquisards* through a village in the centre of France there were a number of summary executions. No; wait a minute. It's not that. I'm getting mixed up with what you've told me yourself. No, it was on an occasion when you were forced to retreat that you killed, or ordered the execution of, a friend of your enemy's. . . ."

"I know what it's about. The young Militiaman. I didn't kill him; it was Ludovic. Without orders from me. Or, rather, there was a misunderstanding, a certain amount of confusion. The chap would have been a terrible nuisance during our retreat. There was certainly no other solution."

"The man I'm talking about seems to regard it as murder, since his friend was your prisoner and one does not shoot prisoners. Anyway, he's taking a high moral line."

"Clearly. And what line do you take?"

"I don't know, my dear chap, I don't know. I should have to know more about the circumstances. Besides, I've no head for politics. . . ."

"Admit that you blame me," said Bernard with more curiosity than reproach.

"No; that's an exaggeration."

"Sit down. What are you standing for? Sit down. We've got plenty of time," he said, looking at his watch. "You're an odd chap," he went on in a friendly way. "When I told you what had happened in those July days in the villages of the Loire, I felt that you were disgusted. You are a funny old Protestant. I look upon you as . . . the embodiment of Moral Law! Yes; in the Kantian sense. Your reactions belong to another age, I mean: excessive in honesty and rectitude, to the point of strictness in fact; but it's no bad criterion, one can trust in it. . . ."

"Stop! You mustn't think me so severe. Only three months ago, someone told me a few home truths about my severity which enlightened me. Go on."

"Anyway, I felt that you judged me severely and perhaps condemned me."

"Your story of lynch-law did shock me rather."

" 'Lynch' is going too far. The man was flogged in public and thrown into prison. I presume he is now free again."

"If I remember correctly, you said that he was flogged in the presence of his family?"

"I believe some members of his family were present."

"Had he sons? In your place, I should watch out for them."

"Your ideas of worldly behaviour derive from Corneille. The

sons of that traitor who was flogged are undoubtedly engaged in the black market at this moment, or are learning swing. We're not living in Corsica or Castille."

"If you despise the inhabitants of this country so much, I wonder why you thought it your duty to take part in their liberation."

François was surprised at his own audacity. He had never been so outspoken with Bernard before. But tonight he had decided to go to extremes, to bring his quarrel with him out into the open. But what in fact was his quarrel?

"You make me laugh," Bernard said. "But I warn you, if you're trying to make me lose my temper, you're wasting your time. My conscience is perfectly clear."

"Forgive me, but it seems to me that your conscience isn't as clear as all that. . . . I guessed when you first told me of these 'acts of violence'—it's your own term. You were very excited about it; you had seen blood flow, men die, things you had never had the chance of seeing before, not even in Spain, where you had missed your opportunities. And suddenly, last summer, in this village of the Loiret, you saw acts of violence committed before your eyes, a tornado of violence of which you lost control, so you said, and you allowed yourself to be carried away by it too, while remaining, I'm quoting you again, 'perfectly lucid'. But you admitted one detail which has its importance: while this orgy of violence was going on, you had to go away for five minutes, to vomit, because one particular sight had shaken you. . . ."

Bernard liked to hear his friends talking of him, decrying him, discussing him, and he made no attempt to hide his pleasure, which was clearly shown in his expression.

"What do you expect?" he asked. "I was accustomed to violence. I had come to it from far away, from the most decadent zones of the bourgeoisie. . . ."

"I'm not sure that you were such a stranger to violence. I remember other things you told me: the Militiaman you hit in the attic of the Hôtel de Ville—before letting him go, of course —but you hit him brutally: the act surprised you, yourself. Another time you beat up a friend of yours, a certain Nick, who had no doubt threatened you, but you hurled yourself upon him when he was already down. . . ."

"God, what a terrifying memory you've got!"

"You see, I'm a dangerous chap: I remember everything. At least everything the more interesting people I know tell me and, naturally, you're the most interesting of the lot."

Bernard bowed.

"I appreciate it. I appreciate it. But to come back to my occasional acts of violence, I do see. It's because I can't stand opposition, a certain kind of opposition. I can't stand opposition to the extent that it imperils my freedom, to the extent that it tends to . . . to class me once and for all, to place me in an absurd, even a gross context. This was the case with the young Militiaman in the Hôtel de Ville, and with Nicholas Gaudie too. The first must certainly have been anti-Semite and the second called me a 'filthy Jew' and explained my politics, my opinions and my ideas from the fact of my being a Jew, which was absolutely intolerable, don't you see? That explains my violence, which was no more than a reflex of revolt. . . . Revolt against a conception which was directed at identifying me with my race, whereas I feel very strongly, with profound conviction, that I cannot be explained away by the fact of my race, any more than by the fact of my being bourgeois. Those are mere incidents which I surpass, transcend, as they say. So, you see, against ideas that place you, that deprive you of your liberty, there is no other recourse but violence, because you can't argue with people who have already transformed you into objects, labelled you once and for all as 'the Jew', 'the bourgeois'. And I admit that these acts of mine you have just recalled manifest the Jew's reflex of revolt in the face of anti-Semitism. As far as the young Militiaman in the Hôtel de Ville was concerned, don't forget that it happened last August at the end of four years of peculiar experience for people of my race. A slap in the face seems a pretty mild sort of revenge."

François smiled. At that moment he felt friendly towards him again. One often had these happy surprises with Bernard: during the course of a conversation with him there would be an astonishingly sincere avowal, a witticism, a strikingly just analysis, which reconciled you again if by chance your sympathy had cooled towards him. He was a good chap, all the same, François thought. His love for truth was as ardent and passionate as his love for women. It had almost the same quality of carnality.

Roland Oyarzun. He had to speak of Roland Oyarzun at whatever cost.

"The sad thing about all these stories," he went on, "is that on both sides people have suffered for being right."

"What do you mean?"

"I'm expressing myself badly. I mean to say that France today is morally divided into two practically irreconcilable camps and that, in each camp, there has been enough suffering and enough sincerity to disconcert, to discountenance anyone who sets himself up to judge categorically, brutally. You see, I was thinking of the chap who hates you so much. It happens that I've known him for a long time. I had lost sight of him and then I met him again the other evening. It was pretty horrible. I wanted to run away. He's our age and he's a lost man."

"What happened to him?"

"He was purged, slightly. Well, three months in Fresnes and National Indignity for five years. And I really think that his crime, if it was a crime, was committed with the best intentions. He went all out for the Youth Organisations, for the Pétain mystique; I suppose he made the noisiest kind of Vichyite propaganda like the tub-thumper he is, and went on doing it right up to the last minute, you understand, right up to the eve of the Liberation. He has the ideological frenzy of an old disciple of Maurras who has turned Fascist—he was for some time with Bucart, but left him when he saw that Bucart was no good—and finally he was absorbed into the new evangelism of the National Revolution. His antecedents are shortly these: an officer's son who from his childhood was imbued with military idealism, his education was somewhat chaotic and he was shuttled between two parents who fought all day long; he was involved in riots in the Latin Quarter between 1937 and 1939, behaved in exemplary fashion during the war. What more? He's not very intelligent. That's the most one can say. . . . Muddled and confused, he sometimes does the most incredibly stupid things, while at others, has moments of lucidity which take your breath away. No; not exactly lucid. It's rather a sort of logical despair, a sadness. Anyhow, it's harrowing. I assure you that when I was at his house the other night, I was shaken by it. And I'll add this, stupid though you may think me, I felt that I was a little, just a very little, to blame."

"Oh, no!" Bernard protested, laughing. "You're a masochist, I know that, you're full of all sorts of horrible complexes, but, really, to feel that you're to blame for this . . . 'victim' as you call him! No; you've got nothing to do with it."

"In his eyes I represented the other side, I was in league with his enemies."

"Yes, and I suppose it didn't for a single instant occur to you that this victim of his own convictions was, and doubtless still is, anti-republican, anti-Communist of course, anti-Semitic, a racial purist."

"It did occur to me. He's still filled with hatred. But hatred's sad too, it's pathetic."

Bernard made a fatalistic gesture, like a man who is abandoning an argument.

"Well, of course, if you're going to pity those who hate! Frankly, Mauriac's articles are charity enough for me."

"Well, it's something that the purge is not being carried on in total silence."

"After all," cried Bernard with an impatience tinged with irritation, "ought the traitors to be punished or not? Your insistence on defending the collaborators is really rather excessive. I must admit I didn't expect it from you."

'Here we are,' thought François; 'the quarrel's beginning.' He felt rather embarrassed, but at the same time perfectly resolute: the important thing was not so much to be right, but to dare to stand up to Bernard, to oppose him properly for once.

"Listen," he said gently, "I'm not in any way defending the collaborators, even though there is something to be said in their defence. But as regards those you call 'traitors' . . ."

"Well?"

"We must define the term."

"Everyone knows what to betray means. There's no clearer term today."

"On condition that the object betrayed has previously been defined. I'm afraid that the historians of the future won't have quite the same ideas on that point that we have."

"I know what you're going to say next: the legitimacy of the Vichy Government. It's a pity you don't read the excellent leading articles in *Horizons*," he added with rather a wry smile. "They might convert you from the *Figaro*, and you'd learn something about the pretensions to legitimacy of the Vichy Government."

"I remember that particular leading article perfectly well. I couldn't recapitulate all the arguments, but I know that they didn't altogether convince me. Besides, that isn't really the point. Traitors or not, there were some people who criminally caused the deaths of their fellow-countrymen, who denounced them and tortured them. It is just and necessary that they should be punished, even if it's only for the sake of social hygiene. But you'll admit that the Tribunals of the Purge also condemn men whose only fault was to make a mistake in all sincerity. People have a right to make mistakes, supposing that to collaborate was a mistake. Crime should be punished, but not mistakes. That's all I wanted to say. The man I was talking about is clearly, in this sense, a victim. He was thunderstruck, horrified by his punishment. He's still bewildered by it. And you know as well as I do that there are thousands of victims of the same kind, and that one day those victims or their sons will demand a reckoning."

"In fact, according to you, the France of today is like the Atrides or, better still, it's Argos with the Furies waiting to come to life in every nook and corner?"

"You know, I think we carry the Furies in ourselves, whichever side we belong to. Anyhow, yes, if you put it like that, it seems to me we're living through a tragedy and will go on doing so for a long time to come."

"Very well, then; but, as you know, that's one of my favourite theories: the continuous civil war of the twentieth century, all that's most frantic and inexpiable in contemporary conflicts, the apocalyptic aspect of the world. Personally, I like it: I was made to live in a Shakespearian epoch. We shan't be bored; so much to the good."

"Don't be frivolous, or pretend to be so. We were talking of the outlaws the purge has created. They'll form a marginal society of their own. What's to be done about them?"

"The opposition has always existed in the Republic."

"The opposition expresses itself, discusses, votes, gets elected, takes part in the conduct of affairs. To outlaws, there's no means available but conspiracy."

"Well, let them conspire," cried Bernard. "It'll add a little life and excitement to political life."

He got up to show that the interview was at an end. His expression was more mocking than cordial.

"You're not the first, you know, to criticise the processes of the Purge. The tendency to do so is in the air."

"I'm not trying to be original. I'm trying to be just."

Bernard was filing away papers in the drawers of his desk.

"What's your article on?" he asked.

"On two Resistance films, one French, the other Italian."

"I hope you haven't been too slashing?"

"Is being slashing no longer suitable to the tone of *Horizons*?"

"For some time," Bernard said, his voice still sounding annoyed, "you've been savagely criticising that type of film, even the good ones. One might think it was systematic."

"Are you afraid of censure or that they'll lower your quota of paper?"

Bernard shrugged his shoulders. He went on filing papers, tidied his desk, and then suddenly came and stood in front of François, pinning him with a cold stare.

"You know that you're perfectly free to hand in your resignation," he said drily.

"It's yours. It's yours," said François with the utmost calm, and went towards the door.

"Come back, you idiot!"

Bernard's laugh seemed hardly forced at all.

"Did you think I was serious? Good Lord, you're angry. Oh, when you shy people go into action!"

He gave him several little punches like schoolboys do.

"You've changed a lot recently, you know. It's growing up, I suppose. . . ."

"Yes; it's never too late to become a man," said François with the pale ghost of a smile.

"Is it because you've become a man that you . . . that you rebel?" asked Bernard in a friendly, teasing voice. "Because you're rebelling against the paper, against me, and against the right causes."

"No doubt, no doubt. . . . I've noticed that the paper, you and just causes are not always to be taken seriously."

"I see. And so my stock's going down, is that it?"

"Yes; a little. But I'm very fond of you all the same. You see, when I met you in '39, in the Army, I was a little boy, more ingenuous than the average of little boys. You dazzled me, absolutely dazzled me. But now it's five years later and . . ."

"My prestige has been shaken?"

He tried to make his voice sound easy and good-humoured, but did not quite succeed.

"That's it; yes," said François. "When one becomes a man, one ceases to worship the gods of one's childhood. But don't worry, I've reserved a beautiful purple shroud for you."

Bernard cut short a dry laugh.

"You amuse me," he said. "But let's change the subject. I'm going to get married."

"Congratulations. Though it's the second announcement you've made this year."

"You don't take me seriously about this either?"

"Not altogether; no."

"Nor do I!"

He smiled and inclined his head sideways towards his shoulder. His eyes looked like velvet and with his fine brown hands he outlined a curve in the air. At that moment, the Editor-in-chief of *Horizons* looked exactly what he was, among other disparate truths: a gentle pleasure-loving Oriental, a young Caliph intoxicated among the warm labyrinths of the seraglio. On the office walls were hung a number of accessories: a map of Europe stuck with little tricolour flags, lists of statistics, three photographs; André Malraux as a colonel of the *Maquis*, General de Gaulle, Georges Bidault. On the desk, a calendar showed the date: it was the 13th of December, 1944.

"*La donna e la piu bella cosa nel mondo*," said Bernard and, leaning back his head, he almost completely lowered his tawny, rather heavy eyelids. "Do you remember? It was the favourite, hackneyed saying of Giuseppe Savelli in London? He was quite right. Christiane has spoken to me of a friend of hers. If it would amuse you, we could all four go out together tonight. Are you on? At nine o'clock, then. We'll meet at my house. I'll telephone Christiane. It'll make you forget the sorrows of the purge, and me those of the twilight of a god."

3

From the Rue Mazarine, François went to the *Deux Magots*, where he had arranged to meet Roland Oyarzun. The cold was

Arctic, and the passers-by were hurrying through the fog. Roland, in a grey mackintosh, was at the very back of the hall hunched and sunken on the bench. At François' approach, he raised eyes like those of a beaten dog and, before even shaking hands, muttered, "How did it go?"

François had dreaded this moment.

"She refused," he said, and turned his head away so as not to see his friend's face collapse, decompose as if under the action of a violent acid.

He sat down opposite him, so as to hide the tragedy of his expression from the other customers in the café. Roland, besotted, his eyes unfocused, remained several seconds without speaking. Then he said, "I didn't expect a refusal. I didn't believe that she could refuse to help me."

"You ought to have gone to see her yourself."

"That's what Simone keeps telling me. So, a man must choose between humiliation and dying of hunger."

"There's no question of humiliation. Your going there would have been the most natural thing in the world. Anyhow, you must understand that to send me as your ambassador lacked sense. I went because you insisted, but I was pretty sure beforehand that she would refuse. You should have gone yourself."

"You don't understand. You'd have to know what my life with my parents was like, its details, its atmosphere. You can't really understand a man till you know his past, his childhood. You can't judge from outside."

François did not reply, but he thought that people were really very tiresome with their family histories, always so complicated, so strange and so excessive. After another long silence, Roland said in a quavering voice, "There's nothing left for it but to turn on the gas this evening."

"Don't say silly things like that. You know very well that you won't do anything of the kind."

François was exasperated: one simply does not say things like that, "I'm going to turn on the gas", when one's sitting with a Viandox in front of one in the *Café des Deux Magots*.

"You'd do better to drink your Viandox; it'll get cold. And there are other solutions besides that one, which isn't one at all. Look for work."

"It's easy enough for you to talk. I haven't a penny in the

world. My parents-in-law are fed up with supporting us all this time. Look for work, indeed. How? Where? What work?"

Nevertheless, he was prepared to consider certain extreme solutions, "the solutions of despair", he sighed, but they seemed to be the only ones to which he could have recourse: a workman in a factory, for example. Many were being taken on and there was a shortage of manpower. François opened the *Figaro* and ran his eye over the classified advertisements. He did not dare say that there seemed to be a considerable number of vacant places for domestic servants: Oyarzun would have started a riot in the café. However, looking at the advertisements over his friend's shoulder, the outlaw observed sadly, "Simone and I could always take jobs as servants. She could be cook-housemaid and I could be chauffeur-footman. That is, if anyone would take us on without references. But perhaps you have to have been in the Resistance to get a job as a flunkey?"

"After the last war the Russian refugees didn't mind becoming servants, even those who had been great nobles in their own country. No work is dishonourable. One must bow to necessity. In fact, I don't think it would be at all a bad idea for you and Simone."

Roland was furious. He had counted on horrified protests—"You can't be serious! What, you become a servant! The son of an Oyarzun!" He exploded.

"You think it'd be a good idea, do you? Thanks very much. You're a nice chap. You flatter us, Simone and me. It's polite of you. My God, you produce the clichés like a schoolmistress giving her class moral instruction! 'One must bow to necessity, no work is dishonourable.' You'd make a first-class preaching brother! Damned Huguenot! Tell me, would you consent to become a flunkey? Can you see yourself, in a white coat, announcing that dinner is served? Can you see yourself in the pantry cleaning the master's shoes?"

"The job I've got at the moment's not much higher in the scale."

"Nonsense. You must admit it's absolutely different! You're a motor-car salesman, you deal with smartly-dressed clients, you don't dirty your hands."

"Seen from a bit higher up, my job and a servant's are much the same. We're both proletarians."

"But there's a difference! Your job's not degrading. Besides, you bamboozle the public. I should love it. And what's more, if it's a question of having the gift of the gab, I should be much more successful than you are. You know nothing about mechanics. Can you even tell a plug from a battery? You haven't even got a driving licence! And yet you sell cars. All the same, it's a pretty unhappy state of affairs. Clearly, there had to be a period of disorder and confusion of values for a Donadieu to be salesman in a motor-car showroom!"

François smiled. "Well, you must clearly be feeling better; you've recovered your powers of indignation."

"I shan't conceal from you, Donadieu, that you've vexed me by suggesting that I should try to get work as a servant. Oh yes, you've vexed me, and you've hurt me, and I shan't forget it. Yes, you've wounded me, you know."

"But, my dear chap, I swear that I had no intention to hurt you! As far as I'm concerned, there's nothing dishonourable about a servant's job. If I were reduced to it, I should do it without the least shame in the world, I assure you. Don't you believe me? By my daughter's head, I swear to you that I'm telling you the truth."

"You can't have much self-conceit, then."

"No; I haven't much. I believe I've got pride, but no conceit."

"I dare say you're right," said Oyarzun meditatively. "At bottom you Huguenots are quite different from Catholics. You've got a different kind of mentality. You're all simpletons."

As far as François was concerned, he had now calmed down, but his 'powers of indignation' were soon aroused once more. This time they were directed at the young men and girls who were sitting here and there about the café. He disliked their crew-cut hair, their fantastic clothes—leather jerkins, trousers of whipcord or corduroy—their really rather amusing demeanour of young intellectual terrorists; had they got incendiary bombs or merely rhyming dictionaries under their jerkins? Roland wanted to know whether these were Resistance youth, whether these 'puppies' had been 'in the *maquis*'. With a fine catholicity he called them 'monkeys', 'bandits', 'spongers', 'parasites', 'little bastards', and other still ruder things. Such spite and hatred seemed odd to François, particularly as they appeared out of proportion to their object, nor could one tell whether they were directed at youth, at pretentiousness, or at the political orthodoxy of the period as personified in these young people. Oyarzun appeared to dislike the young men most, showing himself much more indulgent towards the girls, doubtless due to the normal reflex of a man who professed to adore the fair sex. François suddenly remembered an embarrassing little scene to which he had been an unwilling witness. He had one day met Roland, Simone and Jacques, Simone's brother, in the Underground some short time after the Armistice—in '41 or '42 it must have been. Simone was carrying her eldest daughter in her arms, a child a few months old at the time, and she was visibly about to become a mother again. Every seat in the train was taken. Then Roland espied a boy who, sitting in the rear, had his back turned and so could not see them. He rushed at him, pulled him up by the coat collar and wildly abused him, to the dismay of the other passengers, including Germans: "So you won't get up and give your seat to the mother of a family! You think of nothing but dolling yourself up. *Zazou*! The young people of today . . . cissies . . . in the middle of a war . . . no respect for anything. . . . Why aren't you in the Army at your age? . . . You all need your bottoms kicking and sending to the labour camps. A rotten generation. . . . Decadent youth. . . . Not fit to have children himself and lets the mother of a family stand!" Shouting aloud, furiously angry, his face purple, his eyes crazed, he foamed at the mouth. It was in vain for Simone to implore him to be quiet, or for Jacques to smile in an attempt to calm him and minimise the incident; nothing had any effect. Oyarzun went on worse than ever, taking François to witness, when all François wanted to do was to crawl under the seats, taking the other passengers to witness: talked of his wife as a sacred receptacle, the august procreatrix of future generations of Frenchmen, pointing to her with one hand; with the other he pointed at the sterile young male (he was a schoolboy aged about seventeen) who had omitted to perceive, behind him, the presence of a standing "mother of a family". He seemed demented. Indeed, one had the impression that he was not conscious of his actions and no doubt, thought François, this condition must have a name in pathological medicine, paranoia perhaps. François looked at the unknown boy who was the object of this furious diatribe, and tried to make him understand, by an imperceptible movement of his head, that none of this had any importance, that he must forgive someone so irresponsible, and how extremely sorry about it he, François, was. . . . But the poor child, pale, wan, overcome with shame, kept his eyes lowered while trying to keep his feelings under control, his pallor accentuating the noble distinction of his head, his rather equivocal Florentine delicacy. Certainly, Roland Oyarzun's outbursts were inexplicably violent. Again today, he had shown himself absurdly angry with these poor young people. . . .

"Why get so hot and bothered about things that aren't worth it? It only stirs up your blood and bile and is bad for the liver. Leave these boys and girls alone. They haven't done you any harm after all."

"They're . . . they're disgusting!"

"But, no, really, they seem nice enough to me."

"If the world as it is doesn't infuriate you," said Oyarzun, "I don't think much of your taste. It seems to me positively frightful."

'Because you haven't achieved the place in it you coveted,' thought François. But there are truths that must not be said out loud, for they sear.

"Are you happy?" Oyarzun asked suddenly.

François, disconcerted by the unexpectedness of the question, did not answer at once. He found himself blushing.

"Quite, I see," said Oyarzun with a satisfied air. "You needn't argue about it. If you were happy you would have replied at once: 'Yes, I am.' But you hesitated, so you aren't happy either. Well, I'm not alone. I find that consoling."

This question haunted François Donadieu in the days that followed upon their conversation. Was he happy? Had he been happy during the last six months, since his return to France? He had succeeded in becoming free. There was no paralysing presence at his side, no witness, no judge, no one to make him control his moods, conceal his tempers, no stranger conscience he must consider, and to whom he must render his account. He was wonderfully free, without any tie but that of his daily work. He paid for this freedom in loneliness, though it was a relatively populated loneliness: a few friends, an occasional woman, and above all, little Juliette, who was not yet living with him but who was beginning to occupy an ever larger place in his thoughts. She was now a pretty little girl of eight, sweet and good. François had managed to spend three weeks with her in Béarn in the month of October, and he intended going back there for two or three days at Christmas. 'Later on,' he thought, 'when I've got better accommodation, and she's a bit older, I'll have her to live with me. In three years. . . .' Juliette seemed to value him highly, and he had a profound tenderness for her. But she seemed to him a long way off, clothed in the mystery of childhood, and who could tell whether they would ever become very close to each other since the early years of her young life had been spent apart? . . . Catherine paid practically no attention to her daughter, and took hardly any interest in her husband either for that matter. The question of their divorce had been left in suspense. They had come to an arrangement over material matters. Catherine had gone back to her family's flat and had left the two rooms on the Rue de Vaugirard to François, having first removed all her belongings, furniture, books and so on. François made himself solely responsible for Juliette's keep: he was the father, the breadwinner. . . . "It would be more convenient if we were to remain legally married, it would be more practical for a number of reasons, particularly financial ones. Let's spare ourselves the expensive processes of divorce for the moment. We can think about it again later. Moreover, I can see no reason why we shouldn't meet from time to time, if only to make certain decisions concerning Juliette." While saying these words she had adopted a cold and resolute expression, very much the 'business woman', or the 'modern-woman-with-a-head-on-her-shoulders', and François suddenly hated her for this ridiculous affectation, this part that suited her so ill. He knew her—didn't he?—she lacked all foresight, was hopelessly casual, lived in appalling disorder. He bore her a grudge, too, because she had been so harsh to him, had insulted and humiliated him when they had met on that famous Thursday of the Liberation. 'She's an egoist, she's wicked, she never loved me,' he thought angrily. 'I lived with her for years, she cast a spell over me. She's had the power to hurt me, to make me jealous to the point of torture. What a mess, what folly! And above all she's driven me mad with boredom. Well, it's all over: boredom, love, suffering, they're all over. Let her disappear, let her be forgotten for ever,' and he gazed with a certain puritanical severity upon this woman whose face was already faded, whose hair was dyed, upon this unknown who had been his wife, asking himself how he could ever have desired her. Today, she seemed older than he was, 'a little actress who would finish up as an understudy on provincial tours.' A little less than two years' absence had sufficed to make them utter strangers to each other.

("That's what comes," Roland Oyarzun would have said, "of going to be a play-boy about London.") Another time he met her in the entrance hall of a cinema on the Champs-Elysées. She was with a woman friend. She ran up to him and kissed him on both cheeks. "My ex-husband," she cried in a facetious voice, introducing him to her friend. "And above all, the best of companions. Isn't it true, François, that we've remained the best friends in the world?" She was again playing the breathless rôle from the repertory of 1925: 'the girl-bobbed-hair-courageous-without-prejudices-good companion', but this time she was playing it in the gay mood. Confound Catherine. . . . She had just signed a contract with Marchat for a part in a Spanish piece, something absolutely sensational, she wasn't playing the lead, no, that was Germaine Montero, who had the leading part, but she had a sketch, one of those sketches that 'pay off', and Jean Marchat was a darling, an absolute sweet, a wonderful friend, "you know, my dear man, he's got . . . it!" she put her hand on her left breast, rolled her eyes, and gasped for breath as if she were suffering from a heart attack. This meant that Jean Marchat had gallantry. Confound Catherine. . . . François watched her as she walked away down the avenue with her friend. His lip curled. 'This is all that I hate most,' he thought: 'affectation, the false coin of conventional attitudes, artificiality, smartness, automatic reactions, the whole social and fashionable performance which is the only sincerity of the mediocre. . . . I shall never become a sociable animal.' But could one really say that Catherine was a mediocre sort of woman? 'She's summed me up pretty well. That Thursday evening, when she told me a few home truths, she was certainly not mediocre then. Terrifying, but certainly not mediocre. Indeed, it's probably the best thing you ever did, Catherine: make me see myself clearly, purge me of my silly lies, strip me naked. I've remembered that lesson.' But how could she, lucid, hard and unpitying as she was, show herself at other times so silly and so affected? Was it due to the presence of her friend, of the 'public'? But people were not simple, and Catherine perhaps less simple than most. Unless, of course, she was playing at affectation deliberately, or from boredom, or as one gets drunk? No doubt, she was not very happy either. . . .

'During those twenty months in England I was happy. Catherine was right about that. I know now that I was happy over there because I was free of all responsibility, as one is in the Army, because I was free from the slavery of a job—the economic necessity. I was "serving my country", I had no immediate responsibility for the maintenance of my wife and child, I no longer suffered the sorrow of being poor, there were neither poor nor rich over there, we were all companions in arms. I recovered my lost youth over there among an indomitable and vital people. I was full of joy and used to surprise myself singing as I dressed in the mornings, I who had not sung for years. . . . There was an exaltation about life. I was in a huge, variegated city, I had a language to learn, I had many friends. Each day was an adventure. My work in the office interested me. And when they sent me to Spain last May . . .' That appalling, interminable night march through the mountains behind a Basque silent as Fate. Arrival at Saint-Jean-Pied-de-Port, making contact with the Abbé X. . . . He had very nearly retraced his steps over the same route which, twenty months earlier, he had taken with Bernard when they had left.

'Bernard was also in his element in London, but in a different way. He loved palace intrigue, political gossip, the atmosphere of the backstairs. He had a wonderful time in London from this point of view. God, how he enjoyed himself! Nearly every day he used to give us new details about the composition of the projected Government of Free France, about the clashes between de Gaulle and Churchill, about the relations between the B.C.R.A. and the Internal Resistance, about the differences with Giraud. He always had first-hand information. . . . All this excited him, put him into a fever of happiness. . . . On a different level it was the same kind of excitement that some boys show at school over the rivalries between their masters, the small internal daily dramas, the plots of rival factions. . . . Between the little dancers of the Prince of Wales Theatre, the waitresses of the Stage Door Canteen and the daily details of de Gaulle's Government, he lived, as he liked to say, "intensely". . . . Real danger he only knew later in the *maquis* and, moreover, at the very moment that the Resistance began to disappoint him because it had begun to rot. . . . In London I was always fond of Bernard. I still am fond of him. But it was at that period that I first saw him clearly, that I tired to sum him up once and for all. Before then, I hadn't really seen him, I was dazzled. During those twenty months in London, I discovered that he was, well, rather frivolous beneath his terrific political activity. "Frivolous" isn't quite the right word; I'll find a better later. Anyhow, while I still admired him, I ceased being dazzled.'

While, three years earlier . . . François remembered. He had come back to barracks late one night. It was nearly midnight. He hadn't turned on the light so as not to wake the others who were already in bed. But they weren't asleep. They were listening. They were listening to a fine, resonant voice reciting:

"*Voix lactée, O sœur lumineuse*
Des blancs ruisseaux de Chanaan. . . ."

François stood still in the darkness at the foot of a bed. He listened too, amazed by the unknown's audacity, by the extraordinary assurance with which he dared to recite a poem of Apollinaire's in a room full of soldiers. It was almost unbelievable! Certainly the majority of the soldiers in the barrack-room were a cut above the ordinary—students for the most part, young schoolmasters, who had been grouped together to make a squad of potential officers. But all the same! One must be very sure of oneself, one must have considerable authority, to chance such things at the risk of ridicule before an audience of French private soldiers. Yet they all listened in a religious silence. The unknown voice declaimed each line of the lovely poem with admirable clarity; and when it ceased, the applause broke out, spontaneous and sincere.

The next morning, when he woke up, François looked round from bed to bed to discover who could have been the speaker of the night before. Then he had heard one of the soldiers say the name, "Bernard". At roll-call someone replied to "Bernard". François raised his eyes and saw a young man with an Oriental look about him and bright, intelligent eyes.

'He was a charming friend,' François thought; 'tactful and kind. And how much he taught me! It's simple really: I was a young ignoramus, a barbarian, and I owe it to him that practically everything of interest that I have read was on his advice; I owe to him whatever I know of art; in fact, he educated me, he revealed to me what the life of the intellect could be. . . . For that I shall always be grateful to him. Besides, he enjoyed the part of "master". And then my admiration for him, doubtlessly so ingenuously evident, amused and flattered him. He has, too, a passion to dominate and direct, to exercise a sort of moral tutelage. . . . It's one of the more harmless manifestations of his lust for power. I was the living daily proof of his authority, of his prestige, of the empire he could exercise over others. But that didn't prevent his friendship being beneficent. When war broke out, I was sinking in a quicksand. The war and Bernard saved me from that. From September, 1939, life took on a new savour. I regained confidence in myself. I regained hope. . . .'

That was why, when Bernard had come to Paris from the Free Zone to arrange certain matters before his departure and had suggested that François should accompany him to England, François had seen a possibility of ultimate freedom. Life with Catherine had become dreary and impossible. So unhoped for an opportunity could not be lost.

'I thought that I was embarking upon a Malraux-like adventure, that at last I was becoming a real man of my epoch. The night before my departure was a vigil of arms. I knew what I was risking, but it was not that that frightened me, my sense of danger is not acute, it costs me little to be brave. No. It was not fear that gripped me, but rather a sort of vertigo. I was plunging into the unknown, the future was drawing me on like an abyss. But in the end, except for crossing the Pyrenees, everything turned out to be pretty prosaic. . . . The first weeks in England were depressing: I was overwhelmed with remorse when I thought of Catherine and the child. Then I adopted a soldier's heedlessness. The bombing gave me an excuse, reassured me, appeased my conscience. After all, I was exposed almost every day to the risk of death, I was a "fighter for freedom", and Bernard communicated some of his own personal excitement, made me share in the myth of "twentieth-century man", which is his great intellectual hobby-horse. I was still dazzled by Bernard, seeing him as a slightly less-talented Malraux, but pretty good all the same. . . . I can speak of him now without restraint, with a quite new irony; I am also performing a sort of retrospective self-analysis after the event, because Catherine's words tore down a veil. But, at the time, I could not be introspective with such clarity, I was still floating upon an illusion, upon a lie. Nor could I understand that Bernard, in his own way, was acting a part. But Bernard must suspect it, for in him lucidity, spontaneity and acting a part are eternally playing hide and seek. . . . One day I must talk to him about this. He won't mind, since nothing interests him so much as talking about himself. He'll be delighted to blacken his own character; and that, too, will be acting a part: "Admire my lucidity", and there'll be something of literature in it as well: "What an interesting character I am!" Dear Bernard!'

* * *

Two days before Christmas, François went to see Roland Oyarzun, and took him some toys for his little girls. Roland accepted the toys—seemed, indeed, rather touched.

"I'm very fond of my daughters," he said, "but I shan't hide the fact that I should much prefer a son. Do you see these dolls you're kind enough to give my poor girls? Well, if instead of them there was a drum, a soldier's fancy-dress, a gun with percussion caps, I should be the happiest man in the world. A son! Naturally, as long as we're so meanly lodged and so poor, it's not to be thought of: real fatherhood is denied me."

François asked him if he had found work.

"Yes, in a preserved-food factory, in the packing department. You see, I make the cardboard boxes. We're paid on piece-rates; it's a real stakhanovite system. Yesterday, my boy, in preparation for Christmas, I made two hundred and sixty-three boxes; a record, it appears. I thought I was going crazy, like Chaplin in *Modern Times*.

"That's a start. Perhaps in a few days' time you'll be put in a more interesting and more remunerative department."

"If I manage to become foreman, I shall give my wife a son," he said, his eyes bright with hope, and in the tone of voice one uses to announce: "If I get a rise, I shall go to Switzerland. I've dreamed of it for ten years."

"Athalie," muttered François.

"What?"

"When you played Athalie at school. . . . Just now you made exactly the same gesture, had exactly the same expression that you had then, when you said to Eliacin: 'You see, I am Queen and have no heir.' "

Roland smiled.

"I remember. How odd I must have looked!"

"You were pretty impressive, I must say."

"But what a success it was! Well, old man, like Athalie I need an heir. It must be a great happiness to bring up a child, to watch him day by day grow into a talented man. You see, I want my son to be my revenge. I'm nothing but a poor old bugger, a no-good; I've had no luck; in fact, I'm finished, old before my time. . . . I should like my son to be a sort of living miracle, a miracle of strength and beauty; and, later on, I should like him to have power, the necessary power to crush my enemies, make the unclean bastards who have turned me into what I am bite the dust. . . ."

"You talk like an Old Testament prophet: 'Crush my enemies', 'the unclean', 'bite the dust'; it's the tone of the Bible. That's what comes of having played Athalie at school."

"You see, I'm an implacable sort of chap. I've got the temperament of a judge."

He pointed to a photograph on the mantelpiece.

"You see, Jacques and I dreamed sometimes of being the redressers of wrongs, the two avengers, the implacable young leaders. Jacques even used to say 'the Horsemen of the Apocalypse', and that's a Biblical expression too. Of course, Jacques was still a child at the time. When he spoke to me of things like that, I used to laugh rather. I used to tell Jacques not to be a fool. But it does tend to show you what our ideals were, the sort of moral atmosphere in which we both lived."

"Yes, of course I understand. . . ."

"When we were with Bucard, we were nicknamed Roland and Olivier."

He gazed at the photograph in a melancholy way. In the presence of the dead youth the silence became heavy and oppressive. Roland Oyarzun suddenly snorted and turned about. Accustomed as he was to the sudden and dramatic alternations of mood in his friend, François was none the less taken aback, for Roland's expression was menacing.

"He's got a nerve!" Roland cried.

"What do you mean?"

"The things he dares write about us!"

"Who are you talking about?" François muttered nervously.

"Who? Who do you think I'm talking about but that frightful Yid, that friend of yours, Bernard, damn his eyes, who's always hounding me!"

"Do you mean the last number of *Horizons*?"

"Yes; I do! That article called 'The Excluded from the Feast', which makes me vomit. I read it at my barber's the other day. I thought I was going to choke with rage. And straight away I, who never buy a Resistance rag, went out and bought it, so that I might always have a proof of his caddishness, an object for anger, at hand!"

He opened a drawer, pulled out a newspaper and, wild-eyed, began to read the damning article. François knew the text. He was even indirectly responsible for it: in fact, Bernard had written it after their difference of opinion about the justice of the Purge. It was a means of answering him, of gaining the upper hand in their dubious quarrel, of finally persuading himself that he was right, since this is the final necessity of all ideological passions. The article was by turns violent and measured, aggressive and supercilious, it was redolent not so much of bad faith as of a profound and invincible unease; one felt that Bernard was very uncertain of his position. The argument hesitated between objective exposition and passionate pleading, without care to preserve that unity of tone which reveals the true writer (or anyway those who have a sense of writing). In the first place Bernard spoke of the 'reproaches' made to the Purge by those who were 'excluded from the Feast' (a first distortion of the truth: in fact, no 'reproach' had been officially issued, and for good reason, by the legal methods of propaganda, the radio or the Press. One could merely point to certain appeals, more or less insistent, more or less urgent, for indulgence and moderation, even for a more serene justice—appeals emanating from personalities who were far from being 'excluded from the Feast', François Mauriac for example. At this time, towards the end of 1944, nonconforming opinion had absolutely no means of making itself heard). Then he took up the principal points of a previous argument about the illegitimacy of the Vichy Government and defined the concept of treason, the basis upon which rested the judgments of the High Court and the Tribunals. And finally he contrasted the relatively small number of the "Purged" with the innumerable victims of the extermination camps (as if purely quantitative values could alter the terms of a purely moral problem). He recalled certain hideous memories of the Occupation, mentioned two or three sinister figures of those overcast times and concluded by saying that 'the people of France demand that justice be done', that there were times when 'vengeance is holy'. He counselled those 'excluded from the Feast' to perform a loyal examination of conscience and make sincere recognition of their faults and errors, this being the only condition upon which, at some future date, when France should have bound up her wounds and forgotten her suffering, they might receive forgiveness and deserve to be reintegrated with the French community.

This leading article was not only ill-composed from the point of view of its dialectic. It was not only uncertain in its thought. It was above all stupid. 'By far the worst article Bernard has written,' François thought. 'How could he have forgotten himself so far as to write this low polemical stuff when, normally, he is so full of respect for others, so little of a sectarian, so very conciliating?' The most jarring thing about the article was a certain tone of 'I-am-on-the-right-side-of-the-barricades-and-I-have-therefore-the-right-to-speak'. (François remembered Catherine's fury: "You, the Righteous. . . .") This tone was the worst thing about the Press at that time: almost everyone adopted it, 'September Resistants', whose numbers were continually increasing, as well as the failures in politics or letters whose voices were raised in proportion to the sins for which they needed to be forgiven. Nevertheless, Bernard freely said of himself: "I have no Resistance complex," and it was true. "I'm like Daddy Gide," he used to say, too, "always prepared to abandon my own positions to become wedded to my opponent's." And François had to admit that in a large measure this was true too.

The article was stupid and disloyal because it omitted to differentiate between the people who had acted with the Germans, denounced their fellow countrymen and so on, and those who had stopped short at accepting the Marshal as the legitimate head of the country; between the very rare Frenchmen who had become Nazified and the very numerous Frenchmen who had accepted Vichy; between a young killer of the Gestapo and the boy who had enlisted in the Legion against Bolshevism out of political conviction. Bernard confounded all the categories, placed everyone in the same boat and labelled it 'the traitors'. This was a grossly dishonest thing to do, unworthy of him and of the paper he had founded.

Roland read aloud, declaimed rather: "We are tired of hearing the ex-collaborators, the ex-'patriotic' followers of the Marshal, who never flinched before the massacre of millions of Europeans, cry scandal at the execution of a few traitors. We have not the heart to pity the fate of Brasillach or the suicide of Drieu la Rochelle, because our pity goes in the first place, and in its entirety, to those whom Drieu and Brasillach dared to call 'terrorists'. The disproportion between the severities of the Purge and those of Buchenwald is too great—I mean to say that measured against the scale of the crime, the punishment is derisory. One has the right to expect a minimum of shame from those who are excluded from the Feast. Let them be silent, and in the silence of shame find the courage to look their errors and their faults in the face. One day France, having at last bound up her wounds, will know how to forgive those strayed sheep who have found once more the way of repentance and will permit them to be restored to their places in the national community."

"I'm suffocating!" Roland cried in a hoarse voice. "I'm suffocating!"

He ran to the window and opened it wide. The icy cold of the December evening rushed into the little, unheated room.

Suffocating, crimson in the face, Roland undid his shirt-collar. He was puffing like a man out of breath.

"Calm down, calm down, for goodness sake!"

"I'm suffocating! Let me get at the bastard and kill him like a dog!"

"Shut up. You're out of your senses. Shut the window. Sit down and relax."

"Leave me alone, Donadieu, can't you? I want to be angry! You're in league with the brutes, so leave me alone! Go and find them, go on. And you'd better warn Bernard. Because I've got something in store for him. . . . I've got something . . ."

The words seemed to stick in his throat. Unable to complete

the sentence, he dashed to the cupboard, opened it, and began searching frantically in a drawer. At last he brought out a little metal object and began brandishing it about.

"This is what I've got in store for him! And there are two bullets left, Donadieu. One for him and one for me. Oh, I've done well, bloody well, to keep this revolver. There are two bullets, Donadieu, I tell you: I'll put a hole in him, the brute! Jacques, you'll be avenged!" he cried, addressing the photograph.

Exhausted, he fell back into a chair. François was dismayed. 'He must have roused the neighbourhood,' he thought. 'What a business!' The strange scene had not frightened him because he knew too well the inordinate quality of Roland Oyarzun, his ridiculous but harmless bouts of violence, but it was none the less upsetting: it illustrated, on a sort of miniature scale which was half tragedy, half caricature, and doubtless on a rather low human level, the extent, the gravity of the moral abyss into which the country had fallen. For Roland Oyarzun was but one victim among thousands. There were more noble ones than he, but there were none more innocent. But, noble or not, they were tortured by the injustice done them. History could show many examples of social or moral sanctions imposed by a winning side upon their opponents; but the sanctions had never been so ignominious in character, nor outlawry so bitter and so implacable. At the same time, François remembered his conversation with Bernard, the allusion made to the Furies, the remark upon their timeless and subjective nature: "they are in ourselves", or "each of us has his own Furies." He remembered that he had said the phrase in obscure reference to Roland Oyarzun and his destiny.... The exterior world and its accidents only intervene in our lives as pretexts, they derive their reality only from the ghosts that haunt us. This man, collapsed there in the chair, this man with the mask of tragedy—his mouth hanging open, his eyes dilated—suggested some mysterious relationship between the life of the individual and the great events which cross his path. The fury which shook him was not the simple effect of fortuitous events, but the expression of its own profound truth, the eternal cry of the Furies; and the weapon he had brandished at an enemy, created out of his own imagination for the mere necessity of his cause, was not in reality directed at Bernard's death—Bernard was but the pretext, the exterior projection of another hatred, as secret as it was agonising, and which would never be known by its true name.

"Forgive me, Donadieu, forgive me," he said. "I've been making a ridiculous scene, and you're not responsible for any of this. All you've done is to come so kindly with Christmas presents for my daughters. . . . Forgive me."

The revolver, slipping from his hanging hand, fell to the floor. "Two bullets," he said again in a scarcely audible voice, "but I think I shall be too much of a coward to fire them."

PART TWO

CHAPTER I

THE YOUNG WARRIORS

From THIBAULT FONTANES, S.P. 5073, to Mademoiselle LORRAINE GUILLOT, Paris

November, 1944.

Dear friend,—I left rather hurriedly for the war and had no time to say goodbye to you. You know the very funny scene of Anne Vercors' departure in l'Annonce faite *à* Marie*? He's been thinking of going to the Crusades for ten years and suddenly, bang, he makes up his mind and leaves the same evening, direct for Jerusalem, having told his justly alarmed wife to prepare him a picnic basket. And note the fact that he can't wait one minute more. . . . Well, I enlisted two months ago pretty much as Anne Vercors did. To have done nothing for France suddenly seemed to me quite intolerable. I must add that being in the Army is much more amusing than being at the School of Administration, where I had to work for diplomas in Political Science. Politics interest me very much, but as for diplomas . . .*

We are out of breath from chasing the Germans. Unfortunately, they run faster than we do. They are a very perverse people. However, it appears that we have now caught them up and that we are shortly to make their acquaintance. The battalion I am with goes up to the line tonight. That is why I am hastily writing this note to you, in case I get killed. One must leave tender memories among one's friends.

The First French Army is a young and charming place, full of brave boys who have done all kinds of brilliant things in the maquis, the militia and so on. I am on friendly terms with a certain Philippe, an ex-policeman of the French Gestapo, who has appalling crimes on his conscience but is none the more proud for that. Anyway, I mean to say he hasn't attempted to deceive me, I who am as innocent as a lamb. He has told me dreadful stories with the utmost simplicity. For the rest, a first-class chap. He has complete trust in me, which I find slightly disquieting. He is convinced

I shan't betray him, and he's right, but it's a bit worrying all the same, don't you think? There is another traitor, with a name like an Alphonse Daudet choirboy. I'd take my oath he was a militia-man and have sworn to make him admit it one of these days. But don't be alarmed, most of the other soldiers are honest chaps, as sound as brass and French to the marrow: they become convulsed with masculine gaiety every time the Colonel tells them what it is that every patriot ought to have.[1] *Do you know that I am discovering France? Hitherto, I have only known the Plaine Monceau, a somewhat restricted area. My companions reveal to me Auvergne, Morvan, and the Pays Basque. Besides, I didn't know what a peasant, a metal-worker, or an odd-job man were like. Well, dear Lorraine, they're worth all our little friends put together. Cover your face, I'm becoming democratic.*

In short, this charming Army has taught me a lot. Notably from the point of view of vocabulary. I don't know why so much was kept hidden from me at school. Our secondary education needs reforming. It doubtless soon will be, the Fourth Republic seems so restless.

I would be grateful to you for some new books. We have a weekly paper here called Patrie, *respectable but a little trite. I read in the* Revue de Presse *the other day some extracts from articles signed Martin-Chauffier, Aragon, J.-P. Sartre, O. Bernard, etc. These gentlemen speak of man with a certain licking of the lips. Indeed, Man has been somewhat neglected since 1940. I see that a great number of journals and reviews are being launched and that the editorial battle is joined. I somewhat regret being far away from this vicious fermentation, which represents an abortive civil war. I should like to be in the first row of the stalls, even if I couldn't throw myself into the fight. Prevent Mauriac and Camus coming to blows, if you please, by representing to them that the Purge is a quite negligible incident, a mere froth on the margin of history on the march. I should hate to see these two great chaps grappling with each other for the sake of a few mere hundreds or thousands of victims. The others don't make so much fuss about it. They have grasped the fact that a firing squad is as good a way as another of debating with an adversary. The new slogan of Free French Radio: "Frenchmen are shooting Frenchmen."*

[1] *This esoteric passage is only comprehensible to men who have served in the Army. Do not, my dear friend, seek to interpret it.*

And by the way, "debating" in this sense is part of the new fashionable vocabulary—which is not exactly that of the First Army. One day, I shall make a little anthology of the language of our time: collaboration, resistance, presence (of), message (from) debate, purge, fraternity, weltanschaung, revolt, transcendence, justice, High Court, conscience (I perceive that certain juxtapositions clash a little), witness, and valid, well yes, valid. The terminology of the First Army is far more concrete.

You tell me delightful things about the secret night-clubs of the Left Bank. Who is Claude Luter? Of course jazz means nothing to me, either. So everyone drinks cocktails in cellars and disguises himself as a terrorist? It must all be great fun. In fact, those charming young people have mistaken their post-war period? So much the better. 1925 sounds a most delightful epoch, if one may believe certain good writers, such as Drieu la Rochelle.

Dear Lorraine, moriturus te salutat.

From the same to M. MICHEL DE BARS, Paris

Late November.

Dear Michel,—You ask me for a "detailed account of the taking of Remiremont". My word, you've become bellicose! In a student of the Polytechnic, it's far from normal, I promise you. You bloodthirsty tiger, I've already written an account of the affair to Lorraine. Go and ask her to read you my letter. It's odd: to Lorraine I talk of war, politics and literature. To you I'd rather talk of the latest fashions. Imagine me wearing a ravishing little military number, a two-piece, blouse and trousers, in khaki gaberdine, trimmed with all sorts of chevrons and lanyards in quite the smartest way, with side pockets, musketeer cuffs, V neck and wasp waist. A creation in the shape of a cap, given a swagger tilt over the right eyebrow, lends this soberly military outline a note of wit which is excessively French. Only the boots embarrass me a little. Alas, my bootmaker is the 43rd Light Infantry.

After all, I find I want to do something for the young, so I shall relate an episode of the Vosges campaign. It will give you nearly as great a thrill as reading about Tarzan—you still do read about Tarzan, don't you, my little Michel? Well, we went up the line in an icy first light, through a wonderfully Wagnerian forest, fir trees like enchanted paladins, bushes sculpted in frost. We progressed in a religious silence, only broken by the noise of the guns near at hand echoing among the "ballons". You know, of course, that the mountains of the Vosges are called "ballons". All the same, I emphasise the silence of our procession through the snow-laden undergrowth: this first assignation with death for several hundred boys of whom the eldest is, I believe, twenty-five. My company relieved another company which for two days had occupied a sort of wooded peak. The Germans were in position at the base of this peak and on every side, except the one by which we had come. After being given vague orders, we were distributed about the place. I fooled about all day, trying through the branches to locate the German positions six hundred feet below. The rain dripped from the branches as in one of Charles Trenet's songs. And when evening came, it was minen *that dripped on us. They're noisy engines of war. We took cover in sort of human burrows that our predecessors had dug the night before, and it was exactly as if we were sheathed in wet, icy clay. I am sensitive to damp and was in despair: supposing one spent the whole war catching colds! At length, towards midnight, I was sent on patrol with a corporal and another chap. A wire had been stretched six inches from the ground all round the peak. Attached to it were empty tins and other rattling things. A Sioux trick, you understand, to give the alarm should an enemy patrol think of adventuring in our direction. Naturally, I had forgotten the existence of the wire. Awkward as you know me to be, I tripped over the wire, releasing upon the night a tintinnabulation which filled my soul with legitimate fear. I took cover among the heather while the machine-guns came into action, the sub-machine-gun that I was clasping in one trembling hand went off of its own accord and the chaps down below replied—in brief, my dear boy, a hellish row, which did not fail to cause me considerable anxiety, since I was between two fires and the bullets were mewing about my ears like a thousand furious cats. Besides, I hate cats. In the violence of my quite understandable emotion, I had lost my spare magazines, a tiresome piece of thoughtlessness in the middle of a battle. A black mass fell down beside me, and I thought it was one of my companions on the patrol. Since he didn't move, I felt with my hand approximately where his face ought to have been—remember that the whole thing was taking place at night, under the pines, among bushes, heather and what have you. Well, it was wet, but not with rain. So I worked like a convict to drag this weighty sort of puppet up the hill, behind our entrenchments. And then I saw, from his helmet and his boots, that he was a German, dead too. When the hurly-burly was done, as they say in* Macbeth, *the battle was found to be neither won nor lost, and the night drew to a close without further incident.*

In your next letter, tell me what you think of J.-P. Sartre, supposing you think of him at all. I find the man stimulating, yes, stimulating. Goodbye.

From the same to LORRAINE GUILLOT

March, 1945.

Yesterday I set foot in Germany after having spent the night firing a few shots on the banks of the Rhine. So, the war is practically over. They say the Germans are hastily organising a secret Resistance movement, a maquis, *a werewolf, a Sainte Vehme. Really, they're a strikingly immoral people. Our democracies will shortly be crying in a scandalised way: what, a German* maquis*! Can one believe such devilish obstinacy? Eternal Germania! Tacitus was quite right. What can you expect, these people have already resisted the Roman conquest.*

The ex-policeman of the Gestapo, the Philippe about whom I once wrote to you, came to the most fantastic end in the Vosges, while we were resting: he was killed by a machine-gun while skiing. As night was falling we brought back a frozen corpse, his face rigid with cold and fury. I think you would have admired this David of the shadows, eternally raging upon his bed of snow. I could feel my shoulders shivering: I do not know whether it was death or beauty; both the one and the other, perhaps. We have had many soldiers killed during the course of the campaign: the honour of the regiment is safe.

Alphonse Daudet's little choirboy is well. He's wild with joy since we entered Germany. His face lights up at the news, whether true or false, of a Werewolf organisation. He doubtless plans to join it. He seems to be pondering some low mass, some black mass. Notwithstanding my esteem for the Militia—desperate Evil is always beautiful—I find his rejoicing rather disgusting.

We pass like a whirlwind through villages mute with horror.

They are neat, spring-like and funereal. From time to time, a boy with flat blond hair fires at us from a hedge or an attic window. We arrest him. Then he wakes from the long German dream, raises frightened eyes to us, recognises his defeat and takes refuge in tears. We give him chocolate.

I want to understand the meaning of this tragedy in which we are living—if it has a meaning, and I believe it has. The Marxists interpret it in terms of the social structure, the class war, the distribution of goods. The Fascists make a crusade of it, a war on a European scale. The Democrats, always a bit schoolmasterish, talk of Prussian greed and French humanitarianism, of freedom and despotism, and are prudently silent about the empire of the Czars. The Germans dreamed of an Apocalypse, they're such a catastrophic people, and believed themselves in a sort of Bayreuth raised to the power of n. *Of course all these interpretations contain part of the truth, but they don't coalesce, and I want a synthesis. For a long time past, I have thought that it was like the struggle between Sparta and Athens, between the "heroic" principle and the "humanistic" principle, but this agreeable manicheism does not take into account the third thief, the Czar. . . . Sparta, however, symbolises Germany fairly well: nationalism, the exalting of the body, the race, the blood, while helots were not lacking: Jews, foreigners. Nor were there lacking the politics of birth and eugenics. A certain Delphic delirium had to be added: Hitler as a pythoness, a prey to the Gods of Valhalla. The parallel between France and Athens appears less apt: the democratic chaos of the thirties recalls the Athenian popular front well enough, but M. Lebrun can only with difficulty be made to figure in the part of Pericles. In short, I renounce comparative History, and in any case it is not a discipline which has yet been recognised by the Sorbonne.*

I have been promoted Corporal. I don't hide my pleasure at it. I hope to finish the war as a sergeant-major. Ambition gnaws at my flank like a vulture.

Dear Lorraine, you are "devouring" Camus' Mythe de Sysyphe. *This frivolity saddens me. Why don't you read serious writers, such as Benjamin Constant, Mme de la Fayette, Valéry Larbaud. They will take you into a dimension that our contemporaries have ceased to explore: that of the heart. Besides such reading will go well with your delicious modern figure. When you feel the need for red corpuscles, read Retz, Bussy-Rabutin, Diderot. I salute you.*

From the same to MICHEL DE BARS, Paris

May, 1945.

Dear little boy, your observations on diplomacy have amused me very much. Anyway, if it amuses you to stamp passports and ply the French business-men of Santiago with champagne on the 14th of July, I certainly shall not try to stop you. But it does seem strange that, in this agonised world, amid these funeral marches, these avenging powers, this breaking of empires, this huge conflagration of falling gods, a nice little French boy should be soberly mugging up the examination for becoming attaché to an Embassy. Dear Michel, I'm very fond of you.

We are established in a somewhat ruined city, Stuttgart, from which, it so happens, the Americans are forever trying to turn us out. Alas, it is easier to expel the French from Stuttgart than the Russians from Berlin. My first day here was spent searching for my Company Office among the ruins. I saw a pretty horrible sight: in an air-raid shelter, a hundred feet below ground-level, were a dozen "suspects", German civilian prisoners. They were sweating with heat between the metal walls. A group of French soldiers was playing cards while guarding them. One of the Germans was barefooted, and his toes, my dear Michel, had no nails: the night before, one of our boys had amused himself cutting them out with his pocket-knife. It was an act of vengeance: last year he fell into the hands of the Militia and suffered the same treatment. War would be all very fine if it were all honour and no hatred. But where is the honour?

In the evening, after seeing this sight, I wandered alone about the streets. I could no longer stand the presence of my comrades, the officers, etc. In a brotherly way, a G.I. invited me to share a case of brandy he had found somewhere or other. I drank. He had been drinking more than I had and for much longer. The Americans become pugnacious in their cups. A French warrant officer having permitted himself to reprimand us ("the exhibition we were making of ourselves before the Krauts", and so on), the G.I. drew his revolver exactly as if he were in a saloon in Arizona. I do not know what impelled me—was it humanity, do you think? —to throw myself, a living shield, between the weapon and the warrant officer. Such is the folly of man. For, having come through a campaign unscathed, was it worth risking death for a sergeant-major? This Boy Scout valour resulted in a black eye and sundry bruises in the fight which followed. We succeeded in subduing the American. The warrant officer confiscated the brandy without leaving me a single bottle, which seemed to me to smack of the blackest ingratitude.

If I were to speak to you seriously, I should tell you that the disaster that has overtaken this nation never fails to move me, despite the chronicle of its crimes; that one sees the beautiful faces of children and girls like hostages among the burned-out ruins; that Siegfried's horn can still be heard by the poetic ear sounding in the Forest of Sillenburg; that the insolence of the young Frenchmen of the occupation, together with their kindness, forms a comedy at once gracious and cruel; that our smart young Army—the average age is twenty—marching through the gutted streets of this German Pompeii makes me dream of such childish things as the grandeur of France. . . .[1] *But I never do speak seriously to you, Michel, so I shall merely say: the occupation is going very well, we drink the wines of Wurtemburg and tease the Germans.*

You, apparently, are teasing yourself with Political Economy: each to his own taste, it takes all sorts to make a world. Take care of yourself.

From the same to LORRAINE GUILLOT

Late May, 1945.

You call me "eloquent and grave". I must doubtless translate this into: "discursive and pompous". Do you know that here I pass for a wit? Just at first, no one found me funny: I disconcerted, I displeased, I even sometimes irritated. Little by little, they began to understand and I must say, though my modesty suffers from it, that today there exists in my Company, if not in the Regiment, a sort of "Fontanes tone", though naturally much degraded. But let's leave it at that and lower the eyes.

Your photograph is beautiful. Thank you. I am shocked to hear that your father is in prison. He ought not to have come back so soon: after all, Switzerland is a hospitable country and its watchmakers live outside the times, which is very convenient. If my memory serves, your father was weak enough to sell a few lorries to the Wehrmacht. It's much less serious than if he had written five

[1] *There's a Fascist sentiment for you!*

lines for a newspaper of the Occupation. He'll come back to you, full of virile experiences and happy memories: the French prisons must be crowded with interesting people.

We had fireworks the other night. The war, so it appeared, was over. Tracer bullets tore across the velvet of the spring night. As a sign of our joy, we emptied our magazines upon the Milky Way. Then we swam in Wurtemburg wine and strong drink. It may be that this was not a very delicate way of welcoming the Armistice, but our period is not one for delicacy. It is true that in the afternoon we had saluted the colours in the Schlossplatz.

What more can I tell you? Huge posters, stuck up on the walls of the town, have revealed to us the existence of certain country resorts called Buchenwald, Dachau, Auschwitz. . . . With photographs to support them. We were staggered. This is a scandal that no brain in the world can assimilate. Moreover, we shall make haste to forget it. A religion can be built upon a crucified prophet, but not upon several million slaves burnt in crematory furnaces. We shall go on dancing and searching the map for a pleasant beach for our holidays. All the same, the topography of the camps creates a new dimension in our picture of the world: the dimension of fear. And we shall always feel that some blame more or less sticks to ourselves.

When they saw those posters, my companions reacted in the pathetic way children do. They spread, an undisciplined horde, through the houses of the district, breaking the furniture, tearing up family photographs, behaving in fact like vandals animated by a sacrilegious rage. God forgive me, I fear they molested a few old women and boys—the mothers and the rejects of the German male population, the only population of the city beside ourselves. This explosion of childish anger lasted two hours, after which the exhausted avengers went and slept. The next morning they revisited the devastated homes of the previous day: this time, their arms were laden with tins of food, they walked delicately on the tips of their toes, while their lips smiled their excuses. . . . They are French soldiers, French children. They're not disciplined. They're not well-behaved. Violence and charity take the place of education in them.

So, there has been no war in France. The High Constable de Gaulle has, with the utmost rectitude, turned a blind eye to it. The man is a prey to pious scruples: to admit the communists to the government, to have recourse to a plebiscite, these are generosities that will cost him dear. They'll cost him power. Last September the country needed a surgical operation. Instead, laxatives (the Purge) and poultices (the three-party system) were administered. It will therefore keep its boils and they'll suppurate horribly for years. We dreamed of being militant. We shall only be seditious. If action is denied us, we shall still have literature. Anyway, we shall always have our fun. This period suits me. We who are twenty owe nothing to anyone. We have the luck to belong to an innocent generation. And if our teeth are set on edge by the unripe grapes our fathers ate, well, there's a practical way of putting an end to it: that's to bite.

Goodbye, my beautiful. Whenever I think of you, I'm sorry that you should be a year older than I am and that you should always take me for a nice, rather shy schoolboy. I'm no longer a schoolboy, Lorraine, by God, I'm not. Six months' campaigning and the amenities of the Occupation favour growth. Goodbye. I long for longer letters.

From the same, The Palatinate, to MICHEL DE BARS, Paris

July 1945.

You should not go out so much with Lorraine, you exercise a detestable influence over her. She's an intelligent girl. Your snobbery is no good to her. It is true that she finds creatures of your sort, when used in moderation, refreshing: from time to time nature does not abhor a vacuum. You must be a good companion to swim with at Molitor or dance with in night-clubs. In fact, you've got quite a passable figure. But remember that my shoulders have broadened in six months, and that I don't do the crawl too badly either. All this is to suggest that you might very conveniently hunt elsewhere. There is no lack in your circle of good-looking young ladies. There are even some with titles, an additional attraction to which a future diplomat should not be insensible. Besides, we all know that a coat of arms makes you . . . I was going to be coarse . . . that a coat of arms puts you into a state of exaltation. So, you leave Lorraine alone. I have a weakness for that well-bred commoner.

We linger indolently in the Palatinate, a rich country of vines and flaxen-haired, chubby peasant girls. I wear shorts all day and stuff myself with grapes. I shall not say what I do at night. I have been put into the quartermaster's department. God and our Colonel alone knows why. The battalion has never been so ill equipped. The other day I was peacefully reading Bernanos in the office with my feet on the table when my chief stalked silently in; there's something quite feline about that man. "When you have finished reading," he murmured, "you might perhaps occupy yourself with issuing the battalion with white gaiters." I leapt to my feet and replied, blushing: "Certainly, I could." "You have, of course, taken note of the order about it?" "It has not escaped me, sir. I found it most moving. . . ." "What's more, we shall have to get rid of three tons of odd clothing we've been dragging round with us for the last six months. There's all sorts of stuff among it: coats from the Youth Camps, horizon blue greatcoats, red trousers. . . ." "I didn't suppose we were going to lug the whole shop all the way to Tokio. . . . Supposing we distributed the uniforms to the Germans as souvenirs?" He didn't even smile. He looked at me suspiciously. "You're going to be demobilised in a few days," he went on. "We shall all be able to breathe again. Have you been wounded? Or mentioned in dispatches?" Myself, suavely: "No, sir; I'm intact: neither mentions nor wounds." He imperceptibly shrugged his shoulders and pursued the conversation no further. You see, so much candour annihilates them.

De Lattre de Tassigny is absolutely incredible. The profile of a condottiere, *the ostentation of Louis XIV, the pride of Napoleon and the capriciousness of Caligula. One trembles before him. He makes the generals get into shorts and run the hundred yards on the sports ground at dawn. I should like to see those large, starred behinds shivering with cold and humiliation in the morning dew. But I wake up at ten o'clock and have my breakfast in bed. De Lattre is very kind to the other ranks. He must be a democrat after all.*

So, you see, I think I shall be seeing you again very soon.

The same to LORRAINE GUILLOT, Paris

August, 1945.

I have told you that nearly every evening I go to see an extremely beautiful and virtuous young woman called Inge. She lives in a charming little villa on the high ground behind the town and lives in terror of a neighbouring company of Moroccan Goumiers. (And, indeed, those chaps with their shaved heads are frightening enough, in spite of their long, striped woollen robes which at a distance give them the appearance of characters out of the Bible). Inge's husband is a prisoner of the Russians. She receives me in evening dress and with considerable ceremony—careful to give a Frenchman the most impressive picture possible of German good manners. She is a fanatical Nazi and she has not concealed from me (the strange way people always confide in me!) that she suffers a hundred deaths since "l'écroulement de son rêve"*—those are her actual words: "now that my dream is shattered". I forgot to say that she talks to me in English. I suspect her of hating us, myself first, and above all, of ferociously despising us: the French are filthy monkeys, hardly less savage than their African mercenaries. . . .*

But her contempt does not prevent her from accepting my presents of cigarettes, tins of food and Nescafé. We argue calmly with each other, scratching each other dexterously, like two civilised wild beasts—she, adjusting a wry smile upon her beautiful, angelic, wicked face; I, though my heart is often bursting with anger, maintain a serene expression while I gently utter extremely complicated insults. And do you know what powers confront each other in these daily battles? Quite simply, France and Germany, Democracy and Fascism. The funniest thing about it is that I represent Democracy. And with conviction.

The other night she overwhelmed me with the Hiroshima bomb. She was triumphant. "Well, well!" she said. "You blame us for having let a few thousand Europeans die in concentration camps during four years of war. But you Democrats do much better than that: you atomise two hundred thousand Japanese in three seconds."

What could I answer? I had not foreseen this poser.

How has Hiroshima been "taken" in Paris?

So, we who are twenty and, unlike our immediate elders, suffer from no complexes, have got to attend to serious things, have we? What a bore!

And yet, no, it isn't a bore. I rather think it may be amusing. Oh, how I long to be in Paris and to be able to give you a kiss. I have exhausted the "experience" of the army. (There, I'm expressing myself like our immediate elders. . . .) Is it true that Bernanos has returned from Brazil? Is it true that Maurras is in prison? Is it true that royalist students were demonstrating on the Boulevard Saint-Michel the other day? God, how strong I feel, and how I long to be confronted with this new world!

Ever yours. . . .

CHAPTER II

THIS NEW WORLD

1

"War is very agreeable," said Thibault Fontanes to himself, "but how comfortable one is at home!" Feeling chilly, he drew the skirts of his dressing-gown about his calves and sank into an armchair. The little electric fire dispensed a miserly warmth. In this winter of 1945, there was still no wood, no coal, hardly enough to eat and no strong drink. But Thibault appreciated the softness of his dressing-gown even though it had become too tight for him and too short: he had grown during the German campaign. . . . He had grown and lived splendidly: that holiday time among the snows of the Vosges with interludes of little battles of which, like Fabrice at Waterloo, one never saw more than a tiny corner; these forced marches in Alsace where war with a face of terror crawled from the shattered cellars; the wild joy of the break into Germany, that saraband of festivity and foulness; then the young conquerors entering the great ruined city, as silent as a necropolis. There were too, of course, those things of which one did not speak: the pride of belonging to this smart French army, of having blotted out an embarrassing memory (the disaster of 1940), and those noble, childish feelings which give you an odd sensation in the pit of the stomach. But with the summer all this began to drag a little. Thibault quickly exhausted both people and things. He had absorbed all that was charming and vivifying in a soldier's life. He had garnered its absurdities. Now, he could only see the mess, the stupidity and the futility. From the beginning of August it had already begun to be a tiresome routine, in which you were compelled to be constantly busy with grotesque chores such as, for instance, blancoing gaiters or cleaning a rifle which had become quite useless since the Armistice and the atomic bomb. But the sergeant-major insisted that one should continue polishing a weapon which had now become as medieval as an arquebus. It was intolerable. Even the evenings with Inge ended by becoming a bore: that courteous quarrel, always the same, which every evening went round its appointed circle. Thibault almost wished that Inge might be raped by the Goums. In the first place, he would have had the pleasure of rescuing her; in the second, it would have taught the obstinate German that the mercenaries of the great democracies are not quibblers and casuists. In brief, Thibault welcomed demobilisation with enthusiasm.

What now remained of that year of war? Well, a great deal of pleasure, an increased knowledge of the world and humanity, two or three wonderfully romantic memories. "Transform as much experience as possible into knowledge", to which Thibault added: "Don't forget to be happy even when you are doing your duty, or pretending to do it", which was both more fecund and more Stendhalien.

On the table beside him were a pile of newspapers and reviews: the liberated Press. Through them Thibault breathed in the odour of the new world which had just been born—it was barely three months old—in the great fireworks of Hiroshima. The judges were sitting at Nuremberg, since in modern wars generals become criminals the moment they are defeated. The old Marshal was imprisoned in a fortress in the valley of Aspe, while Thorez and Marty were relieved of national disgrace, brought out of pawn, carried to power. Laval tried to poison himself in his prison cell. However, he was restored to life and the stake. "Shoot the living!" The Communists demanded the portfolios of War, Home and Foreign Affairs, but de Gaulle was not prepared to give them to them. It was all very interesting. Thibault had happy moments. Sometimes he interrupted his reading to write a few lines in a notebook open upon his knees; then, an expression of malice crossed his moody schoolboy face. He smiled with real pleasure when he read an editorial by Mauriac on Pierre Hervé, and another of Camus. "*The perilous honour of presenting the young intellectual Communist to the eyes of the profane, I was about to write of the idolatrous, has fallen to the lot of M. Hervé. Each week, this clever young man does his turn before the footlights with so much specious argument that we can no longer see the leash at whose end he dances and whose other end is held in the wings by the firm hand of the Party. Yet yesterday's contribution was so brilliant that I cannot resist the pleasure of giving M. Hervé a little praise. . . .*" Or "*M. Camus, as we know, rolls his little weekly rock on the first page of* Combat. *Sysiphus has voluntarily condemned himself to the ultimate torture: journalism. He performs his vain labours with a perfect dignity of tact and tone, with a somewhat formal eloquence. This child of exuberant Latin Africa, transplanted to Paris, will not completely let himself go before us Nordics. Nevertheless, not long ago, he was singing the nuptials of earth and sun with a Barrés-like lyricism.*" Thibault took a *Combat* from the pile of newspapers and read: "*We must submit to the evidence, our society tolerates executioners better than it does victims. The first, indeed, arouse only our fear and hatred, the second demand our pity. The ghosts of Buchenwald and Auschwitz scandalise us, when all we ask is to be happy at last and to forget.*" Thibault read the article through to the end with somewhat restrained enthusiasm. True, he judged Camus' thought and prose to have a noble perfection, but tonight he was more in the humour for laughter than nobility. Perhaps Sartre would be more stimulating. Thibault took up an edition of *Temps Modernes*. It was really very kind of Michel to have kept all the newspapers and reviews that might interest his friend. "Like this, in a few hours' reading, you'll be able to learn everything that's been done, said or written during this last year while you've been at the war." A kindly thought. "*The war has ended in anguish,*" wrote Sartre, "*because the end of the war is also the end of hope. For four years we awaited the Liberation, and it was simply a matter of holding out till then. Today it is a question of living in a world that has lost all its traditional vindications, and whose very foundations have been destroyed. The war has been fought immediately for those small provinces of the world known as France, England and Germany, but they know that they count for nothing in the conflict between the two huge empires which confront each other. The war is over, but the little bomb dropped on Hiroshima makes it plain that, as with civilisation, the human race itself is mortal. So are the last ramparts of our faith destroyed: we have no longer the right to speculate about the future of Mankind. Already deprived of religious hope, the last rags of a humanist faith have been torn from us. The war has not only destroyed our cities, it has destroyed our last illusions: our helplessness is complete at last and, by the same measure, our freedom is limitless.*" Thibault admired the way the philosopher associated the extremes of freedom with the extremes of necessity: that he had thus been able to declare that the French had never been so free as under the German occupation. Since his return, Thibault had read all the works of Sartre's he had been able to get hold of. He was delighted with the writer's superb rhetoric, and sometimes a little irritated. Reading Sartre was as invigorating for the mind as a run was for the body. While those works which are described as "action stories" and considered healthy for the young, Thibault was never able to get through them. In the Army a friend had lent him a book called *Hommes et Glaciers*. On returning it, Thibault had said, "It has charm and excitement, but, you know, this business of climbing mountains, as far as I am concerned. . . . I get giddy six feet off the ground." Sartre, on the other hand . . . God, how clever the man was, and how nice it would be to be able to confute him! Because, of course, Thibault was far from being in agreement on all points with the official philosopher of the régime. And if it came to that, the régime. . . . Thibault remembered the Popular Front; he had only been a child at the time, but he had preserved certain memories: the strikers crowding the streets, the occupied factories (particularly M. Fontanes' own), his father's indignation at dinner, the drama of the 6th of February re-enacted by the children in the school yard. . . . No, no. Thibault felt himself to be conservative to the marrow. After all, Joan of Arc and St. Louis have a different aura from la Passionaria and Maurice Thorez. France (he thought) was a beautiful country beloved of God, a beautiful country full of cathedrals, poets and conscripts in red trousers, and it imposed its laws and its fashions upon the rest of the world. The sad incompetents of the Third Republic had made of it a conquered nation. Happily, a great pole of a man, with an unpleasant face and awkward gestures had arisen and recovered a quality that the boys of Thibault's age cruelly missed: honour. Not *all* the boys, no: a few, a small number of difficult cases. . . . Another review, *Horizons*. Who was this O. Bernard? His articles exasperated Thibault, who could not bear the non-Communist left. The Communists, he thought, were logical, and so were the men who, during the war, had enlisted in the anti-Bolshevik Legion. The Militiamen were logical in their sinister way. So were the Nihilists. (Besides, were not the Militiamen Nihilists in the last analysis?) But Thibault refused all logical consistency to the non-Communist Left. 'They talk of principles while the Communists talk of the proletariat and of the Revolution, Maurrassiens, of the *pays réel* and the monarchy, and the Fascists, of force and of blood. The proletariat, the Revolution, the *pays réel*, force and blood are concrete things for which it may be logical to fight. But the humanitarian principles of the Left are so many foggy abstractions,' Thibault thought. Besides, they were a pretty ridiculous lot on the whole, with their spectacles and their floppy collars. A young Communist is not ridiculous—indeed, he may be the reflection of historical necessity. A Militiaman is not absurd, he may be the reflection of tragedy itself. But a humanitarian usher *is* ridiculous. Much could be forgiven Sartre, because he was so wonderfully talented, so superbly the rhetorician. But M. Bernard, Thibault could not forgive. The article he had happened to come upon was an old one. It dated from 1944 and dealt with collaborators. 'It would be difficult,' Thibault thought, 'to be at once more idiotic and more cynical.' As he read, counter-arguments sprang to his lips: 'I must write an answer to this, even if I can find no one to publish it,' he thought. He took up another, more recent paper, and his eye fell upon the announcement of a competition: Grey's Pills (for liver trouble) asked their readers to find a good commercial slogan for them. Thibault looked up the firm's telephone number in the directory and lifted the receiver.

"Hullo, is that Messrs. Grey? I want the advertising department. Hullo? I'm ringing you about your slogan competition. I've found one for you." He raised his voice: "Take Grey's Pills, they resisted."

He hung up as his uncle came into the room.

"Who resisted?" he asked.

"It's a joke. I'm in process of educating myself, Georges. And well, old man, it's a hell of a Press and a hell of a Republic. The Liberation was already absurd enough in certain ways, but I thought that, after a year, things would have begun to get a bit organised."

"The puritanism of the young warrior."

"Sit down. You're still a warrior, and I'm sure you still preserve the puritanism of your twentieth year."

Thibault was very fond of his uncle, "even though you are a bloody soldier," he used to say, "and a bloody professional soldier at that." Captain de Montmort had courteous manners, an air of youth and of Saint-Cyr, and a charming smile. In Thibault's eyes he had the very rare merit, or so the young man thought, of being at once a man of action and a scholar, of combining courage and culture. And, indeed, the hero had read everything. "In fact," his nephew used to say, "you are the only Maurrassien I know who has read Maurras from end to end." And lastly, he was, as was Thibault himself, infatuated with General de Gaulle, on whose staff he had been since his return to France. Thibault was never tired of hearing this young uncle of his with the greying temples tell the story of London during the war: it became a thrilling sort of serial. The rivalries between the General's first companions, who were politically nearly all to the Right, and the envoys of the interior Resistance movement, who on the whole were much more to the Left, the difficulties over Admiral Muselier and his final eviction, the life of the Central Office of Information, the organisation of which Georges de Montmort had been a member from the beginning and which recruited many of its members from the extreme Right (Georges had met in it old friends who were ex-Camelots du Roi) up till July, 1942, at which time important jobs were given to the Socialists, the rivalry between a diversity of political tendencies and interests, the General's moments of impatience, his moods, his tiffs with the British Government, the stir (enthusiasm among some, uneasiness among others) caused by the adherence of the Communist Party in 1943—the whole rather complicated political saga entranced Thibault, it was as full of colour, as alive as the *Memoires* of Cardinal de Retz, "and nearly as realistic," added the young man, but this last remark was doubtless only intended as a joke. . . . His uncle told the story well, with liveliness and precision, and sometimes with an ingenuousness which the nephew found rather touching: 'It's the old campaigner's, the out-of-date student's, side to his character,' he thought. 'I'm older than he is, more sophisticated. . . .'

"In fact, Georges, you think as I do that the Fourth Republic should have a new motto? For example: Liberation, Purgation,

Restriction. . . . Or perhaps, Resistentialism, Existentialism, Directionism, since terminations in 'ism' are so fashionable, and so happily effective too. . . ."

"All the same, one shouldn't criticise too much. There are some things that are all right, and some men too. Malraux is all right. And de Gaulle. . . ."

"Wait! We'll award them marks. Let's consider everything that's happened in the past year, both men and events, and award them marks from nought to twenty. Honour to whom honour is due: De Gaulle?"

"Nineteen and a half."

"Too generous. His manner of pardoning Pétain has done him harm in my opinion. I give him sixteen. Malraux? I give him nineteen. You agree? Very well. We'll compromise with seventeen. The Communist Party?"

"Ten out of twenty."

"I give them fifteen for cunning and opportunism, eighteen for courage, nought for candour, which is on the whole a fair distribution."

"The Constituent Assembly?"

"Seven out of twenty. Sartre?"

"Three."

"You're hard on him. I like that man. He's intelligent, you know. He's got rather fewer ideas than Léon Blum, but he's intelligent. I give him sixteen. By the way, do you know a certain Bernard?"

"The editor of *Horizons*? I saw him once or twice in London."

"What sort of chap is he?"

"The aristocratic Jew, elegant, thoroughbred, assimilated. Before the war his father owned a weekly Radical-Socialist review called *Germinal*, in which people like Cassou wrote."

"A type you hate, don't you?"

"A type I did hate, as you know very well!" Georges said with a frank laugh. "But since then I've changed my point of view. My Maurrassisme has become more tolerant. For instance, I'm no longer anti-Semitic. I never was fanatically so, mark you, but after what we've seen, it's become absolutely untenable."

"Of course! So this Bernard is j. decent, is he?"

"You say 'j. decent' today, do you? You must teach me the schoolboy slang of 1945. I'm sure you no longer say 'spiffing'?"

"No, we say 'sensational' or 'wizard'. But I must inform you that I am no longer a schoolboy. What about Bernard?"

"Well, yes, I think he is all right. From what I've heard, he behaved very well in the *maquis*. He's plucky enough."

Thibault repressed a smile: "plucky" was typical of his uncle's vocabulary. He had said it in a simple, manly way, with an undertone of admiration, of loyal esteem. . . . Good old Georges! It was charming of him to have preserved, at thirty-seven, some of his boyish simplicity, without being any kind of a fool for it.

"He's plucky, is he? I'm delighted. I would rather attack an adversary who is both plucky and elegant."

"An adversary?"

"I tell you I very much want to get my claws into this estimable Bernard. His articles annoy me. How old is he?"

"About thirty, I think."

"He's not too old, then. Do you know if he was writing before the war?"

"I don't know at all, but if you're interested I'll ask one of my friends who used to know Bernard well and who should be able to give me the information you want."

"That would be kind of you. I'll tell you another time what I want to do."

And indeed, a fortnight later, furnished with all the necessary documents (he had found more than he had dared to hope), Thibault wrote an article in a few minutes and asked his uncle to listen to it while he read it aloud:

"*The National Library is an admirable institution. The other day I found there several numbers of a rare, confidential little review which were published two or three years before the war. This review, called* Méduse, *contained among other things several poems by a certain M. Bernard, of which here are a few verses:*

> "*Larbins du Caudillo, évêques franquistes,*
> *C'est encore trop d'honneur qu'on vous fait,*
> *De vous fusiller,*
> *C'est un service qu'on vous rend,*
> *Car sans le martyre vous n'iriez pas au Ciel,*
> *Au ciel des culottes de peau et des peaux de vache,*
> *Au ciel des vieilles badernes et des chats-fourrés,*
> *De Tartuffe et de Basile,*

De Mac-Mahon et de Déroulède,
Nous vous y enverrons franco de port,
Avec ce porc de Franco et tous les Caudillos de la terre,
Avec tous le colonels et les duchesses de droit divin,
Et l'idéal chrétien auquel vous feignez d'aspirer,
Aspirateurs O'dare-dare de la France éternelle,
Avec les Académiciens, les Archontes, les Archidiacres
Et les Archicons des lignes Nationalistes,
Tous les patriotes avec leurs patries,
Arriba España on gesta Dei per Francos,
Et tous les pères franc-coquins du sabre,
Des autels at des Banques.
Avec cette patrie qui nous fait horreur,
Et que nous nous jurons bien de déserter
Quand on l'attaquera.

"*They are a somewhat naïve expression of his Popular Front period of 1937, nor are they of an exquisite delicacy, but rather evidence of a certain ill nature which could at a pinch pass for revolt if one does not look at them too closely. Eight years pass, the tone has changed and the song too:*

" '*One day, France, having at last bound up her wounds, will know how to forgive those who strayed, but have found the way to repentance and will consent to reintegrate them with the community.*'

"*That is still M. Bernard speaking.*

"*This would be a mere trifle if M. Bernard today were not in a position to exercise a leadership of a new kind in a weekly paper of some importance: the leadership of the resistentialist intelligentsia. In this capacity, I imagine, M. Bernard is read by numbers of jerseyed schoolchildren and good young undergraduates who believe in all good faith that they are acquiring the precious gift of the most 'advanced' French thought.*

"*We know very well the moral type to which M. Bernard belongs. He flourished through those delightful years between the wars, the years of the charleston and surrealism. He is the anarch-Socialist, the sort of inverse equivalent of Déroulède. Of the various intellectual absurdities of the period, this is the most out of date, I mean the most venerable, with a sort of after-taste of Gavroche and Louis Michel, somewhat soured from long soaking in the brackish juice of anti-clericalism. In the end we relegated this ridiculous scarecrow to the attics with much other lumber of our bourgeois childhood. But these cast-offs have come to life again: galvanised by some extraordinary miracle, they have become resistentialist.*

"*The men and boys whom M. Bernard condemns to shame thought they were serving their country by obeying a leader whom practically the whole of France still revered on the eve of the Liberation. This is not the place to defend Marshal Pétain. Perhaps he was a perfidious old man and these men and boys were cruelly duped by him or his ministers. We should extend our hand in mute affection to these brothers less happy than ourselves.*

Bernard counsels them to feel ashamed.

"*Up till the moment war was declared, M. Bernard did his best to ruin the prestige and strength of his country with a thousand, thousand pinpricks, and if his individual actions remained insignificant, it was through no lack of perseverance, but rather through lack of intelligence. A single bacillus cannot affect the health of an organism. A million bacilli can destroy it. M. Bernard was one of these untiring bacilli whose concerted action achieved, in 1939, the transformation of France into an anti-nationalist nation, and the French, with a few exceptions, into those rabbits the Germans chased before them playing a mouth-organ.*

"*We have no hate for the anarchist-Socialist, but we love logic; and when we see M. Bernard, who scoffed yesterday at the mere idea of country, setting himself up today as a professor of patriotism, our sense of logic is offended. But incoherence is the last thing to trouble these dynamiters of God and Country who have been converted to the cult of Man and have become in a trice humanitarian terrorists.*

"*At about the same time that M. Bernard was writing the poem given above, Bernanos was publishing his terrible indictment:* Les Grands Cimetières sous la Lune. *He, too, was stigmatising the Spanish bishops who were accomplices to Franco's purge. 'Whatever may have been the true origins, still so obscure, of the Civil War, it taught us nothing about the men of disorder that we did not already know. But, on the other hand, it has thrown a prodigious light upon the morality of the men of order.'*

"*One can see that Bernanos has style. M. Bernard has nothing but vulgarity.*

"Come back, Bernanos, to judge the judges, to judge the 'men of disorder' who will bear before history the responsibility for the French purge of 1944-5. It is time your great voice came to pulverise our little scribblers."

When the reading was over, Georges remained silent for some moments. Then he took his pipe from his mouth and said:

"As a whole, it's good. Everything you say is true, but I make one reservation: it's perhaps rather too solemn. You see, it's heavy artillery and the target's not worth it. You're using a 15-inch gun to shoot a badger or a weasel. Bernard and his article doesn't really count for much in the world of today, you're giving them too much importance."

"Bernard is a pretext. What is important is not so much his article as the state of mind that it implies."

"No doubt, but your reply is too weighty. Your conclusion for instance, that vocative, that invocation. Too solemn! You must make it all lighter. I should like you to write as you talk: by fits and starts, incisive little phrases, an odd, original manner at first sight. Write sarcastically! You should be able to succeed very well with a humorous style, an off-hand manner, with insolence as pointed as a banderilla. The best thing in your reply is the part that comes immediately after Bernard's poem, the whole paragraph about the 'moral type who is contemporary with the charleston', and the one about the cast-offs coming to life and so on. All that's first class. After that you become too serious!"

"But, Georges, I am terribly serious."

"I know. But the only thing is that the most effective way for you to be serious is to preserve a certain lightness of touch."

Thibault thought for a moment.

"You know, my dear uncle, you're not a bad critic. . . ."

"You recognise it now, do you? And another thing, what are you going to do with this answer? To publish it at this moment is, of course, out of the question: no paper would accept it."

It was true. Thibault had five copies typed and sent them to five papers. One of them returned the article in forty-eight hours as if it burnt their fingers. To it was affixed a courteous but firm rejection. Another replied with threats and insults. From the three others no more was heard.

Several months elapsed. Thibault was absorbed by two matters of varying importance: a novel he had begun in the Army and his love for Lorraine Guillot. This love of his suffered certain frustrations, due principally to the fact that Lorraine seemed to divide her affections between Thibault and a friend of Thibault's, Michel de Bars, a charming boy who was both attractive and extremely rich. Thibault consoled himself with writing his masterpiece. With all this he spent a winter so variously rich in emotion that he hardly noticed that General de Gaulle had resigned—an event to which he would not have been insensible three months earlier. Towards the end of May, 1946, he received a letter, signed Henri Marcellin: "Sir, chance and an old friendship have brought to my notice an article of yours entitled *Our Scribblers*. You intended it for publication. I have, therefore, not thought it indiscreet to read it and have it read by my friends. You would be surprised by the reception it has received. I know neither your age, your faith, nor your beliefs, but it gives me great pleasure to salute both your courage and your talent. I should indeed be very happy to have the opportunity of meeting you." Thibault knew who Marcellin was. He had heard his Uncle Georges, who had known Marcellin round about 1925, when they were young together, talk of him: they were both the age of the century and lived in the same world. The Occupation had separated these old friends, sending one to London with General de Gaulle, and the other to Vichy with Maurras. Marcellin had published two books during the Occupation, *La France dans la Tourmente*, an objective account of the defeat, and *Perspectives Européennes*, an essay in political philosophy whose title sufficiently implied its tendencies. Published in the southern zone, the book was withdrawn from circulation when the Germans took over the whole country. That is to say that if, in its main outlines, it appeared to be in accord with the contemporary orthodoxy, its tone was nevertheless sufficiently liberal and some of its conclusions sufficiently ambiguous to shock the occupying power. Marcellin owed his relative security to the protection of an old friend of his who was a high functionary in the Government. At the Liberation, he had some trouble with the Tribunals dealing with the purge (the destiny of some men of this century irrevocably evokes the tribulations of Candide), but escaped the arm of the law.

Thibault thought that it would be amusing to bring together

at the dinner table both Marcellin and Georges de Montmort, those two ex-Maurrassiens of whom one had apostatised (Marcellin had previously looked upon Georges as a renegade). But his uncle refused the invitation.

"I don't blame Marcellin," he said. "I know him well enough to know that his integrity is above suspicion. He thought he was doing his duty as I thought that I was doing mine. Unfortunately, our conceptions of duty are at variance. Nevertheless, before meeting him, I should like to be assured that he forgives me my loyalty to General de Gaulle as I forgive him his to Marshal Pétain. Nothing, however, can be less certain than that. The rancour of a man such as Marcellin must be strong enough to sap his friendships as soon as it becomes a matter of opposite ideologies. The worst feature of our contemporary quarrels is that everything is sacrificed to the urge to be right, to rancour or to the sorrow of defeat."

Thibault was charmed by Marcellin from the first. He had been afraid of meeting a bitter man, an "untouchable" conscious of proscription and whose susceptibilities must be carefully considered. But he recognised that he had to deal with a rather jovial sort of elderly undergraduate, rather bohemian in his clothes and manner, one of those people who live on the perimeter of society and its rules, or at least of its bustle: Marcellin appeared to have infinite leisure, and to have preserved from his student days (of which he spoke with nostalgia, as of a golden age forever lost) the wonderful faculty that boys have of accompanying each other home an indefinite number of times while prolonging into the dawn the combined pleasures of walking and discussion. Despite his physical ugliness or, perhaps, in part due to it, he was attractive, 'as must have been Socrates,' thought Thibault. He spoke very fast, with a jerky, rather feverish delivery, and his hoarse voice stumbled over words owing to his great haste to express himself. Then his eyes would light up, the corners of his mouth curve, while he stopped abruptly, seizing his companion by the sleeve, shaking his arm, and staring straight into his eyes as if the better to convince him; after which, having delivered himself of the final climax of his argument in an explosive voice, he rushed on, pressing the pace, his head drawn down between his shoulders, like a man who is conscious of having had the last word and can expect no worthwhile reply.

Thibault was very amused by his manner and by his impetuous, spontaneous oratory.

"We were staggered by your article—that's to say, some friends of mine and myself. You see, it's the first time we have read anything that seems to have any virility about it. I mean, they were the words of a free man and, God knows, freedom of thought today is no more than a phrase, a fiction, a memory, isn't that so? Yes, I know, you're going to quote Mauriac, of course, he protests, he defends us, he does what he can to spare us, but in fact, honest though he may be, he went into alliance with the others, you see, he's entangled in their lies, he could not have told Bernard what he thought of him as you could with your freedom and your style—mark well that I have no rancour against Bernard, after all he is only playing up to his part in trying to justify the purge and one must not forget that he has very likely suffered a good deal, himself or his relations, from Vichy and the Germans. One can understand his feelings, if one cannot agree with his point of view—but, after all, there were truths that needed saying, basic truths, about that anarchical Left which but yesterday made no small contribution to sapping the morale of the French, to destroying French patriotism, and which today, with its Resistentialism, imposes a rigorous Jacobinism—in short, there exists, as you say, a section of philosophy called Logic, though no one dares remember it, and that is why your article has made us literally enthusiastic, it produced the effect upon us of a gust of fresh air blowing away the miasmas of this poisonous period. And the fact that you are young is so wonderful, I thought at first that the author of the article was a man of my own age, a man in the same boat as I am, too, yet, not at all, you're twenty and one of the young warriors from that First Army which, quite frankly, and I mean this, nearly reconciles me to General de Gaulle, because in short, that army is the youth of France, the future of France, and, good God, it purges no one, judges no one, and doesn't write in the newspapers, but is content to win battles and add another page to the history of France, so, you see, if there is one thing to which a man of my age and persuasion is sensitive, it is certainly heroism, in short, I mean to say to everything that can give the country back some of its prestige and grandeur—mark well that I am utterly persuaded that the Resistance counted among its members a good number of wonderful fellows, merely consider the pluck, the superhuman courage needed to stand up to torture—I cannot approve of them, because I cannot approve of dissidence, you see, as far as I am concerned, Pétain represented legitimate authority, I shan't yield on that point, and everything that was done against that authority was nothing but rebellion and subversion, I therefore cannot approve their actions, but I have the right to admire their virtues—but, well, the only thing is that the greater part of those magnificent fellows are dead, and the people who make the laws today are those who had enough sense to avoid danger and enjoy the moral and material benefits conferred upon them by the blood others spilt—never has history shown a more striking example of 'faith degraded into politics' and what politics!"

The legitimacy of the Vichy Government was the pivot about which Marcellin assembled his argument. The ambassadors of foreign powers, he said, had remained accredited to the Government, which was a proof that they considered it legitimate. The civil servants who obeyed the Vichy Government should not be prosecuted, because that which is done under the orders of the legitimate authority is itself legal.

Thibault was not much impressed by this rather too juridical argument. At bottom, it mattered very little to him whether the vote of the National Assembly on the 10th July, 1940, were legal or not, whether the delegation of constituent power by the National Assembly were legal or not, or whether the Vichy Government were a legal government or merely the fictional creation of a pronunciamento. In that particular domain, he thought, in those particular historical circumstances, principles counted for less than emotions: it was better to defend the honour of France than some principle or method of procedure. He said so to Marcellin.

"But, my dear boy, you must understand that's the whole point!" he cried without realising how familiarly he was addressing Thibault. "You must understand that if one holds the principle of legitimacy to be unimportant, everything falls to the ground, there is no more government and no more nation, there is even no more society! The Resistance has created a terrible and perhaps mortal precedent: because, if one allows the individual to be the judge of the honour or interest of the nation, any form of rebellion becomes permissible, the Communists can later on commit every kind of sabotage in the name of the Communist interest, the colonial populations will have the right to rebel against us in the name of independence—and if those things should happen, by virtue of what principle, may I ask, will the Resistants of today be able to blame them? A protestantism much more grave than religious Protestantism is being instilled into the nation—you talk of honour, my dear friend, and I am grateful to you for uttering the word, it suits both your youth and your character, but I pray you to reflect a moment, I pray you to reflect a little upon the character of the adherence to the Resistance, which, in short, was as follows: a handful of men about General de Gaulle on the 18th June, 1940, then a new contingent after Montoire, then the whole of the Communist Party in a block in June, 1941, after the Russo-German declaration of war, and then others who joined during 1943 and 1944—so, my dear chap, I ask you: at exactly what date does the honour of having resisted begin or end?—no, you see it's a sophism, without taking into account the fact that the notion of honour can be indifferently applied, I mean to say that there can be as much honour in obedience and loyalty, as there is in non-acceptance and revolt."

This fierce criticism, associated as it was with a no less ardent apologia for what was termed Pétainism (for Marcellin discoursed upon the benefits of the Vichy Government, the immense services it had rendered the nation, its practical usefulness, in short its merits) was not without its embarrassing effect upon Thibault, who did his best to oppose his companion with the dialectic of non-consent to the accomplished fact.

"I have no doubt," he said to Marcellin, "that you are right on several points, if you place yourself in the perspective of past events; but you were not right in '41 or '42, before the events occurred, the cards had not been dealt, England was still fighting, Russia had declared war, France's future opportunities and her place alongside the Allies, the future victors, needed to be considered."

"That's an interesting idea, but I think it's misunderstood hegelianism," said Marcellin, laughing, "and there's a good deal to be said about the Allies feeling towards us and their opinion of the possibilities of success for the Resistance, but one can't go into everything at once and I'm afraid of boring you."

Thibault said no more. He thought merely that Marcellin, in all good faith, had fallen into an error which could only grow and spread: that of depicting the Resistance as a futile and criminal enterprise—as disastrous an error as that other, still in the ascendant that year, which contended that the Resistance numbered forty million French, less ten or twelve thousand "traitors", and that it had won the war.

He saw Marcellin again several times. The latter received each week in his studio in the Rue Bonaparte a group of men who belonged to that class of "outcasts" which had been created by the severities of the purge. Among them were several journalists, civil servants, politicians of the second rank and various indeterminate characters who made so favourable a first impression that one wondered why they had not succeeded in escaping undetected.

All these formed a sort of freemasonry, possessing, as do all societies of that kind, an experience in common (in this case, prison and proscription), similar prejudices, and passwords. They were linked in fairly firm solidarity. Week by week, the group increased by one or more new members, and Marcellin laughingly talked of taking a hall—for instance, the Geographical Hall in the Boulevard Saint-Germain—where those condemned by the Liberation could hold weekly meetings under the cover of spiritualism or yoga. Marcellin was full of a spirit of enterprise, and aimed at nothing less than founding a sort of Committee of Defence", bringing together as members those whom Bernard had called "the excluded from the Feast", a Committee of Defence which would be at the same time a Committee of Mutual Assistance, an Employment Office and a Centre for Readjustment.

Several of these people had read *Our Scribblers* (Marcellin had distributed roneoed copies). One night, a man in his thirties, whose face was convulsed with nervous tics, came up to Thibault and said: I have read your reply to that foul Bernard's article. It was perfect. Properly knocked off. I beg your pardon. First-class stuff. It must have made mincemeat of him, if you'll forgive the vulgar expression. You can't think what pleasure your reply gave me. I felt myself avenged. Because I must tell you: I've got a hell of a bone to pick with that Bernard. I must tell you the story. It's worth it. It'll interest you, I know. You can add it to your dossier on Bernard."

He told his story. It was somewhat confused. It concerned a lost friendship, a "summary" execution by the *maquis*. It resembled all the other stories of the day: Thibault had already heard several dozen similar anecdotes. He listened to the hesitant, incompetent narrative with half an ear. The man struck him as being a bore and a "poor type".

"So you can see," the man concluded, "I've got it in for Bernard. We should rid the country of men like that; it would be a purification."

"Indeed, yes!" cried Thibault, grave as a judge. "From the statistical reports the extermination camps fell far short of the figures one should have been able to count on. Many too many, people escaped unscathed, it's scandalous; and then there are all the Jews who have taken refuge in England and America. I'm with you in thinking that we ought to create a maffia to finish off the refugees once and for all."

The man looked at him, slightly perplexed as to whether all this was put forward seriously or merely as a leg-pull.

"I didn't say that all the Yids ought to be massacred," he declared in an impartial and moderate tone, like a man who desires to modify the excessive emphasis of a first statement. "They have been persecuted enough. All one wants is that they should get out of the country: let them go to Israel. But I do say that men like Bernard are snakes who should be crushed."

Thibault was enjoying himself very much. And, whenever he was enjoying himself in this particular way, he modestly lowered his eyes and pouted his lips like a scolded child.

"That's it," he said. "We shall found a new secret society and each of us will have his own particular victim to kill. After all, there's no reason why the Resistance should not be prolonged indefinitely by the Left, the Right, the Democrats and the Fascists, turn and turn about. . . ."

Once again the man looked slightly disconcerted. At last he said, "I like you. You're the right sort of young man, tough and decisive, and we need a few like you. I believe in you. Besides, you hate Bernard: that's enough to make me feel we'll be friends."

He extended his hand, giving Thibault a virile look straight in the eyes.

"My name's Roland Oyarzun," he said.

From then on Roland attached himself to Thibault Fontanes like a shadow. As soon as the latter appeared at Marcellin's, Roland rushed up to him, exuding that dumb, worshipping admiration one sometimes sees in schoolboys. The epigram, the joke with a double meaning, and a sort of roguish insolence were Thibault's most natural means of expression, nor did they fail to confuse part of his audience. Roland, naturally, did not always understand, and on these occasions he watched the expressions of the more intelligent listeners for some sign, response or indication which might put him on the right track. But if he had happened to understand what he called a "wiliness", his face at once broke into a happy smile, he clucked like a hen, and closing his right fist, he extended the thumb vertically above it (a gesture which, in the repertory of the period, signified: excellent, perfect, bravo). He took those present to witness, winked at them, gestured towards Thibault with his raised chin, as if to say: "Did you hear that one? The little 'un's brilliant, isn't he?" and he devoured the "little 'un" (who was in fact at least five foot ten) with eyes moist, tender and admiring.

"You remind me exactly of my friend Jacques," he told him one night. "He was a wit like you. A real joker."

"Really!" murmured Thibault, his eyes half closed. "Remind me of the nicknames they gave you when you were with Bucart. Nisus and Euryalus, wasn't it? Oh, no, it was Roland and Oliver. . . . Of course you come from Roncevaux or the surrounding district. Naturally, Bigorre is less classical than Latium, but then all that doughty, ivory-horn business suits your complexion."

He moved away, leaving Oyarzun dumbfounded and frowning, endeavouring to resolve these enigmas which were perhaps balm, perhaps so much poison.

Thibault visited Marcellin half a dozen times, often enough to get to know some of these marginal personalities, who were often amiable, sometimes brilliant, sometimes shady, or frankly detestable, whom the young Republic had turned into "emigrants of the interior". Through them he tried to understand the complex phenomenon known as "collaboration", its psychological structure, its social ramifications, and its ethical and metaphysical connotations. Even within the group a variety of categories soon became apparent, differing from each other by a whole system of minor gradations: there were extremists, moderates, diehards, penitents, differentiated by the degree of their pro-Germanism or their Germanophobia, by their loyalty to the Marshal or some other eminent figure of the Occupation, in short by their degree of hostility to the new régime: some admired de Gaulle "in spite of everything", others voted him to the gallows, some found themselves returning to republicanism, others remained fiercely anti-democratic. A large number declared themselves to be violently anti-capitalist and this was true: the "National Revolution" had been, in principle, Socialist, day by day it had condemned Wall Street, the City, the Trusts. . . . As with the Resistance itself, the Collaboration was not one, but almost Protean in its multiformity. Its theories and doctrines were so varied, often so little reconcilable, that it seemed in the first instance to be a pretext for infinitely obscure individual decisions, much more emotional than reasonable, and which only a few intellectuals succeeded in systematising. It had not been a mass phenomenon any more than had the Resistance, but rather a solitary passion glowing in the individual heart.

Already various sets were forming from which certain people were excluded. Within the little group of the "purged" who met at Marcellin's, a purge in the second degree tended to exclude certain extremists, those whose pro-German sympathies had been too exuberant or had attracted too much attention, or whose affiliation with certain Fascist organisations had become too well known.

"We consist," said Marcellin to Thibault, "of thousands of Frenchmen from whom, together with their honour as citizens, all sense of civic obligation has been torn. We form an opposition minority or, in any case, a heedless one. We shall never again fight for a cause, we no longer believe in causes. We merely go on loving a physical country, the land and people of France, but we have ceased being interested in what passes for, or pretends to pass for, the state as such."

"It seems to me that that's an old distinction," said Thibault, "and that there was no need to wait for 1944 to underline it. In fact, it's an idea that goes back to 1789."

He had decided to be open with Marcellin, as he was about the "idols" of the day, because it was not worth while guarding against one sort of conformism merely to fall into an opposite one. Marcellin raised his eyebrows a little, but he appreciated Thibault's frankness, the deep pride of a young man who held to his beliefs and refused to give his assent out of mere compliance. One day, twisting his face up into one of his expressive grimaces that gave him the appearance of an extremely intelligent clown, he said, "Whether you wish it or not, you are yourself one of those for whom the physical country is more important than the state, you're one of us, my dear Fontanes, but you don't as yet want to admit it, you don't want to derive your beliefs from us, you'll have to work them out for yourself. In any case, allow me, since I am so much your senior, to warn you against a danger that lies in wait for you and for so many of your generation: that of independence at all costs, lack of discipline and irresponsibility. You must choose the people you are going into battle with."

"Oh, no!" protested Thibault, "we've enough Sartres to preach 'engagement' to us! If you're going to begin doing it too! . . . No, it's not funny any more. Besides, you know, I'm not particularly keen to join your side. I like you well enough, you're clubbable, but frankly, my dear chap, you've got some pretty odd types on that sort of committee of yours. You've got some appalling hangers on who would make me wish to cherish all the Bernards of the world, anti-Semites who make me want to become a naturalised subject of Israel, and a selection of half-wits like Oyarzun, who . . ."

"Those are the rank and file," interrupted Marcellin, "the infantry, the foot-sloggers. You mustn't despise them, you know. They're the dough of history; everyone can't be the leaven. Go and look at the rank and file of the left and tell me sincerely what you think of it."

"I know it a little. I prefer it to its masters and its guides."

"Of course, of course," Marcellin said with a smile. "If you hadn't some love for the people, you wouldn't be an intellectual."

2

François met Roland Oyarzun by chance in the Rue de Sèvres. Roland was on his way to an Institute of Physical Culture, where he had at last found a job as an assistant. He invited François to accompany him.

"I got the job through an advertisement," he explained. "The proprietor asked me for my references and I was unable to conceal from him the fact that I had had certain difficulties at the time of the Liberation. He took me on all the same: the Liberation's fading into the past. The proprietor's a good sort, a tough one: he did his service in the Marines. He's given me the department that copes with the elderly, since I'm no longer fit enough for the young. Besides, an assistant must have a good appearance. But, what can you expect, after all the misfortunes I've been through and the conditions I've had to live in for the last two years. I'm in much poorer physical condition. I've no longer the pectoral muscles I used to have," he said, shaking his head nostalgically. "My abdominal muscles are relaxed. It's lucky I'm so thin or I should have a stomach on me. My deltoids are still in a pretty good state, but my abductors have gone soft because of their enforced lack of use in the factory; my greater denticulated are not too bad. Anyway, for the fat women I have to deal with it's good enough. Yes, my dear chap, every day from four till six, I have to take half a dozen hags with flaccid breasts and thighs like *mousse de foie*, horrible creatures who are enough to disgust one with the act of love for ever, even with humanity in general. But one has to earn one's living; anyway, it's better than making cardboard boxes like a robot. . . . Simone's well, thanks. So are the children. Yes, they're still living with my mother-in-law. As long as we're housed in the hovel you've seen, we can't keep the children with us. What are those Resistance politicians of yours waiting for to give the French houses? Of course, I've been condemned to National Indignity and have no right to ask for anything, but what about the others, the real French, who lack proper housing? What are our liberators waiting for?" he repeated in that tone of sarcasm which he always used towards the members of the hated government. "Your General de Gaulle's pretty hot, you know. Now he's demanding new legislative elections, and with a majority scrutiny, if you please, when he himself is responsible for the law of proportional representation—and all this on the pretext that his party had a great success in the municipal elections. And he wants to dissolve the Assembly, the satrap! Of course, I don't care a damn,

I take no interest at all in the political destiny of the country. But it's amusing to see all these Resistance bastards fighting today among themselves. But we who have been purged merely look at the mess from a distance with contempt and disgust, and laugh quietly to ourselves."

François turned to look at his companion. He had a feeling that Roland Oyarzun was finished, a terrible certainty that he was fixed, would never alter, except with the progressive alteration of physical deterioration. The die was cast for Roland Oyarzun: a wife and two children clinging to him like a triple chain and ball, a wife and two children who gave him no real happiness; life had nothing to give him any more; whatever he did, life would never be happier for him, more beautiful or more significant; he was congealed behind his already blighted face in spiritual indigence, until the day death came to efface this man who was already dead, and put a term to a tragic farce. Until then he would be able to suffer, and that was all; he had lost everything but the capacity for suffering. . . . "*Tel qu'en lui-meme enfin.*" . . . The modern philosophers, whom the Press and the public called "existentialists", asserted that man was a freedom always begun anew, that the future was always open, and that death alone transformed a life into destiny. But some men find their destiny before they die. One had only to look at Roland Oyarzun to *foresee* him. Perhaps tragedy was no more than knowledge of an ineluctable condemnation, of a slow and ceremonious strangling. . . . François began shivering. He thought: 'Are my chances any better?' A dim yellow light lay across the street, the autumn sky showed dirty grey above the city.

At the Institute of Physical Culture, M. Clément, the retired Marine, red as a Viking and with a chest on him like a fairground prize-fighter's, was drilling a group of boys in shorts. Next door, Roland began laying out mats on the floor. He got into his working clothes: flannel trousers and white jersey. François watched him curiously as if he were attending a circus act. Roland hit himself on the chest.

"My chest's still solid," he said. "If only I could eat better, I should get back into form. In 1939, when I was in Morocco, I weighed over thirteen stone. Today I'm barely ten. I ought to have a beef-steak every day and more bread and sugar, but what would you? Good afternoon, Madame Rappaport," he went on politely to a lady who had just come in. "Let me introduce you to a friend. François, this is my best pupil. Yes, yes, I mean it. My friend would like to watch the lesson. I hope you won't object."

The best pupil, who was about fifty and had jowls like an ogress, went into a cubicle. "That old bitch," whispered Roland, has got to lose three stone, the hag. Just about what I need to put on. She's doing a slimming cure, can you imagine? God, it's a hard life! And there am I sweating blood in order the Madame may regain her figure. It would be enough to turn one into a Communist, if one had no Christian convictions. That's what I've come down to to earn a living: making a lot of old bourgeois bitches lift their thighs rhythmically."

"But after all, you're used to it as a profession."

"Oh, but you can't compare it with this! At Vichy and at the school I was instructing youngsters, the flower of the youth of France; it was a religion. Taking these old hags today is merely a business."

More ladies arrived, and soon the assistant started work. An odd sight! As soon as the six pupils, obese creatures tied into brief shorts, had taken their places on their respective mats, a sudden metamorphosis seemed to come over Roland, a prodigy similar to those we read about in Homer and the Ancients, when a god quivers alive in the carnal envelope of a simple mortal or of a prophetess, transfiguring, borrowing a voice. Roland became the *Assistant*. He seemed to grow taller by three or four inches, his thorax swelled, he vibrated all over with an unaccustomed energy, accentuating the vigour with which he moved his legs as he walked round the room. With rapid movements of his hand he slapped his thigh with an imaginary whip, as if he remembered having been a horse-breaker or a cavalry officer. Even his voice had gone up a tone and seemed to have changed in quality: from being hoarse it had become dry and nasal, with extraordinary variations in delivery and register, but fixed variations, as if the formulae of the gymnasium must of necessity be announced in a definite ritualistic melody, a sacred repetition, not unlike plain-song or the monotonous chanting of the Congo. It was as if a demiurge had wound up some invisible spring in Roland Oyarzun's back or side: a wonderful marionette, an extraordinary living automaton had suddenly come into being.

"On the feet, up, legs together, arms extended, simultaneous raising and lowering of the arms and rotation of the forearms inwards," the Assistant announced all in one breath, and with that curious fluency which always strikes one when hearing a man use the jargon of his profession. "Won, two, won, two, a little faster, Madame Germain, won, two, pull that stomach in if you please, won, two, breathe in on raising the arms, breathe out on lowering the arms, won, two." He went from one to another, without ceasing his running commentary, rectifying a position here and there, with the quick eye and the easy, graceful precision of a ballet-master or, again, if the occasion seemed to him worth the trouble, with the patient attention to detail of a Pre-Raphaelite painter touching up a shade of colour. "Won, two, and halt! Breathe slowly while rising on to the toes, breathe with the abdomen *and* the chest; Madame Leroux, *and* the chest! Pull those shoulders back, if you please. Good. Take position lying on the back, hands behind the head, raise and extend the legs, alternate bending and raising from the knee, put your back into it!" He moved about between the ladies as they lay on their mats, dodging about between the huge pink, marbled thighs as they endeavoured to reach the vertical and kick into the void, slapping his leg with the imaginary whip, as if he were training seals or some heavy, jelly-like submarine monsters. Every now and then he caught François' eye and raised his own to heaven, as if imploring him to bear witness to the appalling misery he suffered in the profession of training seals; or he winked while giving his voice a honey-sweet quality as he said: "Won, two, legs at the vertical, Madame Rappaport!" or, again, he sketched an indecent gesture that only François could see. These winks, these ironic gestures, constituted an affirmation of his independence as a man within the frame of his mechanical professionalism, but, with Roland Oyarzun, such an affirmation, by its very outrageousness, by the effect it had, of which he was only half conscious, of making him out to be a "card", became part of the general unreality of this role of Assistant in a gymnasium into which he had been so strangely metamorphosed.

François marvelled.

When the lesson was over, the ladies went into the showers. They could be heard splashing about under the water, uttering little cries of suffocation or voluptuous purrings according to its temperature. Roland controlled a tap placed on the outside.

"I always want to boil them," he whispered with a melodramatic expression; "it's a terrible temptation. Or to freeze them."

He turned the tap almost down to zero. The unfortunate ladies, whipped by an icy jet, uttered strangled protests: "Monsieur Roland, stop. It's too cold!" "Good for the circulation!" he replied in a decided professional voice, and he rubbed his hands and winked with a jubilant expression. François thought that he would never forget the sight of an hilarious Roland Oyarzun submitting six fat women to the torture of an icy shower.

"It's like this every day, old man," Roland whispered. "I give them hardship. I humble them. And they adore me. Imagine what it'll be like when I've picked up physically again: sheer delirium!"

He turned the tap the other way; the ladies screamed.

"It's burning! Monsieur Roland, you're doing it on purpose!"

"Very good for the skin, ladies," he said sententiously, and pummelled François with an air of complicity.

When the ladies had gone, Roland undressed and took a shower himself. He went on chattering through the sound of the cleansing waters.

"It stinks here after the old faggots have been wagging their bottoms about for half an hour."

He developed the theme in considerable detail and with the vulgar jokes one may hear among men when the talk turns to women and sex.

"Chaps stink too, but it's not quite the same thing. I've got a very acute sense of smell and I can tell, merely from the stink, the age and sex of the people concerned."

He elaborated at length the differences between the respective smells of the "old faggots" and the "chaps". He seemed to take pleasure in the comparison. François listened, half disgusted by his vulgarity, half amused by the unconscious caricature he was making of himself. Roland Oyarzun always produced the same complex effect upon him: mingled amusement and contempt, some curiosity, some compassion, and some disgust.

"The good thing about this job is that I can have a shower bath whenever I like. I love showers. It's almost a vice with me."

Dressed once more, the Assistant's language became more respectable, and his preoccupations rose to a higher level.

"We never see each other nowadays, you and I; it's almost as if you were avoiding me. I've written to you twice this year asking you to come and dine at home. On each occasion you found an excuse. I know it's not much fun with us, we're just poor pariahs, but all the same an old friend such as yourself . . . Ah, well, that's life, I suppose. By the way, I've made some friends during the last six months. Do you know Marcellin? Henri Marcellin, the author of *La France dans la Tourmente* and of *Perspectives Européennes*? You don't know him? By God, except for Malraux, Bernanos, Montherlant, and Mauriac, you don't know your French literature. Marcellin's a remarkable chap. Some of us old inhabitants of Fresnes and Drancy meet at his place once a month. We discuss things, talk of friends who are still in prison, see if there is anything we can do to help them, or their families, or to hasten their release. It's a mutual aid society, if you like. Since I've known Marcellin and moved in his circle, I feel less alone, I seem to be coming alive again. Marcellin has a great regard for me. At his place I've met another writer, a young man: Thibault Fontanes. Do you know him?"

"The author of *Une Étoile de Sang*?"

"Yes. What do you think of him?"

"I don't know him personally. I've read his book, which is good, and I read his articles. He has a brilliant talent, but he's a bit of a poseur, isn't he?"

"I haven't read his book. I know that his articles annoy everyone, because he subtly tells the bastards the truth. I can take Fontanes, myself. He makes jokes all the time, but he's a good youngster. He's very fond of me, too."

The idea that the author of *Une Étoile de Sang* could be "very fond" of Roland Oyarzun was unexpected enough. 'Poor bastard,' François said to himself, 'he needs sympathy and friendship; he's been cut off from them for so long.'

"Fontanes's got amazing pluck, he sends fuming articles to the papers, exactly as if the Press were free. Half of them are subbed out of existence, of course. You know what subbing means?"

"Yes."

"Good, good. You always know everything, you do! Marcellin's going to try and publish his collected articles in volume form. I've read one of them, directed at your friend Bernard. It was brilliant. I'm sorry. I bow to your superior knowledge. By the way, what's happened to your friend Bernard?"

"Do you still hate him as much as ever?"

Roland gave him a piercing glance.

"You remember what I said two years ago, one evening before Christmas?"

"About Bernard? Yes, I remember."

"I showed you a revolver and I said . . . Anyway, you remember. Well, look me in the face: I'm a coward. If I wasn't a coward, I would already have . . ."

"Don't talk nonsense. You're not a coward; you're merely a reasonable chap. Killing Bernard wouldn't bring Jacques back to life, and it would do you a hell of a lot of good, and your wife and children too."

"No excuses!" Roland growled as if he were talking about someone else. "Oyarzun used to be a man; today Oyarzun is nothing but the rag of a man. When I catch sight of myself in the looking-glass I want to spit on myself. Bernard is poisoning me. Some nights I start awake crying: 'You'll pay for it, you swine!' It makes my wife tremble for hours on end. That's what I'm like. A coward. Don't deny it, Donadieu, I forbid you to deny it."

François shrugged his shoulders.

"If you like to make yourself unhappy . . ."

"Oh, yes, I'm an agoniser. I always have been, even as a child. An agoniser. I'm going to tell you something. Don't mention it to Simone; she knows nothing about it. One day I went and stood in front of the house at Neuilly where my mother lives. I've told you she lives with a chap? I waited for hours, shivering, it was in December. A copper asked me what I was waiting for. I said, 'My girl friend,' so that he should leave me in peace. At bottom I didn't know myself what I'd come there for. And then I saw them come out, both together. He was wearing a camel-hair coat, you know, brown and warm, and rings on all his fingers, or nearly. She was as smartly dressed as he was and her expression was as hard, as if she had been sculpted in marble. They got into a Citroën, a black fifteen-horse and drove away.

And I stayed there in the shadows, against the railings, shivering all the time, and crying like a baby, I don't know why: rage, emotion, sorrow, I suppose. Or perhaps I was thinking of my father, whom those two dishonour every moment of their lives. Perhaps because I was thinking of myself. I don't know; it's too complicated, there are days when I seem to be living in a fog. I ought, I ought, to have hurled myself on the man, bashed his face in with my fists, crushed him beneath my heels, there, on the pavement. In front of her eyes as she screamed murder. I should have, but I did nothing. Out of cowardice. I wonder even if what stopped me, paralysed me, was not the chap's camel-hair overcoat, his suède shoes, his motor-car, his closely shaven, powdered chin, while I looked like a tramp. Besides, shall I tell you? I was no longer sure enough of my own strength."

He said the last words with a sort of bewilderment, as if it were an almost incredible, almost unutterable avowal.

"Do you understand? I, who before the war was the most celebrated fighter in the whole of the Latin Quarter, I was afraid that I might not be able to beat that pimp. But I'm boring you with my stories! I expect you're saying to yourself: 'He's gone crazy, the poor old chap!' "

"No, I wasn't thinking anything of the kind, but I'm not sure that it wouldn't be a good idea for you to consult a . . ." he cleared his throat ". . . a neurologist. It seems to me that your nerves are in a pretty bad way."

"A neurologist? Do you mean a psychiatrist?"

"Not at all. A specialist who deals with the nervous system."

"Because, if you were thinking of sending me to a psychiatrist I should have replied: One, I'm not mad, whatever you may think. Two, psychiatrists are lewd types who invent stories that are enough to make a monkey blush. And, three, a pauper like me doesn't go and consult doctors for millionaires."

"Excellent reasoning. But I was talking of a neurologist; neurology has nothing to do with psycho-analysis."

"Yes, it has: the fee for the consultation."

He meditated for a moment or two, then said, "You're a cultivated chap, at least more or less cultivated, can you tell me what the Theban Legion is?"

"I think it was the Legion of Saint Maurice, at the beginning of the Christian era, about the second or third century. When the soldiers refused to sacrifice to idols, they were all martyred with their commander. It's the subject of a picture by El Grego."

"So he must undoubtedly have meant that I was prepared to suffer martyrdom for my convictions."

"Who said that?"

"Thibault Fontanes. The other day I was telling him that my real vocation was to be a soldier. He said: 'You ought to enlist in the Theban Legion.' And, you see, I asked him whether it was in garrison at Sidi-bel-Abbès. 'No,' he said, laughing, 'Sidi-bel-Abbès is a branch establishment.' Young Fontanes is a very funny fellow, but half the time you can't understand his jokes, they're too esoretic."

"Esoteric."

"What?"

"Esoteric, not esoretic."

"Damn you for a pedant!" he grumbled. "You're always wanting to teach someone a lesson! Your character hasn't changed at all. I say your character, because physically you've become as soft as a louse!" he said with a sort of surly rage.

Such was Roland Oyarzun. Whenever he imagined himself offended—and it happened ten times a day—he immediately tried to hit back; but, completely innocent as he was of any gift for repartee, he was compelled to fall back upon whatever weapons he could find, upon the first insult that crossed his mind however absurd, obscene, or irrelevant it might be. François had never really felt hurt by the puerile brutalities of his old friend: coming from a man one holds to be one's inferior, insults have no importance. Moreover, the greatest charity that can be rendered to the professionally humiliated, is to allow them to insult you.

3

Bernard was greeting people with a little nod of the head, he shook hands, he knew everyone—that is to say the two or three hundred people in Paris whom he deigned to call "dear friend". François followed him like a shadow: as for him, he knew no one. The audience was composed for the greater part of critics, journalists, and fashionable people, that minority of the happy few who form, or think they form, opinion. It was not a particularly brilliant First Night, not even a full dress First Night. Few of the audience were wearing evening clothes. It was not a Claudel, Cocteau, Anouilh, Montherlant or Mauriac First Night, but merely one of those minor weekly occasions of the theatrical season. Bernard and François went to their seats in the dress circle. Bernard was wearing a dinner jacket. It added to the effect of his particular romantic type. François admired his friend's elegance and the fact that someone so favoured and sought after in society, for whom the choice of a companion was so easy, should have had the kindness to invite anyone as obscure as himself to the theatre. In a society where everything is a matter of calculation even the opportunity of "showing" oneself at the theatre with such and such a male or female companion, this disinterested gesture was wholly estimable. "I would forgive him anything, because he's kind." But there was nothing to forgive Bernard: on the level of human relationships, and in matters of friendship, he was irreproachable.

François had never before had the chance of attending a First Night. He recognised among the audience several faces well known in the theatre, the cinema, or the literary world, whose features had been popularised by the Press. Bernard pointed out others. It was a reasonably smart audience. Such were the minor privileged of the democracy (the great, the really privileged, don't go to First Nights or go incognito) the people who never pay for a seat, who never buy a book, the eternally invited. They seemed nice enough. Certainly many of them were of the Left and had strong proletarian sympathies. Bernard himself, for instance. This intellectual and beribboned élite loved the people, periodically signed manifestos on its behalf, and hated the middle class.

François looked at his programme. The play was called *L'Exécution.* Three acts. The author's name. The producer's name. The designer's name. Mlle Catherine Vallier is gowned by Lanvin, her hair dressed by Georges. Catherine's photograph: masterly shadows, retouching, expert composition, signed Harcourt. She was pretty with a banal, stereotyped prettiness. Her smile was without expression or soul. An advertisement for Pepsodent or Colgate. François could not quite believe that this sophisticated creature was Catherine Monnet, Catherine Donadieu, his wife, the mother of Juliette. It seemed unbelievably unlikely. He thought of the long road they had come since a certain Sunday in summer at the Colonne concert. That young girl with fair hair, who was so reserved, so decorous, who blushed and stammered, who talked so soberly of Bruno Walter, had nothing in common with this actress with the glossy smile, this "rising star" as the journalists called her. Catherine Vallier was a stranger. "I can hardly believe that I lived with her in the most complete intimacy for more than five years, that I called her 'darling', that I was jealous of her." He remembered the first months of their marriage when he used to go to fetch her from the dramatic school in the evenings. "I suffered cruelly from seeing her surrounded by those smart, overdressed boys, whose language shocked me. I felt myself excluded and unwanted. She was escaping me, moving in another world where I could not join her, where there was no place for me." He remembered the morning of the wedding, the poor, shabby little ceremony, Catherine's tears after the breakfast, and he felt his forehead, his cheeks and the back of his neck turning red, as they always did at the thought of the humiliating sadness of that day among days. He remembered the lugubrious fortnight they had spent in the hotel on the Basque coast amid the Atlantic storms. He recalled a quarrel here, a sulky Sunday there, some silent evening filled with mutual reproaches. But he suffered most from the memory of his own faults, his own deficiencies, his own absurd behaviour on such and such an occasion. He had doubtless often been difficult, not to say unbearable. He blushed redder yet—a phrase that he had once uttered having crossed his mind: "I intend to recultivate my mind, as it were, from the beginning." He could hear the intonation of his own voice, imagine the precious, stilted, supercilious expression he must have worn when he uttered this nonsense. And Catherine—all the details of that evening were painfully, concretely present to him—Catherine had barely smiled: "That's right; a good idea; you recultivate your mind from the beginning." He turned scarlet and wriggled in his seat so unhappy did he feel: crucified by his own past stupidity. Catherine at the time had been absorbed in a delicate operation: she was painting her toe-nails. 'In my house,' he said to himself bitterly, 'the butter was often rancid, but the nail varnish was always of the highest quality.' Alas, such a grievance as that could not efface the embarrassing little memory.

'I was only twenty-one or twenty-two at the time,' he told himself. Indeed, he had been no more than a naïve, ignorant young provincial, full of goodwill, but whom the protestant education of the Sault-en-Labourd of the period had done nothing to enlighten. 'All the same, everything would have come right if Catherine had loved me more, if she had taken the trouble to understand me, if she had had the necessary tact and sensibility. But she didn't *really* love me. When night came, she ceased loving me. She escaped from her body like the princesses in fairy tales who are submitted to a magic ordeal. I was alone, clasping an absent one in my arms.' That was the basic cause of all the trouble: of our embarrassment, of our constraint, of our mutual incomprehension, of our progressive disaffection. 'But I was not responsible for it, in spite of making every possible blunder at the start. The fault was hers. Later on, she more or less admitted it.' Later on, and too late, our rupture had already taken place. But what point was there in ceaselessly going over the whole business, common doubtless to so many other couples? Think of it no more. Dispel these obstinate shadows.

He turned the page of the programme and absent-mindedly read the advertisement of the play:

"*The play takes place in a central European country, which has been occupied for the last two months by the army of an enemy nation. Michael, a young bourgeois intellectual, because he is unemployed, has joined a group of revolutionaries hiding in the mountains. There he finds Sabine, a beautiful anarchist, whom he has known before the war when she was the centre of a circle of modernist painters. Having been taken prisoner, and with no illusions as to the fate that awaits them, they endeavour, during the few hours that remain to them before their execution, to find a meaning in their lives. Beside them, Gregor, the sceptic, is the incarnation of denial and negation. The action takes place over a period of exactly twenty-four hours. By the use of dramatic compression, as well as by the singular power of his language, the author has endeavoured to capture the true climate of modern tragedy.*"

"Do you think it's going to be interesting?" he asked rather dubiously.

"Yes, I think so," said Bernard. "The author, Minjeot, is a

subtle sort of chap. I knew him at Louis-le-Grand. Anyway, it's the kind of theatre we need today, don't you think?"

François did not reply. Bernard's literary ideas annoyed him. He thought them either childish or artificial. Mere finical subtlety was about the last quality for which François would have thought of praising a dramatist. There was a certain silliness about Bernard: he threw himself upon the fashionable cliché, like a chicken upon corn. "If I were a critic with a play such as this, I should have no need to hear the dialogue in order to formulate a judgment. Before the rise of the curtain even, my article would be half written. In the first place, the title, *The Execution*, deliberately abstract to give an impression of profundity, intellectuality and mythopoeism, like Kafka's works, *The Trial* and *The Transformation*. The title alone would make me think that the author was a plagiarist, a clever assembler of detached pieces, a manufacturer of the up-to-date, a well-informed dolt infatuated by the prevailing fashion and with absolutely nothing to say. The main fault of this *Execution* is that it comes after *Le Malentendu* and other works of the same kind. But let's pass on. If you analyse the play the result is no more encouraging. This business of a central European country. . . . It's an old, old gag which has already seen much use. Central Europe has had to put up with a good deal. And what's more, this particular geographical setting, at once precise and indeterminate, is jolly useful: there's little risk of being contradicted, one can avoid historical error, and at the same time one has every chance of being believed on one's side: because central Europe was well and truly invaded by the Germans. At once, therefore, one can set the piece against a background of vivid actuality, while giving it a timeless and mythical dimension. A trick from the start: the piece is already compromised as far as I'm concerned. Let's go on. The two leading characters: a beautiful anarchist and a "bourgeois intellectual". Exhumed from the props department of 1925, or even 1905. As for the third character, he is "the incarnation of denial and negation". He is therefore symbolical. So are the others: Sabine represents "engagement"; Michael, irresolution; Gregor, individual denial, the cult of self, the search for happiness, etc. Modern tragedy must be stuffed with implications and ideas. And intellectual ideas come first, well to the fore, and labelled at that. The last word in smart intellectual ideas on sale at three hundred and fifty to seven hundred francs a seat. If the author had one ounce of vitality, originality or dramatic power, he would have put three dimensional people on the stage, characters, pitiful, odd, terrifying, droll, or all of them at once, in short—characters—not boring symbols cut out of vague intellectual ectoplasm. Ingenuously he would rid himself of his own anger, his love and his suffering, he'd burst out laughing, he'd tremble with emotion or sorrow—ingenuously, but with that ambiguous ingenuousness peculiar to creators—which excludes neither strength, critical judgment, nor thought. He would use none of the old recipes, whether classical (the "twenty-four hours") or not, he would never promise "to capture the true climate of modern tragedy", because a creator never promises anything in advance, never explains or makes a commentary: the work completed, he is silent.

The curtain went up. Ten "revolutionaries" were sitting or standing, motionless, in a sort of *tableau vivant* whose mass, balance and general ordering must have been the result of prolonged study: it was clearly visible. It evidently belonged to a more elaborate form of art than the photographs of country weddings. The result was very nearly as natural. A limelight posited these revolutionaries in the centre of a vague, neutral place: no *décor*, the tragedy is timeless. One might have thought that they were about to sing some swinging chorus, like the smugglers in *Carmen*, but not at all. They were sad. Infinitely sad. They were silent. A long silence. So was the audience. The whole thing was sombre. Infinitely sombre. Suddenly, the "singular power of the language" was heard:

"A thousand brothels!" said one of the revolutionaries, sombrely.

No one replied to this fraternal and despairing remark.

"My village is wiped out," said another.

"They have burnt the harvest," said a third.

"They have cut down the trees," said a fourth.

"They have stabled the horses in the church," said a fifth (who must have been rather clerical and reactionary. Doubtless an M.R.P.)

"They have shot Anton, the blacksmith's son," said a sixth.

"They have raped Maria," said a seventh. "They parted her white thighs. She bled beneath them."

(This had the real, true freshness of popular language, the crude imagery both physiological and poetic at the same time, a sort of Gionesque quality, hadn't it, so shatteringly singular. . . .)

Silence. Sombreness. No one had moved, not even the lover of the unfortunate girl with the white thighs. Their gaze was lost in the void, their faces expressionless. Silence. Then the second revolutionary with the voice of a sleepwalker, took up the litany once more:

"My village is wiped out."

The audience, however, was not so as yet. In fact, it had just made an interesting discovery. It had grasped that the ten revolutionaries were the chorus. Not a chorus of smugglers as in *Carmen*, no. The chorus. The Chorus of Greek Tragedy. Powerful. A wonderful transposition. Subtle. It's not every week you can see so original an innovation in the theatre as this.

Sabine made her entrance. She was wearing narrow trousers of khaki gaberdine, a shirt of large red checks like those worn by the herdsmen in the Camargue, it was very open across the chest; and a yellow scarf for a belt. A pistol stuck out of her right hip-pocket. Her hair was done like Veronica Lake's, a long lock falling over her eyes. The restraint with which she played her part bordered upon stupor. Not a gesture. Arms stuck to her sides. Her face utterly expressionless. Her eyes lack-lustre. A mask. Tragic, of course. She advanced upon the group and shouted, "Shut up, you men!" with the energy of a corporal cook shouting, "Come and get it!" The revolutionaries fell silent, subjugated. They had need to be. The fair Sabine was a compromise between a Nordic Passionaria and a Peter Chesney "doll". Monolithic, her hands by the seams of her trousers, her gaze fixed twenty yards away upon the navel of a cherub carved on the proscenium, she intoned a long monologue, a sort of monotonous chant, which from the point of view of sense was not easy to understand. After the recitative of the chorus, this was clearly a sort of aria, one of those lyrical moments when the singular power of the language was really almost ready to explode:

"The sheaves are bleeding. The sky is dark. Pluck those funereal poppies. Cut down the oaks of fidelity. They have bludgeoned the gerboa with their rifle butts. They have placed the lark upon the index. They have exiled the kingfisher. I cry out with all the heat of my entrails. I cry out with the round stones of my shoulders. I cry out with the tenebrous elasticity of my muscles. I cry out with the vegetable patience of my breasts." Extremely embarrassed, François wondered what she was going to cry out with next, but this particular passage was over. "Furrow your faces with your nails. The stars are howling. . . ." Etc. It was the great poetry of the cosmos put to the service of an underground movement. This sort of mystical song put into the mouth of a "beautiful anarchist who, before the war, was the centre of a circle of modernist painters", might surprise not a few. But the sublime conventions of tragedy can but give an effect of reality and credibility. François felt for Catherine. He suffered from seeing her so clearly lacking in all gift of expression, from hearing her declaim such appalling nonsense, the product of a literary convention already out of fashion. "She acts like Nathalie did ten years ago. Immobility and monotony, on the pretext that they are powerful, because she neither knows how to move on the stage nor speak her lines intelligently." It was true that it was difficult to speak intelligently lines so cruelly lacking in intelligence. What François most disliked was not the work's lack of authenticity but its indecency: the way it transmuted into pretentious, dramatic tinsel what had been some people's suffering, fighting and nobility.

Beside him, Bernard was conscientiously taking notes for an article in *Horizons*.

During the interval, François glanced sideways at the notebook. He read: ". . . appears to have attained to a real tragic dimension. . . . The crucial problems of our time . . . theatre profoundly based upon the actual. . . . Catherine Vallier manifests astounding gifts . . . an admirable sobriety . . . sustained power. . . ."

"Do you really like it?" he asked.

"Well enough. Don't you?"

François did not dare say that the play bored him beyond endurance. It would not have been polite to Bernard, who had invited him.

"Personally, it's a theme that doesn't interest me very much," he said.

"Perhaps, but it doesn't alter the fact that there's an individual voice there," said Bernard rather stiffly, "a sort of concrete lyricism that I find attractive enough. There's a tone of voice, a style."

"We haven't got the same tastes. And the woman, what do you think of her?"

"Catherine Vallier? Excellent."

"You make a good audience."

"Well, she knows how to say her lines, doesn't she? She's got a sort of restraint, a reserve, a capacity for 'understatement'. Besides, she's a pretty girl. A good chassis. I wouldn't mind having her at all. Would you?"

"Oh, I already have," said François modestly.

Bernard raised his eyebrows.

"You're joking, aren't you?"

"Not at all. Catherine Vallier is my wife."

* * *

'God, how bad it is,' thought Thibault. 'And how conventional that poor girl is! However, she's got an eloquent and agreeable bosom, and that's something.' In fact, he had not come to see *The Execution*, a play from which he did not expect much intellectual profit. He had come to the theatre because, the week before, he had drawn by lot the young actress with whom he was to fall in love. He had selected twenty names among the young actresses on the verge of fame (for, naturally, Edwige Feuillère, Madeleine Robinson, Danièle Delorme, etc., were excluded out of modesty). He had written their names on pieces of paper and placed them in a hat. He had sent for his young cousin Patrick—for the hand of innocence should designate the pleasures of the libertine (brr! . . .). Catherine Vallier's name had come out of the hat. And why shouldn't it be her? Thibault consulted the theatrical announcements and saw that this young person was shortly to appear in a play called *The Execution*. 'Perfect,' he thought. 'The title's a good augury. I shall take her.' He had published, a few months earlier, a novel which had made a certain stir. He was working on another. Lorraine could still not make up her mind in his favour, but life was very interesting all the same. Besides, one must have one or two sources of suffering, for without them no spiritual enrichment was possible and one ran the risk of becoming sterile—at least that is what great writers like Benjamin Constant, Max du Veuzit, Admiral Lacazes, etc., had affirmed. He contributed to several distinguished reviews—*La Table Ronde*, for instance. He went a good deal into society. A reasonably decorative mistress would do much to assure his position. Thibault intended later on to take up politics in an old-fashioned Barrésian-cum-panache sort of way. And it is traditional for ministers and statesmen in the French Republic to have actresses for mistresses. With a bit of luck he would become deputy for the 17th arrondissement just as Catherine Vallier signed on permanently at the Théâtre Français. All this was merely a matter of sustained effort, talent and attention—easy enough. He would weave a little sentiment into their relationship, because it was necessary to take lessons in the practical psychology of love if one wanted to be a writer—re-reading Mme de Lafayette was not enough. Thibault was certain of being able to love Catherine (or Jeanne, or Hélène, or Colette) for a year or two at least, nay even for forty-eight hours. One can love quite easily wherever one wishes to, the object has no importance in itself, all women resemble each other. . . . Thibault had hoped that Lorraine would be present at this First Night. He had desperately hoped for it, even if she were accompanied by Michel de Bars. But Lorraine was not in the theatre. Thibault got up and went to the foyer. He met several friends, shook hands and exchanged vague remarks about the play. He said good evening to Jean-Jacques Gautier.

"It's not quite as thrilling as *Oedipus Rex* or *Roger la Honte*," he said to him with modestly lowered eyes, "but the author is full of good intentions, don't you think, and there are a few faults of language which are quite overwhelming. Of course, in the last analysis it's the audience who are executed in cold blood, it must be what one might call the Theatre of Cruelty. I have been told that a certain general was hiding behind the pseudonym of Minjeot—Charles de Gaulle, if I remember correctly. But it can't be true, can it? No; I'd take a bet that the author is really O. Bernard: I thought I recognised here and there, though not quite so well expressed, the moral tone of *Horizons*. . . ."

"Not so loud," whispered Jean-Jacques Gautier, "Bernard is just behind you."

Thibault turned and glanced quickly behind him.

"I didn't know him by sight," he said. "Well, he looks quite tame. It's just as I thought: at bottom there's nothing more cow-like than these ravening progressives."

* * *

"Do you mean to say she's your wife?" repeated Bernard incredulously. "Really, you are a funny, secretive chap. Why haven't you ever told me?"

"You never asked me."

"I knew you had married a young actress, and that you had separated. I knew that her name was Catherine, but oddly enough I never connected her with Catherine Vallier."

"Only three months ago her name would have meant nothing to you. People only began to talk about her last February."

"But why the devil didn't you tell me tonight that we were going to see your wife, or ex-wife, act?"

"I wanted to wait to find out what you would think of her."

"Traitor! Supposing I had thought badly of her?"

"It wouldn't have mattered. I'm completely indifferent to her."

Bernard looked at him with a curious and perplexed expression.

"You are a funny chap," he said. "Secretive, so wildly secretive at bottom. I've known you for years and here, suddenly, by chance, I find things out about you: you've got a brother, a little daughter, and you're married to Catherine Vallier."

François smiled.

"Yes, as it happens, I've got a private life. Isn't it extraordinary? What sort of person did you think I was? Suspended in the void, without a single tie to anyone in the world?"

"Good God, I must say . . ."

"You must say that you've never really thought about the matter? Shall we go out for a little? It's stifling in here and, in any case, we shall never get near the bar."

"Who's that young man talking to Jean-Jacques Gautier? It isn't Fontanes, is it? I seem to recognise him from the photographs."

"It may be."

"I'm properly taking him down a peg in the next number of *Horizons*. You remember his article about me in *France Nouvelle*?"

"Yes. It was pretty disgusting, but I must say the chap's not altogether wrong."

"You are a brute," said Bernard, laughing. "You covenant with my enemies. What a frightful fellow you are."

They went into a little café near the theatre and ordered a couple of beers at the bar.

"All the same, I don't understand," Bernard went on. "Catherine Vallier, your wife. . . . I say again: why did you coneal it from me?"

"I haven't concealed anything from you. What you call my secretiveness is simply your own absence of curiosity. There are people who talk about themselves to everybody all the time: their life, their interests, their worries, their love affairs are the things they find most passionately interesting, and because they find them so, they are so. One can listen to them with pleasure. There are others who never speak of themselves unless they're asked, and even then they only tell the curt essentials, from modesty, humility, or a morbid fear of being a bore. I belong to the second category. I listen. I'm a born receiver of confidences. And receivers of confidences, as everyone knows, have no private life. Can one imagine Pylade indulging an intrigue with Céphise parallel to that of Pyrrhus and Andromaque? It's impossible, isn't it? Confidants exist merely as a function of the protagonists, their lives are dependent on others, parasitic perhaps, I don't know. For the rest, I'll say this: I had a wife, but it didn't last long: today she has become the property of the public, if I may express it thus."

He laughed shortly and drank his beer down at a gulp. Bernard watched him from under hooded eyes.

"The conclusion I'm to draw from your little speech," he said, "is that I am one of the inexhaustible talkers who are so full of themselves?"

"Of course!" said François, still in a friendly, joking tone of voice. "But it's quite natural: you're one of those great individualists who have chosen to play their own personalities to the limit, to sculpt their eternal form *in vivo*. And, to achieve that, it's not enough to act, one must talk, or write. The word is the necessary complement to action, in a sense it acts as its fixative, it prevents it from evaporating. That's why you run a journal and why you never stop telling your own story, to me in particular."

"You're bitter!"

"Not at all, I assure you."

"I don't mean that you're possessed with bitterness. I mean that the portrait you draw of me is pretty tart."

"No; not at all. One's always glad to listen to you, you're extremely interesting. I've been listening to you since September, 1939, and I'm not tired of it yet."

They went back to the theatre, where the bell was ringing for the second act.

"What effect does seeing Catherine on the stage have on you?" Bernard asked as they returned to their seats.

"At first I felt a bit distressed. But, in that disguise and with that make-up, she's someone else. I barely recognised the person I lived with."

"You meet occasionally?"

"Two or three times a year, generally because of our daughter. We went to the South together to see her."

"And you've really ceased to love Catherine?"

"Yes."

"Even sensually?"

"Yes."

"All the same, living with her can't have been too boring."

"Appallingly so. But I must admit that at that time she was much thinner, did her hair badly, and didn't wear extremely decolletées tartan shirts."

When the play was over, part of the audience went backstage, according to custom.

I shall leave you," said François. I've got to meet someone at the *Flore* in half an hour's time."

Won't you come and congratulate Catherine?"

"She doesn't even know I'm in the theatre. She didn't think of sending me an invitation."

"Why don't you come all the same?"

"Yes, after all, why not?"

He feigned ease under his friend's scrutiny. He did not wish to give the appearance of wanting to avoid a meeting which might be thought to be embarrassing.

"You shall introduce me," said Bernard.

The passages and stairs backstage were crowded with people. They made their way to Catherine's dressing-room.

"I ought to have some flowers," said François. "I'm not a modern husband. Nor a man of the world."

In the tiny, brilliantly lighted cabin, which was her dressing-room, a number of Catherine's friends had already gathered. They had to wait until this first contingent of visitors had left. François could see his wife's face and shoulders between two large masculine necks. She saw him and gave him a discreet little smile, as if to a particular friend, while continuing to talk to two men who were standing face to face with her. The stage make-up gave her that hard, disquieting mask that the footlights humanise but which, under ordinary lighting, accentuates so strangely whatever is hard or inflexible in an individual's character. She lit a cigarette with slow, measured gestures. She was perfectly mistress of herself.

"Come in! Come in!" she cried as soon as the visitors had made way. "My dearest François, how pleased I am to see you. Let me kiss you. It's nice of you to have come. I wanted to send you an invitation, but I didn't know where to find you. You've changed your address, and I didn't even know whether you were in Paris."

François had the presence of mind to smile. These poor lies, spoken with so much ease, froze him. One can always get hold of someone in Paris. Letters are forwarded from one address to another. Why did she bother to excuse herself? And why did she excuse herself so awkwardly, so manifestly insincerely? Was it possible that there was some latent intention to wound him? No. No, not that.

"Thank you for the thought," he said gaily. "You know very well that I wouldn't have missed this First Night for an empire. I was able to come thanks to my friend Bernard here, of whom you have often heard me speak."

He made room for Bernard to come forward. Catherine fluttered her eyelids, and lifted a hand upon which Bernard placed his lips.

"Ah, you are the famous Bernard. I've met you at last! François has always sworn by you. And I religiously read the editorials of *Horizons*."

"Too flattered," said Bernard. "But in that case you'll shortly read an article upon yourself. You see, kindness always finds its recompense."

"Bernard absolutely insisted upon coming to congratulate you," said François.

"Did you really like it?" she asked, her eyelashes aflutter.

"I hate complimenting actors in their dressing-rooms after the show. It always rings false. But François can bear me out." He assumed a tone of simplicity and directness: "What you're doing is very remarkable indeed."

"Thank you," said Catherine. "I had appalling stage fright, no doubt that's why. Shut the door, my dears, do you mind, there are a mass of people in the passage waiting to come in, God damn it! I'm exhausted. Sit down if you can find anywhere to sit."

She sat down lightly on the edge of the dressing-table, placed her cigarette in an ashtray and picked up a jar of cold cream. She opened it and spread a layer of the white cream on her cheeks.

"Do you mind? I'm longing to get rid of this beastly make-up. François, you never told me that your friend was good-looking. You've talked of his talents, his intelligence, of this and that, but you forgot the essential. Men always forget the essential."

"Do you want to make me run away?" cried Bernard, laughing.

"Be reassured," said François, "Catherine is merely putting on her act of brutal frankness and cynicism."

Catherine threw him a steely glance and continued to spread the greasy cream on her cheeks and forehead. As the grease mingled with the make-up, her face soon became shiny and streaked.

"I was merely stating a fact," she said. "Bernard is good-looking, that's all."

"Please," said Bernard, "let's rather talk of you and of the play. Is Minjeot in the theatre tonight?"

"He was here a moment ago. I think he'll come back."

Someone knocked at the door.

"Come in," called Catherine.

A tall young man with a sulky face and disordered hair appeared in the opening of the door. He was wearing a dinner jacket and his butterfly tie was rather crooked. He held out a visiting card to Catherine.

"Forgive me. I see you're busy," he stammered in a voice in which one felt, nevertheless, that there was much more of insolence than timidity. "I merely wanted to introduce myself. You know there's still a queue outside your door. I am the second. Till later, then."

He went out quickly, like a puppet being whisked away. Catherine, a little taken aback, looked at the card. She burst out laughing.

"There's a boy with nerve!" she cried.

She showed the card to Bernard and François. Above the printed name of Thibault Fontanes had been written in ink: "A Coming Man."

"Fontanes, that's the author of *Une Étoile de Sang*?" said François.

"Yes; he's the chap I pointed out to you in the foyer during the interval. His present affectation is this sort of waggish frolicsomeness. One part baroque fantasy, one part lack of constraint, one part poetry and elegance of style. I suspect he wants to be the Charles Trénet of literature, or something of the kind."

"Hell! Are you malicious too?" said Catherine.

"No," said François. "He's preparing a slating for Fontanes. He knows his subject well. He's merely trying out its contents on us. In fact, we are having the advantage of a preview."

"We're a pretty trio!" cried Catherine. "I wonder which of the three of us is the most false."

She was bathing her face, now no longer made up and naked, with toilet water. A murmur of conversation came from the passages and neighbouring dressing-rooms.

"Besides," said François, "you're prejudiced against Fontanes. He's worth a great deal more than you make out. His book's good."

"I don't deny his talent," said Bernard in a slightly impatient voice. "I say that that particular talent has no relevance. It's all happening in Sirius, or in 1925, which is pretty much the same thing. It's a gratuitous game, a firework."

"I like fireworks. But Fontanes has got more than that. He's got both vitality and character. He'll become someone."

With a disdainful gesture Bernard discarded this eventuality.

"All these little Fascists are simply trying to escape their responsibilities, to avoid coming face to face with an epoch that condemns them. Their affectation of frivolity and recklessness springs from this cause. And so does their choice of subjects: love, happiness—and their conception of a timeless literature. And from this, too, their hatred for Sartre."

"Fontanes a Fascist?"

"I use the term for the purpose of simplification. If you like, we'll call him a reactionary. Or a conservative. . . . But we're boring Catherine."

"Not at all. I love hearing men talk; it's always so interesting. I'm captivated."

"You're laughing at us," said Bernard, "and you're quite right. I was listening to Leroy just now," he went on, getting up. "I think you'll get a good notice from him."

"And Gautier, do you know about him?"

"I don't know. He may not have liked the play."

"Between ourselves," said François, "I can't blame him."

Whether it was that he made this remark in a low voice, like someone who is not sure of his ground, or whether his judgment seemed to the other two insufficiently important to be taken into consideration, they went on discussing the play without paying more attention to François than if he had been a piece of furniture.

"It's *written*, isn't it?"

"A sort of poetic tension."

"It's clearly the sort of thing to write today."

"It carries you with it, it pays off."

"A sense of the formulae of the age."

"And the presentation, no recourse to hackneyed tricks."

"A fine experiment in pure tragedy."

François watched the two sycophants: Bernard was undoubtedly intelligent and sincere, but fettered in a narrow doctrinal system by a host of prejudices as profoundly part of him as his reflexes, and spoilt by the old, old habits of worldly "exhibitionism" and snobbery: while Catherine was a perfect stranger to any authentic emotion, and quite indifferent to anything that did not make for her own personal success, contribute to the figure she cut in the world—but instinctively prepared to respond to exterior stimuli, to adjust her attitude, her expression, her words, to whatever she thought was required of her.

"When I read *Execution*, I said to Lambert: "My sweet Lambert, I absolutely must play this piece, it'll be utterly damned, we shall have a howling failure and go quite broke, but I want to play it, for years I've been sighing for a play like this, you do understand don't you, when for once one does happen to come upon a work of art. . . ."

She was posing as the intelligent and disinterested actress, who is not deterred by the period's lack of comprehension, popular failure, poverty even, to *serve* an author of quality, an 'authentic' work, when in fact she would have agreed to play anything, including *Le Tampon du Capiston*, because it's better to play anything than to be out of work. She was posing as the actress who chooses, who has the stature to choose, whereas Lambert must have said to her on the telephone, "Vallier, come round to the theatre tomorrow. There's a contract for you," without even bothering to tell her what the contract was for, because she was only small-time, and in no position to make conditions. She could take it or leave it. And she must have replied in a small voice, hoarse with gratitude and respect: "Oh, thank you, Monsieur Lambert!" Oh, but she knew the rules of the game only too well, the laws of the jungle: cheek, more cheek, cheek all the time. Hang on, bluff, throw sand in their eyes, hang on at all costs and be a bit tougher than the rest. And to crown all, she talked of the subject of the play (which was the Resistance) as if it lay close to her heart, she, she, that very Catherine who, on the Thursday of the Liberation, had asked François in a tone of cold sarcasm: "Do you belong to the . . . what do you call them? Free French Forces?" Oh, it was altogether too much, too contrived. And Bernard listened, sympathetic, friendly, understanding, as if he believed in these charming fictions, and perhaps he did half believe in them? Sycophants, sycophants! The whole scene was on the level of "let's pretend", falsification and lies, one was still in the theatre, one could never get away from the theatre. François got up, he felt a shaft of burning anger mounting inside him. No, he would no longer let people play their sinister little act in front of him with impunity. For too long he had pretended to be their dupe, from timidity, cowardice, politeness or laziness. It was over. He would tear their masks from them even if he had to tear their flesh too.

"Between ourselves, Catherine," he said in a toneless voice, "playing this piece was not much of a risk. I'm not pretending that it's very good, but it's confected according to the recipe of the taste of today. On the whole it'll have a pretty good Press, because of its subject—at least a sympathetic Press. And don't try to make Lambert out to be an apostle of the theatre of the type of Georges Pitoëff. It so happens that we know him, Bernard and I."

He saw himself in the looking-glass on the dressing-table: his face was pale, his smile taut. Catherine's eyes flashed. He went on: "There are people waiting in the passage. Good night, my sweet. I'm very glad for your sake, you know. I hope it will run for three hundred performances."

He kissed her lightly and went towards the door. Catherine remained still as if nailed to the spot.

"Are you coming?" he said to Bernard.

"Dear friend, good night," Bernard murmured, raising Catherine's hand to his lips. "I'll send you the paper."

They had hardly reached the street when Bernard said: "What came over you?"

"I can't bear affectation."

"Catherine isn't affected."

"Well, I don't know what you call it, then."

"All the same, my dear chap, you might have spared us that exit. It was a bit embarrassing for me."

"I decided to stop restraining myself."

"You're undergoing a second crisis of adolescence. Misanthropy, revolt against the social conventions. It's a bit old-fashioned, isn't it? And you wouldn't do it, if you could only see yourself at such moments: one might think you were going to have an epileptic fit, you go pale and tremble, it's really painful."

"I expect it's because to tell the truth is painful. Even more painful than discovering it. Well, I must leave you or I shall be late for my date, I've just got the time to get there in a taxi. Good night. Thanks for the evening."

Bernard held on to his hand for several seconds.

"You've changed a lot, my dear chap. You're becoming uncivil, sensitive and off-hand. Is there anything wrong?"

He looked at him frankly and intently, an admirable look. He was going to offer his help. Fraternally. He was going to be fraternal, it was his particular speciality. The word "fraternal" often cropped up in his articles.

"Thank you, everything is going very well," said François drily.

"Good. So much the better. Well, good night. Go to you date. Is she sweet?" he asked in a low voice.

François smiled.

"Very sweet."

"What does she do in life?"

"She looks after the cloak-room and sells flowers in a night-club."

"Oh, wonderful!" said Bernard, throwing back his head. "I hope you don't think I'm being indiscreet asking you these questions. You know, nothing that has to do with women is indifferent to me. I envy you. I wish I were in your shoes."

"You ought to be ashamed of yourself with all the women you'ue got already."

"That's just it. I always want someone else's: the one I haven't got. My life is terribly organised, subject to exact time-tables, there's no place in it for the unforeseen, for adventure. All these dates at fixed times become so boring. I long for someone fresh and kind these days. Your little flower-girl, for instance! God, how the creatures make us waste our time. I haven't worked, what you can call work, for five or six weeks. And my novel that's still waiting to be begun. God, how difficult life is! Sex is certainly my greatest problem," he concluded with a serious and meditative air.

"My poor chap!" said François. "As if you hadn't enough on your mind already with North Africa, the Madagascans, Indo-China, and the wage level."

Bernard gave him a quick, youthful, laughing look.

"You're an old bastard!" he said gaily. "Go away, get out of my sight, you beast!"

* * *

At the same time Thibault Fontanes entered Catherine's dressing-room like whirlwind.

"At last, at last," he cried, closing the door behind him, "I thought my turn was never coming. It's frightful how people can't get out of the habit of forming queues. You've seen my visiting card, so you know that I'm not one of those important and successful journalists like that M. Bernard who left this room barely ten minutes ago."

He extended his arm in search of the hand that Catherine had not given him. It lay on the dressing-table next to the ash-tray. He kissed it devotedly.

"You're very beautiful and very kind," he said with stammering effusion. "You wear trousers wonderfully well and you make a wonderful revolutionary of a kind that no longer exists today. Of course, the play's enough to make one die laughing, but you save it, you save it by your grace and spirit. One can see that you don't believe in what you're doing for a single second, but you say your lines with such ravishing grace, with so ironic a detachment, with such an air of making fun both of the author and us, that is simply marvellous. One looks at you, one admires you, one listens to your voice, and one doesn't hear the lines, so that's something gained."

"Monsieur . . . " began Catherine.

"Call me Thibault. Yes, I know it's a ridiculous Christian name; one might think that I'd come back from the Crusades, or that I was about to mount my palfrey to go and massacre some neighbouring caitiff, but what can I do about it? I can't imagine why I didn't think of sending you my book last year. You haven't read it, by any chance? I'll send it to you. It's an exquisite masterpiece in the line of Gérard de Nerval, Radiguet, Cocteau, Henri Bordeaux, etc., and so funny! I laugh till the tears pour down my face every time I reread it—that's to say, every day."

"If you would allow me to get in a single word . . ." said Catherine.

"Get in, my dear friend? One must never hesitate to talk, even when one has nothing to say, it's the simple secret of popularity and success. That's why modern literature is so exuberant."

"I would be obliged if you would get out."

"I understand," cried Thibault. "You want to change your dress. What exquisite propriety! I'll wait for you in the passage. I shall write my article while waiting. I've forgotten to tell you that I've been dramatic critic to *France Nouvelle* for the last eight days and that later on I shall be able to publish an article on you in the *Delta* review, even though I don't cover the theatre for it, but I'll do a stylish fantastical little thing exclusively about you, not about *Execution*, of course. By the way, an urgent question: do you eat grapefruit for breakfast?"

"No," said Catherine.

"Another thing: have you ever read the *Critique of Pure Reason*?"

"No," said Catherine.

"Thank you. It's for my article about you; now I know enough. However, one more question, but a private one this time: what would you say to a wing of cold chicken and a glass of Veuve Cliquot?"

"I'd adore it," said Catherine in a gentle voice.

"And a cocktail at the *Tabou* afterwards?"

"Wonderful," said Catherine.

"Bravo. Hurry up. After that *Execution* one needs building up a bit. But really, my dear friend, how on earth does anyone write that sort of stuff? It's really too indecent! You must have split yourself laughing when you were learning those litanies by heart?"

"I wept laughing!" she cried, her eyes brilliant.

"The funniest part about it is that it's sure to be a success, you know!"

"A real farce!" she cried, and her eyes fluttered with happy malice.

4

François received a note from Simone Oyarzun. She asked him to come and see her as soon as possible, "because I am very anxious about Roland and want to ask your advice."

"What a bore! When on earth am I going to get rid of these people?" But the following evening he went to the distant suburb where they lived, a district bristling with factory chimneys and gasometers. He climbed the six storeys, which were saturated with the smell of burnt cooking-fat. As he entered the tiny flat, another smell, stale and medicinal, seized him by the throat: someone had been ill here and the windows had been kept closed. Indeed, Roland was in bed, his cheeks sunken, his forehead clammy and with a three days' growth of beard on his chin.

"Ah, there you are," he said feebly. "It's kind of you to come and see me. I've been very ill, you know. A temperature for the last three days. I'm better today: only ninety-nine."

François sat down on the edge of the bed.

"What's been the matter with you?"

"The doctor said it was a reaction due to over-fatigue," Simone intervened.

"Doctors are all fools," said Roland. "I know what's been the matter with me. Simone, darling, give our friend a drink."

"I'm afraid we haven't got such a thing in the house," she said, blushing.

"Well, go down and get something from the bar at the corner, will you?"

"Please don't, Simone. I never drink at this time of day," said François quickly.

The stuffiness and smell of illness already made him feel sick, and he did not want to aggravate the feeling by drinking one of those syrupy apéritifs which he in any case hated.

"Darling," the patient said again with a sort of imperious gentleness, "go down and buy something at the bar on the corner."

With a gesture he cut short François' protestations. When Simone had gone out, he said: "I know that you never drink apéritifs, idiot; it was a pretext to get rid of my wife. While she's going up and down the six flights, we shall have five minutes' peace. I can't confide in Simone. She's a good girl, and she adores me, but she doesn't understand. Men and women, and it hardly needs saying, are two different worlds, which only meet in the bed, and, between ourselves, the bed doesn't count for all that. I'm very much alone."

He raised his arm and let it fall back again.

"You understand what it means, having to send your wife to the bar on the corner every time you wish to talk privately to a friend? Living, two of you, in such a tiny place, in two small communicating rooms, is frightful. Luckily," he added with a sombre air, "the lavatory is on the landing. If it had been in the flat, the size it is, I think I should have divorced in spite of my religious convictions. . . . Or arranged a legal separation. It's being on the landing is less embarrassing, but all the same . . . It makes you laugh? All right, laugh then. I always know when you're trying to restrain your laughter: your nostrils quiver, so does your chin, and you put on an expression like an undertaker. I'm quite aware that what I've just told you is sordid, or ridiculous, or what you will, but all the same it's been one of my obsessions since we've lived in this hovel. A presence continually at one's side, well, some days, you know, it's hell. But you know that, since you've been married yourself. By the way, have you seen your wife since your separation?"

"Yes, I see her from time to time. When my daughter came to

Paris last year, we used to go out all three together. It was best for the child's sake."

"In fact, you and Catherine have remained friends?"

"Yes, more or less."

"She seems to be getting on pretty well on the stage. I saw in *France-Dimanche* that she was playing the leading part in something, I don't remember where."

"Yes; that's right. But to come back to you, it's not what you say that makes me laugh, but the way you say it in that inimitable way of yours. When I'm with you, you never speak of anyone but yourself; without ever interrupting yourself, you advance irresistibly like a tank."

"You ought to be flattered by the confidence I repose in you. But if I bore you, say so."

"You don't bore me."

"But what do you expect, old man? You've always been my confidant. Do you remember? 'I'll open my heart to you, follow me, sweet Receptacle.' Well, you continue to be it. There are people who are born to be confidants, and others born to play out their drama in public. The Oyarzun family belong to the second class."

"What have you got to confide this time?"

Roland did not answer at once. He shut his eyes to collect his thoughts. He sighed and crossed his hands on his breast.

"I should like to answer you precisely, but I can't. One thing's certain: my illness is not physical. The doctor said it was due to overwork. Nonsense!"

"Did the fever attack you suddenly without apparent cause?"

Roland kept his eyes shut. His hands lightly clenched themselves.

"Not without a cause, no. There was a cause. But I must tell you. . . . Oh, it's not easy! Well, it's like this: for some time I've felt that . . . that I was not at all easy in my mind. And then I've had sort of vague fears. As if something were threatening me, from outside or inside, I don't know which. All this suddenly came to a head the other day. It had to do with something I was reading."

"What were you reading?"

Roland opened his eyes. He smiled strangely and François saw the sweat forming on his forehead and at his temples.

"Guess."

"How can I guess?"

François remembered that this was one of Roland Oyarzun's childish characteristics: before confiding anything of importance, or if the avowal were difficult to make, he deferred it or endeavoured to escape it by inviting his companion to find out for himself what it was all about. "Guess." It was a childish game.

Roland stared at his friend, his eyes bright and fixed. He made a visible effort to speak.

"It was a dictionary."

"There are all sorts of things to be found in dictionaries," said François, laughing.

"A medical dictionary," Roland went on.

He shut his eyes again and swallowed with an air of suffering.

"I understand," said François. "You're just the type to frighten yourself with a medical dictionary."

"A cancer," murmured Roland. "I discovered that for years, without my knowing it, a cancer had been rotting me to the marrow. The dictionary told the whole history of this cancer, from antiquity to the present day."

"What do you . . . ?"

"It seems absurd to you, doesn't it?"

Roland emitted a long, hollow laugh. And then suddenly stopped short.

"It is absurd," he said more lightly. "I think I've gone off the rails. I expect the quack's right after all: overwork, damned overwork. Both physical and mental. Don't look like that. I must still have a temperature. Overwork. And with all my worries: this impossible flat, my children, my mother and that man she lives with, and then Bernard, still alive, whose articles I read merely to put myself in a rage, and it succeeds every time, beyond expectation."

"What! Do you mean to say you're still bothering about Bernard?"

"I've told you once already that the thought of him poisons my life."

"Couldn't you try to forget that business? After all, you can't do anything about it."

"Look behind you."

François turned round.

"There, the photograph on the mantelpiece. It's of my friend, my brother Jacques, killed by that cad of a Jew."

François picked up the photograph to examine it better. He vaguely recognised the young man he had met one day with Roland and Simone in the Underground. There was something rather brutal about the face which tarnished its youth. He put the photograph back on the mantelpiece.

"I repeat," he said, "that I think you ought to try to banish these painful memories. Time has moved on and it seems to me to be unhealthy to be eternally resuscitating old regrets and old hatreds. Without counting the fact that Bernard had very little responsibility for his death. Your hatred for him . . ."

"In Bernard I hate the whole Jewish race."

"What do you expect me to say to that? If you insist on poisoning your life with ridiculous hatreds of that kind, go ahead, but in that case no one can do anything for you."

"Clearly I'm boring you with my concerns. I can see I am. Perhaps you're not so good a confidant after all. In the first place you don't understand things at the first telling, nor even at the second, and besides, it's impossible to explain some things to you, because fundamentally you've remained very ingenuous. Innocent, in fact. And an utter infidel. One would think there was a screen, a sort of opaque glass between you Huguenots and certain aspects of life."

He looked at François with an expression of irritable condescension.

"Forget what I've told you, old man," he added. "Let's change the subject. Have you found out about a flat, as I asked you?"

"Yes. It's not easy. They're asking considerable premiums. I've got something in view in the Batignolles district. Could you find fifty thousand francs premium?"

"Fifty thousand? Christ, no!"

"Your mother might lend them to you. Have you been to see her?"

"Not yet."

"You should. The flat I've heard of has three rooms, a hall and a little kitchen. It doesn't sound too bad. Better than here, anyway."

Roland looked dejected.

"There or here," he murmured, "life would always be the

same. My job, my worries, my wife, my children. The same, day after day, till the end. It's intolerable!"

"And I thought I was doing something to please you!" François cried in feigned indignation. "What's the use of doing your friends a service?"

"Forgive me, old man. I'm ungrateful, I know. But you're face to face with a broken man."

"Come, come, Oyarzun, have courage. Remember your one great desire."

"What the hell are you talking about? I have no desires left, great or small."

"The desire whose realisation is in fact linked with your getting a larger and more convenient flat: your desire to have a son."

Roland winced.

"Don't talk of it!" he said loudly. "A son? Why should I put a son into the world? To bequeath him my misery? To turn him into a wreck like myself? No, no. And, besides, being a father's not always much fun. For instance, there was a time when my father and I meant everything to each other; while today . . ."

Once more he made the fatalistic gesture of raising his hand and letting it fall back again.

"I no longer desire anything," he said after a silence. "Except perhaps, sometimes . . ."

He fell silent again, and then asked dreamily: "Have you read *Li Fan Tchou et les Pirates*?"

"No," said François, frightened. ('He's gone off his head,' he thought.)

"I read it in *L'Intrépide* when I was a boy. I must have been ten or twelve then. It was a serial with coloured illustrations. It must have lasted for eighteen months, that serial. You can't imagine with what excitement I read it week by week. It was the story of a little Chinese boy, Li Fan Tchou, who was kidnapped by pirates. I can still see the pirate chief: Yen, his name was. He was a superb fellow, with wonderful pectoral muscles, and slit eyes, but not too slit, and the good looks of an intelligent brute. He was always naked to the waist, with a black cloth round his head and black, tight trousers with a large red sash. He scoured the Yellow River in a sampan. He wanted to make a real pirate out of Li Fan Tchou, a more successful one even than he was himself, but Li Fan Tchou wouldn't have anything to do with it, probably owing to Confucian morality. My God, that story fascinated me! Those two characters overwhelmed me, I couldn't make up my mind which I wanted to be: Li Fan Tchou, the brave and honest little boy, or Yen, the terrible great pirate."

He broke off, frowning.

"Why the devil am I telling you these idiocies? I'm going off the rails."

"It had something to do with what you were still able to desire."

"Oh, yes, of course. Asia. You see this serial was full of gambling-hells and opium-dens, which were always hidden in junks and flowered sampans on the river. There were also mysterious pagodas lost in the depths of the jungle, secret sanctuaries whose entrances were hidden by curtains of lianas. And when you went in, you suddenly saw, fearfully but too late, that, by God, the sanctuary was guarded by a giant cobra. Well, you'll laugh because it's funny enough at my age to have a desire like that, but I'd like to see all that, all those Asiatic things: gambling-hells, opium-dens, Chinese servants in long robes who understand everything without having to be told and who lead you silently down long shadowy roads. Along the streets of the Cholon district swarming with Chinese, prostitutes and sailors. Merely the sound of the word: Asia. Shut your eyes and say it. It has the effect of a drug on me. You see, there one has no more responsibilities, no more past, no more future, all links with Europe, with one's past habits, with one's duty, even with God perhaps, have been cut. There nothing is left but the present, and you can let yourself dissolve in the moment like a chip of metal in an acid bath. It must be absolutely wonderful, and I believe only possible in Asia, because over there putrefaction is in the ascendant. Asia. It seems to me to be much more than merely a section of the world. It seems to me to be . . . you'll laugh, because what I'm going to say sounds idiotic . . . it seems to me that it's a way of life. And, above all, a way of dying. And I think perhaps that that is what attracts me in the first place."

He had talked as if he were dreaming, with such a monotonous, such a "distant" tone of voice, that François was struck with it. And the strangeness of what he said worried him, too: Roland Oyarzun had never talked so strangely before. François could not understand what the man was driving at. The conversation had merely seemed to him unhealthy and rather embarrassing. He tried to make a joke of it: "You must admit that for a man who believes in order, and is a disciple of Maurras, it's a somewhat unexpected desire."

Once more Oyarzun gazed at him insistently, his expression troubled and at the same time a little ironical.

"Order. Order, my dear chap, it's a long time since order has had a place in my life. Besides, have I ever really been what you call a man of order?"

"Good gracious! I don't understand you."

Roland gave a little laugh which made his shoulders shake; but his eyes were not gay.

"You don't understand? That goes to show that there's a hell of a difference between an Asiatic servant and a French Huguenot. My good Donadieu, you're as pure as a spring morning. You don't even suspect what can stir in a man's heart. Ah, there's my wife."

A few minutes later François said goodbye.

"I'll come with you," said Simone. "I've some shopping to do. Is there anything you want, darling? I'll buy a paper."

She was not a very good actress. Her husband looked heavily at her.

"I thought you'd done all your shopping this morning."

"I see that I've forgotten to buy any oil," she said, blushing.

"Very well, very well. If you've got secrets to talk over with our friend, I shan't keep you."

She laughed, protesting awkwardly, "Good heavens, what'll you think of next!"

François would have liked to make his escape.

"I'm very anxious," Simone said when they had reached the street. "I asked you to come because you're our only friend and I know you're very fond of Roland. How did you think he was?"

"Not very well, perhaps, but not too bad."

"Did he say anything odd?"

"Well, you know as well as I do, if not better, his usual sort of worries: his mother, your flat, and that wretched Bernard who still obsesses him."

"Yes, yes; I know. But was there nothing else?"

"He seemed rather depressed," said François cautiously.

Simone took out a handkerchief and wiped her eyes.

"I had a terrible fright, the other night, when he fell ill. He came in and didn't say a word. He was as pale, as pale. I questioned him, I was terrified. It was as if he'd gone dumb, couldn't open his lips, had a sort of rigor from head to foot. He was shivering and rolling his eyes in the most terrible way, and without being able to see anything what's more. I went downstairs and asked the concierge to call the doctor, who arrived twenty minutes later. I had made Roland lie down, he was still shivering, even had convulsions, while his lips were so tightly compressed that they had gone almost white. The doctor gave him an intra-muscular injection. Little by little Roland went to sleep. He slept for a long time, but his sleep was very disturbed and, touching him, I could tell that he had a high temperature. The doctor came back the next day and gave him another injection. I went down to the street with him and he told me some very complicated things. I didn't understand, and haven't even remembered, them all. You know what difficult words doctors use. He used a word like 'tetanus', only it wasn't tetanus, it was something like 'catotonous' or 'cotatonous', I couldn't find it in the dictionary: 'catotonous state', he said. He also spoke—and I remember this because I put it down at once on a piece of paper—of anxiety and neurosis. 'Periodical neurosis' was his exact phrase. And also of 'psychasthenia'. I looked up the word in the dictionary, but it was not very well explained and I was frightened because I thought it meant the early stages of madness. When the doctor came back, I asked him. He reassured me: 'It's got nothing to do with lunacy,' he said, 'but it's mental just the same. Your husband is suffering from a psychological trouble. I don't think he's really ill. Rather, I'd say that he was escaping into illness.' He asked me some very embarrassing questions on Roland's behaviour towards me. You know what I mean, don't you? I told him that, as far as that was concerned, I hadn't noticed anything out of the ordinary. Naturally, Roland isn't . . . well, you understand, as he was in the early days of our marriage, but that's normal: physical love doesn't last for ever. But Roland was never very demanding in that way. In words he gives the impression of what's vulgarly known as pretty sexy, you know him: those soldiers' songs that used to shock me so much, and his Marseillais stories. But in fact, as far as I can judge, I should think he's pretty average. You know,

François, I can only talk to you about these intimate things because I have confidence in you and because you're our friend. Then the doctor asked me whether Roland was fussy, whether he was peculiarly precise, checked the contents of his pockets several times over for instance. 'Doctor,' I said, 'you've placed your finger on the spot: my husband is a real maniac in that way. You've seen the front door, Doctor, it's barred like the entrance to a fortress. Well, every night my husband checks up several times to see that it's properly shut, and every bolt in place, as if he were frightened of burglars or God knows what. He even checks up on it sometimes in the daytime.' But this mania of his may be simply due to the trouble he had at the time of the Liberation. I'm telling you this, François, I didn't tell the doctor, as it wasn't worth the risk of turning him against us: you see, if he was in the Resistance, one never knows. 'Another thing, Doctor,' I said to him, 'my husband is obsessed by illness. At the slightest indisposition he thinks he's going to die. He imagines himself ill. For instance, he's terribly afraid of cancer. And then, as to cleanliness, Doctor. Of course, one must be clean, but my husband could spend his life washing himself. He washes his hands fifty times a day. He insisted on buying a bath and I had to fill it with hot water every night so that he could bathe himself, while I scrubbed his back with a hard brush; goodness me, that was something, I can tell you! Luckily, in the job he's got now, he can have a shower whenever he likes.' Then the doctor asked me what were Roland's relations with his family. I told him what I knew, which is what you know too, doubtless. He listened attentively, nodding his head. He talked of a psychiatrist. It so happened that I had just read an article about psychiatrists in New York in the *Reader's Digest*. Roland often buys the *Reader's Digest*; you know his enthusiasm for the things of the mind. He's very intellectual, isn't he? Always out for culture—she said these last words as if she were placing them in a sort of oral parenthesis, and with a sort of timid pride, while glancing quickly at François with a half anxious, half defiant eye, as if uncertain of the effect she was producing—so I knew that psychiatrists are in general very expensive. I said so to the doctor. He merely shrugged his shoulders as if to say: 'What do you expect me to do about it!' and went away."

"Before this crisis, had you had any previous cause for alarm about Roland?"

"Yes; several times. For instance, one day I was in the kitchen. I went into the dining-room or, that's to say, the other room. I saw Roland in front of the looking-glass that hangs over the mantelpiece. He was looking at himself, or something, I don't know what, and he had an appearance of, an appearance of . . . Well, I don't know, but I very nearly screamed. He saw me. Then he passed his hand across his eyes and sat down. Another time was in the morning, very early. I woke up, feeling vaguely ill at ease. I opened my eyes. I saw Roland leaning over me, resting on an elbow and looking at me without saying anything, as if I were a stranger. He had an odd look on his face, which terrified me."

She began crying again and blew her nose.

"My God, I'm unhappy! You don't know what it means to live side by side with someone who is in a perpetual state of anxiety and disquiet. One becomes a bit crazy oneself."

"And yet, in the old days, your husband was quite stable, wasn't he?"

"Yes, he was, wasn't he? He was a solid sort of man. It all began with the death of my poor brother. Until then, Roland was active, happy, and optimistic. Always nervous, of course: you've noticed his tics, the little muscles that move under the skin of his face. But, anyway, he was all right. Jacques' death was a great shock to him. Jacques amused him, entertained him, he was so young in character, a real boy. I think Roland's bored since Jacques' death. And then all that happened to us at the Liberation on the top of it: the prosecution, the appalling sentence, the shame Roland felt, the three months in prison, National Indignity. All these trials finished him. Just think: a patriot like he was being condemned to National Indignity, it was like an officer being reduced to the ranks. Exactly the same. He's never recovered from it. I no longer know to what saint to pray. The best thing would be to go abroad. I read somewhere that they want agricultural workers in Canada. I very nearly wrote. France is ruined for us, for Roland. We need a free, active life in the open air, without politics, without this poison! Roland needs to face the future like a man. And I think that's where the trouble lies. It took me years to find out that in certain respects Roland was still a little boy. Of course," she corrected herself, blushing, "I don't mean . . . well, from the physical point of view, it's not that," she blushed and stammered all the more. "No, I mean to say from the mental point of view; he's still a schoolboy, still sodden with his own youth, his childhood, his past, his father, his mother, and his school. And even his politics—and God knows he took them seriously enough!—well, I think they were still a kind of school game, a matter of insignia in the button-hole and slogans shouted in chorus. In the old days, when Jacques used to visit us, I used to watch them, hear them talking, the two of them together, and I couldn't help thinking: 'What little boys they are!' At that time Roland was happy: he had Jacques, he had his pupils, he had Marshal Pétain, whom he blindly worshipped, and he had his political ideology. What was it called now? Oh, yes, the National Revolution. Since it made him happy, I let him go on believing in it, you understand, it did no one any harm and was of no particular consequence, at least so I thought. Anyway, it was better than if he had gone running off to brothels, or spent his days playing cards in a café, as so many men do. Personally, I should have preferred him to be fond of doing odd jobs about the house, or making models, like the husband of a friend of mine who is always making model aeroplanes. But, anyway, he was passionately fond of politics and his hobby-horse was the National Revolution: so much for the National Revolution. When I heard them discussing Vichy, Jacques and he, or when I saw them designing projected decorations for Youth Rallies, I used to say to myself: 'My men are contented,' and I used to knit quietly in my corner, my heart full. Unfortunately, those childish things were more serious than I thought. Ah, if only I could have foreseen!"

François stopped walking. He took hold of Simone by the shoulders. He was astonished at this sort of naïve lucidity, this perspicacity without arrogance, this profundity of judgment which yet remained homely and indulgent. What an extraordinary little woman she was, and how she deserved to be happy, was worthy of happiness! She saw her husband as he was, yet continued to love him tenderly, to protect him, to devote herself to him and even, nor was this the least wonderful thing about her love, continued to admire him. François was sorry for her, for that poor, anxious, crumpled little face, which misfortune had not succeeded in rendering ugly, but then misfortune does not render ugly those who have nobility of soul. Suddenly, he pulled her to him and kissed her cheek. She gave a little smile, accompanied by an expression of mild surprise.

"Simone, what you've just said is extraordinarily true. Do you know that his mother said something very similar?"

He told her not to worry, that there was no need: Roland was not seriously ill, and it would all blow over. He said many reassuring things. He said she could count on him, and that he would come whenever she sent for him. As he talked, she seemed to return from the depths of despair, her face brightened, her eyes recaptured the brilliance of youth. As they passed a flower-barrow, he bought her branches of mimosa and bunches of narcissi. He would have bought her sweets if there had been a confectioner in the neighbourhood. As he said goodbye to her, he kissed her on the cheek once more. It was a long time since he had felt so happy.

CHAPTER III

THIS NEW WORLD (CONCLUDED)

1

IT was a long time since he had felt so happy; but it did not last. The pleasures of kindness are as fugitive as any other. A few weeks later he received another letter from Simone Oyarzun, who this time merely asked him to luncheon, and he found it no more than importunate. He did not answer it and remorse at not having done so worried him for several weeks.

At Easter that year he had Juliette and the cousin in whose care she was to stay with him. It was the first time the child had visited her father in Paris. The journey, which had been in prospect for some time, seemed miraculous to her: she dreamed about it every day. Her joy was almost painful to see, so contained and repressed was its expression. The child was so sensitive that she needed very careful handling. François felt a great tenderness for the little girl who somewhat resembled him and to whom he undoubtedly meant a great deal. He would have liked to buy her all the toys in the world, but there was no need of dolls with articulated joints to make Juliette happy; it was enough to take her for a walk, her hand in his, and talk to her affectionately. François naturally took her to the Châtelet, and to the ballet at the Opera, as well as to see animated cartoons at the cinema. One day the child came with her cousin to pick him up at the motor-car showroom where he was employed. François, very smartly dressed, was in process of giving a Belgian customer his line of sales-talk. During three years in the trade he had learnt all the professional tricks of commercial selling, an exercise for which he had previously had no training and in which he would never have believed he could be successful. But, contrary to Roland Oyarzun's opinion, he had succeeded well and was highly thought of by his employers, who valued his skilful presentation of their cars and the good impression he made upon their customers of sincerity and honesty and of taking a discreet interest in their requirements. Moreover, his professional conscience had made him familiarise himself with the arcane mysteries of mechanics to the point, at least, of being able to discuss them with anyone who was not an expert. Juliette opened her eyes wide when she saw her young father moving about the vast showroom with as much authority as if the whole building belonged to him, including the four or five splendid cars which were exposed for sale on a velvet carpet like jewels in a jewel-case. Even her father's voice sounded different. Juliette was surprised. Our intimates always disconcert us a little the first time we see them in the exercise of their profession. In this role, in which we now see them for the first time, they display an ease and certainty which we find disturbing. François was negligently tapping a car's bonnet. "Of course," he was saying in a tone of voice that implied incontestable evidence, "as far as the quality and finish of the coachwork are concerned, we have succeeded in beating pretty nearly every other firm on the European market. Except, of course, for the Italians," he added like a man concerned above all for the truth. (This homage to Italian coachwork was, of course, an improvisation of the moment. At other times the competing coachwork was English or American.) "I won't pretend that we've altogether beaten the Italians. It wouldn't be true. But . . ."

He followed this up with a few complicated technical terms. In the meantime, the Belgian customer was bending over the bonnet, gazing at the unrivalled (except in Milan) coachwork, while François looked across at Juliette and gave her a sly wink, a wink of complicity. At once the child's face lit up with a radiant smile like a wave of light.

He wrote to Catherine to tell her that Juliette had arrived. On the first day the child had examined the small flat in which her father lived on the sixth floor of a block in the Rue de Berri, as if she were trying to find signs of an habitual feminine presence. She found nothing but a photograph of her mother—a photograph which François had put out for the occasion. Though she made no comment, François was ashamed, feeling himself to blame in face of her earnest, innocently inquisitive gaze.

"Mummy is on holiday in Switzerland," he said.

The next day Catherine arrived, elegant, scented, her arms

laden with little presents. She was kind and gay and behaved so naturally to François that he almost had the sensation of having left her but the day before. But Juliette was much less open and much less confident with her than with her father. But these family reunions passed off without incident.

François had several opportunities of being alone with Catherine and discovered that there was no constraint between them. He knew that she was the mistress of young Thibault Fontanes. A few echoes in the Press, a few photographs in the illustrated magazines (*France-Dimanche*, *Match* had shown them together at the *Rose Rouge* and on the beach at Juan-les-Pins) had seemed to suggest a liaison. Then the vague rumours in the social columns had stopped and for long months Catherine Vallier's name was never mentioned. The love of novelty was insatiable. At first François had felt a certain bitterness: but, after all, he too had his private life, and they had been separated for so long now. His bitterness quickly turned into indifference. Besides, Thibault Fontanes was a successor for whom he need not blush. François remembered having seen the young man at a first night at the theatre. He remembered the visiting card he had given Catherine in her dressing-room: "Thibault Fontanes, a Coming Man." He had read the young author's book: *Une Étoile de Sang*. He thought it something of a masterpiece, saw in it something similar in effect to that made after the first war by *Le Songe* of Montherlant, whose influence indeed was discernible in Fontanes. With as much panache as his illustrious elder clothed in the horizon blue of 1914-18, the young warrior, clad in the khaki of 1944-5, showed a greater versatility, a greater subtlety perhaps, and certainly more humour. Beneath the double ensign of war and poetry (the book bore on its title page Apollinaire's line: "*Une étoile de sang me couronne à jamais*"), Fontanes' story was in fact a wonderful hymn to youth, pleasure, and the heedless sacrifice of which a boy of twenty is capable. The plot was unfolded against the background of a fantastic, superbly Wagnerian Germany. The boy soldiers of the First Army moved through the solemn shadows of the huge German forests, their arms slung, a daisy between their teeth; their redolent speech, heavily spiced with military slang, and incredible obscenities, shocked the fairies and the sprites of those ancestral groves. Sometimes the tone rose to a sober lyricism. There was, too, a Loreleï, a tall and beautiful girl, perverse and fatal, who played with the bodies and hearts of two friends (two aspects of the author) and, naturally, the younger of the two, the better and more charming, found death among these games of love, hate and chance. Upon this deliberately conventional and romantically woven plot, Fontanes had embroidered the most dazzling scenes. The book was often very funny, but beneath the laughter quivered a sort of chaste tenderness, an intense awareness of the pathos of life. Such was the book which had achieved a lively and deserved success, even though some of the critics had condemned it with the words, pejorative at that time, of "frivolity" and "brilliance". Bernard, for instance, was obstinately determined to consider Fontanes an author of no importance. It was true that he had other than literary grievances against him.

In his intermittent arguments with Bernard, François had from time to time supported Thibault Fontanes, which irritated Bernard. It was an irritation into which there entered that particular kind of resentment which certain dominating characters are prone to feel when they see the faithful taking a line of their own, their disciples betraying them, and those they thought submissive for ever emancipating themselves. (There are other characters who are so assured of their own superiority, so confident of their own power, so full of themselves, that these defections leave them perfectly indifferent.) François saw in the Fontanes-Bernard rivalry a miniature of a vaster conflict, of a sort of modern political tragedy. No, 'tragedy' was too big a word. Or at least, such a tragedy could only exist on some less obvious level, on the level of the emotions, in the great passionate waves that beat about the shoals, in that mysterious point of fusion where what are called 'ideologies' and 'doctrines' meet the abyss of psychology and are merged with it—François was thinking of Roland Oyarzun. But Fontanes and Bernard were much too intelligent to suffer from the blows they gave each other, and much too intellectual to be opposed to each other in reality. One day their quarrel might well be resolved in a superior smile of complicity.

François saw less and less of Bernard, whose daily life still consisted of an imbroglio of gallant appointments, political conferences, and journalistic tours about Europe, indeed the world. He had recently left for Indo-China whence he intended bringing back a series of articles for *Horizons*. He was to meet Ho Chi Min, the Emperor Bao Dai, and other eminent personages. This globe-trotting role, half adventurer, half journalist (Koestler, Malaparte) gave him great satisfaction. He played it light-heartedly. (Paraphrasing Malraux, he had one day said to François: "I have chosen the lies of heroism.") But it occurred to François that as modern American children like to be given interplanetary travel, 'space-man', outfits for Christmas, so, adult, intelligent and cultured as he was, Bernard remained the spoilt child who demanded the latest fashionable toys, the fine uniform of 'the great political eye-witness', of 'the modern condottière', the trappings of the 'space-man'.

* * *

"Do you mind," Thibault asked, "if I read yesterday's papers while you're dressing? I've hardly had the time to read Bernard's article about me. Sunday morning in bed is the time to appreciate the more important articles of the best contemporary journalism."

He reached out a hand and seized a pile of newspapers from the bedside table. 'If I weren't here,' thought Catherine, 'he would have been up two hours ago, he'd have had his shower, his coffee, and gone to his desk. He must be impatient for me to go.' She looked at him. Leaning back against the pillows, his pyjama jacket wide open, his hair falling untidily over his forehead, he looked like a great, overgrown schoolboy. He had the schoolboy's plump cheeks, his round and beardless chin, his full lips, and a surly, childish air about him. But she well knew the energy that this childish aspect concealed. This young man of twenty-four could work a dozen hours a day for months on end. He could pass whole nights in reading with the voracity of an intellectual ogre. He neither smoked, nor drank, avoided all excess, and lived on grills and fruit-juice. He was capable of any form of self-discipline. He knew what he wanted and where he was going. He was most certainly not a child, even when he amused himself in a childish way. Catherine pondered the fact that she had not yet discovered his zones of weakness and defencelessness, the chink in the armour which in the end one always finds in others and which makes them human. Thibault appeared invulnerable.

She was unable to dissipate a certain sense of dissatisfaction and melancholy. Awake since dawn, oppressed by the weight of the young man's head on her shoulder, his arm on her waist, she had awaited daylight in order to slip from the bed without waking Thibault. In spite of infinite precautions she had woken him, but he had immediately gone to sleep again. In the bathroom, before the looking-glass, she breathed again. Face to face with her own image, she savoured the tender delight of this moment of intimacy with herself. She envied those women who can spend hours at their dressing-tables, induing themselves with the apparatus of beauty, consecrating the most precious hours of the day to their bodies and their faces. 'If I were rich, I should have a bathroom of unimaginable luxury, with looking-glasses everywhere, massage machines, a selection of creams, unguents and make-up, the most expensive scents.' Her dressing-table had always been her favourite distraction, her sin, her vice. Not from vanity exactly, for she was well aware of her physical imperfections and was not unduly concerned about them. No, it was something else. There was a calm, profound, obscure, almost vegetable pleasure to be derived from these hours of minutely attentive ease before the looking-glass, from hands massaging the face with little, delicate gestures, smoothing, soothing, applying emollient oils, from all those expert operations that the women's magazines describe at such length. Here was the domain of pure femininity, impregnated with odours, glittering with scent-bottles, glass caskets and boxes containing a thousand mysterious and magic treasures each of whose virtues it was fascinating to try in turn. Rather than 'bathroom', a cold, clinical word, evoking walls tiled in a cruel white, Catherine would have preferred to speak of a 'boudoir', and it was of a boudoir that she dreamed: a cosy, upholstered place from which man was excluded, a warm, rose-tinted shell within which, sheltered from the world, she might curl up like some happy animal. The old-fashioned word 'boudoir', with its imaginative associations (Mme de Pompadour, Watteau, silks, satins, taffetas, powdered wigs, the indolent grace of the eighteenth century) secretly moved her as, in an allied train of thought, she was moved by the words 'odalisque', 'harem' and 'gynaeceum'.

This morning the rites of her toilet gave her less pleasure than usual. The terrible, naked, wakening face seemed to show up in greater relief than on other days, so she thought, the outrages of the years at the corners of her lips and eyelids, and beneath her chin. She told herself that at times Thibault must think her ugly. She told herself that time was passing and that as yet nothing decisive had supervened in her life. She felt a great lassitude weighing her shoulders down.

Thibault was reading. She went and sat beside him, leaning forward a little so as to be able to read too.

"*In the last number of* Parsifal, *M. Thibault Fontanes once again attacks the intellectual Left, those he calls the Girondins Without attacking me by name, as he did in his earlier diatribe,* The Scribblers, *published in December, 1947, in* France Nouvelle, *he spares the weekly review I have the honour to edit none of his arrows. But in fact M. Fontanes' arrows lack point. Perhaps his polemical style would have had some chance of attaining its mark before the war, for instance during the years 1920-5 for which the author of* Une Étoile de Sang *seems to nurse so tenacious a nostalgia—though in fact he did not live through them—and whose spirit he has apparently determined to reanimate, at least in Letters. Today, however, these witticisms, paradoxes and frivolities have lost much of their effect. . . .*"

"But of course!" cried Thibault, interrupting his reading to point to the last phrase with his finger, "nothing pays today but the tedious! But he's wrong: far from being behind the times, I'm in advance of them, I'm paving the way for a return to classicism, lightness of touch and wit. Isn't that so, darling?"

He turned his head lightly towards her and stroked her cheek with his chin. His eyes shone.

"I am paving the way for a return to classicism, aren't I?" he repeated.

"Yes, you'll be the Cocteau of the second half of the century," Catherine replied, prompt to give her answer the appropriate ring.

"I didn't ask you to say it! But let's go on."

"*M. Fontanes wishes to be non-contemporary, if not old-fashioned. He clearly succeeds in being both one and the other. There is something rather painful in the spectacle of this young writer endeavouring to recapture the sterile frivolity of a decade which, with its fashion in clothes and decorative art, is irremediably buried. We are not unaware that 1925 is a great date in the history of Letters: it witnessed the flowering of surréalism, it was the great period of Morand, Drieu la Rochelle, Chardonne, Cocteau, Giraudoux, Mauriac and Montherlant, a wonderful literary galaxy. Nevertheless, the period of 'exquisite corpses', cocktails and the bachelor girl is well and truly over. Since then we have had some millions of corpses and have failed to find them exquisite. But we are not here concerned with literature. We have said elsewhere . . .*"

"I wonder why he uses the royal 'we'," said Thibault. "It creates such a very humble effect when one doesn't happen to be Louis XIV. It's true, of course, that in order to say 'I', you've got in the first place to be someone."

"*We have said elsewhere how little we care for this author's first work,* Une Étoile de Sang, *a brilliant and useless book. . . .*"

"There," cried Thibault, "there's an admission! A useless book, and useless because it's brilliant. For M. Bernard, presumably, literature should be useful and boring. Clearly, one couldn't be more humble than that. Sartre says the same thing, but with more brio. God, how dull it all is!"

"*It is not as a literary artist that M. Fontanes interests us. He interests us simply to the extent that he represents, and moreover in a limited field, a phenomenon of crystallisation . . .*"

"These poor young men trained in the crude discipline of Marxist dialectic really express themselves in a most extraordinary way. Here I am transmuted into a phenomenon of crystallisation. You'll see, in a moment I shall become a little superstructure or infrastructure, I really don't know which. . . ."

". . . *phenomenon of crystallisation of certain reactionary elements. Every attentive witness of the age cannot fail to discern, in France as in the rest of the world, a sliding, an orientation towards the Right, even a reawakening of Fascism or, at least of the forces of conservatism and reaction. This reaction was to be foreseen. But, at this hour, it is impossible to predict the extent of the orientation or its future effect upon the political life of the country. The causes of this reversal are multiple. And without doubt the most important is the fear inspired by the power of the U.S.S.R. among the middle and managerial classes. The West shows every symptom of an anti-Communist phobia, sometimes even to the point of hysteria, till even the most calm suffer from the contagion. There is another cause, and this is a strictly national one, I mean limited to our own country. France has a minority of ex-Vichyites and collaborators of whom a certain proportion suffered, after the Liberation, the sanctions appropriate to the crimes of which they were guilty. This minority has never forgiven us. They suffer from a corrosive and all-pervading complex, which might be termed the complex of the excluded or of the emigrants. Following Maurras, they always made a distinction between the state and the country, and now they find themselves equally condemned by both, since, having been already convicted by the State, that conglomeration which they call 'the country' holds collaboration and Pétainism in horror and stigmatises it in their persons.*"

"That remains to be proved," Thibault said. "What does M. Bernard know of the country's real opinion about Pétainism? He only knows what the Press says, and this is inspired by a minority who merely hold power provisionally."

"*These pseudo-realists who have always revered the true logic of facts and, through 'realism', bowed before the defeat of 1940, should also bow before the history of 1945 and accept the condemnation of their policies. Drieu had accepted in advance the fact of his own suicide. Laval tried to poison himself. The fact that the Fascists carry a phial of cyanide of potassium shows well enough that they know what risks they run and what their fate will be if they have the misfortune to lose. But it would seem that our ex-Vichyites and ex-collaborators have great difficulty in accepting the rules of the game as applied to themselves. The truth is that in politics one never admits defeat. We appear to have strayed some distance from M. Thibault Fontanes, whom, moreover, the above only indirectly concerns: for indeed, during the occupation, M. Fontanes was at the age of Latin proses and short trousers. In 1944 he enlisted in the First French Army. One can hardly, therefore, accuse him of collaboration or of Vichyism, but his whole cast of mind and everything he writes breathes 'reaction'. Since he is both insolent and what is called 'fashionable', it is natural that certain writers of his own age, or younger, and whose political pasts are less innocent than his own, should group themselves round him as if he were a magnetic pole. Everything they write has a curious quality of angry negation, of snarling hostility, of vindictive acrimony. As for the literary 'doctrine' of this group, in so far as one can speak of a doctrine when as yet there exist no more than tendencies, it may be defined as a return to that formal manner which has been called 'classicism', to art for art's sake and to irresponsibility, the usual refuge of those who have something on their conscience. So here is M. Fontanes installing himself as leader and spokesman to a group of the proscribed, whose hatreds, even more than their past activities, have place on the margin of the community of the nation. But for a long time past it has been the strange and unhappy destiny of those who call themselves nationalists to exist merely on the verge of the great and authentic currents that flow through the nation.*"

"Have you finished?" asked Thibault before turning the page.

"Yes. What are you going to say to him by way of reply?"

"I don't think I shall answer this time. I'm beginning to tire of the controversy. I've already given M. Bernard a drubbing three times, but it's not as if we were playing Molière, where a drubbing's always funny. Naturally, Marcellin will become wildly angry, start shouting and try to persuade me to reply. But I think I shall do no more than add a little note to my next article in *Parsifal.* A postscript of three or four lines, something of this kind: '*One knows that M. Bernard writes the page of political notes, signed "Minotaur", in* Horizons. *The little argument we have had during the last few months looks as if it might go on for ever, and I hereby inform M. Bernard that I am delighted to leave him the last moo.*' "

Catherine smiled. She took a lock of his hair above the forehead, and wound it round her fingers.

"How you hate that man," she said automatically.

"Not at all! I even have a certain feeling of sympathy for him. After all, he's a reasonably honourable opponent. I should like to have a chance of meeting him. His article's not at all bad, you know. Boring, of course, but his analysis of the causes of 'reaction' and so on are reasonably sound."

"Is there anything you don't find boring?" she said.

"At least one thing, my dear. By an unfortunate chance, it just happens to be one of the things that bore you."

She let go of the lock of his hair and slowly rose. She went to the window, lifted the net curtain and looked out.

"Is it raining, is the sun out, what's it like?" he asked.

"It's like Sunday," she said without moving.

He opened a review with a red cover and began to read. There was a fairly long silence.

"Thibault," she said at last. "Look at me, please."

He raised his eyes and turned his head towards her. She was standing with the thin outline of her body dark against the pale religious light of the white screen of the curtains. She had slipped her hands into the pockets of her blue dressing-gown. He guessed she was smiling.

"Could you manage," she went on with some hesitation, "to be quite natural with me just for ten minutes?"

"My dear, what an impertinence! If I'm not natural with you, I don't know what more you want? I can't be more so."

"Oh, no doubt, no doubt. But do you think you could also manage to say and listen to some extremely unpleasant and disagreeable things for the next ten minutes? You might note the fact that I'm not asking you to address me with any intimacy, nor even to call me Catherine instead of 'my dear', I should not do such inconceivable violence to your feelings as that, but . . ."

She went slowly towards him. Her face emerged, tired and a little old, from the shadows.

"Thibault," she said very gently, "you long not to see me any more, don't you?"

"For heaven's sake, don't become mournful; it's extremely uncomfortable any day of the week, but particularly on Sunday morning. Besides, it would be unjust. I'm the most sensitive and tender-hearted chap in the world."

"I've no intention of being mournful. But children get so bored on Sundays, they've got to play to keep them occupied; and since you don't like chess or mah-jongg or whist, I propose the truth game, which is a trifle more disconcerting."

She again sat down beside him and again took a lock of his hair in her fingers. Thibault had closed the review, but kept his forefinger between the pages he had begun reading. He stayed perfectly still, his eyes half closed, his expression suddenly hard.

"Very well," he said in an altered voice. "Begin."

She was playing gently with his hair.

"You don't love me, Monsieur Fontanes."

"I have never told you I loved you," he murmured.

"That's true, but you pretended to, or at least there was an element of make-believe."

"The whole of life has an element of make-believe."

"Perhaps, perhaps. . . . It's very strange. But there are people, you know, for whom love and all that is a very serious business. Of course, they're not novelists."

"That's all very fine. But as far as I know you're not a novelist, and yet there was an element of make-believe about it for you too. I know that you've had all the difficulty in the world in trying to make this particular form of make-believe credible, because there are certain, shall we say sentiments, that even an excellent actress such as yourself can only feign with difficulty."

"Why have we pretended, Thibault?"

"God knows. Probably because we're light-minded and frivolous, as the good M. Bernard would say. A lost generation, aren't we? For instance, one of my friends pushes cynicism so far as even to draw lots for the women he is going to love. He draws lots with pieces of paper in a hat. You can't expect anything of us after that! It's really startlingly amoral. Moreover, this friend of mine is a perfectly intolerable chap."

"Yes. But I don't belong to your generation, Thibault. I'm a good deal older than you, and it was not altogether from frivolity that I pretended to love you. Would you like me to tell you my reasons?"

"No," he said drily.

"Why not? You surely don't want to spare yourself?"

"It's rather you I wish to spare. You see, I guessed your reasons from the first moment."

"Yes, I suppose it's difficult for us to deceive each other. To 'delude' each other, as some of your characters would say."

She continued smiling while she played with his lock of hair. He kept his eyes half closed, smiling too, and the muscles at his temples and jaw contracted at regular intervals.

"Are you bored with this game?" she asked.

"My God, it would be worse if you made a scene. I'm grateful to you for your good behaviour."

"You'd be more grateful to me for silence. Or absence. I prevent your working and you love your work more than anything else. Between nine o'clock in the morning and ten at night we're a nuisance, aren't we? It's a pity no one has invented robot women suitable for the use of workers such as you. In the morning you'd pull out the electric plug and hang the robot up in a cupboard till nightfall. It'd be very handy."

"You've got a romantic novelist's imagination. And a pretty horrible one, I must say."

She got up and walked slowly to the middle of the room. With her hands in her pockets, she gazed towards the light rectangle of the window, and seemed to meditate for a few moments. At last, she said in a toneless voice, "I was thirty-two yesterday."

Thibault opened his eyes.

"You don't look it, my dear," he said lightly.

"Thibault," she went on after a silence, "I must tell you certain things. They don't make sense, but I must express . . . express myself. I don't love you. You know that. At least, what's called love. . . . I agreed to our liaison half for want of something to do, half from calculation. I had no one. I was alone. You came along. I accepted you because you might be useful to me. You're something of a young celebrity, you've made your mark and I think you'll last. Being your mistress gave me a position, might afford me opportunities, new parts. Since you guessed my reasons from the first, I'm not telling you anything you don't know. But I had to tell you this out loud, tell it you. Well, apparently, I was still living in a world of illusions. Our association has not turned out so profitably. For six months I haven't had an offer, not even of the smallest part, nothing. A complete blank. A gulf of silence. Not even an echo in the Press. It's as if I'd never played a part. As if I were still completely unknown. The world moves too quickly, consumes too many things and too many people in too little time. Everything is forgotten between one season and the next, one always has the impression of being at the foot of the wall, of having to regain by force the little one thought one had won and which has been lost again. I feel I'm sinking. You, Thibault, manage to get on all right. You're rich. I mean to say: rich with inexhaustible internal riches. That's why you'll always get on all right. But I'm no more than one little actress among a great many. I know something of my trade, that's all. I'm no longer at the age when all dreams are permissible. I'm at the age when one begins to be panic-stricken when the gap lasts too long. But above all, Thibault, don't show me any pity because of what I've just said. I have a horror of pity, as you have. I've told you all this to show you that I see things clearly, it was a way of making you understand that, from a certain point of view, I deserve better of you that merely politeness, consideration and courtesy. For example, I could do with a little companionship, a little of the warmth of friendship; and, after all, it doesn't let you in for anything. Perhaps, however, it's too much to ask. You don't possess much warmth in the ordinary way. You can dazzle but you don't warm."

Suddenly she looked him straight in the face, smiling, her eyes bright.

"Don't I talk well, when I want to?" she said. "It was a perfect monologue! My poor Thibault, I haven't even got your coffee and toast. How neglectful I always am! And there you are simply dying to get up and get to work! I'll give you your coffee in five minutes and then I'll get out."

She left the room. He heard her moving the cups and saucers in the little kitchen next door. For some seconds he remained lying down, his hands behind his head, his expression serious and thoughtful. Then, he got up and went into the bathroom. Catherine came in and placed the breakfast tray on the table. She took from the tray a little photograph and examined it with intense and eager concentration. Then, she placed it very much in evidence on Thibault's napkin. The latter came out of the bathroom, knotting the cord of his dressing-gown; he saw the photograph at once; the blood flamed in his cheeks.

"Where did you . . ." he began, giving her an angry glance.

Catherine watched him curiously.

"You dropped your notecase and the photograph must have fallen out. I found it on the floor, next to the open notecase, in front of the hanging-cupboard."

He had already hidden the photograph away in his pocket.

"She's very beautiful," Catherine went on calmly. "Very beautiful. I seem to recognise her. I believe you introduced us one day at the *Rose Rouge*. It is Lorraine, isn't it?"

He nodded his head. His ears were still scarlet. He sat down and unfolded his napkin. Catherine, still standing, her hands in her pockets, went on looking at him with her eyes half closed.

"She was with a chap called Michel, a friend of yours, I think. Isn't that so?"

"You've got an excellent memory. I hope this discovery hasn't made you spoil the coffee. I'm like Balzac when it comes to coffee."

He had regained control of himself, his usual defiant, ironic ease.

"So that's it," Catherine murmured. "Lorraine's your weakness?"

* * *

As Thibault had foreseen, Marcellin was furiously angry about Bernard's latest retort.

"You must answer!" he told Thibault. "You simply must answer him. Those fellows are still arrogant" (he meant by "those fellows" the new men of the Liberation—as Roland Oyarzun, more dramatically, referred to them by such harsh epithets as: 'brutish', 'filthy', 'abject', which from time to time he followed by such nouns as 'brutish curs', 'filthy shits', and so on), "they're still arrogant, but they're losing a little more of it each day, they're beginning to realise that they're not taken altogether seriously, that their lies no longer take people in. With the passing of the years, History sits in judgment, and they know they'll be judged, that they, who created the iniquitous Tribunals, are already up for judgment. Every crime committed by the Resistance, and the newspapers reveal a new one nearly every week, open the eyes of Frenchmen a little wider to their horror and imposture. There's a low murmur of indignation throughout the country, and it'll burst out. If you won't reply this time, Fontanes, I'll do it myself, I'll show up this impudent Jew."

As soon as it was a question of his grievances against the Resistance, Marcellin became positively lyrical. Sometimes Thibault had to repress a smile. It astonished him that anyone so intelligent, so exquisitely cultured, so sensitive and kindly, who adored his wife and children, who made a cult of friendship (with what tender emotion he spoke of two of his dearest friends, shot in 1945), who was undoubtedly capable of the greatest generosity, seemed to lose all sense of proportion and restraint, even a great deal of his good sense, the moment it became a matter of political ideology. Thus, for instance, he allowed himself to show an extraordinary hatred for the Jews. His anti-Semitism, which had been much shaken during and immediately after the war by the appalling pogrom, seemed now to reconstitute itself and, three years after the Liberation, to be beginning again with all its pristine fire. It was somewhat painful to hear him give vent to the usual jokes against 'Israel', talk of 'Yids' and 'Sheenies' with much the same tone of bestial aversion that sounded in Roland Oyarzun's voice. It seemed that his intelligence at these moments suffered a momentary eclipse.

Marcellin replied to Bernard in *France Nouvelle*, with a mixture of cold reasoning and passionate violence. He began by contesting the notion of 'error' as applied to the Collaboration. If the Resistance thought it was showing forbearance and magnanimity in excusing the 'sincere Pétainists' on the grounds that they were 'mistaken', they were under a strange misapprehension: for the Pétainists had never for a single moment considered sheltering behind the pitiful excuse of 'error committed in good faith'. And, indeed, on what grounds could the policy of Collaboration be considered erroneous? On one ground only, in that it had failed to triumph. If Germany had ultimately won, it would have been Gaullisme and the Gaullists who would have been condemned. But the truth of a doctrine does not depend upon the fluctuations of history, nor is the justice of a cause affected by the hazards of war; pretending the contrary constituted the fraud of the Purge. Marcellin followed this with the apologia of Collaboration, a necessary and fecund policy which had rendered immense service to the country, both in sparing it the fate of Poland and in limiting the havoc of war. Similarly, the Armistice had saved France from the worst. While, on the other hand, the terrorism of the *Maquis* was a cause of innumerable misfortunes: the execution of hostages, deportations, an increase in the severity of the German domination. What seeming usefulness was served by stabbing an enemy officer in the Underground? But this absurd, mean, vain act was repaid by the death of twenty or thirty innocent Frenchmen. And, considering the matter on a higher level, Marcellin quoted the opinion, and a pretty severe one it was, of an eminent English political personage upon the value and results of underground warfare in occupied countries. Finally, he demanded the revision of the 'infamous prosecutions' and ended his peroration by invoking the urgent necessity, for the moral health of the country, of re-establishing truth and justice.

This reasoning and these arguments were already familiar to an increasing number of Frenchmen, they were indeed the small change of conversation. Marcellin had done no more than put them into vigorous shape and give them a biting, vengeful edge.

Thibault said to himself that in France martyrs get no better Press than executioners; or rather, that everyone tries to forget both the one and the other as quickly as possible. The Resistance horrified many Frenchmen, because the state of public opinion at the time it had burgeoned and flowered, in 1944 and 1945, had been horrifying—those subtle degrees of folly and absurdity which can so decisively accentuate all that is horrible in war. But one tended to forget that it had, too, an aspect of simple honesty, of disinterestedness, and of courage. The lot of the Resistance was very much the lot of Brutus, the lot of all conspirators and tyrannicides: one part nobility and one part mediocrity, inextricably mingled; with the purest of intentions it had committed, or allowed to be committed, the most abject crimes. In its ranks were to be found many a malignant Cassius and foolish Casca for every upright Brutus: but that was no more than the normal proportions to be found in any human enterprise. And the way so many Frenchmen had changed sides to the support of the Resistance resembled the change that had come over the people of Rome when Mark Antony repeated his jeering phrase "for these are honourable men. . . ."

The great imposture of the period, thought Thibault, and its tragedy too, lay in the fact that the dice were loaded and the cards stacked: there was misdealing in both camps. There was pretence of fighting the Germans or the Russians in the name of France and liberty, these were the official justifications for the struggle; but the more cynical or perspicacious of the partisans, on whichever side, knew very well that the real stakes were neither the mystical idea of liberty nor that romantic province of Europe called France; two conceptions of society, two systems for the organisation of the world, were face to face. For an 'enlightened' member of the Resistance, the real enemy was certainly not Germany, but the 'Cagoulard', not the Third Reich, but the 'Synarchy', not Rosenberg but Laval. What was made to appear as a war of nations and imperialism was in the first place a civil war on a world scale.

During the winter of 1946, Thibault had come under the influence of a man whose books he already admired, Bernanos, whom he had been able to meet two or three times through journalist friends. The writer was living at that time in an hotel on the Left Bank. Thibault had been much impressed by the old warrior's ravaged face, his rather disconcerting manner, and his sturdy vitality. Never had he heard anyone denounce the period with such vehement and all-embracing accusations, regardless both of the conventions or the powers that be: Justice herself seemed to be speaking in that rather jay-like voice: Bernanos could be corrosive in the manner of a Bloy or a Veuillot, that is to say with terrifying effect. Thibault could still see this potent man in his mind's eye, sitting in an armchair in the *Cayré* bar, improvising a monologue, his head a little to one side, his grey hair swept back, and his fine eyes yellow with bile, their sadness and brilliance enhanced by the heavy pouches beneath them. He would never forget the presence, nor the voice, nor what was said. Bernanos was a sort of criterion by which he judged the period. He often asked himself: "What would Bernanos have thought, what would he have said of this or that?"

But as the days went by and his young fame became established, Thibault found that the interest he had taken for so long in the stir of political life, in the quarrels of faction and party, was weakening. After all, these were eminently perishable excitements and there were other verities in the world: those of poetry and of the heart.

2

François found a vacant place on the café terrace. The night was mild, almost hot. At this late hour the street had undergone a transformation and was clothed with extraordinary enchantment. This narrow space, delimited by the lights of three or four celebrated cafés, had assumed a magic which seemed to be at once both upon the margin of time and a reflection of the period. It was easy enough to perceive the absurdities, to laugh at the hordes of tourists and provincials who came there in search of absent celebrities, to denounce the commercial exploitation of a myth that had been three-quarters forged by the popular Press. But this myth was sustained in part by a true, though confused, feeling of personal necessity, of defiance of social restraints, of mute revolt against the threats of bondage or death which were manifest upon every one of the earth's horizons. The century had exacerbated the sense of the precariousness of things, of the frailty of life itself. There was an urge towards enjoyment, because it was impossible to believe any longer in the reasons for creation or constructive action. There was a need to exploit one's own youth to the uttermost, because it was the only capital upon which there was no mortgage but time. Above all, there was a need to escape from boredom. Saint-Germain-des-Prés supplied these needs, it was a profitable tourist enterprise, but it was also a phenomenon of social crystallisation. It was also the expression, perhaps misleading and aberrant, of a great need for individual affirmation, anarchy, and happiness. François looked round him at the people on the café terrace. There was a great proportion of young people. Both the men and women had an avid, resolute air. They seemed to him to be without illusions, as if they knew the hard laws of the world and were prepared to conform to them. Many were there simply from indolence, curious to watch the human spectacle. Many, like priests of a new religion, which in their case was Culture, Art or Humanism, bore upon their persons the insignia of their priesthood, long, untidy hair, the strained, needy air of professional intellectuals—or allowed to be seen, when they did not ostentatiously display them, the liturgical accessories: a white book with the red and black rule of the house of Gallimard, a high-brow review, *Les Temps Modernes*, *Critique*, or an illustrated work on Cretan painting. Others, however, only came to these sanctuaries of the intelligence to initiate, by chance encounters, proximity and the abandon of night, intrigues whose object was far from being intellectual: thus the prostitutes of classical times pursued their trade in the shadow of the temples. Since the Liberation this last characteristic had year by year been gaining ground and it was possible to predict that Saint-Germain-des-Prés would soon become no more than a banal amusement fair, a district devoted to those pleasures which are customarily called spurious by those who do not practise them.

A woman came in and sat down at the next table to François. He realised at once that he knew her without, however, being able to place her in his memory. The waiter came over to her. She smiled at him with the air of a well-known customer and called him by his Christian name (since, in default of being an intimate of Sartre's, it gave one a certain standing to be able to speak familiarly to a personage almost as celebrated: Pascal, the waiter at the *Flore*). She said "Good evening, Pascal. How are you keeping? 'Course you'll bring me a Martini as usual."

Then François recognised her: it was Nathalie. The sing-song intonation, the voluptuous rolling of the 'rs' in the roof of the mouth, the amputation of the first word in 'of course', the droll, charming accent of a Lithuanian princess restored at a blow the spatial and temporal conditions of their first meeting: the *Dôme* in Montparnasse. A lost world, more profoundly engulfed than the town of Ys or than Atlantis, suddenly returned from the depths of the abyss: Paris in 1937, the Popular Front, the International Exhibition, *Tout va très bien, madame la Marquise*, Jouvet as a Samurai, "one minute of peace is always worth the having", Catherine at the School of Drama, Juliette out for a Sunday walk in her pram, Roland Oyarzun, the superb fighter, king of the "Boul' Mich", the dying Montparnasse of before the war, Nathalie in a Russian blouse, her feet bare in sandals. To-night, too, her feet were bare. She was no longer disguised as a girl from the steppes, but as the heroine of a mystery story. Her hair hung loose on her shoulders, in the fashion of Juliette Greco. She wore trousers, supported by a large leather belt. She looked superlatively Valkyrie. Nathalie! Oh, one knew her well, on two or three occasions one had even found oneself in the same bed with her. François saw her in profile, she did not seem to have changed much: though a little heavier, her beauty was still striking. He was disquieted, amused, and a little moved, not so much at having found an old friend again, but at being suddenly plunged back into the past, into his own youth. He remembered the quality of the pleasure she had been able to give him and even the special aptitudes she had shown in that direction. He hesitated between making himself known and avoiding a meeting. He was on the point of getting up when she looked in his direction. He was shocked. Full face, she looked ten or fifteen years older, she had aged appallingly. What he had taken for a mere heaviness of the face was in fact puffiness. But it was in the eyes above all that time had performed its tragic offices. Their substance seemed to have become aqueous or gelatinous; the eyelids were red and swollen. There was a vague, distant expression in the huge sea-green pupils, a sort of inspired vagueness, which in the old days could have been called dreaming, but which today one had to attribute to an immoderate use of alcohol. Her gaze passed dully over François. She had not recognised him. 'Have I changed as much as all that?' he thought. She was looking attentively at someone sitting behind him. Automatically, he turned round to see the object of her attention and saw a young man of twenty, thick-lipped, with high Mongolian cheek-bones and an expression of rather bestial sensuality. But he was not looking at Nathalie, as he seemed to be enraptured with a beautiful American girl covered with jewels. As if regretfully, Nathalie brought her eyes back to François, and only then seemed to make an effort at identification, which made her frown. He smiled. She smiled too, and said with an engaging air, "'Course you're Philippe, aren't you?"

"No."

"Not? Well, are you Jean-Claude by any chance?"

"Nor him either."

"Oh, well. Do you know me?"

"Yes."

"I suppose you've seen me at Antonella Favantini's?"

"I don't think so."

"Well, I give up."

He leant towards her and whispered something into her ear. Nathalie's face at once expressed a rather (but very slightly) shocked pleasure, like a marquise to whom an impertinent abbé has whispered some audacious gallantry.

"Well, then," she cooed, "since we know each other so well, I think we might call each other darling. Tell me, at about what date did this occur?"

"Ten years ago."

"Ten years! You must have snatched me from the cradle, you young satyr! Ten years. And you've remembered me as precisely as all that? You really are sweet, darling. All my lovers don't remember me so well," she sighed. "Nor indeed do I remember them. For instance, I'm afraid I don't remember whether you've got a mole on the left of your navel, or anywhere else for that matter. Anyway, who are you?"

"My Christian name is François."

"François. I had a François in Auvergne, but he wore a moustache. . . . François. . . . Wait a minute. Ten years ago, you say? I've got it," she cried. "François! You're the husband of Catherine Monnet. Darling, let me kiss you."

She embraced him, kissed him on the mouth, with no more embarrassment than if they had been out of doors in the depths of the country. In any case, no one paid the slightest attention to them. She was very moved. She recalled a thousand memories, both gay and sad, of her bohemian youth. She asked after Catherine.

"I haven't yet been to see her act, she had a little part in *Assunta*, and now she's playing the lead in *Execution*, it's wonderful. And so you're separated? How strange it is, you seemed so very united, such a sweet young couple, but what do you expect, darling, you can't marry an actress, you know, if you aren't connected with the profession yourself, either as author, critic, actor, producer or director, in fact if you aren't in the same boat. You would have looked like a prince consort. What do you do? Motor-car salesmen? Well, you see, you innocent darling, where would you have been with Catherine? And besides, I tell you, I think Catherine was a gold-digger with her eye on the main chance, she was cold and calculating, she hadn't got—you know what I mean?—it!"

She placed her hand on her heart, opened her mouth and drew in a long breath, her eyes turned upwards like a saint in ecstasy.

François asked her if she had given up the stage. She said she had. She had gone into films, into the technical side: first she had been continuity-girl and was now a cutter.

"But, you see darling, it's only my official occupation, because I must tell you that I've remained a bohemian at heart, I can't submit to regular work, to its constraint, I must have absolute freedom; and then, of course, I never go to bed before four or five in the morning, and I get up at two o'clock in the afternoon, so you see, necessarily, the cutting is bound to suffer. What can you expect, after all I'm a night bird, I love sitting up, I love living when the rest of the world's asleep and I love sleeping when the rest of the world's stupidly earning its living; I love wandering about the streets after midnight. I'm romantic to the core. All the same, I've managed to make two films, short documentaries, one about the rococo monuments of Paris, and one about the more curious animals in the Zoo. I want to make a third about Paul Claudel. A sort of Claudelian retrospect, you know, with family photographs and documents, Claudel in shorts, making his first Communion, as ambassador, and so on. It's a fashionable form at the moment; only I suppose I ought to read the whole of Claudel and the trouble is I find him maddeningly dull. 'Course, I know Carné very well, and Grémillon too. My friend this year is an assistant director and works with Lansky. I must introduce you to him, he's a sweet brute, beats me all the time, oh, my darling François, the boys'll drive me completely crazy in the end, besides, it's all ready begun anyway. . . . So, you remembered my mole after ten years, that's very sweet of you, you're an angel, really, I shall have to tell my Jules about it, he'll die of anger and swear at me, tell me that I'm boasting, that's how he treats me, imagine it, he's jealous of my success, really the boys today are beastly little sluts, you know, oh dear, where is the delicacy of the last generation, your delicacy, darling François, who remembers after ten years my poor modest little attractions? Oh yes, gigolos. I don't know how it is, but since the war, I always seem to get mixed up with gigolos. They make me suffer a thousand deaths; all the same I pet them and spoil them, they can do anything they like with me, I'd give them my shirt and all my underclothes—not, of course, that I should be worried by any question of modesty, I'd walk about quite naked in the summer if the police would allow it—it's simply to show you that I'm an incomparable mistress, besides, without my prompting you, you've admitted that you've retained a thrilling memory of me—well, you've no idea how these beastly boys treat me, just think, I had one who was being kept at the same time by me, by a frightful slut, an Austrian painter who lived exclusively on whisky, and by a singer, you do see, don't you? And do you know what the bastard did? I'll give you a thousand guesses, but you won't find the answer, because there are degrees of meanness that one can't even conceive. Listen: he was actually saving! One night I discovered that he was wearing gold bracelets round his ankles, like a slave out of Baudelaire, you know: '*Et des esclaves nus, tout imprégnés d'odeurs. . . .*' 'Course he was beautiful enough to make one cry, naked like that with just those barbaric jewels round his ankles, you can imagine how I just wanted to eat him up, but with a great effort of will I managed to restrain myself, and I said: 'Darling Claude, what are those bracelets?' And he said, trying to provoke me: 'Those, my poppet, are forty thousand francs, it's my little hoard that no one can take from me without first cutting my feet off. It's my capital. I had them welded on by a jeweller, and when

I'm in the shit I'll have them taken off again.' Can you imagine it? 'Course I asked him how he had made forty thousand francs. I can't possibly tell you what he replied, it was too deliciously scandalous, but I roared like a tigress. There was a terrible scene, fists, teeth, nails. Six months later he hadn't got his bracelets any more, and today he's waiting for clients at the *Reine de Sabbat*, at a special summer price of a thousand francs a time. That's how he began and that's how he ended. And I, Nathalie, I can still support myself, that's my revenge! Look behind you to the left. Do you see that boy with the Negroid lips? I want him madly, but I'm quite sure he's only another cruel vampire. Oh well, to hell with it. I'd do anything to have him. Cheero, darling! Isn't he as beautiful as original sin? You're looking shocked, Jean-Louis. . . ."

"François."

"Sorry! Of course, François. Why did I say Jean-Louis? You look shocked. Perhaps you think I'm a shameless bawd. Well, think again. I'm only an unfortunate woman thirsting for an ideal, searching desperately for love. I've known love, real love, in Auvergne, not with a native of Auvergne, oddly enough, but with a Spaniard; it was wonderful, under the moon, our rifles beside us. 'Course I was in the *Maquis*. An extraordinary experience, wonderful comradeship," she declared in exactly the same tone of voice as she might have said: "central heating, all modern conveniences". "Since the Liberation I've found nothing like it. Were you in the *Maquis*, Philippe?"

"No; I was in London. My name's François."

"Tell me, darling, are you waiting for someone? I see you looking at your watch every other second. Perhaps I'm boring you? You must tell me. You won't hurt me, I'm resigned to it. The people I bore never hesitate to send me about my business, so you see I'm accustomed to it. It's extraordinary really, when you think that in the old days I used to look upon myself as a miracle of wit, how many people there are for whom I'm the queen of bores. One loses one's illusions, Philippe, it's appalling. I don't know why I call you Philippe, when I know perfectly well that your name's François. I very nearly killed myself for Philippe. He was a young acrobat, gentle as a girl, inconstant as a cloud, and as volatile, he never kept an appointment, or at best would turn up twenty-four hours late. I lost two stone over him, I was an absolute skeleton. Are you waiting for a girl friend? She's late and you're afraid she won't turn up? Poor darling, you're quite pale. But that's how the days go by: waiting, waiting, waiting, drinking Martini after Martini. When I grow old and ugly for good, I shall kill myself. Darling François it makes me sad to death to see you so nervous and anxious. Pascal, give us another round, my friend'll pay this time. We're two miserable waifs. No, I wasn't speaking to you, Pascal, but to my friend here. I doubt if she'll come now, you know. Shall we go and look for her?"

No, she would not come now.

He felt an anguished void. Disappointments of this kind disintegrated him. Why had she not come? Where was she? What was she doing? He had been waiting for this night. He felt that this night was vitally necessary to him. Why had she not come? Had she misunderstood him on the telephone? Midnight, at the *Flore*: it was clear and simple enough. He emptied his glass. Disgusting. (He never drank spirits.) Drinking was easy and disgusting. Nathalie got up. Why shouldn't he go on with this crazy creature?

Two o'clock in the morning. At the *Tabou*. Cocktails. Nathalie tried to dance, but gave it up. Wisely.

"You say she works at the *Wigwam*? You should have said so sooner and we could have gone there; it'll be shut now. You poor darling, I hate hurting anyone, but sometimes kindness demands that one should lance a boil. That girl goes with everyone, including the manager of the bar. Bleed, my dear friend, bleed and suffer; afterwards you'll feel better."

Three o'clock at *La Mandragore*. Iced punch.

"Two miserable waifs. Come on, darling. They're going to close. Let's go somewhere else."

"I'm wish you. Mus finish telling you 'bout Catherine."

"I'm listening, little Father. Catherine jus a gold digger, alwaysh thought so. Cold, calc'lating. Perfectly odioush and cruel to me, hic."

"Well, ash I was shaying, she was always quite horrid 'cause I use t'go fesh her at the school. 'Course I was jealous. Shee what I mean?"

"Hic. Got hiccups again. Chronic wish me."

"Nashalie, don't walk so fasht, can't keep up. Nashalie!"

"Shtop calling me Nashalie, so boring. I don't call you Anchois."

Four o'clock in the morning at *La Reine de Sabbat*. Two beers.

"I'm sad to death. And there's nothing to be done. Those who create, they can survive, but people like ourselves. . . . I, for instance, draw. I've made two thousand drawings of boys. But I know, when I've had a drink or two, that those drawings are trash. Drink makes me wonderfully lucid."

"Yesh, you're very lushid. Well, as I wash telling you, my lil' girl, she's call' Juyette. She's darling lil' girl, if I didn't have her, don' know what'd become of me. . . . Juyette."

". . . Gethsemane, the eternal cup of bitterness, hic, which one can never empty. . . ."

". . . I sh'd like t'have her here, but how ca' a shingle man manage in Parish when he hash a job. . . ."

". . . We are two miserable waifs, you and I, we are two poor beings crushed by life, 'course we are. . . ."

Five o'clock in the morning. Even the *Reine de Sabbat* closes at that hour.

* * *

François woke up in the early afternoon. His head felt as if it were in a leaden vice, his mouth full of ashes. He got up and discovered that he was completely clothed. He was ashamed of himself for days and days afterwards and what worried him most was to have allowed himself to mention among his drunken confidences—and it was the first time in his life that he had ever allowed himself to be overcome by drink—the name of the little creature who held so sacred a place in his heart.

At the beginning of the holidays he took four days' leave to go to Sault. Juliette had to be entered at the school. He went to fetch the child from the village where she had until then been living. He had not seen her for three months and thought her grown, shooting up. With her long legs, her nervous thinness and awkwardness she was like a young hind, one of those charming, graceful, and yet gawky creatures, who succeed so well in combining wildness with a sort of touching clumsiness; and she still had that deep, concentrated gaze whose impact was almost unbearable. Juliette was torn between joy at seeing her father again, excitement caused by the prospect of a new life, and sorrow at leaving the good people who had brought her up and the familiar scenes of her childhood. Of course, the village was not far from Sault-en-Labourd, barely eight miles. Visits could frequently be arranged, every week in fact, but it was nonetheless a separation and a wrench. Once more she took her father round the farm and the outbuildings, she dragged him from the yard to the stable, from the coach-house to the barn, and he felt her little brown hand quivering in his own, warm with an inviolate and mysterious life. She spoke Béarnais fluently, talked to the men servants, young and old, on intimate terms, as well as the bailiff and his children, who had been her companions at the local school. She talked familiarly to all the animals on the farm, including the turkeys, and knew how to vary her tone of voice for each one of them: one does not speak in the same way to chickens as to cows and pigs. The horse, an aristocrat, was the only animal who could be addressed in French which, moreover, he perfectly understood. François regretted having more or less forgotten his Béarnais: whenever he did try to speak it, he had the impression of sounding rather affected, of being the condescending city-man in spite of himself, and this annoyed him because of Juliette, it was another obstacle in the way of their intimacy, because children, who are so completely natural themselves, perceive the unnatural at once and withdraw themselves from it. The day of departure was a wrench. François was upset by the little girl's distress, he had forgotten how one can suffer and weep at eleven years old.

He barely recognised the Sault-en-Labourd of the past. Not that the changes were obvious at first sight: the size of the population had not varied, the vistas of the streets had remained pretty much the same, neon lighting only appeared above an occasional shop. The startling metamorphosis was in the customs and the minds of the people. The town was no longer provincial in the old sense. Sault-en-Labourd would never again be the little town sleeping in the hollow of a valley, softly dreaming away the days in its half-country quietude, with its domestic comedies, its personalities marked by toil and custom, its bow-fronted cupboards from which escaped an odour of starch and lavender, the long, hot, emptiness of July afternoons when, behind closed shutters, the kitchen was cool and shadowy, haunted by the buzzing of flies, and from the deserted, cobbled street came the grinding of wheels of an ox-wagon, a sound of wood and metal, ever diminishing, never disappearing, across the burning spaces of the sunlit silence. The bow-fronted cupboards had been relegated to the attic, the picturesque characters had died one by one because no one took any interest in them any more, the relaxation of morals had taken much of their excitement from the domestic comedies, the social levelling-down had destroyed the fantastic and the individual. A uniformly educated youth left every October for the universities. The cinema, the radio, and the popular Press played their part in rendering the population indistinguishable. Linked to Paris by a thousand ties and to all the novelties of the age, Sault-en-Labourd ceased beating to its own rhythm in order to keep time with the pulsation of the world. François no longer recognised this crowded holiday resort, filled with tourists, huge red buses in its streets, American cars, and young people in shorts. The fishmonger went to her shop in a car with front-wheel drive. Two students passed close to him and he heard them talking of Henry Miller and *The Tropic of Capricorn.* Like the cars, the children pullulated, they were everywhere: since the state had subsidised having children, France had become a country with a growing birth-rate. The smart thing to do was to marry at eighteen. And the innumerable children of Sault-en-Labourd had no longer anything provincial about them except their accent; one realised, in watching them, and listening to them, so certain of themselves were they, so expansive, so arrogant, that education had been radically transformed, that the children were kings at home, at school, in the street, everywhere, and that everything favoured this absurd cult, the heritage of Vichy and the various forms, either of the Right or the Left, of European Fascism: the myth of youth, stupidly accepted by everyone, with the complaisance of the central Power, and the general abnegation of critical sense. The world would perish, strangled by the myth of Number, the number of frigidaires, of radios, of motor-cars, of journalists, of contemporary problems and of children. Sault-en-Labourd presented all the symptoms of this hideous modern malady of Number, the social manifestation of a cancerous proliferation, the town was being gradually hollowed away like an ant's nest, it had changed more since 1940 than during the two preceding centuries; and when, at the swimming bath, François heard a boy of thirteen or fourteen say to his companion: "You've got an inferiority complex," he realised that Sault-en-Labourd was no longer a little French provincial town, a mere village of the South-West, but a locality upon the map of the world, an indistinguishable cell in the body of the planet where, as elsewhere, flourished the stupidity and boredom of the epoch.

The social categories of the past had also disappeared. François remembered having known at Sault an artisan class, a fine class of independent workers who loved their individual trade, had exquisite taste and quite often, on their own modest level, a sort of creative genius. Since the crisis of 1930, this artisan class had entered upon a long and proud agony, until the time came when the governments of the Liberation had tried to deal it its death blow and had in fact savagely decimated these last individualists of manual labour, who were but little richer than the labourers they sometimes employed, but whose inexpiable crime was not to be salaried. François also remembered having once known a certain kind of small bourgeois society, somewhat retrograde perhaps, and without political or even municipal influence, but which was nonetheless of some importance and maintained certain traditions of honesty and humanity. This society no longer existed. Already, between 1930 and 1940, it had been eclipsed by elements rising from below and more or less tainted by 'enlightened secularism': M. Homais succeeded M. Prud-homme. Today M. Homais was himself finished. The managerial class of Sault-en-Labourd was recruited, so it seemed, from a new aristocracy of greengrocers and sausage-makers, who owed their fortune to the Germans and their certificate of good citizenship to the local Maquis, whom they had prudently supplied.

Thus the town was no longer recognisable, at least in its profounder aspects and in the physiognomy of its inhabitants. François felt almost a stranger. He walked up the hill to the Navailles Tower, the scene of his adolescent dreams. By some curious mischance it had not yet occurred to anyone to divide up the hill into lots for the building of blocks of flats, or to turn the castle into a school, a cinema, or a dance-hall. Here, nothing disturbed the charm of ageless things. The ruined castle beneath its mantle of ivy defied the passing of the days and generations. On the horizon, the mountains still described that blue, hazy outline towards which men dressed in the skins of beasts had turned their fearful gaze from the threshold of echoing caves at dawn, and which the last mortal, beneath the lightning of some atomic disaster, might perhaps salute as the ultimate, radiant vision of the world, before falling dead among his brothers upon the charred earth. François looked out across the wavy line of grey and rose-coloured roofs, and thought that the flag with the swastika had floated for four years over the town and that it was not beyond the realms of imagination that one day, for a longer or shorter but equally ephemeral period, for all Powers crumble, the Russian flag might fly there in its turn. Would there be an opposition, a resistance, a collaborating government? No doubt. The same murderous and sinister performance would take place all over again, people would still speak of honour and treason, torture once more in the name of a unified and proletarian Europe, as they had in the name of a hypothetical Fascist Europe. Only the heroes and the traitors would not be the same as those of yesterday, would they perhaps have exchanged places? Only suffering remained unchanged, and hatred, and hunger, and death.

And if such a conflict were to be avoided and men show themselves wise enough and strong enough to postpone the apocalypse indefinitely, there could still be no assurance that the world would ever know a golden age. Moreover, in so far as it was possible to conjecture about a future state of "happiness', it did not appear to be altogether of a kind to arouse unmixed joy in the hearts of men. It appeared, indeed, that the promoters of Utopia, and their disciples, wished once and for all to do away with those curious whims which had been handed down for thousands upon thousands of years, and which go by such names as: love of solitude, personal independence, disregard of historical necessity, the right to love, enjoy and suffer in uncodified and unpredictable ways. They went about proclaiming that the era of individualism was at an end, that the era of collectivism must be brought into being, but they omitted to give their reasons for supposing that a conglomeration of little individual souls had greater significance, or a greater prescriptive right, than one of the little souls of which it was composed. If a single man, considered in his unique individuality, was of no greater value than a fly, two hundred million flies of that order had no greater value than one, and one could asphyxiate them in the mass with a good conscience, or keep them alive beneath the permanent threat of asphyxiation, and therefore bend them to one's will: and this, at bottom, was the devilish dream which haunted the imaginations of the fanatical apostles who so oddly preferred the History of Man to men themselves, Utopia to the poor, fragile citadels of the flesh.

This 'sacralisation' of History, a logical term used by moralists and philosophers and founded upon a contempt for mankind, was in fact no longer a peculiar characteristic of Fascism. One could discern it in people who noisily professed revolutionary Socialism. Thus, what had been the indubitable language of an obscure desire to oppress had become, through the most insidious imposture of the century, the official language of a certain kind of 'humanism'.

François told himself that he had changed a good deal since the period when he had read *Jean Christophe*. At that time he had been imbued with an idea of the future, both optimistic and vaguely sentimental, the heritage of the nineteenth century, which constituted in the Donadieu family a perfectly clear political doctrine, handed down from father to son together with the family Bible and an ancient edition of *Rêveries d'un Promeneur Solitaire*. He had himself believed in the coming of a Golden Age. "*Et ego in Utopia.*" But, doubtless like many men of his generation, it was one more faith that he had lost. Sometimes Bernard laughingly took him to task over what he called his 'apostasy'. "You're becoming a frightful reactionary," he would say. It was not the case. And yet there was some truth in it. Certainly, he very well knew which side he would be on in the case of internal dissension: without hope as without anger, he would be on the side of the weakest. If there were barricades on one side and tanks, troops and police on the other, he would be behind the barricades. Not from conviction, but by instinct, loyalty, or simply from some feeling of moral decency. But not from conviction, because he no longer believed in the possibility of Utopia. The belief in the future happiness of the human race was in his eyes as fallacious and hypothetical as the promise of heavenly felicity. These articles of faith had their value. Naturally, it was not forbidden, indeed it was even desirable, to labour as best one could for the onset of a better world, but without believing that in this lay the only key, the only truth, worth the seeking. If there were any truth in the world, he thought, it was imprinted upon the faces of those whom we love, of that small number of particular individuals for whom we really care. The rest was merely brain-washing.

On this romantic height overlooking the town, François evoked something of the melancholy of the past, of those hours in which he had pondered the insignificance of his own being lost amid the innumerable multitude. And since he had reached middle age, that mature period when one takes stock of one's life, he could better discern, with a more certain, more concrete awareness, how precarious human existence was and how derisively short. The new world revived once more the vertiginous sensation of the flight of time; perhaps it would accelerate time itself? One day, soon, too quickly, the inexplicable end would have arrived. Some men are never affected by the idea of their own death. Others, with wise resolution, put it from them. Others again (François thought of Bernard) drug themselves with amusements: sport or love, or those yet more frivolous forms of diversion: business, political passion, social ambition. But nothing from now on would distract François from himself and his own destiny, nothing, except perhaps his love for Juliette; only those whom we love have the power to protect us from the image of death.

He went down towards the town by the same road that he had walked in the past. Familiar details rose to greet him at every step. Upon this milestone generations of schoolboys had carved their names. At this turning the cold winds of winter evenings leapt upon you like a savage enemy and one had to hold on to the hood of one's cloak with both hands. At this ironmonger's shop one used to buy marbles or those aluminium propellers that can be thrown by means of a bar twisted in the shape of an endless screw. Here was the Oyarzun's house, transformed today into a furniture shop. At the top of this slope Roland Oyarzun had given way to one of his typical crises of anger and despair. ("Laugh! Joke! Humiliate me! I'm misunderstood.") All this was at once near and infinitely far off. Rather more than twelve years, rather less then twenty.

The odour of hides and bark had evaporated from the house by the stream. There were no longer dark hides drying in the sun or soaking in the huge vats in the basement. Empty as tombs, they grew a little moss and lichen on their grey sides. Death had touched this house where a half-blind old woman, a Bible in her worn hands, awaited without fear the hour of her own passing. Mme Donadieu had long ago forgiven her son what she called his "error" and which, in fact, was no more than that. She cherished Juliette. She drew the child to her and with the tips of her fingers touched with a sort of tender respect the young face she could no longer see, the young life which was her promise of survival.

"She's like us, isn't she?" she asked François.

"Yes, she's like us."

He knew that for his mother it was not a question of physical resemblance.

Mme Donadieu kissed the little girl.

"When you're grown up, you must live in this house. You'll see, it can be made comfortable and gay. It'll be your holiday house, for you and your cousins. You mustn't sell it."

Thus, in the evening of her life, this woman, whose religious faith was strong and sure, took pleasure, as indeed do most human beings, in those visions which oppose the certainty of individual death with the illusion of survival: the survival of the line, of the race. As if names and families did not become extinct like all else.

François spent the last evening at his younger brother's house with Juliette. He was upset by the child's sad gaze, by its mute intensity, the abandon of her kisses, the restrained violence of her forlorn unhappiness. He saw with mixed emotions of joy and vague disquiet the place he held in her young heart. He marvelled at this love which he had done nothing to deserve. 'For I *have* done nothing,' he thought. 'Until today I haven't even seriously tried to be a father, I've evaded that obligation with many others. Two or three visits a year, a few little kindnesses, a few short letters, and that's all. Certainly, I've never scolded her, I've never spoken harshly to her, besides it wasn't necessary.' Until now she had been a rather distant little being, tenderly loved, no doubt, but from afar. Now, he realised that she counted for him more than anything else in the world, that she had become the pole about which his life revolved. The future must be thought of in terms of Juliette.

This last night was warm and starlit. Walking along the deserted street to the sound of his own footfalls, François thought of all the years that had vanished since he left school. Vanished but for a residue of recollections, a little handful of memories. His youth seemed to him now to have no more consistency than a dream. Those first months in the pastor's house, Juliette's birth, Catherine, the end of their life together, the war, Bernard, the return home, his secret departure, London, the Liberation, his recovered freedom, his strange job that was no more than a means of earning a living, efforts he had made in other directions and which had soon been discouraged, the mild happiness of an existence in which there was no effort either of competition or creation. It was not a brilliant tale. A life among others. A man among others. An indeterminate destiny. With, however, its occasional moments of exaltation, even of joy. Joys, exaltations, sorrows, which had almost never been occasioned by the external world. Everything of any importance in his life was of a purely private nature, owing nothing to History. At first glance, the political circumstances of the war, the defeat, the resistance, held a considerable place in those fourteen years; and, indeed, these things had taken up a great deal of time—many days, months and years; they had demanded much attention and much patience, oppressive as they were with a sort of compelling sombreness (and for others they had meant separation from loved ones, solitude, a huge sum of brute suffering, sometimes torture and death). Nevertheless, in that dimension which is neither spatial nor temporal, the true dimension in which life exists, they had no place. Fortunately, François had not been affected by those vague fatalities which were as blind as natural cataclysms; or at least he had not been profoundly affected by them; and the same thought that had come to him one night at Roland Oyarzun's, as he watched his face mask-like in its tragedy, returned now: before we inhabited cities of stone, we wandered for aeons, and we have not ceased to wander through the labyrinth of our own internal city—a city enclosed by no wall, but of which we are nonetheless prisoners for ever, subject to its strange laws which we die without ever having understood, its hidden Powers, its terrifying trials by ordeal, and its unforgiving Gods.

3

He thought it his duty to invite the Oyarzuns once. His daily life was oppressed by all sorts of obligations, imprisoned in a network of tyrannical and inconsistent imperatives, which infuriated him, but to which he scrupulously submitted. Every time he thought of the Oyarzuns he swore and determined to eliminate them for ever. Then, he felt a certain pity which made him revoke a decision taken in anger—or was it merely sensitivity, weakness, a fear of wounding, an instinctive retreat in face of the risk of hurting someone one knew to be vulnerable? Whether courage or cowardice, it was a strain on the nerves, a fatigue to the eyes. Should not a "free" man rise above this? Should he not consider himself first and systematically above all others? Should he not consider others only in the measure of his own pleasure, enrichment, or interest? François admitted to himself that he was far from making the grade. With death in his soul he sacrificed a free evening (which might well have been spent in reading, pleasure or anyhow in a few hours of personal existence). He invited Roland and Simone to dinner.

Roland that night was, unusually for him, in excellent form. "In wonderful form!" he declared, beating his chest with his fists. He beamed. He was in superb form. He was in superb form because he could say "an old friend asked my wife and me to dinner, we ate damned well, and it's a great pleasure to dine together when one has worn out the seats of one's pants on the benches of the same school," and so on. The intolerable ambience of solitude was destroyed for a single night. Man cannot live in total isolation, without contact with society. For a man of Oyarzun's type, proscription, ostracism, was equivalent to a sentence of death. Without talent for arousing or sustaining friendship, Roland, before even the first wrinkles had overtaken him, had watched the numerous acquaintances that his turbulent youth had gained him, evaporate. People did not remain faithful to him: married, grown old, he ceased to be interesting. His trial and his poverty had created a vacuum around him. And thus he suffocated, because this vacuum and silence was the counterpart of an interior vacuum, of that vertiginous void into which we must never look at any price because, as before the face of

Medusa, it carries with it a sentence of death. But here was someone afloat above the shipwreck extending a hand: someone whom Roland did not very much care for, someone whom he would have savagely trampled upon had their respective positions been reversed (François proscribed and poverty stricken, Roland fortunate), someone for whom he had never felt more than an uncertain mingling of contempt, envy and vaguely intermittent affection: François Donadieu, despised for his timidity, his harmless appearance, those odd Huguenot ideas, humanitarian and socialist; envied for his success at school, his knowledge of literature, for the odious luxury which is called culture; and yet liked because he was a constant figure from that past which in Roland Oyarzun's heart was still a sharp, deep wound. Sitting at a table in the picturesque restaurant on the island of Saint-Louis, where the meat was red and rare, and the wine strong, Roland could not contain himself for joy. There was even something abnormal about his exuberance, something that suggested the morbid rhythm of certain lunatics by which they are carried to an extreme degree of excitability before relapsing into the depths of a languid despair, in a cycle almost as constant as the phases of the moon. He was overflowing with vitality and euphoria. He told funny stories and succeeded in being funny in the telling. He made puns, not the highest form of intellectual exercise but one at which he excelled when "in form". He made spoonerisms and nearly choked himself laughing when François, who never understood them at first hearing—"your Huguenot candour!"—asked him to explain them. Between the cheese and the *tarte maison nappée de crème fraiche*, he remembered that he was a man of the twentieth century, had been to school and was an assiduous reader of various *Digests*: he paid his due to the things of the mind.

"Tell me, since you're up in these things," he asked, "what do you think of Existentialism?"

The restaurant with its marble tables and red-tiled floor was one of those small places which are popular in the right way; completely unknown to the general public, appreciated by a small number of connoisseurs and snobs, its food was simple and delicious. With its usual clients of mechanics and artisans were mingled a few young Americans, emigrants from Greenwich Village to Saint-Germain-des-Prés, one or two writers, and from time to time a few fashionable women, who came to breathe an air of youth and adventure on the Left Bank. Thus, as neighbours, in an equality before the high cost of living, which was perhaps the best thing about the period, were a mason, his cheeks white with plaster, and a very young girl in black jumper and trousers, her eyebrows plucked and short hair about her shoulders. One single jewel relieved the darkness of her clothes, a huge bracelet of pure gold, a priceless Merovingian fantasy. At another table, two Boston aesthetes, disguised as cowboys in the style inspired by Christian Bérard, did not appear embarrassed, rather the contrary, by the near proximity of an athletic bargee, who exuded an aroma of tar and the romance of ships. Elsewhere, was an extremely elegant couple: the woman had a Florentine beauty and wore a dress which left her shoulders naked, the man had the appearance of a tanned Count Mosca with white hair; they were drinking a heavy red wine and eating a strong *cassoulet* which was priced on the rather dirty menu at eighty-five francs. All these people from different social levels tolerated each other with more than mere good humour: with a certain pleasure indeed, the proletarians were amused by the picturesqueness of these unexpected diners whose presence they owed to monetary or poetic inflation (Jacques Prévert was fashionable at the time), while the intellectuals felt a certain exaltation in the presence of the lower classes. In any case, whatever the reasons, there was a certain evident atmosphere of goodwill, a sort of microcosm of fraternity. Thus, Roland Oyarzun, having thought he had recognised from their clothes two or three specimens of what the popular Press and the tourist agencies had baptised 'Existentialists', asked to be informed about a movement of which the *Reader's Digest* had not revealed to him all the arcana. "Now tell me," he asked with the air of a man who had decided, once and for all, to get to the bottom of the matter, "what, ultimately, are these Existentialists after?"

"Who are you calling 'Existentialists'?"

"Why, those oddly dressed boys and girls, who dance to swing music in night-clubs and call themselves disciplies of Sartre. That girl over there, for instance, or those two chaps in check shirts."

"They're no more Existentialists than you or I. It's the public who call them that, the public that reads the sensational Press. They've got nothing to do with Sartre, nor with a certain philosophy. They're quite simply boys and girls who like jazz music, companionship and freedom. They want to have a good time and forget because they've come out of four years of hardship and the future may not be much fun for them, that's all."

"All right. But, all the same, Sartre's their leader and inspiration, isn't he?"

"Not at all. Some of them read and appreciate Sartre's books because he deals with contemporary preoccupations, that's all one can say."

"Well, anyway, tell me in a couple of words what Sartre's philosophy is about."

"In a couple of words? How can I? Sartre took eight hundred pages to explain it."

"Have you read his book? You have? Very well, then, tell me the gist of it."

"What an oaf!" François thought. He went on insisting, stupidly, hilariously, his napkin tucked into his collar, like a Bouvard or a Pécuchet of the twentieth century who for his instruction counted upon 'digests' and 'tabloids' rather than upon his own hard work. The girl in black trousers stared for an instant at this loud-mouthed fool who assumed the scepticism of a superior intellect about things of which he knew nothing and appeared never likely to know anything. Roland picked up a teaspoon and banged his glass as though demanding silence. The people at the neighbouring tables looked up and stopped talking. Roland was slightly drunk.

"Ladies and gentlemen," he cried, "you are about to hear an account of Existentialism by Professor Nimbus."

François blushed scarlet. The two aesthetes from Boston, the athletic bargee, the dark girl, the Sanseverina and Count Mosca, the garage hand and the typist realised at once that it was a question of a decent shy young man at the mercy of an uncontrollable nitwit. For François' sake they tactfully looked the other way and resumed their interrupted conversations. Roland was delighted with the effect he had created. He went on still louder, "Come on then, come on, tell us what this wonderful Existentialism's about!"

"Roland!" Simone implored him, hiding her distress behind

an embarrassed little laugh. "Don't you see you're annoying your friend?"

"We'll talk about it some other time," said François.

"Here and now. I want to know what the hell this fellow Sartre's about."

"Don't make a fool of yourself."

"No, no. You don't get out of it as easily as that! Do you know what this Existentialist philosophy is about, yes or no?"

"Frankly, I know no more about it than you do."

"Don't pretend! You're merely equivocating. Come on, Donadieu, get on with it, by God! Come on, come on. Look, I'll help you. What's it about, basically? Living one's own life? That's it, isn't it?" he cried triumphantly.

"Not quite, no. It's about being free, rather," François said, his embarrassment making him stutter.

"Being free," Roland repeated as if he were making a mental note. "Very interesting. Go on."

How could he put an end to this scene? The fool would not give up till he had got his 'digest', his 'what everyone ought to know about Existentialism' for the use of Kanakas. François wondered where to begin. With the experience of nausea, the essence of existence, engagement, authenticity and bad faith? God, how humiliating it was! God, how debasing contact with mediocrity could become! François suddenly remembered Sartre's metaphor at the beginning of his own digest, "Existentialism is a humanism. . . ."

"Imagine a gherkin," he said fiercely.

"A gherkin," Roland repeated with a knowing smile. "A gherkin. Splendid."

"A gherkin grows according to a certain plan, in accordance with the preconceived idea of a gherkin, thus one can foresee its development, its future colour, its taste, in short all its properties, with reference that is to an ideal gherkin. You give me that?"

"There is no such thing as an ideal gherkin," Roland objected tiresomely.

"No; but the whole thing happens as if all the gherkins in the world grew and developed in the image of, and in resemblance to, an ideal gherkin. You admit that?"

"Very well."

"With gherkins then, essence precedes existence."

Roland gave an olympian frown.

"I don't follow you," he said.

"The objects called gherkins exist in conformity with their ideal image, with the essence of a gherkin—good God! what things you're making me say!—which may be considered independently of their existence and previously to it, because, for example, man can think it. Do you understand?"

"No, I've got lost on the way. What can man think?"

"The essence of a gherkin."

"The essence of a gherkin is thought by man," Roland repeated in perplexity. "It's funny. Go on though."

"Men, unlike gherkins, grow and develop without reference to an ideal image of man, an eternal prototype which would be human nature. It's in the actual process of living that they become defined, that they gradually take shape. In man, existence precedes essence."

"Take care!" cried Roland as if their table had burst into flames (their neighbours all turned round, startled). "Take care! You've spoken of human nature. Men develop in accordance with human nature. That is their essence."

"Where is it?"

"What?"

"Human nature?"

"What do you mean, where is it?"

"Where is it except in men's minds who have created the idea after the event?"

"Again, I don't follow you," Roland sighed, discouraged.

"You agreed a moment ago that the essence of a gherkin is a thought in man's mind. Very well. But the essence of man has not been thought by anybody except by man himself, therefore he must first exist in order to be able to have thoughts about his own nature."

"I beg your pardon," said Roland reproachfully. "The essence of man was thought by God. 'God created man in His own image.' "

"But that's exactly the point, because Sartre won't accept the idea of God. He says that God is a useful hypothesis invented by man in order not to have the bear the burden of his own freedom."

"He's got a nerve, that Sartre of yours! If he begins by denying God, he can obviously affirm anything he likes."

Simone approved the dialectical discussion of the two men with discreet smiles.

At last, Roland appeared to give up all desire to learn more of this obviously ridiculous philosophy. He placed the palms of his hands round his glass of brandy and warmed it with a voluptuous air. Having lost the habit of drinking, the slight excesses of the dinner—cocktails, burgundy, Three Star brandy—had empurpled his face and given him a vague look about the eyes.

"Stop talking to me about intellectuals," he said. "They're all bastards. Except you, of course. You're a reasonable sort of chap. I've great confidence in your future," he declared decisively, in the same pompous tone of voice in which he might have said: "I have faith in the destiny of the country." "Yes, yes. I expect great things of you, Donadieu. How old you are? How stupid I am, of course we were in the same age group at school! Thirty-two. Of course, till now, you've done nothing out of the ordinary," he added with impartiality, "but then there was the war, wasn't there? Darling," he said, turning to his wife, "don't forget what I'm saying: our friend Donadieu will be heard of. Don't forget that, you hear me?" he repeated.

It was exactly as if he were telling her to tie a knot in her handkerchief. Simone shook her head several times to signify that she would indeed not forget his words.

"You see, Donadieu was already very promising at school," Roland went on, carried away by the exaggeration of his southern temperament. (These eulogies were also an ingenuous and elementary method of showing his gratitude to François Donadieu for the pleasant evening.) "He was a real phoenix. What?" he cried in indignation, as if his silent wife had questioned François' quality. "Him?" (Simone at once began nodding her head: yes, yes, of course she believed it.) "But, my poor sweet, he beat us all! Donadieu was a real ace! Good God! How I remember those prize-givings with the fellow bagging all the prizes."

He was overcome by the excesses of his own generosity, in a few words he sketched the portrait of a young Pic de la Mirandole astounding the doctors of the College of Sault-en-Labourd with his precocious learning. At that moment, Roland was thoroughly enjoying the part he was playing: that of a sincere, warm-hearted, integrated man, who could not be stopped once he had embarked upon the eulogy of his friends. Moreover, he ended by believing in the myth he was creating and, with the assistance of the brandy, felt himself flattered to be the intimate friend of such a paragon, moved to tears by the mere fact of being able to call himself his friend; and he gazed at François with moist and tender admiration.

"Yes, indeed!" he said. "Upon my honour, you outstripped us all. You left us all behind. Yes, you did. You're a wonderful chap, my dear Donadieu. But at least there's one thing that a poor devil like myself can take pride in: to count you among his friends."

The "wonderful chap", overwhelmed with embarrassment, bowed his head. At last they went out. Roland took his friend by the arm. His gait was somewhat unsteady. He belched magnificently.

"Darling," he said to his wife, "I believe I've lost my handkerchief. Would you mind going to see if by any chance it fell under the table?" And when she had gone: "A pretext!" he said, pummelling François' ribs. "I merely wanted to ask you to forget everything I said the last time you came to see us. You know, when I was recovering from my illness. Everything I told you about the medical dictionary and my fear of . . . of having cancer, and my longing to go to Asia. It was all nonsense. When it comes to the point there's no saner man than I am. I'm feeling in splendid form these days. Splendid form! Wonderfully fit!"

And since the road was dark and deserted, he began singing stridently:

"*Et voilà la vie, la vie, la vie chérie, ha, ha,*
Et voilà la vie que tous les moines font,"

then stopped abruptly, "Damn it," he said, "I suppose I oughtn't to sing that now that Papa's gone into a monastery?"

He thought for a moment and then began again:

"*Les filles de Camaret*
Se disent toutes vierges."

* * *

For some weeks François heard no more of the Oyarzuns: there were no messages, no appeals for help. 'That's fixed,' François said to himself, relieved. He thought of Roland as he had last seen him, optimistic, full of energy and the joy of life. At last old rancours, bitternesses, rages, and the desire for vengeance were fading. The autumn of 1944 was getting further away, dissolving into forgetfulness. Three years had already elapsed. Soon an amnesty would give Roland Oyarzun back his prerogatives as a French citizen, his honour and his good conscience. His material circumstances must improve with time. Life, both for him and his poor little wife, would flower anew. 'So much the better,' thought François, 'they have suffered a cruel injustice, it is time they were happy at last.' In order not to appear to have completely forgotten them, he went to see them one evening. 'At the cost of one visit every three months, I'm prepared to maintain relations with them.' The suburb. The six storeys. Breathlessness. Noise of locks and chains. François had hardly entered before he realised that nothing was changed. Roland's face was lugubrious, his eyes were red.

"Oh, it's you? I thought it was Simone," he said sadly. "She went out with the children. It's an eternity since we saw you. We haven't communicated with you for fear of being bored. Come in."

There was a certain constraint between them as their exchanged the usual banalities. Roland turned his head away, perhaps to hide the signs of recent tears. Suddenly, he looked his visitor in the face and said, "After all, I needn't be ashamed with you. When you came in I was crying."

François at once lowered his eyes.

"I'm sorry," he muttered.

"I was crying because I was alone," Roland said with such poignant simplicity that François felt its pathos. "A man of nearly thirty-three in tears cannot be a very pretty sight. Forgive me. It was a moment of weakness. Simone had been gone a long time. I was alone here, between these four walls. I turned on the radio. And do you know what I heard? A song. A song that went like this: *Qu'as-tu fait, toi que voilà, Pleurant sans cesse, Dis, qu'as-to fait, toi que voilà, De ta jeunesse?* And so I began crying like a child."

"It can happen. There's nothing to be ashamed of."

"Yes. It has happened to me now for some time past. It's idiotic. It's just that I think all the time of my youth. It's over, finished, done with. I wonder about life, whether it's worth it or not, and of the chances that make on a success or a failure, happy or unhappy. And then, oddly enough, I think a good deal about death. In the old days, I never thought of it. Never, you understand. It must be a sign of growing older. Because we've reached an age when the die has been cast and there's nothing left but to continue along the well-known road, without hope that it will lead us anywhere in particular: indeed, one knows where it leads and what's at the end of it. You will say: thirty-three is the prime of life in a man, it's still youth. And, indeed, in a certain sense it still is youth. But for someone like myself, married, with children, it's middle age, you see. Middle age. I find the fruits of middle age rather bitter."

How odd it was to hear from the poor devil's lips the very same words one had murmured to oneself but a few weeks earlier, beneath the shadow of an old house touched by the hand of death. François was astonished. How did Oyarzun manage to be sometimes so odious, so grotesque, and on others so sensitive, so perceptive and so pitiable?

"Listen, you mustn't say things like that. You mustn't even think them. You're young, Roland, that is a fact. You've got a wonderful wife, children you love, a job. You've got friends."

"My poor chap, you're my only friend."

"You've got others, Marcellin, Fontanes. . . ."

"Don't ever speak to me of Fontanes again," he said forcibly. He paused and then went on sombrely, "Fontanes not a completely bad type, but he amuses himself. . . . He laughs at the sufferings of others."

He got up and went to the window. He pressed his forehead against the pane. It was only at this point that François became aware that the looking-glass over the fireplace had been entirely covered with a large red cotton sheet. He remembered what Simone had told him.

"You've hidden the looking-glass?" he said.

Roland turned round. His face, sad to the point of despair, with bald forehead, and lines at the corner of the mouth, twitched spasmodically. That face he remembered as young and beautiful.

"Yes, I don't like seeing myself in looking-glasses. When I'm not here, Simone uncovers it. She's not frightened."

"Frightened?"

"I mean she doesn't mind."

They fell silent. From the kitchen next door an alarm clock piercingly broke the silence. When François had gone, Roland sat down, put his elbows on the table and took his head in his hands. He stayed thus, motionless, for long minutes. With regular, obsessive monotony, the alarum clock continued beating in the heavy silence. Roland spread out his hands with the slowness of a sleep-walker. His temples were beaded with sweat. He gazed besottedly round the room. He held his breath as if he had perceived, behind the rhythmic beating of the alarum, a tenuous sound which was the indication of another presence. He rose with such care that he seemed to be unfolding his body. He opened his mouth as if he were out of breath. As he let his eyes roam from object to object, they seemed dilated with terror or with some other more obscure emotion. The silence seemed to hold him in its grasp like inexorably mounting water, while the spasmodic ringing of the alarum seemed to grow louder from moment to moment like a crazy tocsin. Roland placed his hand on his breast as if to relieve the beating of his heart. He went over to the fireplace. The sweat was pouring down his cheeks. He raised his eyes. The thumping of his heart answered the frightful tocsin from the neighbouring room. With a mad gesture, Roland tore down the sheet and saw in the looking-glass a figure gazing at him with unblinking eyes. Behind and around this figure was shadow, a shadow in which something invisible moved, drew nearer. . . . Roland clung to the chimney-piece with both hands. His breath came in gasps. His right hand moved along the shelf, searching like a blind animal till it touched the metal of a photograph frame; the fingers trembled, clutched the frame. Roland leapt backwards, raised his arm, and brought it down with all his strength. The world burst into joyous sound, a cascade of little shining daggers leapt from the wall. The cotton sheet was a red foam at his feet. Roland gazed at his hand, from which flowed a thin trickle of blood.

4

Bernard said to his clerk that he was on no account to be disturbed for at least an hour. Callers must wait! The clerk nodded and went out. As soon as the baize door was closed, Bernard heaved a sigh of relief.

In front of him on the desk was a large note-book bound in

leather. It was open at a page filled with fine, regular writing. Bernard enjoyed reading his journal. It was, he thought, admirable literature. He had just begun to read an exciting chapter upon his life in the *Maquis*, when he was interrupted by the ringing of the telephone.

"Hullo. Is that Bernard?" said a feminine voice with a somewhat exotic accent. "How are you, my dear friend? You haven't forgotten that you're dining with me tonight? I'm reminding you because you have so often thrown me over. . . . No, don't protest, you're a terrible debauchée, the merest hint of a skirt is enough to turn you from your duties, particularly the most important, your social duties. . . . I should like you to come a little earlier than usual tonight, a little before eight o'clock if possible. . . . I've read your article in yesterday's *Horizons*. Wonderful. Very much to the point. I don't remember exactly what you were writing about and besides, you know me, I understand nothing about Indo-Chinese affairs or about politics, anyway, but at the time I was certainly struck by your arguments. Riveted. Of course, you're devilish clever, my dear, as someone was only saying the other day. . . ." (Bernard tried to get a word in edgeways, but on the telephone Letitia Dolfus-Gomez never stopped. One had to hang up. In ordinary conversation she never stopped either. One had to talk louder than she did.) "Tonight I've got a little surprise for you. You'll meet a new friend of mine, an extremely nice and interesting man. I can't wait to see you together. No, no. Don't ask me who he is. . . . I want it to be a surprise! Till tonight then. Remember to be here a little before eight o'clock."

"You remember, Letitia, that you've also asked a M. Donadieu?"

"Donadieu? Who is he? I know no one of that name."

"Of course you don't know him, but I asked you to invite him. He's a friend of mine, a rather shy chap whom I want to bring out."

"Oh, I remember now. Yes, of course, he must come. Besides, I'm sure he's been asked. I think Alice has already asked him."

He hung up and dialled another number.

"I want to speak to M. Donadieu," he said. "Hullo, is that you? I'm sorry to bother you, but you haven't forgotten that you're dining at Mme Dolfus' tonight with me? You hadn't forgotten? Good. I've just been speaking to Letitia, she she's very keen to meet you, because it appears that you were at school with her son. . . . Yes, he was a bit older than you, four or five years, but you remember him, don't you? You must talk to her about him, it'll please her. She was quite insistent that I should bring you. Come and pick me up at about twenty to eight. . . . No, no; a lounge suit. Goodbye, old boy. See you tonight."

He hung up and went on reading, but rather distractedly. The interruption had broken his concentration.

'Luckily, I was not engaged in writing,' he said to himself. 'Impossible, absolutely impossible to work under such conditions, when one's interrupted every other minute by the telephone, visitors, a thousand odd jobs. The hell of living a social life! One should isolate oneself. Spend the winter in Sicily and give no one one's address. Or perhaps a little house in Haute-Provence. I can see it now, a tiled roof ending five feet from the ground; little green shutters, a vine and ivy. . . . "*A la rose s'allie. . . .*" Or perhaps even a room in a hotel at Rambouillet or Montmorency for a month, four wretched little weeks. In a month I should have time to get my novel started, the novel I've been thinking about for years, ever since my adolescence, without ever finding a quiet week in which to get it going. First there were my studies, then journeys, Spain, Czechoslovakia, Munich, then the war, Vichy, Nice, London, the Liberation. Then the exciting life of Paris, old friends recovered, old habits renewed, First Nights, and this weekly paper which takes up too much of my time, and with no real profit to me: I mean without real moral or intellectual profit, or social for that matter, since it is only read by a small, politically inactive public. A novel. A big, rich, densely woven book, an ultimate expression of myself; a summation of all the problems of our period. Its tone: halfway between Malraux' *Espoir* and Sartre's *L'Age de Raison*. Its theme and its characters are all ready. And don't anyone talk to me about talent. I don't know what's meant by talent, or rather I know only too well: it's a dishonest word. And don't let anyone talk to me of "interior necessity" or "romantic temperament" either. They're nothing but vague ideas, without any true basis. The whole thing is a question of work and method. Technique. As far as I am concerned there is but one difficulty: time, time, time.'

He went on reading his journal. During the last three years there had been a few small alterations in the appearance of the office of *Horizons*' Editor. The photograph of Malraux in the uniform of a Colonel of the Free French Forces was still there, but it had been placed in a dark corner. (Malraux was "in the corner" like a naughty schoolboy. What had he done to deserve the disgrace?) On the other hand, the photographs of General de Gaulle and of Georges Bidault had been removed. *Sic transit* . . . In their place had been hung two pictures, Bernard's private property: a Labisse of a cadaverous green which represented a fight to the death between two huge insects, carapaced and caparisoned, bristling with prying antennae and huge, globulous eyes—the artist had most effectively reproduced the stupid, dumb, implacable cruelty of that appallingly aggressive world; the other picture was of a woman with the head or mask of a cat, clothed in a huge, tenebrous robe, and was signed Leonor Fini: a phantasmal apparition placed against a background of truncated columns, filled with a dark romanticism and painted with a violent surréalist pungency. The work would have been all the stronger if the wild and rather lunatic quality of the inspiration had not been somewhat ameliorated by the exquisite elegance of the composition. Bernard was very fond of these two paintings which reminded him of the enthusiasms of his youth, of his Maldoror period. The map of Europe with its little flags had also been relegated to the archives. In its place was an enormous advertisement for *Huis Clos*, Sartre's play. The office of the Editor of *Horizons* had obviously considerably changed since the Liberation.

Bernard was reading:

"*March 12th. Thibault Fontanes goes on attacking me, this time in a new review called* Parsifal, *which incidentally has some pretty old contributors. He seems to set the tone for a team of young reactionaries about whose past I should very much like to know. Fontanes throws the usual complaints of the Right in my face: lack of realism, sentimentality, incoherence, muddled thinking. His diatribe is written in a staccato, pointed, offensive style, filled with annoying childish witticisms. I've recently reread* Une Étoile de Sang. *It doesn't move me (as it does Donadieu, for instance, but his literary judgments are not very sound). The book has brio, destructiveness, an insolent brilliance and prodigious technique. But it has no importance: he might as well be playing the flute. These pointless tales have nothing to say to us. His romantic psychology is old-fashioned. His gestures and pirouettes are terribly dated. In the era of Stalingrad and Hiroshima, how can one be interested in the loves and infidelities of a man and a woman? In the age of behaviourism and the American novel, of Sartre and brute realism, 'Jules thought that' is on the same level as 'the Marchioness went out at five o'clock'. It corresponds to an out-moded metaphysic. And don't quote Proust at me. Proust had his uses, but the Proustian conception of the world is as old as that expressed in the romances of the Arthurian Cycle.*

"*March 16th. If I had to sum up in a single phrase, a single word, the essence of my beliefs, my faith and my hopes, I could do no better than to repeat Oedipus' reply to the Sphinx: Man. I could only quote the most ancient formula of humanism, that of Protagoras: 'Man is the measure of everything', or the most recent, Gide's: 'Man will become God.' I think that with the destruction of all the religious myths, this century will crown the last myth of all (the last in date and, doubtless, the last in an absolute sense), the myth of the Man-King. I know, as Malraux does, that our culture is threatened, that there is no Ark, no interplanetary ship in which we can take refuge, with our statues, our pictures, our gramophone records and our books, that there exist no means of taking these precious vestiges of our terrestrial civilisation into space, far from this pulverised earth. I know with Sartre that if the world can do without literature (art and literature), it can do more easily still without man. I know that the Apocalypse has never been so close, or so possible, I do not want to write: so probable. None the less, I declare that the humanistic hope must survive all our fears and all our doubts, and that we must fight with all our strength to bring about a better world, a happier one, more just and more free.*"

The telephone rang. Frowning, Bernard lifted the receiver. Almost at once his expression changed to one of tender, infinitely tender, rapture.

"Oh, it's you, Josette?" he murmured. "I'm delighted that you're back, darling; it's been so long since . . . What was that? Yes . . . yes. . . . Of course I understand. . . . I love you! When are you coming to see me? . . . Just a minute, darling, while I look in my book. You know how terribly engaged I always am, so many meetings. . . . No, you are silly, darling! Hang on. . . . When did you say? Wednesday?"

He turned the pages of a little diary. *Wednesday: 7 p.m. Martine.*

"No, darling. Wednesday's impossible. I've got a Board meeting at exactly seven o'clock. What's that? You could come later? At nine? . . . Oh, but you see, I'm afraid of being rather tired; these Board meetings are so exhausting. . . . And I wouldn't like to be tired for you, darling, not after two months. I should like it to be a special occasion," he said, lowering his voice caressingly and meaningfully. There was a distraught, libertine expression on his face which curiously loosened the outline of his features. There was suddenly something rather vulgar about his appearance. "Friday?" he went on. "Wait a minute. . . ."

He turned a page of his diary to Friday: *3 p.m., Claudine; 5 p.m., F. Donadieu.*

"What time did you say on Friday? Five o'clock? You couldn't make it six, could you? Because at three I've got an extremely important business meeting which is bound to take me till five. You can? You are sweet. You know, I had another meeting at six, but I can get out of it. . . . You know I'd much rather that you could have made it another day, because I'm bound to be a bit tired on Friday too, but since you really can't . . . Good-bye, Josette darling. You really are an angel. Thank you, darling. All my love."

He hung up and remained thinking languorously for several seconds, as if the telephone conversation had been a wave, a voluptuous surge bearing him up. His eyes were bright, his pale cheeks were slightly flushed, he was vaguely smiling, and his eyes were half closed, like an Eastern prince engaged in a secret and delicious reverie. At last, his expression returned to normal, and with renewed calm he began to read his journal again:

"*March 28th. Quite decidedly one can no longer listen to the Porto-Riche theatre. Uterine literature (I mean* Amoureuse).

"*March 29th. How happily one would give oneself to Marxism if only. . . .*

"*If only one believed that the class-war was really the means to the affranchisement, the total liberation of humanity. If one believed that the class war, as state the Marxists, was a necessary step towards a reconciled society. If one really believed that*

Marxist values were worth sacrificing everything to, including oneself.

"*These make up a number of improbable beliefs which lie between my adherence to Marxism and my actual position, which I well know to be in the balance.*

"*I used to believe that it was possible to travel with the Communists without any profound agreement with their doctrine, without the Marxist faith: simply from a desire for solidarity with the working classes, a taste for action, and a wish to be in 'the current of History'. Today, this solution appears to me to be impracticable.*

"*What we have learnt in recent years about the evolution of public morality in the U.S.S.R. (orthodoxy all along the line, monogamy, divorce quasi impossible, the adulterer held in disrepute) is one of the things which has contributed to turn me away from the Communism of Stalin at a time when I might have adhered to it. I give this reason for what it is worth. I do not pretend that it is either a noble one or a particularly convincing one, indeed I can well understand that it may raise a smile, but this journal would have no value had I not long ago determined that it should contain only 'the truth, the whole truth, and nothing but the truth.*

"*The incalculable strength of Communism, which in the long run must assure its certain triumph, is precisely the strength of Christianity at its beginning: it is constructed out of the infinite weakness of all the oppressed who are a prey to want and famine throughout the world. Never lose sight of this fact.*"

Bernard ceased reading. He was aware of a vague unease. Remarks of this nature were thickly strewn throughout the three or four hundred pages of his journal. For the last ten years he had been dancing this sort of hesitation waltz before the Communist Party. One step forward, one step backwards, and turn, "am I going, am I not going? . . ." For ten years he had been juggling with his highly distinguished scruples, his reticences, his reserves, whose sincere avowal must palliate his wholly bourgeois and egotistical character. He always felt a great regard and respect for the Party. He burnt incense before it—from a distance, but he nevertheless burnt incense. Above all, he venerated the proletariat, the Working Class. Never had he said a word against these mysterious, but vaguely redoubtable, entities. No consideration on earth could have persuaded his liberal spirit to be guilty of the crime of lése-Proletariat. In one's time one had been both a nihilist and an anarchist. One had taught oneself, while still quite young, to sift every accepted idea, every opinion of the day, every concept. Nothing was to be accepted that had not first been examined, scrutinised and analysed in accordance with the most rigorous methods of criticism. With Alain, Paul Valéry and Gide, one had refused to sacrifice to the idols. But there was one concept which was outside all discussion: the affranchisement of the Proletariat. Bernard had been able to mock, to scoff at, to trample metaphorically underfoot no matter what constitutional organisation (the Army, the Church, the Law), no matter what economic or cultural school, he had violently and pleasurably attacked the class called bourgeois, nor had he spared the peasantry to the extent that it was conservative, or indeed any other social category. But for the Proletariat, he had nothing but respect. A courtier at Versailles can have been no more subjugated by the person of the King; and he can have pronounced that name with no more fervour, no more reverential awe than Bernard uttered the two words "Working Class". From time to time, Bernard heard himself speaking these two august words; he apprehended, with a sort of fugutive, divided intuition, that he was himself the intellectual and even sentimental slave of these obscure powers. At these times he was a prey to a certain irritation. A doubt, as obstinate and intimate as a familiar demon, haunted him. "*These dilemmas, these abstract and insoluble problems, these weary questionings, are they more than a pretence, a make-believe, an alibi for my easy life? Which am I really most concerned about? The affranchisement of the Proletarian classes, or my own reputation as an advanced intellectual? And the reverence I pay these entities, this sort of interior standing to attention, as precise as a reflex, which is my reaction to the single word Proletariat, is it more than a new sort of conforming, as lazy, as stupid and as hypocritical as any other, one moreover beneath whose shelter I tranquilly pursue a life of pleasure, of minor vanities, of 'spiritual enrichment', which is essentially similar to Barrés' ideal of the 'Cult of Self'? Am I not indeed something resembling a respectable whore of the progressive Left?*"

Questions such as these Bernard found extremely embarrassing. He took up his fountain-pen and wrote at the foot of the last paragraph of his journal:

"*April 3rd. The most profound and essential thing about me is my scepticism.*"

Then he went on reading the last pages with his mind temporarily at rest.

"*March 18th. There is no longer any doubt today that the destiny of the twentieth century is the destiny of the human race, and that it will be played out between the two opposing blocs of America and Russia. Thus the world, in contrast to the growing complexity of its economic structures, of its technical and scientific conquests, etc., will become simplified. This progress towards unification torments us and is doubtless our misfortune. At the same time it is our only hope.*

"*March 19th. Have reread* Les Liaisons Dangereuses *with wondering admiration. The famous seduction scene between Cécile and Valmont threw me into a state. I very nearly telephoned Claudine to implore her to come at once.*

"*François Donadieu. I used to take him for granted. I never reconsidered him. He was Donadieu: easy, familiar, someone I was accustomed to. A good sort who was devoted to me. Loyal, faithful, kind. And he admired me. He took my least word for Gospel. I, too, was friendly and kind, without having to make any effort about it. Perhaps because kindness has never been very difficult for me. Perhaps because his rather ingenuous admiration flattered me a little without my realising it. After all, Donadieu was not a fool. I even appreciated in him a sort of puritanical protestantism, the severity of a provincial Huguenot. He was the Moral Law, the Categorical Imperative. Distrustful in his probity, he had violent and rather absurd aversions. However, in a world of infinite complaisance such as ours, these things did not displease me. And all this time, I had no doubt that he was judging me, too. Calmly, silently, he was judging me, he was judging me. He was very far from sharing my point of view, my ideas and opinions. If he did not oppose me, it was through modesty and self-effacement. But, since a few months ago, he has opposed me. And now I can measure the distance that separates us. I am not affected by it. It is only that it is always a curious experience for me to discover that others are autonomous.*

"*March 28th. For a long time I had been wanting to see Gide again. As I knew that he was overwhelmed with invitations and visitors since his return to France, I was discreet enough not to go to Rue Vaneau. The other night, dining at Letitia's with Jean Denoël, who sees Gide fairly regularly, I asked him to make my desire known. A week later, Denoël telephoned me that I was expected at Rue Vaneau at six o'clock the following day.*

"*I had not seen Gide since the spring of 1941. At that time I used to meet him fairly often at Nice. The last time was at the Ruhl at a luncheon where were, among others, Pierre Hérbart, Roger Stéphane and Titania Orloff. Seven years later, I still found him as astonishingly young and alert as ever—and he is nearly eighty. Always chilly, he was wearing a shawl of thick Pyrenean wool thrown over his shoulders, while on his head was an unspeakable smoking-cap made of ribbed velvet, a sort of Phrygian bonnet whose point fell swaggeringly on one side. But, with him, this rather eccentric get-up only adds a touch of aristocratic negligence to his distinction: a great lord taking his ease. His long, narrow eye retains all its acuteness; the mouth is firm and framed by the two long furrows which are etched into his Chinese bronze-like mask. He came to meet me, smiling, his hands extended, with a noble, cordial warmth which really touched me very much. He at once asked after my family. He hoped they had not suffered too much under the occupation. He remembers my father perfectly well and expressed his regret at not having had more frequent opportunities of meeting him. He spoke to me of Léon Blum with lively and affectionate admiration. Our conversation lasted forty minutes, at the end of which a certain weakening in Gide's voice gave me the signal to leave. Our conversation was, I think, perfectly free and easy, without the least embarrassment on either side. As for me, I had almost (I say: almost) the impression of talking to a companion of my own age so extraordinary is the old man's wonderful vitality still. Malraux and Breton alone have given me the same impression of flowing riches. But in their presence I remain silent, I feel stupid and uncultivated. With Gide, on the other hand, my little mental cells function at full blast. Once or twice I repressed a desire to laugh: when Gide used the word* 'dégueulasse' *with superbly precious diction and an altogether episcopal unction, separating the syllables thus:* 'dé-gueu-la-sse, *my dear fellow!*', *and his eyes sparkled as he went off into a little cascading laugh, at once grave and schoolboyish, as if to underline the incongruity of the nasty slang word in his mouth—indeed, it was at once unexpected, naïve and charming. He used the epithet in the same manner, and hideously enough to tell the truth, that a writer, a member of the C.N.E., had used it against him in an article written a little while after the Liberation (it was over some pages of Gide's* Journal, 1939-1942). *He asked me a number of questions about Sartre, whom he holds in the highest esteem, though I thought I detected, oh, by almost imperceptible signs—a slight clouding of his expression, among others—I thought I detected, I say, that he fears his growing influence over many of the young. (Does this octogenarian prince of letters feel that he has lost the ear of the younger generations? The young men who were twenty in 1945, and* a fortiori *their juniors, know nothing of Gide. They read Malraux, Aragon, Eluard, Sartre, Camus,—and some, Cocteau. I am one of the last of the younger French to have suffered the imprint of Gide.) I tell him I adhere to the general principles of what is called Existentialism. He seemed rather surprised.*

"'*I do not know,' he said at this point in our conversation, 'that Christian ethics have ever been surpassed.*'

"*He admires Sartre as a playwright without reserve.* Huis Clos *is, he said, 'astonishing'.*

"*I noticed a book on his desk:* Pompes Funèbres. *He followed my glance and smiled.*

"'*What do you think of Genet?' he asked.*

"*I reply that I look upon Genet as an excellent writer of prose, but that his range seems to me singularly limited.*

"'*I cannot conceal from myself the fact,' he said with almost ecclesiastical gravity, 'that it is I, after all, who have made the success of a Genet possible, isn't that so? I opened the way.*'

"*He also admires Genet's talent but admits that he finds his sordid scenes disagreeable and chilling.*

"*He told me that the event this year which has shocked him most is Gandhi's assassination.*

"'*An event of con-si-der-able import! The apostle of non-violence falling at the hands of a fanatic. It's beautifully symbolic in the Ibsen manner. And it's appalling! It gives one a chill at the heart. The world is rushing to disaster. There are days when I can think of nothing else, when I am incapable of being distracted from contemplating the spectacle of History on the march. It's ag-on-is-ing!*'

"*I dare to reply that, as far as I am concerned, I am enormously interested by our period and that for nothing in the world would I have wished to live in another century (if one can make so absurd an hypothesis). I tell him that the influence of History upon our individual destinies is in process of totally upsetting our traditional conceptions of literature, in particular the novel, as Sartre has shown. The psychological and analytical novel has had its day. I develop this argument with ardour. Gide listens to me with great attention, which encourages me. He comments upon it by shaking his head and sceptically pursing his lips.*

"*'Yes, yes. . . . Nevertheless, all this seems to me to be rather obscure.'*

"*The manner in which he pronounces the word ('ob-scure!' with a peculiar emphasis) flattens me! But without giving me time to answer, he goes on: 'I mean that it seems to be somewhat premature, too easy a conclusion, I would even say: something of a car-ic-a-ture, like Moliére's doctors, isn't that so: "We have changed all that. . . ." But after all, you may be right. But, I don't want to argue about it with you, for I know only too well my propensity to follow another's lead: at the end of ten minutes, I should have abandoned my own positions in order to adopt yours. Well, I'd rather keep my own ideas At my age one can no longer allow oneself to veer in this way. I've already veered too often in my too-long life. . . .'*

"*All this was said with great art and inimitable humour, with a wonderfully attractive air of youth and gaiety. He added: 'The tiresome thing about arguments is that they're so often convincing.'*

"*He went off into a gale of laughter which seemed to prolong itself indefinitely. I laughed too and bow, as if paying homage to his epigram. Then with shining eyes he said, 'It's not mine, it's Wilde's!' And goes on laughing louder than ever.*"

There was a knock on the door. The office boy came in and announced that there was a gentleman wishing to see Bernard. "A M. Bourgoin, I think."

"Bourgoin? Don't know him. Ask him if he's got an appointment. You know very well that I only see people by appointment."

"He says you know him."

"Perhaps, but I don't remember him. . . . All right, show him in all the same."

By almost unconscious habit, he pretended to be absorbed in his work, a harmless piece of play-acting which was intended to give him a superiority over his visitor from the start. The visitor had to wait respectfully till the busy young editor could suspend his business. Sometimes, if his visitor appeared worth it, he carried the act to the point of picking up the telephone receiver and pretending to hold a conversation. And while talking to this fictitious correspondent ("Right, my dear chap. Come and see me at three o'clock tomorrow. No. Wait a minute. I've got a Board meeting at that time. Let's say five o'clock. Right. See you tomorrow then."), he smiled conventionally but engagingly at his visitor, and with a gesture invited him to take a seat. Then having hung up, he rose to his feet, excused himself with such exquisite frankness and politeness that his visitor, while being kept at a distance, was most favourably impressed. On this occasion, as the name Bourgoin meant nothing to him, he did not go so far as to perform the pantomime with the telephone but merely contented himself with writing a few lines in his journal, as if in a hurry to complete a sentence which had already been begun. Thus, he waited till M. Bourgoin had come sufficiently near his desk. But suddenly he had a vague impression of familiarity. First he looked at the unknown's shoes, which shone like two little black stars, then he raised his eyes up the beautifully creased trousers. This inspection lasted no more than a second. Bernard leapt to his feet, crying: "Nick!"

He went round the desk.

"Nick!" he repeated several times in amazement. "It's not possible! Where have you sprung from?"

He took Nick's hands in his. He was excited, stuttering, asking a thousand questions. His face was red with excitement. Good God, it was unbelievable! Nick fallen out of the sky! What had happened to him? Where had he been hiding?

"I've been looking for you for over three years. As soon as I got back to Paris in 1944, I went straight to your flat. There was no one there. The Gaudies had disappeared into thin air. No one could give me any information. Utter silence. Could one disappear, become invisible, in the middle of the twentieth century? I thought you must have been deported, or God knows what. Oh, my dear old Nick, I can hardly believe that it's you, here in my office, that it's really you. . . . It's overwhelming."

Nick smiled politely, perfectly calm, perfectly master of himself. He looked at Bernard with an expression of friendly indulgence. When he could get a word in, he said, "I'm glad to see you again, too, Odilon."

"Why are you masquerading under the name of Bourgoin? Why didn't you give your real name to the porter?"

"Well, I just wanted to surprise you, watch your reactions. Bourgoin's my wife's maiden name . . .

"You mean to say you're married?"

". . . and it's also my journalistic pseudonym."

"You're a journalist. . . . But let's look at you, Nick. I haven't seen you properly yet. I hadn't noticed . . . Have I gone blind? Nick," he cried, "you're looking fantastically smart!"

And, indeed, Nicholas Gaudie was very well dressed indeed. He was clean. His linen was white. He was wearing a self-coloured tie of a discreet dark red. His suit was dark blue. His overcoat raglan, in the 'Prince of Wales' style. His felt hat was black with a turned up brim. He carried gloves. It was unbelievable.

"You're so smart I wouldn't have recognised you in the street. All the same, you haven't changed. You've got a little fatter. And it suits you very well, too. You're better off than you used to be. But, Nick, I'm bewildered! Explain things, tell me. Sit down and talk! Where have you been? What have you been doing? Are you in league with the Devil or what?"

Nick smiled drily.

"Yes; that's it more or less. I've been in league with the Devil. But I'll tell you all about that some other time. Let's talk about you."

"No, no, please! I want to know! Explain yourself. So, you're married? But that's wonderful, Nick. I couldn't be more surprised. Nick Gaudie married! Well, I've grasped the fact. What's the next surprise?"

"We'll talk about that another time, Odilon. I've only come in for five minutes, simply to make contact again. I've not got much time today. I'm merely in Paris between two trains. I live at Montpellier."

"You live at Montpellier. . . . Your wife too?"

"Yes. She's a chemist and works in a chemical factory."

"How long have you been married?"

"A year. I met my wife on the Thursday of the Liberation in Paris; we got married two years later."

"The Thursday of the Liberation. . . . But where were you? Who with? With Leclerc's army perhaps?"

Nick shook his head and again smiled drily.

"No. I was in my room and, as our journalist colleagues would say, lying in a bath of my own blood. My wife arrived in the nick of time and, well . . . rescued me. But let's talk about you, Odilon."

"For God's sake, don't call me Odilon! What's the matter with you? You never called me that in the old days. Your wife rescued you? You were lying in a bath of your own blood? For goodness sake, Nick, tell me!"

"Are you sure I didn't use to call you Odilon? That's very odd. It seems to me that we knew each other well enough to use our Christian names."

He was not joking. He did not seem to be joking. Bernard went and sat down at his editorial desk. His head felt as empty as a sounding bell. The whole thing was a dream, one of those dreams which are neither good nor bad, but merely odd and disconcerting, when one has the impression of being off-centre, to one side of things, of failing to understand or grasp the essence of what is going on. He had very nearly reached the point of rubbing his eyes. What *was* going on? He looked at Nicholas Gaudie. He recognised him: a tall, loose-limbed man, with hair that was so fair that it was almost white. But this gloved and cravated gentleman, turned out like a business-man or a doctor with a rich practice, who gazed at him kindly, politely, sitting there in front of his desk with his scrubbed, close-shaven face, his carefully brushed, silky hair, could it be Nicholas Gaudie? Bernard gazed at the walls, as if wishing to assure himself of their reality. Yes, Labisse's rabid insects were still there, and Leonor Fini's cat-women. Nick's eyes followed his glance.

"You didn't have these pictures in the old days," he said. "You still like that sort of rubbish?"

"What did you call them, Nick?"

"Rubbish. Those charming pieces of nonsense turned out by the devotees of surréalism. Mark well that I'm not saying they're altogether negligible. They've remarkable technique, even talent. But ultimately they're of no importance. From the aesthetic point of view they're not much more important than the 'make my flesh creep' children. 'Oh, oh, how frightened I am!' You should have something, I don't know what, but something true, solid and honest, even if it were only a reproduction of a Courbet."

Bernard was so stunned that he had not the strength to utter a word. He seemed to be floating about in a fog. Nicholas Gaudie asked him about his activities during the war, about his stay in London, his present job; he replied automatically, fascinated by his visitor's staggering transformation. The whole thing was a dream.

"I hope," Nick said, "that I shall have an opportunity to discuss *Horizons* with you at greater length one day. I've often discussed you in my local rag at Montpellier, but I should like to have the opportunity of discussing things frankly with you."

"Oh, so you run a paper at Montpellier?"

"Yes. *Le Progrés de Languedoc*. It's only a little local rag, of course, and can in no way be compared with *Horizons*. But in an area which is perhaps not quite so poor as one might suppose at first glance, we can make quite a bit of money."

"You make quite a bit of money?" repeated Bernard weakly.

He was stunned.

"You'll forgive my speaking frankly," Nick went on, "but your policies seem to me to be somewhat out of date." (He smilingly indicated with his chin the pictures hanging on the walls.) "Well, they're dated, like those amusing objects there."

"You think so?" stuttered Bernard.

"Yes, well, individualism at all costs, the problems of the liberty of the individual, all that bourgeois luxury. It smells of 1930, not to say 1925—or 1895 for that matter. But we happen to be in the middle of the century. We happen to have had Stalingrad, the unification of China and Hiroshima. The notion of liberty to which you refer in your editorials is purely formal. It's a mental conception. What do you suppose it can mean to millions of Hindus dying of famine, to the Hong Kong coolie, or to the half-breed spitting out his lungs in the silver mines of Peru? As for the problem of the end and the means upon which you were playing your little variations a fortnight ago, I find it pretty rancid; for two thousand years it's served as an alibi for the egoism of the possessing classes and for the dishonesty of their followers. The end and the means, it's the greatest deception in the supposedly spiritual arsenal of the directing classes. I don't know how you can still go on falling into that trap. If I remember correctly, you even used the word 'soul' in that article of yours of a fortnight ago. You may be sure it made me laugh."

"It was a sort of metaphor," Bernard muttered.

"Yes. I gathered that. But, you see, I don't care a damn for metaphors and there are several hundred thousand men like me who don't care a damn for metaphors like that either. It doesn't make sense, Odilon. And you know it."

He got up. He had been speaking without anger or irony. His comments had been made calmly, in a perfectly objective manner, like a man who is merely concerned to convince a friend in error, but has no intention of wounding him or being ironical over his wrong-headedness. He spoke like a man devoted to the cold and impartial examination of things as they are, who was not affected by personal sentiments or considerations.

"I must go," he said. "I merely came in to say how do you do. We shall see each other again. I come to Paris once or twice a year to look up my friends."

Bernard also got up. He was stupefied.

"Nick," he stuttered, "you're . . . you're not by any chance trying to pull my leg, are you? . . . A sort of surréalist leg-pull?"

"No. Why should I?" Nick said coldly.

"God knows. I merely remember you as you were, you see. I remember you, for instance, disguised as an Austrian girl, a refugee from the Anschluss, or, again, as a great admirer of Jean Richepin."

"If you would oblige me," said Nick, "you'll never make any allusion at all to that particular past. All that's finished. I was a perverse and wicked boy. I went on being one till 1944. I went to extremes that you can't even suspect. But I'm detached from all that now, it's finished with, obliterated. Besides, I've expiated it, if the word means anything."

Bernard found strength enough to smile sketchily.

"A true redemption, Nick. . . . It's got a sort of devilish Tolstoy quality."

Nick lowered his eyes and quickly raised them again.

"Irony's an old-fashioned amusement, too," he said, "and an alibi for bad faith as well. Too easy. But I hope you'll understand one day. At the moment you don't seem to have attained to maturity, or truth. You're still an anarchistic schoolboy. You're concerned with false problems, problems that for me are as sterile and remote as the arguments of the schoolmen. The end and the means, for instance, is as absurd a conception as any of the Universalists. It's all much simpler than that. The one thing that matters is efficacy: it resolves all the incompatibles. What matters is to finish as soon as possible with injustice and the reign of money. But I hope that one day you'll see the importance of these things as clearly as I do. I'll come back."

There was a short silence.

"You must introduce me to your wife," Bernard said.

"Of course," said Nick, his face suddenly lighting up. "You'll see, she's . . . wonderful! She's frightfully intelligent. She's . . ."

He hesitated. A vague little smile trembled at the corners of his mouth. There was a strange glow in his eyes, and his eyelids flickered. He raised one hand, and his finger seemed to grasp some invisible object.

". . . She's terrific!" he said breathlessly.

For a second or two, his eyes shut, his face wore an expression of intense and happy exhaustion. Then he recovered himself, relaxed, smiling, very much at ease.

"Goodbye, Odilon. Oh, I'd forgotten," he went on. "You don't like being called that. As you will. All the same, I thought I remembered . . ."

"You always used to call me Bernard!"

"All right. Goodbye, Bernard. We shall see each other again. As for Christian names, I've got my little fads too. Do you mind not calling me Nick? Call me Nicholas. Or just simply Gaudie."

When he had gone Bernard stood for several moments by the door as if turned to stone. As soon as he moved he became a prey to a sort of violent agitation. He began marching up and down the room, his hands behind his back, his head lowered. From time to time he stopped and uttered a muffled expletive. Then he'd give vent to a burst of laughter. A sardonic laugh. Then he'd wipe his forehead with his handkerchief. Twice he called, "Nick." Then he sat down behind his desk and began writing feverishly. He covered three or four pages in forty minutes. He reread what he had written in an undertone in order to judge its rhythm and force. Here and there he made a few small corrections. He closed the notebook, leaned back in his chair and uttered a sigh. He interlaced his hands behind his head and let his eyes wander over the ceiling. He smiled vaguely. He murmured: "You haven't yet attained to maturity, or truth," and laughed silently. He shook his head and pouted his lips commiseratingly. He looked at his watch and lit a cigarette. He was on the point of getting to his feet, when the office boy knocked at the door and came in.

"Monsieur Bernard," he said, "there's a gentleman wants to see you."

"Has he an appointment?"

"No."

"Tell him to telephone and make an appointment. I can't see anyone now, it's already six o'clock and too late."

"He says he simply must see you."

"He does, does he! What's his name?"

"A name like Orzon, if I caught it right."

Bernard started.

"It's not Orson Welles, is it? Show him in at once!"

The office-boy smiled.

"No, Monsieur Bernard, it isn't Orson Welles. I saw him in *Citizen Kane*."

"Of course; and, anyway, what would Orson Welles want with *Horizons*? Show him in. But what a nerve people have!"

He pretended to be absorbed in his notebook. The baize door opened again. A man came in. He was carrying a leather brief-case.

"Monsieur Bernard?" he enquired.

His voice was low and hoarse.

"Yes; that's me."

Bernard indicated a chair with a wave of his hand. The man sat down, placed the brief-case on his knee and his two hands upon it. He had an indefinable expression—hardly a normal one, in any case. Bernard said to himself: "Begging money. Some social object. I'll get rid of him in two minutes." As his visitor remained silent, he asked, "Would you mind telling me the object of your call?"

"You."

"I beg your pardon?"

"You. You are the object of my call," the stranger said with a sort of weighty mockery.

"I heard you," Bernard said drily. "But my time's limited. Perhaps you could be more precise."

He looked at the man opposite more carefully. The most extraordinary thing about his expression was that it seemed at once fixed and slightly wandering. The man's eyes seemed alight. 'A visionary,' Bernard thought. 'A yogi. He's going to suggest that I should start a campaign in *Horizons* for vegetarianism or self-control through deep breathing.' The man seemed to be about thirty-five years old. His features had a certain degraded and disintegrating nobility. He must once have been very good-looking. His hair was dark, thick and in disorder. His appearance uncared for.

"I've been wanting to meet you for a long time," the stranger said. "For over three years. Three years and a half. But I hesitated. I've hesitated for three years."

"Well, that's a long time certainly. I hope you'll manage to be more prompt in explaining your business."

"Just one question. I simply want to ask you one question."

"Ask it, sir, ask it."

The stranger was silent for a moment or two. The burning fixity of his glance was almost unbearable.

"Do you believe," he asked, "that one has the right to take the law into one's own hands?"

Bernard repressed a start. He was fiddling with a paper-knife on his desk. He put it down and looked up.

"I beg your pardon, but are you by any change interviewing me for some newspaper or periodical? If you are, I must ask you to show me your journalist's card."

"You're wrong, sir. I'm asking you the question for purely personal reasons. It's a question that has had a particular interest for me for rather over three years."

'It's neither charity nor yoga. He's mad,' Bernard thought. He got up to his feet and went round the desk so that he could be on his guard if the stranger tried to do anything foolish. He put his right hand on the desk near the bell. He had only to put his finger on it and the office-boy would come at once. He was aware upon the instant that the stranger had noticed the bell and that there was a half-smile upon his lips.

"Are you afraid, sir?" the stranger asked gently.

"Afraid?"

"I think you'd be well advised to leave that bell alone. Supposing I intend killing you, do you really think that bell could prevent me? You're turning pale, sir."

"I'm exasperated," said Bernard curtly. "Do you mind getting out of here?"

"But you haven't answered my question about the right to take the law into one's own hands."

He slipped one hand under the flap of the brief-case, raising it slightly. Then he waited.

'He may be armed. I must keep cool.' Bernard's emotions were mixed, there was something of fear, something of curiosity and the excitement of meeting with an interesting adventure. It was the same mixture of emotions that he had felt once or twice in the past: at the time of his departure for England, then in the spring of 1944 in the *maquis*. He would have to write about it. . . . He went back and sat down in his chair. He was dominating the situation. He began playing with the paper-knife again and smiled courteously.

"May I ask on what grounds you wish to know my opinion about taking the law into one's hands?"

"It's about a boy you killed or ordered to be killed on the 25th May, 1944, at Saint-Ferréol, in the Creuse."

In a flash Bernard remembered something François Donadieu had told him three years before. Now he knew whom he had to deal with.

"A boy I killed?" he repeated. "I think you must be talking of a Militiaman we took prisoner in those parts. If it's of any interest to you, I didn't kill him myself. It was one of my subordinates who took charge of the business and without awaiting my orders either. More precisely, there was some sort of misunderstanding. But I had to recognise, later on, that the execution of that Militiaman was inevitable in the circumstances."

Bernard thought he saw the man begin to tremble. Yes; there was a sort of trembling, or nervous contractions, rather, an almost imperceptible jerking of the shoulders and arms. The telephone bell rang. Bernard put out his hand towards the receiver. He looked at the man and smiled.

"Do you mind?"

He lifted the receiver. He was playing a part, and it was very exciting: a moment of intense living.

"Hullo," enquired a small, anxious voice at the other end of the wire. "Is that you, Bernard? This is François. I've got someone here whose husband . . . Listen, I spoke to you one day of a chap who . . ."

"How very odd!" cried Bernard in his most social voice.

"What?" said the little voice with stupefaction.

"The gentleman in question is in my office. Hang on a minute, will you?"

He covered the receiver with his free hand and turned towards Roland Oyarzun.

"An amusing coincidence. I've got one of your friends on the line, François Donadieu."

He took his hand off the receiver. The distant voice went on in a sort of low murmur through which sounded a note of horror, "He's in your office? My God, I was afraid he'd gone round to you! Take care. He's not near the telephone, is he? He can't hear? For God's sake, look out. His wife tells me that he's been in a crazy state since last night. He went out without saying anything to her. She was terrified, and came round to see me."

"Very well. Very well, that's all right. Goodbye, my dear chap. We're meeting tonight, aren't we? You'll come round and pick me up about twenty to eight, then."

He hung up and smiled broadly.

"François Donadieu asked me to give you his respects."

"You're lying," said Oyarzun. "He's just warned you about me. My wife must have given him the alarm."

Bernard burst out laughing.

"I can see it's no good pretending with you. Well, my dear sir, let's put our cards on the table. What exactly do you want with me?"

Oyarzun made an effort to suppress the tremblings which were shaking his whole body. He was like a man benumbed, trying to get a grip of himself, contracting his jaws so that his teeth should not chatter. His right hand was still slipped under the flap of his brief-case.

"You're finding this amusing, aren't you?" he said. "So am I. I had imagined every possible circumstance of our meeting, except being amused by it. Perhaps I've waited too long."

"Vengeance is a dish that can be eaten cold, so they say."

Bernard smiled as he played with the paper-knife.

"You're pretty sure of yourself," Oyarzun said. "But the Jews, it seems, have become brave as the result of being persecuted. So you're an old member of the Resistance, are you, a real one? I've often wondered what you look like. I imagined you hideously ugly. And yet by and large you're a good-looking man. Odd, isn't it? I'd even go so far as to say that you appear to be quite a decent chap, at a first meeting."

Bernard leant back in his chair and laughed frankly. He was no longer in the least frightened. This intrusive idiot's visit was really fantastic. Quite fantastic! A huge joke. He'd tell the whole story at Letitia's tonight and have quite a little success.

"You see how stupid it is to have preconceived ideas about your enemies before you've met them! Now you've got to revise all your ideas about Jews in general and myself in particular. 'Treat your enemies as if one day they were to become your friends.' Who said that?"

"I didn't, anyway," said Roland, his teeth chattering.

"You're trembling, sir. Are you cold?"

"Yes; I'm trembling. I'm trembling with fear," Roland said, his voice quavering. "I'm trembling at the thought of what's going to happen to you. I'm going to kill you."

Bernard sketched a vague gesture. 'Perhaps I should ring after all?' he thought.

"Enough nonsense!" Oyarzun said suddenly in a curt, vulgar tone. "Nonsense is all very fine, but it's time we came down to brass tacks. So, Bernard, you don't in the least regret having killed that young militiaman on the 25th May, 1944? You believe the execution to have been perfectly just? You believe that the young Militiaman was a traitor? But, supposing, in my view, you were the traitors? You of the Resistance, with de Gaulle at your head, the greatest criminal of modern times after Hitler? And supposing I'm right? And supposing the future proves me to have been right, what then, Bernard. In that case, perhaps I should be right in killing you for the bastard you are, eh? I repeat, leave that bell alone."

There was extraordinary hatred in his voice, and a mad, murderous decisiveness shining in his eyes. Bernard stopped smiling. He felt his skin grow cold across the temples. If only the office-boy would come in. . . . 'No, I'm not going to die like this, killed by this fool. It would be too stupid. I've got faith in my star. I shan't die today. I've still got too many things to do.'

"You held other people's lives pretty cheap in the Resistance. Well, supposing I hold yours cheap too, you foul Jew?"

"The Germans held people's lives pretty cheap too!" Bernard shouted, half from anger, half to attract the office-boy's attention in the next room.

With a decisive movement Roland opened the flap of the brief-case. In his right hand was a revolver, its muzzle pointing at Bernard.

"Don't shout!" he said savagely. "Stand up. Go on, stand up!"

Bernard stood up. His legs felt weak. Through his panic he was conscious of a fragment of thought: 'Find some shift, some means of distracting this madman's attention. . . .'

"Say your prayers, Bernard. If you believe in the God of the Jews, say your prayers."

Roland stood up. His brief-case fell to the floor. As if led by his revolver, he advanced upon Bernard, who moved backwards and away from him. His face was inhuman, convulsed; he moved like a sleepwalker. The ringing of the telephone tore the silence apart.

"Too late," said Roland. "You no longer belong to this world."

The telephone rang and rang again, strident in the void. Then the door opened and the office-boy appeared. He stared at them wide eyed, glued to the spot. At that moment Roland pulled the trigger.

Nothing happened.

Roland looked down at the weapon and pulled again.

Nothing.

"It's out of order," Bernard whispered. "You've waited too long."

He gave it a sharp blow with his hand. The revolver fell to the floor. Bernard put his foot on it.

"It's you, Fernand, is it?" he said to the office-boy. "You can come in. This gentleman was giving me a demonstration of revolver shooting. Unfortunately, his weapon is out of order."

The telephone was still ringing.

"Do you mind if I answer it?" Bernard asked.

He kicked the revolver with his foot.

"Pick it up," he said to the office-boy. "And go and put it in the archives."

Roland was looking at his hands with a bewildered expression. The office-boy picked up the revolver, and glanced with horror at the stranger. Bernard picked up the receiver.

"Hullo," he said. "It's you again, is it? You want to come round? Come on, then. . . . No, no. . . . Everything went off very well, as you can see." He gave a laugh. "Yes; of course your friend's still here. Do you want to speak to him? Here he is."

He turned to Oyarzun.

"Your friend Donadieu would like a word with you."

He handed him the receiver. Roland took it like an automaton, and put it to his ear.

"Yes, it's me," he said in the thin, broken voice of a convalescent. "Yes. . . . Yes. . . . It's all right. . . . Of course, of course. She's with you? You shouldn't have been anxious. Simone always gets worked up about nothing. No, no. . . . If you like. . . . In how long? Ten minutes? All right. I'll wait for you."

He hung up.

"They're coming to call for me," he said without looking at Bernard.

"Fine. Sit down. What are you waiting for?" he said to the boy. "Why did you come in, in the first place? I didn't ring for you."

"I heard you shouting. And then the telephone was ringing, and you didn't answer it."

"Good. Well done. Listen, Fernand. Not a word of what you've seen. Understand? Not a word to anyone. Or I'll give you a week's notice."

"Very well, sir."

"And look, bring me a brandy. Two brandies. This gentleman will doubtless take one too."

The office-boy went out. He held the revolver with the tips of his fingers as if it were some disgusting object. Bernard took a handkerchief from his pocket and wiped his hands. His eyes were bright with a happy, cruel excitement.

"I feel groggy," Roland said complainingly, as if he had just woken from a daydream.

"A mouthful of brandy will do you good," said Bernard,

going over to him. "It's jolly lucky all the same, both for you and for me, that that revolver was out of order. You'd have killed me; and what good would that have done you? None at all, and it wouldn't have helped France either. You must see, my dear chap, that the world today moves too quickly: after three years it's not worth avenging anyone and, however you look at it, it doesn't make any sense. Let the dead bury their dead.

CHAPTER IV

THE BANQUET

*

THERE were already two guests in Mme Dolfus-Gomez' drawing-room: a girl and a young man, whose modernity was apparent from the fact that they smoked American cigarettes, drank neat whisky and seemed terribly bored. The girl, nineteen or twenty and very pretty, was sprawled on a yellow sofa. The boy, of similar age, was not bad-looking either, in a rather taurine way. Standing by a bookcase, he was looking at the titles of the books. When Bernard and François came in, he extended his hand and muttered an unintelligible name. Without getting up from the sofa, the girl also extended a hand and murmured, "Beatrice Marcillac", then let her arm fall back as if the effort had exhausted her. She drank a gulp of whisky, puffed at her cigarette and said languidly, "At last someone's arrived. We were beginning to get terribly bored. Is either of you anyone particularly interesting?"

"Good Lord . . ." said Bernard, taken aback.

"Are you geniuses or anything like that?" asked Beatrice.

"Not exactly," said Bernard.

"So much the better," she sighed. "Geniuses are a frightful bore when there are too many of them about."

"Did I hear you say 'Bernard'?" the boy asked. "You aren't by any chance the Bernard of *Horizons*?"

"Yes; that's me."

"Yours is not a bad paper," the boy said lethargically. "At least it makes sense from the political angle, even though you do ape the *New Statesman and Nation* in tone and layout. But who's your film critic? You'd do well to sack him and replace him by someone who makes sense."

François blushed scarlet and fidgeted his feet.

"Here's our film critic!" said Bernard, bursting into laughter.

The boy was not to be put out by so little a thing as that. He looked François up and down.

"You're a quarter of a century out of date," he said coldly. "Your values are basically emotional and aesthetic, as they were in 1925. For you the film is purely pleasurable, with no ulterior significance. But, if one wants to make a sound criticism, it is essential to posit the film in relation to a contemporary dialectic, with particular reference to Socialist . . ."

"Michel!" cried Beatrice. "Shut up! Stop quoting your article! You're being a bore! And don't you worry," she said, turning to François, "about your criticism. Michel has been practising intellectual masturbation since he was eight and a half. Besides, he's the most monumental dropper of bricks, as you've just seen. Help yourself to a drink. It's a much better idea."

She had quite the manner, at once knowing, nonchalant and authoritative, of those dangerous women, the gangsters' molls of the American films. Bernard, smiling and attracted, devoured the chubby, sophisticated child with his eyes. François, on the other hand, suffering from the shock of young Michel's brutal assault, wore the embarrassed, circumspect expression of an honest bourgeois who has strayed into some low haunt, and in a certain measure, Mme Dolfus-Gomez' salon could be as disconcerting and intimidating as any low haunt, though only reputations were assassinated there and the victims remained in excellent health. From time to time Mme Dolfus received people of whom her staff, pursing their lips, disapproved. Sometimes Mme Dolfus called her housekeeper to the drawing-room, an elderly laidy of extreme correctitude, and on these occasions an immutable little play was enacted before the guests which threw the hostess into ecstasies of pleasure:

MME DOLFUS: Louise, tell us about the day M. Arpoudijan came to luncheon here.

LOUISE (*still in a tremble at the memory of the occasion*): Oh, madame, we were terribly put about. . . .

MME DOLFUS (*her eyes shining*): Who was put about, Louise?

LOUISE: The staff, madame. We were very put about in the servant's hall. We were concerned for Madame's silver, and works of art, and window panes.

MME DOLFUS (*in ecstasy*): Why were you put about, Louise?

LOUISE: Because of M. Arpoudijan, madame. Really, madame, he looked like a tramp. Hector didn't want to let him in.

MME DOLFUS (*hardly able to control herself, speaking to her guests*): It's quite true, you know. Hector simply did not want to let him in! (*To Louise*) What was it you were saying in the servants' hall, Louise?

LOUISE (*knowing that her reply constituted the whole point of the play*): We were saying, "Of course, Madame often invites very odd people here, but, after all, really . . ."

MME DOLFUS (*screaming with laughter, and clapping her hands*): Say it again, Louise! Say it again! Of course, Madame often invites . . . who, Louise? . . . Who?

LOUISE (*obediently*): . . . very odd people, madame, but we were saying among ourselves in the servants' hall that, really, M. Arpoudijan was the limit.

General laughter, Mme Dolfus almost in tears. The house-keeper made a little curtsy and retired. Madame no longer needed her.

The savour of the joke consisted in the fact that M. Arpoudijan was a poet much admired in a certain circle of connoisseurs and that his work had been published owing to the munificence of Mme Dolfus.

François had learnt from Bernard a good deal about the personality of his hostess. The anecdote about M. Arpoudijan gave him cold shivers down the spine, but Bernard assured him that there was no malice in the spoilt-child exuberances of Mme Dolfus. François gazed round the room into which they had been shown by a white-coated servant—doubtless the very Hector who refused to admit ragged poets. It was a huge room decorated with the most fashionable sobriety. The eye was immediately caught by four little pictures of the Impressionist school: chubby pink and white little girls scattered about a wild garden heavy with summer light and heat; a dancer in a vaporous *tutu* suspended above the footlights in an opalescent mist; a sketch of white water-lilies; a beach painted in melting tones with a little liquid orange sun upon the horizon, shining through iridescent clouds. There were some contemporary works too, notably a portrait of Mme Dolfus by Marie Laurençin, done at a period when Mme Dolfus was a young woman with a rose-and-ivory complexion and astonished eyes.

François admired the beautiful pictures and thought how extremely agreeable it must be to live within such a frame, so warm, so wonderfully luxurious, decorated with exquisite pictures, precious china, and every kind of object which could testify to the beauty of the world and the greatness of mankind. It must be easy here to be good, intelligent and happy. He sat down in an armchair and selected an amber coloured drink, in which floated little pieces of ice, from the tray the servant handed him. He helped himself to almonds, black olives and nuts from a saucer. Bernard sat on a footstool near the reclining beauty, and he so obviously wished to charm, captivate and attract her that he was quite radiantly transfigured. The boy, who found that so very little was "sound" here below, did not deign to enter into conversation with François. He went on examining the books. Another guest appeared, a tall young man with untidy hair and the round cheeks of a healthy schoolboy. His tie was slightly lopsided, but this in no way detracted from his air of distinction; rather the opposite. He advanced upon the group, though not without catching the toe of his shoe in the carpet; he modestly lowered his eyes. Bernard and François got up.

"Fontanes," stuttered the new arrival. "I recognise you," he said to Bernard. "I might have guessed that you were the surprise-packet."

"I beg your pardon?"

"Our darling Letitia has been promising me a surprise for the last week. It was you. She firmly believes that we shall come to blows, but then she doesn't know very much about writers."

Bernard looked at him with a mixture of sympathy and mistrust, and one could see that sympathy (or some similar emotion, curiosity perhaps) would shortly carry the day. Bernard was free from rancour and, what's more, found it extremely difficult to resent attacks as such. This meeting, indeed, was calculated to give him the greatest pleasure; certainly the day was fertile with remarkable incidents: the reappearance of Nicholas Gaudie in his latest avatar, Roland Oyarzun's miscalculated attempt at assassination, and now this meeting face to face with his young opponent, Thibault Fontanes. How rich in excitement life was! Tonight, he would write another thirty pages in his intimate journal.

Bernard introduced the young people and François to Fontanes.

The young man called Michel at once took upon himself the office of making conversation.

"Are you the Fontanes of *Une Étoile de Sang*?" he asked. "Your little book is sound from the point of view of style; indeed, one might say that it was written. From every other point of view it's a gratuitous piece of filth and pretty revolting into the bargain, and of course you know it. You've falsified its affinity to the period, you've drowned tragedy in the easy poetry of words and conceits, you've put militiamen and *maquisards* in the same boat, in short the whole thing manifests the most flagrant lack of integrity. This said, you can write."

Bernard roared with laughter.

"My dear chap," he said, "you've found your match."

Fontanes lowered his eyes and pouted.

"The young people of today are frightfully smart," he said. "I very much like their adherence to the old values, their Dreyfusard side, so delightfully old-fashioned, their taste for Eugène Brieux and François de Curel; and then their way of classifying and cataloguing literature, as if we hadn't already catalogues from the big stores. All this shows a very touching goodwill. You and I, Bernard, we belong to a more perverse generation; we believe in nothing, except perhaps the Prix Goncourt and the prize at the Battle of Flowers at Toulouse."

Fontanes' speech was rapid, flat and slightly stuttering, which accentuated, by contrast, the acid, ironic wit of his mockery. François had heard it said, and by Bernard in particular, that Fontanes tended to disconcert people by his easy, often insolent manner, and that it had made him many enemies. As far as he was concerned, he found himself amused by it. So that's what the author of *Une Étoile de Sang*, that book I liked so much, is really like, he thought. Well, Fontanes was like his work: he had the same brilliance, vitality and humour, the incisive elegance; only, there was no melancholy apparent, but then this evening he was playing a part; he had donned the most artificial of moral uniforms, the worldly. François gazed at this boy, some ten years younger than himself, with a sort of shy admiration; he felt towards him what could only be called respect. 'But,' he thought, 'after all, I belong to a generation, to a locality and to a family where one still maintained a feeling of respect, certain moral values, spiritual distinctions, and where one knew very well how to hold people at a distance as well as to keep one's own. That's all gone, or in process of going. Mediocrity knows neither how to respect or admire, and the whole tendency of modern civilisation is to give even the intelligent the reactions of mediocrity.' The impertinence and pretentious vulgarity of the young man called Michel had disgusted him. He was delighted with the ironic disdain with which Thibault Fontanes had put this typical product of the second post-war period in his place.

"It seems to me," said Bernard, "that you must be nearer in age to M. Argelouve than you are to me."

"I think this young man must have been in the bottom form when I was in the fourth, but then two years at school makes an enormous difference; besides, I always felt nearer to the Philosophy class. . . . By the way, talking of philosophical or sociological terms, you lacerated me by calling me an excrescence, an efflorescence, a phenomenon of crystallisation, and I don't know what else. It took me three weeks to recover. I used to look at myself in the mirror and say sadly: 'Poor little efflorescent head!' or: 'A real excrescence of a face.' I could have wept."

"Well, you said I mooed!"

"Yes, but like the minotaur, a classical comparison, and in the last analysis, flattering."

Everyone got up as Mme Dolfus-Gomez made her entrance. The scent she used preceded her like a herald. An expensively simple black dress floated about her perfect legs and moulded her girlish bust. She was wearing a single piece of jewellery, a collar of diamond brilliants. She described an arc, a kind of rapid circular dance, her arm extended horizontally, as she went from one guest to another. She had a gay, sovereign ease of manner.

"I've missed their meeting!" she cried. "And I told them to be here early on purpose. They arrived too early and I've missed it! Well, what do you think of my surprise? There's not another woman in Paris who can boast of having brought Fontanes and Bernard together at her table. You haven't massacred each other?"

"Never before dinner," Thibault said as he kissed Mme Dolfus-Gomez' hand. "I only kill people with the liqueurs. Particularly in your house. Your dinners are much too good."

"My dear little Michel," said Madame Dolfus as she passed on to another of her guests, "how smart you look this evening. Do you see this boy," she said to the others. "I carried him to the baptismal font. He didn't want to be baptised and made such a scene. He was as wicked as the Devil even then. Is your father well? How much younger has he succeeded in becoming this year, the scandalous man?"

She did not wait for an answer, but kissed Beatrice.

"My child, at least ten people have talked to me about you this last week. I've a thousand things to tell you."

She reached Bernard.

"Dear friend, how are you? I hope you're very angry with Fontanes and that you'll argue a lot during dinner. I've told Alice to take down your replies in shorthand. One mustn't lose anything these days. In twenty years, when you're Prime Minister and Fontanes is in the Academy, it'll be a valuable document. Sit down, everybody. Monsieur Donadieu," she said, giving François her hand, "you come from Sault-en-Labourd, I believe, and you were at school with my son. Do you remember him?"

"Very well indeed. I hardly knew him personally, since he was rather older than I, older enough to make it impossible that we should be friends, but he was celebrated, even among us small boys, for his intelligence and all sorts of exceptional qualities."

Mme Dolfus-Gomez' face brightened.

"Oh, he's intelligent enough, the rascal! And do you know what he's doing with his intelligence, now? He's in California with Huxley and Christopher Isherwood and all that lot, studying the Occidental and Oriental mystics. And he washes out his own shirts!"

"Which, all the evidence goes to show, presupposes a strong tendency towards mysticism, particularly in California," said Fontanes.

"No doubt they're nylon shirts," François suggested.

"Have you heard recently from Patrice?" asked Bernard.

"He writes regularly. He may be coming to France in the autumn."

She lit a cigarette. François was trying to compute Mme Dolfus' age. She must have been nearly sixty. She looked thirty-five. Wealth had preserved her thin, alert and youthful outline, her firm cheeks, and her lustrous, beautifully curled hair. She sat down on a low, backless stool. François admired the way she held herself straight without stiffness, the technical precision with which she posed her arms and legs as she sat down. She was talking to Bernard with animation. The servant with the white coat moved about silently, tray in hand. Two more guests arrived: a man of twenty-eight or thirty with a tired face, whose name François did not catch; from what he was able to gather he was a writer—a novelist for the most part; then a tall, strong, statuesque woman in a sumptuous and rather odd dress; she was dark, rather horse-faced, and examined people through a lorgnette which succeeded in making her look impressive. Mme Dolfus-Gomez rose and ran towards the newcomer with open arms.

"Ariane, darling," she cried. "How delighted I am to see you. It's been age! Well, perhaps not quite, since it's only three weeks. . . . But you look absolutely wonderful. Have you come from a Beauty Parlour?"

"Letitia, darling," the woman said, "I've given up Beauty Parlours since you started going to them. There can be no competition between us, my dear."

She gave a neighing laugh and put up her lorgnette.

"Oh, but you're wearing your diamond collar!" she cried. "It must be a special occasion! Anna Spendrift was only talking about your collar the other day, she was saying that it was Prince Boris who gave it to you in 1910 or so. 'But, no Anna, you're really talking nonsense!' I said. 'Letitia was given it in 1920 or thereabouts. Besides it wasn't Prince Boris, but Achmed Pasha; you do muddle things up so. . . .' But do introduce me to these charming young people," she went on, pointing with her lorgnette. "They're your pages? They're at your feet, of course?"

"It is I who am theirs," said Mme Dolfus. "You can search all Paris and you won't find anywhere such brilliant young men as I have in my house. Not even at Florence's. Of course, Florence has everyone, the whole of classical literature, Jouhandeau, Léautaud, Paulhan. . . . But give me the young. Here is the leading French journalist, Bernard of *Horizons*. And here is Fontanes, whom you know of, of course, the author of *Une Étoile de Sang*."

"A wonderful book," the newcomer sighed.

"Madame Ariane Agropoulos, who was Miss Greece not so long ago."

"Be quiet, you perfidious creature!" groaned Mme Agropoulos.

"You were as beautiful as a statue from the Erectheum," said Mme Dolfus enthusiastically. "And you've kept your beauty, darling, only it's a little more Junoesque. . . . This boy," she said, introducing Michel Argelouve, "hasn't done anything yet, but he will do the most astonishing things. You know what a flair I've got."

"You've an infalliable flair for the young," agreed Mme Agropoulos in a languid voice. "Everyone you've discovered has done something—one doesn't always know quite what, but something, anyway. . . ."

She gave her neighing laugh again and Letitia laughed too.

"So you're the man who writes those clever articles in *Horizons*?" Mme Agropoulos said to Bernard. "What do you see upon the horizons of the world? Not war, I hope? I've already lived through two, and the second one more or less still goes on in my poor country. For goodness' sake don't prophesy a third world war during the next twenty-five years. That's about the time I've still got to live, if God is good to me, and I'd much rather live those twenty-five years in peace."

"Alas, we've been in a permanent state of war ever since 1914," said Bernard. "We're exposed to its risks every day. If I were to tell you that, only this afternoon, I very nearly fell on the field of honour of . . . I don't quite know what, but the field of honour, anyway."

"Not really?" said Mme Agropoulos, raising her lorgnette.

"Oh, do tell us!" cried Mme Dolfus.

"Here we go," thought François. "The Oyarzun story. He's been longing to tell it. It'll be the main event of the evening."

He was still shocked by the pitiable incident. It would be a long time before he forgot this day: Simone Oyarzun, bewildered, in tears, knocking at his door: "I think Roland's gone mad. He went out without a word. I'm frightened." The telephone call to Bernard. His reply: "Yes. Your friend's here." the second telephone call, five minutes later: "Everything went off very well." Then, Roland's voice, a small, broken, toneless voice. Then, the strange sight in the office of *Horizons*: Bernard and Roland, sitting in two leather armchairs, glasses of brandy in their hands, just like two old friends quietly chatting together. Roland Oyarzun's exhausted appearance, his debility, like someone who has just come through a grave nervous crisis. François and Bernard had gone out for a minute or two, leaving Simone with her husband. "What are you going to do? Are you going to hand him over to the police?" François had asked when he had heard the story of the attempt. "Not on your life!" Bernard said. "Why on earth should I hand the poor devil over to the police? His case needs a doctor, not a magistrate." It was true, of course. Simone had left them, taking her husband with her as one takes someone seriously ill, gently and with precaution. She thanked François, who offered to accompany her, but firmly declined, like the brave little woman she was. To crown the tragi-comedy, Roland and Bernard had shaken hands.

The servant interrupted Bernard's story to announce dinner. He opened the double doors and they went into the dining-room.

"But I know Oyarzun!" cried Thibault Fontanes. "Your story's really very funny. I know the fellow very well, and I know that he wanted to bump you off. I believe I even jokingly encouraged him to do it."

"Thanks. Your jokes seem to be on the dangerous side," said Bernard. "You don't seem to realise that it was damned nearly the end of me. If his revolver had not been out of order . . ."

"But after all," said Fontanes, "you chaps, you great adventurers of the twentieth century, surely you dream of nothing else but dying on every battlefield, or am I wrong? Surely a violent death is part of your programme, isn't it?"

"This is delightful," cried Letitia. "They're beginning to go for each other. Alice," she said, turning to the pale, smiling woman who was her secretary, "you've got your pencil and notebook? Get ready to take it all down. Bernard, my dear friend, sit here on my right. Fontanes shall sit opposite you on Mme Agropoulos' left. Alice, help me to arrange the table. Ariane, you shall sit there, at the head of the table, opposite me, between two young novelists."

"How did you come to know Oyarzun?" asked Bernard. "It's a curious coincidence."

"I met him among a society of dissidents. As a result of an article I published in *La France Nouvelle*; he spoke to me of you."

"Oyarzun had a great admiration for you," François intervened. "But he was afraid of your teasing, which, as it happens, he did not always understand."

Fontanes laughed frankly.

"Did you know that he knew Thibault Fontanes?" Bernard asked François.

"Yes; and he was rather proud of it."

"Tell me, Monsieur Bernard," said Mme Agropoulos. "What interests me most in your story are your last seconds of life. What were your thoughts when you saw this man level a revolver at you and you knew that you were going to die?"

"Ariane!" cried Mme Dolfus. "Don't be macabre. Not in my house. You know very well that such subjects are prohibited, forbidden and taboo in my house. I hate table-turning and Black Masses"

"I find that a little of the macabre adds salt to my pleasures," said Mme Agropoulos gravely.

"At last, the very accents of Barrés!" said Fontanes. "I feared that I should never hear them. It's not the best Barrés, I must say, but still, it's a great pleasure nowadays."

"I certainly knew M. Barrés," said Mme Agropoulos. "He had Byzantine eyes."

"Quite a Byzantine heart, too," said Fontanes.

"I should say gipsy rather," said the man sitting on Mme Agropoulos' right, "with that lick of hair on his forehead and the music of his prose."

"Yes, indeed," said Fontanes, leaning forward to look at his brother professional. "Barrés plays heart-breaking czardas, those czardas that invite to suicide, and then, racked with remorse, he brutally attacks *Sambre et Meuse*."

"You haven't answered my question, Monsieur Bernard," said Mme Agropoulos. "What was your last thought before dying?"

"I'm going to disappoint you: I didn't for one instant believe that I was going to die, or that the madman was going to fire. You see, I don't believe in my own death. I've an indestructible faith in my self and I'm sure that I'm going to live to be a hundred."

"You're very lucky," sighed Mme Agropoulos, who, her eyes alight with greed, was in process of helping herself to two huge slices of roast meat. "I'd give anything in the world to be sure of living to a hundred."

Mme Dolfus was talking about her son to François Donadieu, sitting on her left. He was not listening very attentively, since he wanted to hear what Fontanes and the other writer were saying. The conversation had broken up into three or four principal parts which mingled and overlapped like the different parts of a fugue; the sound of their voices gradually rose, from time to time one voice would dominate the others which then fell silent by a sort of common accord to allow the audacious soloist to modulate his improvisation, and preen his verbal virtuosity in an attentive silence. François contemplated the scene before him: the large polished table, the yellow napery, the great procelain basket from which flowers and leaves seemed to pour in a sumptuous flow of vegetable lava whose fringes touched the crystal glasses; the warm light reflected from the walls in a soft phosphorescent glow, the long perspective of the room, in which gleamed the little pictures that art historians, come purposely from San Francisco or Munich, craved Mme Dolfus-Gomez' permission to see: these assembled men and women, whom a silent, well-trained servant, almost invisible in his discretion, served each in turn; they ate delicious food, chatted gaily, crammed with fine knowledge, or, at least, trained to the conventions of an elegant society which demanded a rigorous frivolity. They were fresh-faced, had charming manners, were the guests at a perpetual banquet, and no apocalypse could touch them. And Bernard himself, the ex-partisan, the 'lucid and passionate' prophet of the age, the humanist so profoundly integrated in History, he too was infrangible, wrapped as he was in the hard and brittle shell of fashion which was his natural habitat. And round Letitia Dolfus' throat, so miraculously young and well preserved, the diamonds in her collar darted forth their little incandescent fires.

* * *

At the very same hour Roland Oyarzun and his wife were finishing dinner. After leaving the office in the Rue Mazarine at about six o'clock, they had wandered along the quays, crossed the Pont des Arts, and sought a quiet spot under the trees of the Tuileries. Little by little Roland came out of his daze. His first words, whispered rather tremulously, were, "You're not going to take me to a doctor, Simone, are you? I'm not ill, you know. My nerves are in a bad state, and I had a sort of fit, but I'm not really ill. I'm better now. And I feel I'm going to be quite all right."

She kissed him and took his hand. She made a great effort to smile and to speak cheerfully.

"Yes, Roland. You're quite all right. It's all over now; it was a bad dream. Now it's done with."

"Simone, we must go away. I don't want to live in France any more. We must go abroad."

"Yes; if you wish it. We'll go abroad."

"To Canada or Africa. One can find work in these places. We're still young; we can start a new life," he said with growing excitement. "France is rotten, as far as we're concerned. We must have a change of air and new horizons." He shivered and gave a hoarse little laugh: "Let's change our horizons!" he repeated. "Let's go, Simone. We have often talked of it. And now is the time. I'll go and see my mother. Next week. I'll ask her for money, demand it. I'll go. I promise you I'll go."

"Of course you will. And I'll come with you, if you like."

It was delightful under the trees of the Tuileries. Roland looked at his wife and put his hand on her shoulder.

"Poor darling," he murmured. "I've led you a dog's life. You've not had much luck. And you take it all so bravely. You've got pluck, you know."

They went out of the garden.

"Do you want to go home?" asked Simone. "Or would you like to go and eat in a restaurant? Look. I'll buy you a good dinner. Mummy had given me some money for my birthday. I wanted to buy a mackintosh, but of course, if we're going to Africa, one won't need a mackintosh there."

"Yes, you will. They have the most terrible rainstorms."

"I don't care. Let's enjoy ourselves tonight."

She took his arm with a somewhat forced gaiety.

"This place looks nice," she said, leading him into a restaurant window in the Rue de Seine. They looked at the menu hanging outside.

"We can't go there," said Roland. "It's much too expensive. A single portion of chicken at three hundred francs. It's much too much."

"It doesn't matter," Simone pleaded. "I've got the money. Let's go in, the place really looks quite good."

"No, no; not with prices like that. I couldn't eat a thing. Let's go somewhere else."

And they went on their way down the Rue de Seine, arm in arm, stopping from time to time to look at the menus hanging in the restaurant windows.

* * *

In the meantime the dinner-guests of Letitia Dolfus continued to talk gaily, while the silent Ganymede continued to pour out the wine with precision into the crystal glasses, and a soft, delicious light illuminated the interior of the snug shell. They were talking of the recent books they had read, of the plays and films they had seen: *Uranus*, by Marcel Aymé, *Le Maître de Santiago*, *Les Mains Sales*, *L'Archipel Lenoir*, and the brilliantly intelligent summing up of a period by Nicole Védrès, *Paris, 1900*. Thibault Fontanes was much taken with the humour of *Uranus*.

"You've picked up a habit of Marcel Aymé's," said Bernard, "that of writing words in foreign languages phonetically: *coquetéle*, *ouiquende*, *bohiscoute*, *nioulouque*, and even proper names such as Rita Héoursse. Besides, Marcel Aymé, with Montherlant, is one of your masters. Not only your own particular master, but that of all the young people of your group. One day I shall write an article about you and denounce all your tricks."

"You bear me a peculiarly literary grudge!"

Mme Dolfus-Gomez rose. Her guests went into the drawing-room. The two modern young people, Michel and Beatrice, went over to talk to Thibault Fontanes. Mme Agropoulos evoked the classic charms of Hellas to François and the secretary. Bernard went over to the writer who thought that Barrés was more gipsy than Byzantine.

"I haven't read your last book," he said, "but I've heard people speaking about it. You are one of the few authors of our generation who writes novels in a profoundly romantic way. Is it deliberate or spontaneous? Do you in fact still believe in the novel?"

"I don't quite understand your question. Do you mean: do I believe in what I do? Or do you mean: is the novel still possible as a form in present circumstances?"

"I really mean the second question."

"You know the novel is condemned to death every six months. Its proliferation as a form is clearly rather a disquieting tendency, but I imagine the good God will recognise his own."

"I wasn't thinking so much of its proliferation as of its conventions. You can say what you like, but it's obviously an impure form!"

"Every literary form is conventional. Literature itself is a convention."

"No doubt; but I believe that the novel in its traditional form is exhausted, devitalised, on its death bed. It only seems to survive because the Americans have given it a blood transfusion. But American blood is too heavy and too rich for the body of the French novel. Besides, there are no subjects left."

"I guess that in painting your taste is more for the abstract than for the representational? At least you haven't got an obsession about subject in matters of art? Why do you ask that question of the novel then? As far as I'm concerned I like a novel to have a 'subject', but then I neither am nor wish to be modern. That said, it doesn't seem to me that your remark makes much sense. A man who really has a novelist's instinct is never short of subjects, either because he's always writing about the same one, or because everything he sees is assimilated, digested and transmuted according to his own peculiar chemistry."

"You still believe in those discarded myths: the novelist's mysterious talent, his personal vision and all the rest of it? It's odd. . . . I believe in work, method and technique. Like Valéry."

"Who very well knew of what a Dickens consisted, could take him apart piece by piece, and bet he could write a novel more Dickensian than Dickens, but never kept his wager."

"He disliked even the form too much."

"Yes; of course."

"What you're saying is that the 'chemistry' of the novel operates permanently, if I may so express it? For instance, what do you see in this drawing-room that you could use?"

The novelist smiled.

"Goodness me, a thousand things. You, in particular!"

"Me? Well, that's interesting."

"I don't pretend that I should draw you as you are, but all the same, it seems to me that certain of your characteristics might lend themselves to . . . Listen. You were speaking of subject. The incident that happened to you this afternoon furnishes one."

"A bit thin and anecdotal."

"You think so? But my dear chap, there are immense things behind that anecdote; the antagonism which divides, or has divided, a whole part of French society, the conflict between the Resistance and the Collaboration, or, going further, the conflict between the Progressives and the Conservatives, between Left and Right, which is not at all the same thing, moreover, since there were many in the Resistance who came from Conservative circles, and conversely certain brands of 1939 Socialism formed the cadres of Collaboration. There are anti-Semitism and all sorts of obscure passions. Indeed, it would be interesting to explore, from the point of view of a novelist, the how and the why of political choice, and the psychological bases, social and religious, for that choice. In short, the impact of political ideas as they affect the whole human personality."

"If I understand you, you start from the postulate that political choice is never disinterested?"

"I don't like the word 'disinterested', because it tends to ambiguity. Besides, I know the sense in which you're using it. I should prefer to say: political choice is no more 'pure' than any other, philosophic choice, aesthetic choice, metaphysical choice. . . ."

"I see the analogy, but does it take one any further?"

"Good God, it leads to some pretty important problems: the relations of the individual to society, the world and the individual, truth and playing a part. You see what interests me is the continual bearing upon the personal equation. Political ideas exist on two levels: on the one hand they have an intellectual configuration and on the other they are a source of passion and emotion. These two levels are constantly mingling, and there is the ambiguity. The relationship between 'idea-personality-conditioning' is above all ambiguous, but I believe that it is exactly this ambiguity which is the proper domain of the novel. Or at least of the novel as I conceive it and practise or endeavour to practise it."

"And all this derives from the single incident of a halfwit who tried to kill me. . . ."

"Is he a fool? I've a great weakness for fools. There's a sort of thickness about them, a disturbing opacity. They're so significant, so representative of ordinary humanity. You have doubtless noticed how rare they are in the contemporary novel? Look for them. You won't find a single one in Malraux."

"But Malraux has explained that. He has said that fools don't interest him."

"He's wrong. I'd give all the intellectuals in contemporary fiction for one great foolish character from, shall we say, Balzac or Dickens. Or from Proust. Listen: Proust. . . . How many of the crowd of characters in *A La Recherche du Temps Perdu* are really intelligent? The narrator, who is hardly a character at all; Swann; Charlus, the Duchess of Guermantes, at moments only; and of course the mother and grandmother of the narrator. Oh, and then, Saint-Loup. . . . All the rest of them are wonderful idiots, often cultivated and eloquent, of course. No, no, I'm quite sure," he said with something of a malicious air, "that the successful creation of a fool is the touchstone of a novelist's talent."

"I must say I feel about it as Malraux does: that particular kind of animal leaves me cold."

"Listen, my dear chap. If you need intelligent characters, there's yourself and there's Fontanes. . . . Look. I've got it! Fontanes has also been an adversary of yours, like the wretched fellow of this afternoon's affair, but on an altogether different level. This represents another variation on the major theme of conflict. You see how things are beginning to take shape!" he cried as if he were beginning to enjoy himself.

Thibault Fontanes came over to the two men.

"Our friend here wants to put us both into a novel," Bernard said. "He seems to think that we're sufficiently representative."

"That's it. You put us into a novel," said Fontanes. "I'll furnish you with a complete account of my childhood, my first love affairs and so on. By way of recompense you'll make me into a charming and sympathetic character, while Bernard will be the big, bad wolf."

"Splendid," said the writer. "Childhood and adolescence are extremely important. I like beginnings and rough drafts. As one knows, the child is father to the man. So I shall show Thibault Fontanes organising an anti-parliamentary plot in the school yard."

"You don't know how true what you're saying is!" cried Fontanes. "On the 7th February, 1934, I got myself nominated dictator, almost unanimously, by the citizens of the bottom form in my school. Daladier was most surprised."

"Daladier?"

"The son, a contemporary of ours."

"Excellent. The whole thing must start with the volleys fired on the 6th February, like the three knocks that precede a tragedy. Then the curtain rises, and one sees on the one hand Thibault

Fontanes, in shorts, in the process of fomenting a revolution in the school yard; and on the other hand you, Bernard, who must have been older at that time. . . . Where were you on the 6th February?"

"In the Cours la Reine with a friend who, since . . ."

He shrugged his shoulders and gave a short laugh.

"Louis-le-Grand, at the time, admired his crimes. In short, I mean to say that he's changed now, but at that time, he thought that I was absurd to be concerned with politics. For him, nothing would do but revolution in its pure state."

"So Bernard was among the demonstrators," the writer said as if he were reconstituting history. "A third character: your adversary of this afternoon, where could he have been on the 6th February?"

"Wait a minute," said Bernard, entering into the spirit of the game, "there's someone here who can tell us. François!" he called.

François was talking to the beautiful Greek lady with the lorgnette. He excused himself.

"Please forgive me," said Bernard to Mme Agropoulos, "I'll give him back to you in a moment, but we're in need of some information. François, what were you doing on 7th February, 1934? Where were you?"

"Where was I? I was at school," François said somewhat disconcerted.

"And Oyarzun?"

"He was at school too. We were in the top form. At least I was."

"Can you give us any details, any account of the time? Were you interested in events down there in your village of Sault-en-Labourd? Did you schoolboys ever discuss them?"

"Of course we did. There were Republicans and Monarchists among us, Leftists and Rightists, a good many varieties of opinion. We devoured the newspapers. I remember that it was I, as a serious minded day-boy, who had secretly to bring in the newspapers for the boarders."

"What attitude did Oyarzun take in February, 1934?"

"A purely dramatic one. He foamed at the mouth."

"I can see him doing it!" cried Bernard.

"So can I," said the writer. "And there's your first chapter for you."

"And how do you see the last chapter?" Bernard asked.

"You get killed, of course," said Fontanes, "and you die like Du Guesclin or the young Bara, crying: 'Man is Man and Malraux is his prophet!' An apotheosis of the humanist faith."

"Never!" said the writer, laughing. "Certainly no apotheosis! A novel should never end with such words as peace, liberty, serenity and so on. One should be able to detect them worked like filigree into the web of the book, but the last pages should strike an uncertain note, a sort of lost chord. There must always be ambiguity, you see. Without doubt it's one of the most important laws of the aesthetic of the novel. I'm thinking of 'He had just been awarded the Legion of Honour' in *Madame Bovary*, or of 'I am very anxious to know Caloub' in *Les Faux Monnayeurs*."

"Those phrases seem to me very significant," said François.

"They most certainly are. Flaubert knew very well where he was going and what he wanted, so did Gide, and they both succeeded in gauging very exactly the necessity and effect of their little final phrases. When I say 'a lost chord', I don't mean a false chord, but an ironic and ambiguous one which brings the symphony of the novel to a close."

Letitia wanted to organise a "truth game", and though nobody showed much willingness, she was sufficiently tyrannical to make them all sit down, upon which she asked Thibault the first question.

"You're on the top of a tower with Ariane and myself and you're obliged to throw one of us off, what do you do? Answer quickly."

"I'd throw you both off," he said coldly. "I hate those sort of dilemmas."

"And you, Monsieur Donadieu, what would you do?"

"I'd throw myself off," he said, blushing.

"How nice he is!" cried Mme Agropoulos.

"And you, Bernard? Answer quickly. It's the rule of the game."

"I'll answer for him," said Thibault. "He awakens the universal conscience, cries that such coercion is intolerable to human dignity, sends an article to *Horizons* and starts a poll among its readers. Besides, Bernard's accustomed to that sort of thing: for years now he's been at the top of a tower with two women, one of whom he has got to throw overboard: America or Russia."

"Fontanes has admirably summed up the Fascist and Democratic attitudes," said Bernard, laughing. "He throws off both women, whereas I manage to go on living with them and avoiding the dilemma."

"Another question," said Letitia. "We'll begin with you," she said to the writer who had thought Barrés rather gipsy. "With which of the people here would you like to go to bed tonight?"

"With this girl here," he said, pointing to Beatrice.

"And you, Ariane?"

"I confess I find this most embarrassing. I think I should choose this young man" (she pointed to Argelouve), "but I should deceive him, in my thoughts, with M. Bernard or M. Fontanes or M. Donadieu."

"Beast!" said Letitia, delighted. "You obviously hate dilemmas too. It's your turn, Monsieur Donadieu."

He blushed once again. It was a horrible game. François had never heard anything like it before. All the provincial Huguenot in him came to the surface and was scandalised. Letitia saw his confusion and smiled with pleasure. The whole charm of the game of course consisted in the nervous exasperation and self-hatred into which it threw the participants.

"You're cheating, Monsieur Donadieu. You must answer at once, without thinking. And no politeness, please!"

"It was only the hesitation of Buridan's donkey, madame."

"Oh, I'm deceived. You're lying. Out of politeness to Ariane and me, you don't dare say that you would have chosen this girl here. Anyhow, it's no use going on: all these young men want to go to bed with Beatrice."

Beatrice did not appear to be embarrassed.

"And you haven't answered yet, Letitia," said Bernard.

"My dear, with you of course. You've known it for years."

The servant came in and whispered a word in her ear.

"Monsieur Donadieu, you're wanted on the telephone," she said.

"Me?" he said in surprise. "That's odd. . . . Forgive me." He got up and followed the servant into the hall. He picked up the receiver. He recognised the voice of his concierge and grasped straight away from the way she said "Is that you, Monsieur Donadieu?" that something terrible had happened.

"They're rung me up from the Midi so that I should tell you.

Oh, my God, it's your little girl. She's hurt herself falling in the mountains. On an expedition. Poor Monsieur Donadieu. They said you should go tonight."

He gently replaced the receiver and stood motionless for a few seconds. There, quite close to him, an extraordinary thing had happened, something new, unforeseen, something confusing which would upset his life and undoubtedly cause him much pain. It was there, still in the shadow. For the moment he had to busy himself with small, urgent matters: he must say goodbye to those people in the drawing-room, he must tell Catherine, go and see her perhaps; go home and pack a bag, get himself to the station.... All this must be done properly and decently, He went towards the drawing-room, and then stopped. No; it was impossible. He could not tell them why he was going; nor could he invent some pretext and look as if nothing had happened. The servant appeared. François beckoned to him and put a note in his hand. He talked calmly, with a sort of cautious slowness, as if the slightest error, the slightest solecism ran the risk of causing an explosion.

"Will you please convey my excuses to Madame? I must go at once. I've been called away on a matter of urgency. I'll telephone or write a note."

The servant opened the door and François went off on tiptoe, like a malefactor.

"Another question," said Letitia. "Is there anyone here whom you hate and whom you would wish to see dead? Answer, Fontanes."

"You, when you insist on playing this perfectly beastly game. It's odd, though, when you come to think of it, how very limited the number of shameful questions in fact there are: whom you would like to kill, with whom would you like to go to bed? Aggressiveness and eroticism, one can't get away from them, it becomes exceedingly monotonous. In fact, the game's an amusing attempt at psycho-analysis by administering a treatment of successive and burglarious shocks."

From then on the evening began to drag and the guests started to take their leave. Fontanes and Bernard went out together.

"Shall we go and have a drink at Saint-Germain?" said Bernard. "It's barely half-past eleven; much too early to go to bed."

"Yes, let's. I've got a car here."

He indicated a low, long, black, squat-looking drop-head coupé, with an aggressive radiator.

"What on earth's that monster?" asked Bernard. "It doesn't look very catholic to me."

"No, it's a puritan. It's English. But don't be frightened. It perfectly understands my English. It's true, isn't it, old chap, you do understand my English, don't you?"

He pressed the self-starter. The monster uttered a metallic muttering.

"It said: 'Very well, sir.' Get in, won't you?"

At the wheel, Thibault made a magic pass or two. The monster began groaning in a most disquieting manner and then took off. With his hair blowing in the wind, Thibault had an air of happy expectancy; he appeared the youthful spirit of speed. The car accelerated, the Avenue de la Grande Armée rushed by in a few seconds. Bernard clutched at his seat. The Arc de Triomphe oscillated on its axis, the Champs Elysées swung by with a roar in a fantastic kaleidoscope of illuminated advertisements, the Place de la Concorde was already upon them, the Chamber of Deputies leapt up in front of the monster as if to swallow it up, but it managed to turn in time, and rushed, raging, out into the Boulevard Saint-Germain like a burning meteor. There was a harsh, sharp screaming of brakes. Bernard was thrown from his seat against the windscreen.

"How many pedestrians have you run over?" he asked in a weak voice.

Thibault laughed.

"One should drive as one writes and as one lives," he said, "risking death every second."

They sat down at a table on the terrace of the *Flore*.

"I'm glad," Bernard said, "that our dear Letitia had the idea of bringing us together. I've been wanting to meet you for a long time. It won't prevent our attacking each other in the future, because we're both equally stubborn, but that's another matter. Léon Daudet never hesitated to shake hands with people whom he had insulted at length in *l'Action Française* the day before. Indeed, it would be much more profitable to go about with one's enemies than with one's friends. One of my great regrets is not to have known people like Brasillach and Drieu at a time when

I could easily have done so. I can't forgive myself for having neglected to do so."

"It might have been dangerous, my dear chap. Those fellows would have been quite capable of converting you."

"I don't think they would have done that, but they most certainly would have enlightened me about a great many things. I was curious about them as I'm curious about you. Curious about the way their minds worked. Because how the devil can one be a Fascist? I mean to say, when one's Brasillach or Drieu? I can understand pretty well the mentality of the fifty-year-old member of the Croix de Feu who was an ex-soldier and wore a beret and insignia. I can understand the mentality of the boy Militiaman. There's nothing particularly mysterious about those reactions. But Drieu, Brasillach! I don't understand them. I think in the first place there must be an enormous contempt for humanity that only psycho-analysis could explain. They're pessimists. And, as you know, 'every man who is at once active and pessimistic is or will be a Fascist, unless he has a faith behind him'."

"As far as Brasillach at least is concerned, what strikes me most is a positive, living vitality, a spirit of comradeship and youth, I'd even say a passion for marching songs under a blue sky."

"That is not incompatible with a profound pessimism. Brasillach was the only poet of French Fascism. He liked the '*wandervögel*' side of European totalitarianism, as he liked hitch-hiking, camping out and the open air. He would have forgiven the Popular Front a lot because of its Youth Hostels and its ski-trains. Nevertheless, you must admit that in the first place his attitude was one of denial and proscription: a sort of denial of the world, accompanied by the proscription of certain elements in society, Jews, Communists and so on. Fascism always defines itself by what it wishes to destroy. The myths it elaborates afterwards merely serve to justify previous destruction."

"As for destruction, the humanitarians don't lag far behind."

"That's your knock-down argument," said Bernard, smiling. Your atomic argument. But you forget that the Germans also had nuclear laboratories. They were outdistanced by the Americans, that's all. You're not showing good faith in squashing us with the Hiroshima bomb."

"That bomb's extremely tiresome, I admit. Particularly for

the Japanese, of course, but also for certain Occidentals too. What one can say is that in preparing nuclear machines, the Nazis were logically true to their lust for conquest and destruction, their aggressiveness and their *schadenfreude*. As far as I know, they never pretended to be humanitarian, whereas the Americans . . ."

"In fact, you reproach us with having answered violence with violence instead of allowing ourselves to be piously massacred?"

"I shall merely confine myself to pointing out certain contradictions in which you've been floundering for a long time. From 1918 till 1939 you were all antipatriotic and internationalist. After June, 1940, you became wildly militant and screamed for revenge. You wanted or pretended to want to fight for Danzig. Today you refuse to fight for two-thirds of Europe occupied by a foreign power. You shot or allowed to be shot some of the pacifists of 1938 and 1939, but only a certain category of pacifists, because one can read in the *Editions Communistes* of 1940 these lines which, with the exception of the first two words, could have been signed by a contributor to *Je suis Partout*. Wait a moment. I've got them noted down somewhere. . . ."

He took a little notebook from his pocket and opened it.

" '*The Party shows the way of salvation. And the way of salvation is not that shown you by General de Gaulle, who would like to ally France to the tottering fortunes of the British Empire in decline. . . . The Party which fought against the Treaty of Versailles and for the fraternisation of the German and French people against an imperialist war can hold its head high.*' "

He closed the notebook.

"You do not want to remember those lines because, of course, the Communists took part in the tribunals which condemned to death the non-Communist pacifists of 1938-9, who expressed practically exactly the same views. You resisted the German occupation, but you're divided among yourselves as to what attitude to take towards a possible Russian occupation. You pretended to fight, as nationalists, against the Nazis, while you were fighting as Marxists, against a régime which seemed to uphold the bourgeoisis. . . . I say that these are tiresome contradictions. But they could be resolved at once if you had the guts to make your words accord with your intentions. Don't talk any more of fraternity, liberty and other such trifles, but say: 'Our object is to upset capitalist injustice through revolution and to establish the Marxist order in its place, and we shall use every means at our disposal to arrive at these ends.' At this point I shall undoubtedly continue to oppose you, but I shall cease mocking you."

Thibault spoke without violence or bitterness. Both men were, in fact, extremely careful to maintain the courteous tones of friendly debate.

"What you're saying, Fontanes, is an over-simplification, besides being rather unfair. Above all it isn't true, and you know it. You know very well that the only contradiction, and it's a perfectly conscious one, from which what you call the 'progressive intellectuals' suffer, is in rejecting capitalist injustice without being able to accept Marxism, because in our eyes it appears to be another injustice. You know that, don't you? And have you ever thought that it may not be to the honour of democracy that it should be in a state of permanent contradiction, a very sign of contradiction, a state of delicate equilibrium constantly threatened by order on the one hand and justice on the other?"

He laughed in order to modify a certain solemnity apparent in his last words.

"Good God!" he said. "It may not be the Sermon on the Mount, but it's the sermon of the *Café Flore*. Rest assured. I've no intention of catechising you. Only, I repeat, I'm curious about you and I've retained an adolescent taste for arguing.

* * *

Now, at this very moment, a man leant his forehead against the lateral glass screen of the *Flore's* terrace. He opened his mouth, aghast. He opened wide his eyes, as if he doubted the reality of what he saw; and his pale, stark face behind the glass was the very mask of anguished astonishment. It was Roland Oyarzun. After dinner in a neighbouring restaurant, he had wanted, or more exactly Simone had wanted, to take the air, "go for a little walk" in the mysterious Saint-Germain-des-Prés of which the papers talked so much and to which, as distant suburbans, they had never had the opportunity of coming at night. They had passed the closed doors of the night-clubs, from which came the sound of a sort of witches' music. Like two wandering provincials, they had watched in the street for a long time those strange boys and girls who seemed to be dressed for some funeral rite. They had looked at the foreign tourists through the windows of the famous cafés; and now, on the terrace of the *Flore*, Roland had just discovered, sitting side by side at the same table, chatting like two old friends, smiling affectionately into each other's eyes, the two men whom he had always taken for irreconcilable adversaries, for ruthless enemies: Bernard and Thíbault Fontanes.

He was glued to the spot, struck dumb.

Simone pulled him by the sleeve.

"Are you coming? What are you looking at?"

"There," he said at last.

"What do you mean, there?"

"There. Bernard."

She recognised him and exclaimed in panic:

"My God! Come away, come away. If he were to see you!"

She dragged Roland along the Rue Saint-Benoit. She was terrified.

"If he'd seen you, he would have thought that you were after him again, that you wanted to . . . This time he would have called the police."

"He was with . . . You saw whom he was with?" he asked.

"No. With whom?"

"Thibault Fontanes."

The name did not mean much to Simone. She hurried along the street to escape from Bernard, to escape from the day's bad dream.

"Who is Fontanes?"

"The young chap I met at Marcellin's, don't you remember? The one who wrote terrible things about Bernard. The one who was on my side against Bernard. . . ."

And as his wife did not react, did not seem to understand the enormity of this collusion between Fontanes and Bernard, he went on, almost stammering, "But then, but then, were they all just laughing at me? I was just the poor fool following on while the leaders laughed, as thick as thieves, behind his back. Fontanes' articles were all a joke, were they? He didn't believe a word of them, then? If only I had suspected that. Fontanes to be a friend of Bernard's. Sitting in a café with Bernard. Are they all cheats and double-crossers in that world?"

"What world, Roland?"

"The intellectuals. The chaps who write in the papers, who make speeches. the people who count."

"What do you expect, my poor Roland, they've got their own ideas and their own customs. It's no good trying to understand them."

"Yes; but there's such a thing as loyalty after all?"

"Loyalty? I don't know. . . . Those sort of people are above us, you know, they can do what they like, what amuses them, they don't care. Besides, they've got money, you see."

"And there was I strutting proudly about. Running after Fontanes, admiring him with my mouth hanging open."

They were going along the quay, which was almost deserted at this late hour. The night was deliciously warm.

"We must hurry," said Simone, "if we want to catch the last train at Saint-Lazare. Let's get a move on."

"Really, I can't get over it," he said. "To think of it! It only needed that. It's the last straw."

"Don't think about it any more. Politics have done you enough harm already. Let it rest."

"Bernard and Fontanes together in a café," he repeated. "Laughing together. And I the poor fool who never suspected anything. And now there's nothing I can do about it."

"Don't think about it any more, Roland. . . . What's the matter with you? You're shivering?"

"It's odd: I suddenly feel cold."

* * *

"Besides," went on Bernard, "what always surprises me a little in a man of your intelligence is that in your rather puerile attacks upon what you call the 'humanitarian Left', you seem always to forget one thing: you seem to forget that it's due to this 'humanitarian Left' and to it alone, that there has been any progress on the plane of liberty and justice since the very beginning. You forget the social revolutions and the Socialist prophets of the last century. You forget the statutory limitations of hours of work. You forget that it's the Left, and the Left alone, which invents and propagates the ideas which change the face of the world."

"Yes; we already know that Christ was a Radical-Socialist and would have called himself Emmanuel in the Resistance," said Thibault with the utmost seriousness. "You are right, of course. Only, I believe that the humanitarian Left has ceased to be a living force. It has tried to popularise a religion, but you can't popularise a religion as you popularise some domestic detergent; religion can only be revealed. The goddess Reason had already become a figure of masquerade and the Myth of Man with a capital M has become a figure of masquerade too. The high-priests of the Left, Michelet or Renan, are schoolmasters or strayed seminarists who have never persuaded anybody but other schoolmasters or strayed seminarists. You see, Christianity gave sense to the human adventure. One can respect and love in one's neighbour the image and semblance of God who created him, of God the Father and Saviour. It is much more difficult to love in him the rough sketch of the God he thinks he will become. After all, this sort of promise is too like a leg-pull."

"You've got a nostalgia for bowing the knee."

"My dear chap, on the eve of the disaster in 1940, it wasn't the Fascists who went to worship in Notre-Dame! A proof by absurdity of what I'm saying concerning the defeat of the religious myths of the Left. No, your position is no longer tenable. Communism is a living force, it's the first attempt at a messianic religion without the transcendental, a messianic religion of a purely material kind, one might say. Fascism is also a living force, it's a resurgence of the ancient Chtonian cults, come to reanimate a technical conception of social organisation. Communism seems in process of winning, would have won for certain if it were not for America. Fascism is provisionally defeated. The Left is on its deathbed: there is no longer such a thing as liberalism, even if there are still liberals."

"But there's still one extremely important factor which you always forget: principles always triumph in the end. True realism does not consist in believing in pseudo-realities: blood, race, the too famous 'pays réel' and so on. It consists in believing in abstractions, in principles. Clémenceau understood this very well: 'It's ideas that give people courage.' Ideas not only give courage but, like faith, move mountains. And what's more, my dear Fontanes, since you're very far from being a fool, I strongly suspect that you're already convinced of all this and secretly agree with me. But you're also a spoilt child and a shameless romantic. The spoilt child will continue to have his moods and his whims—your favourite game of 'self-criticism', and the shameless romantic will always prefer the sombre poetry of despair to the prosaic rationalism of his socialist schoolmasters. A spoilt child plus a romantic makes a charming young reactionary. But take care, my dear chap: the elderly reactionary is a horrible sort of animal. . . ."

Thibault did not answer. He was watching a couple whom he knew well passing on the pavement, and his heart stopped beating. A couple: the boy was called Michel, and he had pretty much the same physical appearance as the Michel they had met that evening at Leitita's. The girl was Lorraine. She was leaning on her companion's arm and talking gaily. Neither of them saw Thibault. At that moment, everything for Thibault Fontanes suddenly dissolved into indifference: the fate of the world, politics, his agreement or disagreement with the intelligent Jew sitting beside him, his own success, his career as a writer and even his beloved work, the happiness of those serene hours he spent at his desk, beneath his lamp, a blank page before him, in the silence of the night, with the crowd of shadows waiting to be evoked, waiting to be translated out of the invisible. He became indifferent to everything because a young, radiant face had passed close by without seeing him, because a young heart had not chosen him. People looked round as Lorraine passed, because she had that proud carriage which gives style to beauty.

"Yes," said Bernard, "that girl was marvellous."

Thibault laughed shortly.

"You have distractions like that too, do you, my dear humanitarian? Well, then, let's go and finish the evening at the *Rose Rouge* or at one of those places which are full of distractions of the same sort. Let's occupy ourselves with serious things, such as dancing and love. Tomorrow we can return to our frivolities."

CHAPTER V

THE EUMENIDES

*

"It's you, is it?" said Clothilde Oyarzun without showing much surprise. "Well, it's quite a time since we saw each other."

"How are you, Mamma?" he said, visibly perturbed.

She gave him her cheek cautiously, as if she were afraid of soiling herself or disorganising her appearance. She was unable to repress an imperceptible contraction of disgust at the contact of her son's lips. He took her roughly and clumsily by the shoulders, hiding his face in the hollow of her neck. Clothilde's face expressed embarrassment and alarm. She frowned and drew back, disengaging herself from the uncomfortable embrace.

"Now then," she said. "Where are your manners? You're not going to begin snivelling, I hope."

Roland stood there, his hands raised, his face rather crumpled. He closed his eyes for a moment and his Adam's apple trembled. Clothilde sat on the edge of the table in an attitude to which she was prone. She opened the cigarette box.

"At last you've decided to come and see me," she said. "After more than three years. . . . Last time we met, you were in prison, and it was I who went to visit you. Don't stand there. Sit down. Do you smoke? I no longer remember whether you smoke or not. Oh, no, you don't, of course: athletic types like you don't smoke."

She looked him up and down with the eye of a dealer judging a draught ox.

"You don't look in very good shape from a physical point of view," she remarked. "You don't look at all well!"

He was sitting on a pouf, hands on knees, his head lowered, his whole appearance humble and docile before Clothilde perched above him, dominating him with all her physical arrogance.

"For three years," he said, "I haven't had enough to eat from day to day."

"We've all been in the same boat!" she said. Her magnificent eyes gleamed savagely. "The hardships of the times, the restrictions, the housing crisis, all the post-war horrors. . . . If that's the refrain you've come to sing, you can save your breath. I know it as well as you do."

Roland looked round the room. Except in the cinema he had never seen a similar *décor*: animal skins on the parquet, screens of unpolished glass decorated with curious heraldic figures, massive furniture in pale, precious woods, enormous standard lamps.

"You can't have suffered much from the housing crisis," he said without heat.

She puffed lengthily at her Pall Mall cigarette.

"Don't be bitter, my boy," she said; don't be bitter. Life's too short and I've no intention of allowing what remains of it to be spoilt for me. If you were in difficulties, you only had to come and ask me to help you. You didn't do it, so that's your look-out."

"One has one's pride," he said, lowering his eyes.

"All right. You can die of it, if it pleases you. The trouble is you've got a wife and children. One has no right to be so upstage when one's children are hungry."

He bowed his shoulders even lower.

"Why are you so hard on me? I don't deserve it," he said in a low voice.

She turned her eyes away from him.

"I'm not being hard on you," she said, relenting. "I only know the law of the world: there are those who succeed and those who fail, and the failures always have to pay for it, that's all. How's your wife?" she asked in a different tone of voice.

"Well. Pretty well, thank you."

"And the children? Do they go to school?"

"Yes. They're doing well. The master says they're very clever."

"Really!" said Clothilde, arching her eyebrows with an air of dubiety. "Well, so much the better. I hope later on they'll manage better than you have."

"I had no luck."

"Everyone says that. Personally, I don't believe in luck. It's a word that means nothing; there's nothing behind it. You've asked for what's happened to you; you've brought it on yourself. You've got to play canny in life. Everything counts, you see, the least mistake, the slightest error of judgment has to be fatally paid for some day or other, and the thing you have to pay the most dearly is stupidity. When one has committed a folly, the consequences develop unendingly like links in a chain, it's appalling."

"Do you always know where you're going?"

"Yes, my boy. In any case, I take trouble to play the game as best I can. And in my own line I haven't done too badly."

"I can see that. And I don't ask you what means you've used."

"No; don't ask me," she said calmly. "I never go to confession, and morality gives me a headache. But really, there you go, straight away making disobliging remarks! You come in here looking as if butter wouldn't melt in your mouth, and two minutes later you're already being beastly. Listen, if you think my money stinks, what have you come for? Because you have come for money, haven't you? You sent that little sacristan, young Donadieu, that sort of slippery Jesus, and got nothing by it. So then you decided to come yourself."

He raised his head towards her, towards that image of opulence and success. As in the past, the beautiful golden hair formed a halo round the pure, inexorable face, which he had seen in turn transfigured by triumph, cunning, anger, hate, and fierce gaiety. Fifty years had doubtless marked that face, but only as the centuries and the salt of the sea corrode a sunken statue: erosion eats into its material but without destroying its beauty. Clothilde was wearing a long black dress, fitting tight about the waist, but full below it, and then narrow again about the ankles —one of those dresses known as "*entravées*", which had been fashionable at the beginning of the first war and which a celebrated dressmaker was trying to popularise again three years after the second, since the great periodical holocausts of the planet always so happily inspire those princes of grace and frivolity. On her left hand she wore a single jewel, a huge diamond which glittered with the least movement she made. Her nails were painted a bright red and filed to the shape of claws. Roland remembered a picture he had seen in a school-book: the sphinx on the road to Delphi; and he thought that this

Sphinx, his mother, was crouching with her male by the side of the secret roads, along the frontier between the two zones, to relieve the clandestine travellers of their gold and of their jewels.

He got up.

"Yes; it's true that I have come to ask you for money. But I'm pleased to see you too, in spite of everything."

"How well-spoken you are. A true son, loyal and affectionate. I particularly like the 'in spite of everything'. How much do you want?"

"A lot. You'll refuse to give it to me."

"How much?" she said impatiently. "How much?"

"A hundred thousand francs."

"Chicken-feed. What do you want it for?"

"I want to go away."

"Go away? Where to?"

"Africa."

"Africa," she repeated. "What the hell do you want to go out there for? As a missionary?"

"I want to start a new life."

"He wants to start a new life. Like the other. He wanted to start a new life too. At forty-five. You're both maladjusted, incapable of adapting yourselves to life, that's what you are, you and your father. Maladjusted, neurotics."

"I forbid you to speak of my father."

She annihilated him with a savage glance.

"And I forbid you to come here and give me orders in my own house," she said, volleying each syllable like so many little whistling projectiles. "Arrogant you were, and arrogant you are. You come and ask me for a hundred thousand francs and you try to find a way of taking them with your pride intact, you make insulting allusions, and forbid me to speak of this or that. But you're in my house here," she repeated, "you're in my house as a beggar, and I won't permit—no, I won't permit you to take these liberties. You can change your tone or get out."

She stood straight before him, her nostrils quivering, her teeth clenched, hard with pride, as he had always known her, walled up in the hell of her own pride as he suspected she was walled up in another, obscurer hell of which one must not think under pain of committing a sin. Implacable, and one might have said incorruptible, in the measure that the very excess of a passion, when stripped of everything that is not itself, participates in the purity of a flame or a diamond. "Yield or die", yes, that was the device inscribed on the infernal blason of pride. Roland took a step towards her. He was pale and furious, all the repressed rages of his childhood returned upon him, filling his mouth with acrid saliva. His pupils were contracted, narrowed round a burning, inflexible point in the darkest part of his iris.

"You won't prevent my saying what I want to say and as I wish to say it. Yes; you're quite right, I'd rather die here than take your money. Keep it. I don't want it; it stinks. Keep it, eat it, sleep with it, you wretched little sixpenny tart. It's not your money that'll give you the distinction in which you're so lacking. Common you were and common you are. And now go and look for that sheik of yours. Go on. Go and count your napkin rings and your pots of jam together."

He had spoken with extraordinary ease and fluency, as if a prey to some personal daemon, the delightful daemon of contempt perhaps. For some seconds he stood there swaying slightly, his eyes half closed, his mouth awry, as if drunk with the delight of aggressive action. She gazed at him with staring, outraged eyes. She was quite still. At length, she put out her hand towards a little square of marble that lay on the table and applied her forefinger to it. A bell rang in a neighbouring room and almost at once a servant in a white coat came to the door.

"Jean," she said with an extraordinary gentleness and without taking her eyes from her son for a single second, "is Monsieur still in his room? He is? Go and tell him I want him."

The servant disappeared.

"The sheik will take it upon himself to punish you, my boy," she said in the same gentle voice.

Roland was filled with an almost superhuman joy. He had not felt such abounding strength for a long time. Disdain, revolt, insolence had tautened his muscles. He recovered the wonderful fire of his twentieth year. Battle was upon him. He closed his eyes tight.

"You can't imagine," he murmured, "the pleasure you're giving me. You're bringing me to life again."

A light step made them turn their heads. Alex had entered the room: he was dressed from head to foot in pearl grey, with a gold pin in his tie, his eyes were yellow, his head tufted with hair and the lower part of his face looked as if it had been sculpted out of whipped cream.

"Alex," Clothilde said calmly. "This young man has just insulted me. I think he needs correcting a little."

"Well, well," said Alex.

He remained perfectly impassive.

Roland smiled broadly and foolishly. He turned towards Clothilde, and with a jerk of his thumb over his shoulder pointed to the man at the door.

"Is that Madame's *souteneur*?" he asked in a languid voice.

"Yes. That's right," said Alex softly.

"How comic," said Roland. "Unexpected, but comic."

He turned slowly round and seemed to balance himself on his legs, but without undue haste. He brought his hands round to the front of his belt. He was still smiling.

"Well, are you coming on, Terror?" he asked.

"Yes. I'm coming," said Alex.

Clothilde had sat down on the edge of the table. She crossed her legs. The sheik drew nearer. Roland emitted a short, joyous neigh which was his battle-cry. His head lowered, he suddenly bounded forward like a wild bull.

And dashed himself against the wall. Faced with such ridiculous impetuosity, Alex had merely sidestepped with the discreet precision of an expert at judo. Contemplatively, one finger to his temple, he watched Roland gathering his scattered limbs together on the parquet and get painfully to his feet again. He was waiting. He was in no hurry. Roland pivoted round. His, left cheek was grazed and his hair in disorder. He had that sad, lowering, rather bestial look that men have when they know that the fight can have no other issue but the total annihilation of their opponent. His panting seemed to increase the weight of the silence. He charged a second time.

It was done as quickly and startlingly as a piece of sleight of hand. Alex seemed to be catching a fly in flight, or to be dusting his cuffs: Roland fell to his knees. Alex seemed to be stroking the back of his neck: Roland jerked like a spring and cried out in anguish. Alex pulled him to his feet by his coat-collar and leant him up against the wall; then, with the side of his hand, gave him a few light blows across the region of his vocal cords:

Roland, suffocating, opened his mouth. From then on the man with the tufted hair could manage him as easily as a child can a disjointed doll. Several times he slapped his face with the full weight of his arm. He kneed him in the stomach and the doll broke in two. He straightened him up again with a blow of his fist on the bridge of his nose. . . . At that moment Clothilde raised her hand and said:

"Enough!"

The man with the tufted hair looked at Clothilde, smiled a little and hit the doll once more.

"Enough!" Clothilde cried.

The man with the tufted hair smiled and poked two fingers into the doll's dead eyes.

"Enough!" screamed Clothilde.

The man with the tufted hair smiled yet again, cleared his throat and spat a jet of saliva into the doll's face.

"You're disgusting. Stop!" said Clothilde breathlessly. "Stop! I told you to punish him, not to kill him."

"I've never properly understood these questions of degree," said Alex calmly, and strolled out of the room with his hands in his pockets.

Roland staggered to a chair and fell into it. Blood trickled from his lip, down his chin and neck, on to the single silk tie he possessed and the fine white shirt he had put on for the occasion. ("To impress the mater. . . .") His head seemed to hang loose for several seconds. Then he took a handkerchief from his pocket and dabbed at his mouth. Round his right eye a bruised patch was beginning to turn blue. Clothilde was pale and motionless. At last she got to her feet and went to open a little cabinet. There was a clink of bottles. Without a word she handed her son a glass of brandy. With a suspicious eye, Roland took the glass and threw the contents in her face. There was a brief silence.

"Go away!" screamed Clothilde.

With a mad woman's gesture she wiped herself with the back of her hand.

"Go away! Don't ever come here again! Get out!"

He got up and faced her. In his hand was the empty glass. Whatever it was she saw in his face, in his eyes, it froze her with terror, for she called: "Alex!" in a toneless voice.

"What my father . . ." Roland began.

But he could not finish. He took a pace towards her.

"What? What? What do you want to say?"

She was retreating before him with awkward little steps because of the tightness of her dress about her ankles.

"What my father did not do . . ." Roland went on.

"Your father! Don't call him that. . . . Don't call him that. . . ."

She threw out the words like a jet of poison, as if they were capable of immobilising, of paralysing the man threatening her.

"He isn't your father!"

And, indeed, he did stop abruptly, letting the glass fall on to the parquet where it rang with a clear note.

"What are you? . . ."

"No, no, no," she cried, upright on her high heels, shaking her beautiful golden head. "No, he isn't your father! You idiot, you loved him, you thought you were like him, you imitated him, you were in league with him against me, and he wasn't, he wasn't . . ."

"You're lying," he said in a low voice.

"Lying, am I? Write to him, write to him, ask him. He knows; he has known for a long time."

"It's not true."

"Not true? I'll show you letters. I've got proof. You're not his son. I've wanted to tell you a thousand times, to scream it at you, fool that you are, a thousand times. And it wasn't even out of anger. It was from . . . I don't know, perhaps because I pitied you. It was to free you from him, there! He destroyed you for ever, he . . . oh, I don't know . . . mutilated you, and I pitied you like an invalid, or a cripple. Listen. The day you played Athalie at school, I had a sort of revelation. You looked crazy, you looked like a circus freak. And yet, and yet, how like him you were!"

"I looked like . . ." he stammered.

"Yes, you looked like your real father, you looked incredibly like him, you looked like the whole of your father's family, and that's the truth. I was embarrassed by it, sitting there next to Edmond, in that courtyard; it seemed to me that everyone must know, merely by looking at your face, that you weren't Commandant Oyarzun's son."

She fell silent. He stood there upon the same spot, his arms dangling, his eyes vacant. Suddenly calm, Clothilde went into the bay window and leant her forehead against the pane.

"Who is he?" Roland asked in a small childish voice.

"What?"

"Who is he? Who's my real father?"

She shrugged her shoulders.

"What does it matter? Besides, he's been dead a long time."

"Who is he? I want to know."

"You needn't worry; he was quite all right. You wouldn't have had to blush for him."

"I want to know. Who is he?"

She still stood with her forehead against the pane. Her voice took on a dreamy sentimental tone.

"His family objected to the marriage. I suffered terribly. You see, I belonged to the class of small civil servants. And they belonged to the Weill-Farquart connection, very well known in those days. An old Jewish family of the most distinguished kind, and very rich. The Weill-Farquarts lived in a wonderful house at Auteuil. One of their uncles had been Grand Rabbi. He, your father, that's to say, was an extremely handsome man and very fashionable, if you want to know; quite the son of rich upper class parents and only mingling with the cream of Paris society of the period. . . ."

She turned quickly round. Roland had fallen in a heap and lay on the parquet like a discarded puppet.

* * *

François held a little leather-bound note-book clasped in his hand—a diary which had belonged to Juliette. He clasped it like a sacred reliquary, as by far the most precious thing he would own in this world from now on. The roar of the train beat out the time, making a heart-breaking chant out of his sorrow. François looked out of the window. A thousand shapeless, diverse thoughts, without the least relationship to what should have been his only consideration, succeeded each other in his mind, and he was astonished to find how little one was capable of concentration, even in the particular circumstances where it seemed that one should so easily be able to concentrate upon a single event. But he was aware of nothing but a sort of wayward dispersion of thought; from moment to moment his mind seemed to become distracted, his thoughts to break up into fragments, dissolve into the fugitive, the fortuitous, the unrealisable, as if to avoid coming face to face with something overwhelming and perhaps mortal? Yes, perhaps the distracted state of his mind was the reflex of a blind and obstinate instinct for survival? From time to time, the image of the little girl, pale and motionless upon the sheet, flashed before him—or again it became Juliette's living face, her expression at a certain moment in time, her look, her fresh, shy little laugh. Then, these visions dissolved and once again he knew the emptiness, the despairing effort to conjure from the void and fix for ever an image, a harmony of fluid features which were unceasingly dissolving and renewing themselves. The little leather notebook burned his hand. He had opened it, seen a few lines written in the childish writing he knew so well. He had closed it again, rather shocked, as if on the brink of committing a sacrilege. The roar of the train gradually induced in him a sort of trance. His head rolled against the back of the seat. He suddenly remembered a similar journey, made at the same hour, by the same train; Catherine and himself, thirteen years earlier, returning from the Basque coast. Thirteen years. . . . Rather more than the span of Juliette's whole life. He shivered as he was suddenly struck, as surely as with a knife, by the knowledge that he would never again see Juliette's face, that he would never again hear her voice, that it was finished, that the radiant little being had disappeared for ever. . . . "Never again." He said the two words in his mind, but what overwhelmed him was not the intellectual formulation of the thought, but rather the physical horror of a living certainty, the trembling of a beast before an ascertained danger; this only lasted the fraction of a second and then once more he was plunged into distraction and vacuity as if, for the moment, he had refused to understand, as if he had relegated to some later time the exploration of the truth which had just been revealed to him in a flash. His eyes were dry and he thought of all sorts of indifferent things, things without relation to what had happened. Only the contact of the little notebook, like a burn in the palm of his hand, related him to the immediate event. His sorrow was as monotonous, as impersonal and mechanical as the rhythmic roaring of the train as it crossed the Landes in the night. Someone in the compartment got up to turn off the light. Another traveller folded up his newspaper, wedged himself in his corner and uttered a sigh. The little blue light of the night-light engraved tired faces upon the shadows. François looked at Catherine. She had not moved since the train started. Her eyes were closed. He remembered how she had looked when she had been led to the bed upon which her little girl lay. She had not wept. Her face had remained hard and expressionless. Then, when the others had gone, she had put out her hand and gently touched the forehead and cheeks of the child, already as rigid and strangely cool as marble under one's fingers. Then, she had seemed to break down. Her eyes had remained tearless and her mouth closed, but for several minutes her shoulders had been shaken by stifled groans, and nothing could have been more shocking than this almost animal sound issuing from a face devoid of all expression. François guessed that what was torturing the young woman most at that moment was perhaps less the idea of future deprivation than remorse, remorse for not having loved Juliette sufficiently, or for not having sufficiently shewn her love for her, regret for a simple happiness which she had not known or had not wished to know how to give and receive, self-pity, the consciousness of an enormous, irremediable loss, all the sad, grave lessons of which men become aware too late upon gazing at a dead face.

François opened his eyes again. It was cold. The train was driving through grey, flossy cotton-wool behind which a flat, brown countryside could be vaguely discerned. They would soon reach Paris. "I've slept," he thought. "I've been able to sleep." He turned his head towards Catherine beside him. There were damp traces on her cheeks, as if she had wept in her sleep. With her lips slightly parted she had a disarming, abandoned, childish air. It was the first time he had seen her like this for many a day; he was touched by it. He took one of Catherine's hands in his own. Then he noticed that the little leather note-book had fallen at his feet. He quickly picked it up and dusted it against the lapel of his coat. He opened it. The writing was misted. He wiped his eyes. The feeble light of dawn barely enabled him to read. He closed the note-book again with a beating heart. He had recognised a date, the date of his birthday, and upon the white page Juliette had drawn a little cross and written a few words. . . .

When, at the Gare d'Austerlitz, they were upon the point of

parting, Catherine gave him her hand and said, "Goodbye." He could not bear to part from her thus. "Come on. Let's go and have something to eat," he said, leading her to the refreshment-room. He felt utterly unable to face the days that were before him. The thought came to him that they would no longer be able to leave each other, Catherine and he. Because he had seen that crumpled, childish face in the dawn, because he had felt some pity for her, some affection even, he believed for an instant that something had changed. A conventional phrase crossed his mind, "brought together by misfortune", and indeed there was some truth in it. They sat in a corner of the room to avoid being looked at; a useless precaution since no one was paying the slightest attention to them. It had begun to rain, a small, fine, grey rain which, through the window pane, seemed to turn the landscape to water. The waiter came to take their order. At this early hour of the morning he was alert, eager and precise. He made a judicious remark about the "weather having turned cold again". François nodded. Catherine was looking out through the rain-swept window. The waiter came and placed in front of them two cups of black coffee and a plate of *croissants*, then turned gaily away like a man happy to be alive, who had felt superbly energetic since the dawn. François was frozen. Drinking the hot coffee did him good. He felt rather hungry too, but did not dare to touch the *croissants*, as if there was something indecorous about eating on that particular morning. . . . He said to Catherine, "What are you going to do?"

She shrugged her shoulders without answering. She was still looking out of the window. He remembered their meeting four years earlier, on the Thursday of the Liberation, their conversation over a wretched meal, in the little restaurant where the men were peeping out through the cracks in the closed shutters. He leaned over towards Catherine. His voice was rather hoarse.

"Do you remember how four years ago you asked me whether I didn't think we could take up our life together again, the two of us? I don't know what you plan to do. But today it's I who am asking the question. It seems to me that perhaps . . ."

She did not allow him to finish. She shook her head. She gazed tenderly at him. "Poor François," she said; she took his hand and pressed it in a brief, awkward gesture.

They went out. It was raining harder now. They went to take

shelter in the entrance to the Underground station. They could not manage to part.

"I'll try to find a taxi," said François. "Wait for me here."

He turned up his coat collar, but Catherine held him back.

"No," she said. "It's not worth it. I'll go home by the Underground. Listen. We must meet again soon, in a few days," she said with an effort. "I've got something rather painful to tell you, painful today for me, after what has happened. I had intended to see you about it last week. Listen. We've never done anything official about our separation. But something must be done. . . . I think a divorce will be necessary."

A man passed close to them, carrying heavy suitcases. He threw them down in the passage, grumbling. François took Catherine's arm and led her a little aside, at some distance from the doors which were unceasingly opening to give entrance to a passenger and a gust of rain. Catherine bit her lower lip and turned her head away.

"Lambert has asked me . . . Well, I'm going to marry him," she said in a sorrowful voice.

There was a moment's silence.

"You're going to marry Lambert?" François said gently.

"Yes," she said. "I'm tired—so tired, if only you knew. I long for security and rest. It's a chance for me. . . . An unhoped-for chance."

She turned away her head. François gazed with all his might at that familiar profile which was so deeply woven into the plot of his own life, that pretty profile now merely a little older and so sad, upon that pale cheek moist with rain, upon that well-turned lip now quivering a little. . . . The doors banged and people were swallowed up in the entrance, excited, hurrying, important, with their suitcases and their early morning bad temper. They had fought the wind and the lashing rain, and now they hurried to buy their Underground tickets with the methodical craziness of insects.

"A chance," Catherine murmured. "A chance."

Her face seemed suddenly to crumple, she lowered her head and said with a stifled sob, "I'm so ashamed. . . ."

* * *

About a month after his return, he received a note from Roland Oyarzun. After expressing the usual sympathy, Roland asked him to come and see him as soon as possible: he had things of the first importance to tell him.

'I shall go,' François Donadieu thought, 'but it will be for the last time. It's time I eliminated the useless from my life.'

Naturally, from the very first words of their conversation, he was overwhelmed with embarrassment. Indeed, Roland thought it necessary to renew the expression of his sympathy aloud. He appealed to the terrestrial law of forgetfulness, to the supernatural consolations of Christian hope. He exhorted his friend to find an amelioration of his sorrow in redoubled activity, in the rude discipline of work. Having achieved this prologue within the shortest space of time that decency permitted, Roland heaved a sigh of relief and said, "Now I'm going to talk to you about myself. A most sensational upset has occurred in my life. I've wanted to tell you about it for some time, but I did not want to impose upon your sorrow too early. Out of discretion, you'll understand. Therefore I've preferred to wait a few weeks. Besides," he added ingenuously, "you'll listen more attentively. I've sent Simone and the children to her mother's, so we shan't be disturbed. Sit down. Sit over there," he said, pointing to a huge leather-covered armchair. "That armchair wasn't here last time you came."

As François made no comment, he repeated:

"I don't think that armchair was here last time you came."

"Perhaps not. I don't remember. I don't notice details much."

"Do you mean to say that you can call an armchair that cost eighteen thousand francs and that to be hoisted in through the window because the door was too narrow a 'detail'? That's a good one."

"It certainly takes up a lot of space."

"Oh, yes. Goodness me, it's nearly as big as the room. There's hardly space to turn round since the great thing arrived."

"Why did you buy it?"

"We didn't buy it, idiot! My mother gave it to us."

"You've made it up with her, then?"

"I'll tell you all about it, Sit down. It's comfortable, isn't it? Cumbersome, but comfortable. We're quite pleased to be able to rest in it, Simone and I, Simone during the day and myself at night when I come home from work. We can 'relax', as people say today. Relaxation is very important. I read an article about it in the *Reader's Digest*. Well, my mother made us this present as a result of the circumstances I'm going to tell you. She's eccentric. Imagine choosing this when there are a thousand useful things she could have given us. Oh, I don't know. An electric cooker, a washing-machine, or she could have simply given us the money; it would have been pretty handy. But not at all. She sends us an armchair, without taking into account that we live in a tiny two-roomed flat on the fifth floor. Simone and I were shattered when we saw this mastodon arrive. However, let's leave that. I was telling you that something extraordinary had happened to me. Put your briefcase down. And your newspaper. I hate people having things in their hands when I'm going to speak for some time. It's odd, but it gives me the impression that they're not listening to me. For instance, when I read the newspaper aloud to Simone, she has to stop knitting and look at me, or I get put out. Sometimes she forgets and I become aware that she's counting her stitches. Then I lose my temper and tear up the newspaper. Are you comfortable? You are? Do smoke. No; I shall stand. I prefer standing when I'm going to talk. Listen, then. It all goes back to that famous day which will remain graven for ever on my memory and on yours: the day when I went to see Bernard and you, poor chap, got a telephone call. . . ."

"By the way," François interrupted, "you haven't heard anything more from Bernard?"

"No. Nothing at all. Simone was terrified that he'd go to the police or try to have me shut up. But I wasn't. The fellow took the whole thing as a kind of farce—a tragic farce, if you like. And what's more, he wasn't altogether wrong. When I went to see him, my main intention was to terrify him, to tell him a few home truths at the muzzle of a revolver, and to make him ask my forgiveness, in short. God knows what else! And then, when I found myself face to face with him in his office, it occurred to me that I couldn't retreat or I should appear ridiculous; and then again, I lost my temper at seeing him so much master of himself, laughing at me. . . . But I don't want to conceal the fact that I was terrified at the moment of putting my plan into execution. Torn between terror and fear, I was no longer in control of myself, I no longer knew what I was doing. . . . When he snatched the revolver from me, I came to. That's exactly what happened, like waking up from a nightmare. But that's not the story. Two days after that famous day, I went to see my mother. Simone and I had decided to leave France and go and start a new life in the French Congo. We had read in a newspaper that there are opportunities in the Congo. I intended to ask my mother to lend us a hundred thousand francs."

François was listening to him rather distractedly, because he was observing him so intently. What was different about Roland's personality? His clothes? His haircut? His voice? Certainly, some change had occurred. "It's his face; it's filled out, he looks younger, more alert . . ." And, around Roland, the frame in which he lived had also undergone minor changes. Apart from the magisterial armchair, there were certain new touches of decoration: above the fireplace was a huge new looking-glass in place of the hideous, tarnished, fly-blown, gold-framed one François had seen covered with a piece of red cotton sheeting upon the occasion of his last visit. There were flowers on the table, small pictures had been hung here and there, a parchment shade surrounded the bulb which had remained naked so long. Some attempt had been made to make the room agreeable, attractive and gay. François noticed that the photograph of Jacques, the young Militiaman, had disappeared. However, Roland was still talking.

". . . gave me a terrible beating up, me, me, do you understand? Me, who thought I could kill him easily, and the fellow must be at least fifty and looks hopelessly weak. He had me where he wanted me. All the same, it's a wonderful thing, judo. Besides, I've decided to take lessons in it. . . . But, at the time, I was so humiliated I could have died. Honestly, I really wanted to die. To think that I, Roland Oyarzun, at twenty the best fighter in the Quartier Latin, should have allowed myself to be beaten up like that by an old man! I told myself that I was finished, definitely out. But that's not all. I still had to learn the worst. So, Alex goes out. I remain alone with my mother. She offers me a glass of brandy. What do I do? I don't hesitate a moment, I take it and bang! I chuck it in her face. Drama. Music. But it isn't Dalila's great aria, you know: 'My heart opens as do the flowers at the sound of your voice. . . .' It was more like the shouting in the first act of *Carmen*."

There were subtle changes in face, eyes and speech. 'Tragedy's fading out,' François said to himself. 'He's made it up with his mother, she's helping them, the material situation's improving.

I've hoped for this for them for a long time. They've recovered their desire to live, they're putting flowers in their little den.'

"Well, my dear chap, here comes the sensational revelation. Something absolutely breath-taking, appalling. I was ill for a fortnight afterwards, you know. However, I'm much better now. I'm getting used to it. Look. Try and guess what it is."

"How can I?"

"Try all the same. What could it be about, since it concerns me?"

"I haven't the least idea."

"Think. You've got an imagination, haven't you?"

"Well . . . Someone's left you some money?"

"Prosaic. Unworthy of you. It's not a legacy, not even an important one, that could have upset my life like this. No. Think rather of something on the moral plane. Something of a natural kind," he said with a timid and rather hesitant pomposity, "that would completely and utterly upset my welangstancore."

"Your what?"

"My welangstancore. Don't you know what it means? Conception of the world, in German. After all, it's a term which is in constant use among cultivated people."

"I don't know German, but I expect what you meant to say was *Weltanschauung*, wasn't it?"

Roland frowned irritably.

"Listen to him! Always cleverer than everyone else!" he muttered. "You've got the soul of an usher!" He controlled himself. "Anyway, it doesn't matter. It was something natural which could alter my conception of the world. Guess."

"I don't know. Have you lost your faith?"

"No. At least, I don't think so."

"You abjure Vichy and Pétain?"

"N . . . no. Perhaps, on one or two points. But, as a whole, all the same, no."

"I give up."

Roland's eyes shone.

"I warn you it's . . . fabulous!"

"Enough beating about the bush, old man. Tell me."

"I'm not quite sure of you. I'm afraid you may burst out laughing. Or that you may . . . that you may . . ."

"I've no desire to laugh, whatever it may be."

Roland paced the tiny free space between the armchair, the table and the wall a couple of times. He placed his hands in his pockets, and drew them out again. He turned his back on his guest, then turned sideways on to him. He opened his mouth. He shut it again. He lifted his eyes to the ceiling, and then contemplated the floor. He took a long breath then and said in a low voice:

"I'm a Jew."

". . . ."

"I'm a Jew," he repeated in surprise at the silence.

". . . ."

"Is that all the effect it has on you?" he cried.

"Are you sure you're not ill?" François asked.

"No; I'm no longer ill. Certainly not! All the same, does it shock you? Are you taken aback? Well, it's true. My father was not commandant Oyarzun. My father was a Jew. Scream; pull your hair out. It's the pure and simple truth."

"Did your mother tell you this?"

"Yes, old chap, during a somewhat dramatic scene. I fell down. I lost my senses for ten minutes."

"Between ourselves, there surely wasn't anything to do that about."

"Oh, so you think there wasn't anything to faint about, do you? Thank you very much. That's splendid. That's really good, that is."

"But how can the fact of your knowing that you're half Jewish, as you say, alter your conception of the world?"

"Donadieu, you don't happen to be half-witted by any chance, do you?"

"But, good God! I suppose we've all got Jewish blood in our veins more or less. And German, Latin, Slav, Arab blood and what have you, too. Anyway, it's what the biologists and ethnologists say. Besides, one only has to do a little calculation, count the number of one's ancestors in going back even fifteen generations. It becomes a geometrical progression, and one reaches some fabulous figure, thirty to thirty-two thousand ancestors, if I remember correctly. And a jump of fifteen generations doesn't take one very far: approximately to the beginning of the sixteenth century. Therefore, between your ancestor, alive in fifteen hundred, and yourself, something like thirty thousand men and women have had an influence upon your heredity. I can only imagine that they were not all pure Gauls. Anyway, what is a pure Gaul?"

Roland appeared staggered.

"I had never thought of making that calculation before," he said. "For me racialism was a rigid and absolute notion. I had learnt to distinguish two great categories in the white population of the globe: the Jews and the non-Jews. Have you read Drumont?"

"No; but I didn't need to read him to consider your anti-Semitism a pretty ridiculous sort of mania. As far as I'm concerned, it was absurd. And when I think that you based your political opinions on it. . . ."

"That's exactly it! You've placed your finger on the sore. I was an ardent anti-Semite. And, all the same, Donadieu, you'll admit that a lot of first-class brains were anti-Semitic: Drumont, Maurras, Léon Daudet, Béraud, Rabatet, Céline . . . Saint Louis!" he added in the same tone of voice, as if Saint Louis had been an eminent contributor to the *Action Française* or *Gringoire*. "My faith in the destiny of the country was based upon the mystique of the ancient French race, a race from which Semite contamination must be excluded by constant effort," he said with a sort of mechanical eloquence. (He clearly had the phrase by heart, it was part of his catechism.) "As far as I'm concerned, my hatred of the Jew was no longer an idea or a doctrine, but a reflex action."

"I fear it's always a reflex action."

"Perhaps. But then you see what it means? An anti-Semite of my particular kind discovering one day that he's half a Jew himself?"

"Clearly it's a case of poetic justice."

"But, look, Donadieu. Is the whole thing nonsense, then?"

"What's nonsense?"

Roland gestured with his arms like a man at his wits' end who has given up all hope of seeing anything with clarity in the confusion of the world.

"Why, everything! Everything! Anti-Semitism, the idea of race. Our ideas. Our convictions, political and other. Our beliefs. Are they all, as you say, nothing but reflex actions? The result of hot blood, temperament, habits, personal predilections, dislikes, and eccentric passions, which we transform into wonderful theories? And, good God, at times I've allowed myself to be hacked to pieces to justify my anti-Semitism, to defend my idea of France and the purity and independence of the French, my idea of authority and order, in brief the whole heritage of Maurras, brought up to date by the contribution of Fascism. Well, then? Is it merely our education, our circumstances, the conditions in which we live, that make us what we are? Supposing I was born, a legitimate child, into my father's family—I mean to say my true father's family—I would have been brought up in a Jewish family in easy circumstances, well then, I should probably have become someone rather like . . . like Bernard, Christ almighty! The Jewish intellectual, Left-wing, Gaulliste and worldly. . . ."

"It's very unlikely. Social conditioning doesn't explain everything. In the first place, you would never really have become what one calls an intellectual."

"I should have pretended to be, idiot, and it comes to the same thing! But, do you understand the effect of this discovery? There can therefore be no . . . what is it? . . . Help me!"

"I must first know what you're trying to say."

Roland clicked his fingers with impatience.

"Come on. You know very well what I mean. What do you call—you know what it is . . . the thing that supports, the thing on which you build?"

"Basis? Substructure? Foundation?"

"Foundation! That's the word I was looking for. Do you mean to say that there's no foundation for absolute truth? . . . No; it's not 'absolute' I mean. . . . What do you call a thing that's separated from the human mind, that is no part of ourselves? Something that's independent of our judgment?"

"Objective?"

"That's it, exactly! Therefore, there's no foundation for objective truth? Christ, it's difficult to express oneself. . . . But, if there's no foundation for objective truth, everything is the result of temperament, conditioning, circumstances? So why should one believe in one thing more than another? What value have ideas and doctrines? Who's right? And who's wrong? What's it all based on? Where is the truth? What is truth?"

"Pilate has already asked that question."

"Leave Pilate out of it! This is about me. You see, I'm over thirty-two, I've been concerned with politics for nearly sixteen years. I've voted. I've fought. I've preached my ideas. I've been thrown into prison for them, and all that, and my most profound and sincere convictions were based all the time on . . . on a sort of huge lie, an absolute nonsense? So, for sixteen years of my life I've been a complete fool?"

"Why? The fact that you're a half-Jew doesn't necessarily invalidate anti-Semitism."

"What do you mean?"

Roland started.

"Listen," said François. "Just reflect for a moment. The fact that you're a half-Jew should merely reveal to you the fact that you yourself are subject to the proscription implied by your own anti-Semitism."

"Wait a minute, that sentence is complicated. That I myself am subject . . . Well, really!" he cried, having understood. "You won't succumb to an excess of tact!"

He was exacerbated.

"But listen," François said quickly. "Personally, I find anti-Semitism a ridiculous proposition to hold, but, logically, the mere fact that you happen to be a half-Jew is not sufficient in itself to prove its absurdity. Do you see what I mean? I mean to say that anti-Semitism is absurd in itself, absolutely, quite apart from the proportion of Jewish blood that you say you have in your veins."

"Now I understand," said Roland nodding his head. "At bottom we're agreed, but you must admit that the discovery was enough to shake me?"

"Undoubtedly."

"Wouldn't you have been shaken yourself?"

"Frankly, no. I don't think so. If I were told that I was of Jewish descent, or Slav, or Scandinavian, I shouldn't care one way or the other."

"Slav or Scandinavian, all right. But Jewish, Donadieu, Jewish!'

"It can only be painful precisely for a man that's accustomed to hate Jews and look upon them as an inferior race, as . . ."

". . . the scum of humanity!" Roland finished in a lugubrious voice. "That was, in fact, my point of view."

"What's so odd, though, is that your point of view hasn't changed since the war, since we've learned about the systematic extermination of the Jews by the Germans. After all, one always sympathises with the persecuted, whoever they may be. During the Occupation you could see men, women and children in the streets with yellow stars on their breasts. Didn't that give you a pain at the heart? Weren't you ashamed?"

Roland thought for a moment.

"I must admit that the sight of them was on the whole painful, but I thought that it was a question of a necessary measure. You see, at that time I read *Je suis Partout* a lot, and that paper kept me more or less in a permanent state of anger."

"And it's just that that seems to me to be the fundamental problem."

"What do you mean by the fundamental problem?"

"This anger, this vital need to hate, hold in contempt, condemn and proscribe is always found, always and necessarily, among Fascists. The need to persecute expiatory victims. Of course, Fascism is much more complex than that when considered as a psychological and social phenomenon, but this particular characteristic is an essential part of it. Why? You must remember that you've always been an angry man. At least, I've always known you to be so: perpetually angry, with some faction of society: the Radicals, the Freemasons, the Jews, the Communists, the Resistance. . . . And in the end one has some ground for wondering whether the objects of your anger, of your lust to destroy, are not in the last analysis purely pretexts."

Roland did not answer at once. He sat down on the arm of the chair. His face betrayed a violent effort to think, a first gleam of interior light.

"It's quite extraordinary," he said at last. "What you've just said is the very spit and image of me."

"Of course."

"You know, these last few days, I've been thinking about things. I've been wondering about myself and my past. I was in a complete fog, and then every now and then, I'd see a gleam of light in the distance as if I were about to discover the truth at last . . . and then, bang! I'd be sunk in confusion and darkness again. I'm not intelligent, I've never wanted to be; intelligence is a mere trick for weaklings and foreigners; a man, a real man, can get on very well without it. Mark you," he hastened to correct himself, "I don't mean to say that you're a weakling; there are exceptions. You've enlightened me with a couple of words. It's most extraordinary. That's why I wanted to talk to you. 'Donadieu's a light-weight,' I told myself." He punched his friend's shoulder with little blows of his fist, winking hugely at the same time, like a bad compére in a music-hall. " 'He's a light-weight, but as for dialectic, as they call it today, as for dialectic, Christ, he's pretty hot!' And you see, I was right. You've enlightened me. It's most extraordinary. Because I'd suspected it vaguely at times. I had glimpses. I suspected, as I was saying a moment ago, that I was a huge lie, a sort of enormous moral canker that was choking itself. . . . My love of order, for instance. . . . I couldn't speak of anything else: order, order! Well, I wonder if, basically, my love of order was not really an insane fear of the disorder to which I would have given way if I had let myself go for an instant. Because, in my blood, in my bones, in my very marrow, I am nothing but disorder. Do you understand me, Donadieu? Good Christ! I'm nothing but disorder itself! I was made for anarchy and I imposed an iron discipline on myself. I wanted to become a statue! I was a being of sentiment and passion, and I went against my own nature to play the hard, impassive superman. . . ."

"And pretty badly too, my poor chap," said François, smiling.

"What?"

"You succeeded very ill in giving the impression of a superman. No one can ever have seemed more vulnerable than you."

"Vulnerable. That's exactly it. A mere trifle could have made me cry out with suffering or sorrow. I was more vulnerable than a virgin. And so, thinking that I was fighting for my ideas, I was in reality fighting for or against my passions. On the surface, it was for France and France alone, the national virtues, a sacred hatred for foreigners and Jews. Underneath it was . . . what was it exactly? Perhaps it's better not to ask oneself that question. In any case, it was confusion. . . . My mother made a curious remark, which has given me to think. She said that my father—that is, Commandant Oyarzun—had mutilated me! What do you make of it all?"

He did not wait for François' answer. For the fraction of a second a sudden panic seemed to transform his features. He waved his hands in front of him as a sign of denial.

"Well, no, there isn't really anything to understand. Besides, it's all much too complicated; better not try."

He began walking up and down again in the narrow cage formed by the armchair, the table and the wall. This mechanical going to and fro, this little dance was, in him, a sign of extraordinary mental effervescence. A minute or two elapsed. He stopped abruptly.

"There's one thing I've never told you: in January or February I very nearly went over to *Maquis*. It's quite true. At that time I was a bit fed-up, though I can no longer remember exactly why. I'd had enough. I very nearly left one day to join a *Maquis* in the Landes. It was such an adventurous life, and then the courage of those young men. Of course, I argued with myself. I even reproached myself for entertaining such an idea. But supposing I had gone, that I had joined. . . . There would have been no trial and no Fresnes. I might even have performed some brilliant action and been a hero today. Not a traitor but a hero. My whole life would have been utterly different. Perhaps I would even be a fanatical supporter of de Gaulle! You see upon what details things depend: a sudden whim, a chance, a mere nothing. There again is your 'foundation for objective truth'!"

He began walking up and down again in his narrow cage, frowning, biting his lips. Twice he gently repeated to himself the word "*maquis*", and nodded his head. Suddenly he stopped short as if thunderstruck. He raised his arms above his head.

"Deliverance!" he cried. "Deliverance!"

And he turned red as if all the blood in his body had flowed into his cheeks. François was frightened. A third time Roland cried in exaltation: "Deliverance!" Then in a dying voice: "Donadieu, let me have the armchair a minute, will you? I'm exhausted."

François rose obediently to his feet.

"I think you should rest," he said. "This business has taken too much out of you."

Roland smiled beatifically.

"François," he murmured feebly (it was the first time he had ever used his Christian name), "I'm very fond of you. You're my only friend."

"The only friend" shuffled his feet, hung his head and looked extremely sheepish.

"François," Roland said, "I'm going away. I'm going to Indo-China. Yes, my dear François, I'm going to enlist. For two, three, five years, I don't know. Why didn't I think of it earlier? The idea has only just come to me this second, in a flash while talking of the Maquis and as a result of seeing the word 'Viet-Nam', there, in the newspaper you've got in your hand. A flash, a moment of illumination! Of course, it's the only thing to do. There's no other possible loophole. You can well believe that it's not out of patriotism that I shall enlist. Insofar as Indo-China's a French possession I don't care a damn about it. After what they've done to me, after the way they've rewarded my love for my country, I put patriotism you know where. Ho Chi Minh, Bao Dai, Thierry d'Argenlieu, Truman, Stalin or the Pope—they're all the same to me. Don't make me laugh. The joke's gone on long enough. We've taken the point. We've had it. Patriotism? Of what are you talking, gentlemen? No! It's simply that I like the Army. I've never been so happy as I was in uniform. Well then? Indo-China! Am I fed-up? Indo-China! Indo-China! Indo-China!"

He got up, too excited to be able to sit still in an armchair.

"Sit down," he said. "I can't sit still."

François obediently sat down again.

"For I'm bored, Donadieu, bored as a dead rat. And I've been doing everything I can to hide that from myself too, always, but it's over now, I'm not going to hide anything from myself ever again, ever! I'm bored to death!" he repeated forcefully. "I'm bored while I make my fat women exercise. I come home at night bored. Simone's a sweet little wife, but, there it is, I adore her in boredom. I eat, sleep, come and go in boredom. Well, then? Indo-China!" he chanted ecstatically. "Why have I stood this boredom over the years? Why? Can you tell me? Out of duty? I no longer recognise any duty towards anyone. Love of country? I've just told you what I'd do with that. Fear of God? I don't know that God's done much for me; anyhow, I've never noticed it. Well then? Everything's finished, you see. Everything. The good and the bad, truth and lies. There remains only a chap of thirty-two who knows that he's lost his youth, who's managed to take himself in like a fool, and who's now discovered he's a Jew and so on. To whom do I owe anything? For whom or for what must I go on being bored? Indo-China! What, what, what's all this?" he cried in a tone of voice that riveted François Donadieu with terror. "No, sir. Reporting for duty, sir!"

Turning towards the wall, he stood at attention, clicking his heels, and then came to the salute. François watched wide-eyed.

"The Viet post has been cleaned up in twenty minutes, sir. Three dead, twenty-five prisoners, two of ours wounded," he recited in a martial tone, as if he were making a succinct report. He relaxed and turned towards François.

"I feel as if I were already there," he said simply. "It's marvellous. In the rice-fields. We paddle along, suck, suck, with the water up to our thighs, on reconnaissance patrol with one's comrades, and we remove the leeches that stick to our legs by dozens," he murmured voluptuously. "And then leave in Saigon with a pocket full of money, well turned out, impeccable white coat and trousers, colonial headdress, sun-glasses, a cocktail that twists your guts in an ultra-modern bar, and the beautiful little geishas. . . ." Suddenly his expression changed to one of extraordinary sadness, as if every feature had suddenly grown old, loose and flaccid; his eyes suddenly lost their brightness and became sad and vague; and he went on in a small, distant, broken voice: ". . . and the yellow servants, you know, silent and faithful in their silken robes, their veiled eyes full of a wisdom older than the world, a terrible wisdom. . . . The servants who lead you in silence along the streets of the Cholon quarter. . . . My childhood's dream. The pirates on the river. The opium dens. And that Asiatic decadence by which one can gradually become submerged, with the dumb complicity of the servants to whom one need say nothing as they know everything in advance. . . ."

Turning his eyes away, he paused briefly and then said quietly, "You know, I don't think I shall come back."

Once again François Donadieu felt the shock, the shudder that seized him from time to time in the presence of this man who was at once pathetic and slightly mad. When Roland Oyarzun gesticulated and shouted, one wanted to smile. And then suddenly he said a word, adumbrated an attitude, which took your breath away. A dark chasm opened, and upon its edge you saw a man standing, wearing the mask of tragedy, while all the lightnings of the heavens played about him.

This lasted only a moment. Roland quickly regained control of himself. He moved and smiled.

"Certainly," he said, "there's a pretty good chance of losing one's skin out there. But after all a soldier must be prepared to get killed: that's part of the beauty of his profession. From the practical point of view"—he frowned and talked through his nose, as he always did when he was playing the part of a practical man of affairs—"this solution of Indo-China is obviously most satisfactory. A non-commissioned officer's pay really means something out there. I'll send three-quarters of it to my dear wife: it'll mean no more worry for her. Within six months, she'll be able to find a more convenient flat, buy clothes for herself and the children, toys, little luxuries. It'll be paradise regained. Quite apart from the fact that she won't mind being alone, at least not for a while. Poor Simone, I haven't made her very happy. Alone, with the two children, she'll be able to relax a bit. And if I'm killed, she gets a pension and she's still young enough to start a new life. So everything's for the best from the family point of view. As for me, I get an amnesty: besides, I've only got another year of National Indignity to run, anyhow. I shall get back the rank I held in 1940. Fine. The more I think about it, the better this solution seems to me to be."

He rubbed his hands.

"I shall go to the recruiting office this very week. I shall be free at last! Well, let's take a look at my soldierly face."

He went over and gazed at himself in the new looking-glass.

"My mother paid for this looking-glass. She spoils us. Not bad, not bad," he said, stroking his cheeks and chin. "Older, but not too bad. I still look pretty good. Fine eyes. Semitic ones, so it appears? All right. After all, you're quite correct. Semite, Aryan, Negro, what the hell difference does it make? Life's the same for all of them. Death too. Confound you, Oyarzun!" he said, smiling at his own image. "These last years I haven't dared see myself in looking-glasses. I was frightened, I don't know why. I had the old one covered with a piece of cloth, do you remember? One gets phobias like that. Well, that's all over. I'm no longer afraid. Since these fantastic revelations, since everything has collapsed around me, I'm no longer afraid. In the looking-glass, there's only myself, and nothing more: a void."

A sound of chains and locks warned them that Simone had come in. She also was transformed: she looked fresher and more smiling. They both insisted that François should stay to dinner.

He accepted, because he had the very definite feeling that this would be the last time. When they said good night at the door, Roland took his friend's hands in his and pressed them as hard as he could. He seemed violently moved and his eyes were misty. He muttered a few more words about their youth together, about their schooldays, but he could not finish what he wanted to say because his throat was constricted.

A month later, he embarked for Saigon; and, as he had foreseen, he did not return. Today, his photograph is in the place of honour in front of the new looking-glass. Simone has received, from the High Command in Indo-China, a letter in which she is specially informed that her husband has "redeemed" himself. As the fashion is still for black, Clothilde has not had to discard her wardrobe in order to go into mourning.

* * *

It was a year after their last meeting that François learned of Roland Oyarzun's death. He felt a certain sorrow. Above all, he was struck by the incomprehensible, the extraordinary, or, in the vocabulary then in fashion, the 'absurd' character of such a life. Poor Oyarzun! He had always been hugely agitated, had fought inextricably, but with all his might, against the bonds that he himself had done his best to fasten about him; and except in rare moments of clarity, he had projected outside himself, imposed upon the exterior world, the disquiet, the anguish, which was clearly within. This man, in whom a sensitive being was combined in so disconcerting a manner with an automaton —but are not many men, from certain angles, from certain points of view, automatons?—this man, so much 'all of a piece', whom one thought one knew so thoroughly, had had, even he had had, his shadows, his zones of mystery, his depths. François remembered the strange conversation he had had with him the night Roland had called him to his bedside, the confused monologue about the Far East, about that Asia to which Oyarzun had gone as if to some profound and true vocation, a vocation so curiously discovered, which had become confounded with his death. . . . Poor Roland Oyarzun! "*A tale told by an idiot, full of sound and fury, signifying nothing. . . .*" These words of disillusion, in which the century seemed to have discovered the ultimate truth about the world, could be applied to Oyarzun's destiny, as indeed to many others, perhaps to all? And this feeling, though it might be a source of fear and bitterness, could also, according to one's humour and the colour of the day, be a source of calm. A calm which was neither the indifference of the sceptic nor the frivolity of the hedonist, but rather the bright consciousness of all that is most precious, all that is most essential in this precarious life, this brief flame that glows so feebly between those two equally tenebrous states, inexistence and death, and which belongs so peculiarly to ourselves, independently of any authority but our own—a brittle inalienable treasure whose riches we alone can explore. One night François tried to formulate this notion, which was becoming more and more familiar to him, aloud to Bernard: but he soon gave up the attempt, paralysed by the certainty that such conceptions remained, would always remain, a dead letter to his friend: the sentimental reveries of a dreamer, the stale illusions of another age, that was what Bernard must think of them. Nevertheless he listened with the friendly attention from which he never departed, with the rather elaborate goodwill of a man who has decided, whatever it may cost, that he must be comradely, that he must listen to what people have to say, encourage 'communication'. But, in fact, there was no communication. . . . When François fell silent, Bernard said kindly: "Go on. I'm listening, you know. You were saying: 'the idea of an interior life'? . . ."

François blushed, suddenly embarrassed.

"No," he said, making a vague negative gesture. "I don't . . . Forgive me. I'm afraid of boring you. Besides, this is not the kind of thing I should say to you. It's not that I'm afraid of your misunderstanding, you can understand anything, and better than most of us, but I simply don't think these things interest you, or seem to you outdated, stupidly romantic."

"Not at all," Bernard protested. "Do you take me for a complete extrovert, incapable of introspection? But, my dear chap," he went on with a certain pomposity which was intentionally comical, "you forget that I've been trained in Gide's discipline of the examination of the conscience and that I've been keeping a journal from my earliest youth!"

"Yes, yes. I know that. But this isn't quite a question of the examination of the conscious, nor of analysis, nor of anything of that kind. I should say rather that this was a question of a sort of spiritual flux, of an almost mystic feeling about life. And I imagine that you look upon all that sort of thing as a detestable form of Epicurianism, as the inconsistent caprice of an outmoded individualism. You see, you're so virtuous a man!"

"Virtuous?" exclaimed Bernard, laughing. "It's the last definition I should use."

"But, listen. Of course you're virtuous, in spite of your thirty-six mistresses and the place those particular pleasures occupy in your life. You intellectual progressives are the real puritans of the century. In fact, you're a man of duty! You've got the social religion of the mass. You're engaged in the great fight for the deliverance of humanity. I may be smiling, but I'm serious all the same. I'm not joking the least in the world. It's merely that it's easier to speak of these things with a certain air of frivolity. No, Bernard, I insist, you're a man of duty, you're a puritan, and I intend no paradox. As for me, I'm an appalling egoist. The fate of society doesn't interest me."

He had said this last phrase as quietly as if he were announcing some quite simple and anodyne fact, but Bernard was taken aback and looked astonished, almost scandalised. And indeed, François told himself that Bernard must have been scandalised: what he had just heard was for him a sort of blasphemy. He was like a Christian who is painfully affected when a friend laughs at the Holy Church, mocks the Commandments, and is ironical concerning the Mysteries.

"Have I shocked you?" François asked. "It isn't really quite what I wanted to say. Society exists for me, too, of course, I have to take it into account since I live in it and everything that concerns it has repercussions upon my own life. But, I have to make an effort to be interested in it. I compel myself, from reason and from a sense of duty, to take it into consideration. Instinctively, I'm bored by it. It's a task, an imposition. If there is a hierarchy of problems, an order of urgency, and I believe there to be one, well then, I must say, that for me, the problems of society, and therefore of politics, take second place. In my eyes the essential does not lie there. The essential lies in the invisible and the unutterable and concerns myself alone. I don't know whether I'm right or wrong and, to tell the truth, I don't care. Perhaps, at some future time, the virtuous of the earth will be compelled, with tears in their eyes, to build concentration camps for people who believe as I do. It will be the price of virtue and of liberty. But, for the moment, we have the right to live. Well, there it is; it's on that point, I imagine, that we differ."

It was in fact upon that point. Bernard was entirely in the thrall of another 'mystique', the mystique of 'History on the March', to which many of the young adhered since religions had become moribund. He was passionately concerned with every prognostication of revolution, for the political future of the planet, and, after all, it was an exciting story, filled with sudden climaxes and crises, wild adventure, fertile in heroes and traitors. "The tragedy of today is politics." Bernard could have made this remark of Napoleon's his own. But it was not entirely as a spectator that he was interested in history. He took part in it or, at least, wished to take part in it. He struggled, it was true, for the 'Deliverance of Man', a long-term project which, nevertheless, implied a precise programme. At this moment in time, at the present historical or political 'conjuncture' (it was upon the eve of the second half-century), the 'struggle for the Deliveance of Man' seemed to be divided between two fronts, East and West. "Father, defend yourself on the right! Father, defend yourself on the left!" For several months now, while continuously criticising American policy with acerbity, *Horizons* had nevertheless taken up a definite position against Stalinism and as a result had become the *bête noire* of the whole French Communist Press.

"What you've just said," Bernard replied, "doesn't shock me at all. I think it's a question of a sort of momentary disgust: you don't want to have anything to do with the world, because the world, or its present aspect, horrifies you. I can understand that reaction, and even, with an effort, sympathise with it. It is what I should call the 'Achilles complex', to use a ridiculous phrase: a fit of the sulks in which one retires into one's tent saying, 'get out of your own difficulties, your affairs have nothing to do with me'. Unfortunately, it so happens that the affairs of the world do continue to affect us, and more and more directly. As regards our duty towards society as a whole, remember that it is laid down even in Christian morality: love of one's neighbour and charity include all the other obligations and, indeed, are much the same thing as the love of God."

"That is perfectly true, but in the Christian view a single soul is worth as much as all other souls put together, and that it is better to lose the universe than to fail to assure the salvation of a single soul. Let us consider the theological vocabulary merely in order to retain from it one single idea: the absolute value of the single individual being. But to return to the collective social order, I'm not altogether convinced by what you have just said: to devote oneself to the collective social order is often a handy pretext for avoiding more modest obligations. . . ."

"I know what you're alluding to."

"Yes. I've already spoken to you about it; and I'm becoming more and more certain that I ought not to have followed you to England; I ought to have stayed with my young daughter and my wife. Going seemed superficially to be the greater risk, but it was also the easier course to take."

"Really, really," Bernard murmured, "you shouldn't always blame yourself. You really carry it to extremes, do you know that? You're your own counsel for the prosecution. You're the eternal criminal."

François looked up.

"No. I assure you, I've come to terms with myself in the long run. I'm no longer afflicted by the Furies. I've made my choice."

He hesitated and smiled, because what he was going to say had already been the subject of friendly jokes between them, whose irony had been no more than a mask and a veil.

"I have chosen 'the truths which reduce a man to his own miserable level'; you, on the other hand, have preferred the 'heroic lies'."

"Good God!" Bernard said, laughing. "One has little opportunity of being heroic on *Horizons*."

"But you may have. Who knows? One day you may need heroism to dare to write certain things in your paper. What has always rather concerned me," he added, "is how you manage to reconcile your altruism, let us say, and I don't know by what other name it can be defined—what, indeed, you call your 'fight' —how you manage to reconcile that particular devotion, that active and militant generosity with playing a part, with telling lies and playing a part, because you do play a part, Bernard, like the upper-class individualist that you are, and still remain. You're a thousand times more upper class than I am. In the last resort politics and women are your two diversions, the one as necessary to you as the other."

Bernard was never concerned by personal criticism. On the contrary, he was fascinated by being the subject of discussion, however adverse it might be. He smiled with pleasure and replied in the most lively way. 'How young he is,' François said to himself as he watched him, 'and how he keeps his looks despite the thickening of chin and cheeks, the deepening wrinkles and hair growing grey at the temples. He is a fine example of the civilised man, the white man. He is worthy of being admired and loved. Into what a wonderful White Chief the years will transform him: at once sybarite and sage, egotistical and generous, magnanimous. . . . He really is a man!' He watched him with fascinated curiosity. He thought of poor Roland Oyarzun, who in this very office had wished to destroy the man he hated and whom he believed to be responsible for his own misfortunes. He remembered the unknown who had so impressed him one night in a soldiers' barrack-room by reciting the first lines of a poem by Apollinaire. That had been ten years ago. 'I, too, was young then,' he thought, 'and I was already the father of a little girl to whom I paid very little attention at that time.' The little girl who was no more than a memory, an image, an invisible presence in the most secret places of his heart. He made himself listen to what Bernard was saying.

"You're raising the old problem of sincerity and authenticity. I don't mind admitting that I've left them behind long ago. But supposing you've observed correctly, supposing that I really am, indeed perhaps more than all, a determined individualist, a man who looks in the first place for the egotistical expression of his own powers, or for the enrichment of his own personality, what does it matter? What does it matter, if in the last analysis I contribute, nevertheless, to promoting that deliverance of Man, which is the official reason for my activities? What matters if the achievement of an objective good, not the purity of subjective intentions. Saint Martin may not have had the purest intentions when he cut up his cloak for the benefit of the poor—it was a somewhat theatrical gesture, and who knows if the young soldier was not acting a part to himself? It's of no importance: he placed his cloak about the shoulders of the poor, and the poor man could have protection against the cold, some small part of the suffering of the world was alleviated. You see what I mean? Sometimes I too play a part to myself. But if my little editorials in *Horizons* contribute, in however small a way, to the establishment upon earth of a little more justice, am I not ultimately justified? The tree will be judged by its fruits."

"You plead well. Your sermon seems to me a little masterpiece of casuistry, but you may, after all, be right. Nevertheless, you're adepts at sophistry, you old pupils of our greater schools. And oddly sycophantic at that!"

Bernard laughed frankly.

"I merely wanted to show you that if, in the past, I've stumbled over this question of personal authenticity, well, today it worries me no longer. I, too, have ceased to be tormented by the Furies."

"Doubtless that's what's known as growing up."

* * *

THIBAULT FONTANES, from Paris, to MADAME L. DE BARS, Ambassade de France, Oslo

February, 1951.

Dear Friend,—I met your father the other day. He told me that you very nearly killed yourself ski-ing. Both your father and I disapprove of these violent sports. Please be sensible. Or I shall take the next aeroplane to Oslo and give you a beating.

You will have heard that Gide is dead. (I shall go on with the news, since you say that I happily take the place of the newspapers which you have no desire to read.) Gide, therefore, died the other day with the utmost propriety in the Rue Vaneau. I was not really much impressed by the work of this young author. All the same, his disappearance has to some extent disquieted me. Jean Paulhan says that Gide's death has not been badly received, since it was met by a broadside of insults. It has also cast a certain gloom: with Gide a world is disappearing which had a certain manner of being noble, intelligent and happy. We feel that all that is completely finished. Within five years three great writers have taken leave of this earth upon which there was no longer any place for them, three writers all very different from each other: Giraudoux, Gide, Bernanos. The last Magician. The last Sage. And the last Crusader. After them there is no one left but partisans and specialists. The fireworks of the atomic age can tell me nothing of any value. We have entered upon a long twilight.

Does time fly as quickly in Norway as it does here? Perhaps in the snow, people and things last a little longer than they do elsewhere. Or have you also the feeling that everything is accelerating? I seem to hear the planet revolving with the roar of an express train. For several days now I have been in my twenty-sixth year. Soon the time will come for plans and resolutions. What a bore!

My cousin, Patrick, whom you know, is at this moment turning out my desk, having already threatened me with a couple of revolvers. The child has read too many thrillers which his father leaves lying about all over the house. He began reading the special number of Crapouillot *about the war. With perverse curiosity, I asked him if he knew what was meant by a Resistânt, a Collaborator, or a Maquisard. He had but the vaguest ideas. And to think that he is the son of Georges de Montmort! At his age I was much more concerned with politics than he is. I used to play games imitating all the excitements of the Third Republic. On the other hand, there is nothing Patrick does not know about mechanical things and is prepared to discuss jet-planes with anybody. He swears by America and dreams of going there to make a lot of money and buy a Cadillac. In the meantime, he's the sweetest little boy in the world.*

And this anecdote, which is perfectly true, is something of a sign to me: time is passing, the country is forgetting the dramatic crises of the past, a fatal torpor is upon us. I thought there was something to fight about and have hit out around me: I get no response, I seem to be hitting into a sort of soft paste that gives way on every side. There is nothing to do but to write and be happy. And by the way, I am beginning to forget you, dear Lorraine, so you can breathe again. You are becoming a gracious constellation in my private heaven: a nordic constellation, frosty and brilliant. . . . Yes, happiness is attainable, and since we happen to be at the beginning of the year and the half-century, I send you the customary good wishes. When are you thinking of returning to Paris? Charming as Embassy life must be in Oslo, I suspect that both Michel and you are longing to come back to Paris in the season. Come back. This city is always gay and one moves from a dinner-party to a fancy-dress ball in an eddy of duchesses and dress-designers. Never have we been so wanton. We enjoy ourselves very much. You have my love.